Elijah and Sabrina

Any story can be a great story

— Philip Pink

Elijah and Sabrina

Philip Patrick

Copyright © 2019 by Philip Patrick.

ISBN: Softcover   978-1-7960-3592-6
             eBook   978-1-7960-3591-9

All rights reserved. No part of this book may be reproduced or transmitted in
any form or by any means, electronic or mechanical, including photocopying,
recording, or by any information storage and retrieval system, without permission
in writing from the copyright owner.

This is a work of fiction. Names, characters, places and incidents either are the
product of the author's imagination or are used fictitiously, and any resemblance
to any actual persons, living or dead, events, or locales is entirely coincidental.

Any people depicted in stock imagery provided by Getty Images are models, and
such images are being used for illustrative purposes only.
Certain stock imagery © Getty Images.

Print information available on the last page.

Rev. date: 05/23/2019

To order additional copies of this book, contact:
Xlibris
1-888-795-4274
www.Xlibris.com
Orders@Xlibris.com
794706

CONTENTS

Elijah vii
Sabrina...xix

PART ONE

Birth of Feelings

Chapter 1	Day One of Hundreds 1
Chapter 2	Welcome the Fourth Member............................30
Chapter 3	Talk to Girls 55
Chapter 4	Twelve Years and Counting..............................72
Chapter 5	Definition Perfection 83
Chapter 6	End of an Era 95
Chapter 7	Clarin, Dawson, and Peyton 116
Chapter 8	A Day with June 125
Chapter 9	Bad Vibes 137
Chapter 10	Like the Good Old Days..................................167
Chapter 11	Adult Situations 173
Chapter 12	Elijah has a Heart 194
Chapter 13	Dream Girl..209
Chapter 14	Holiday Spirits..223

PART TWO

Dark Clouds

Chapter 15 The Brave and the Girl 235
Chapter 16 Mystery Valentine......................................250
Chapter 17 Angels..262
Chapter 18 Rhythm of Souls...283
Chapter 19 Absolute Dream..302
Chapter 20 The Professor and The Comedian 313
Chapter 21 Far From Finished 323
Chapter 22 A Clarin's First Challenge 343
Chapter 23 E-4 versus The Serious Bunch 377
Chapter 24 The Final Round 400

PART THREE

Lost and Found

Chapter 25 Another Step Forward.................................... 419
Chapter 26 Dancing the Night Away 435
Chapter 27 An End and a Beginning 460

ELIJAH

June 2000.

The sun shined down during noon hour on William Konkin Elementary School. Students, boys and girls alike, were all around, laughing, chatting and playing. Some were playing on the playground, monkey bars, tire swings, while others would be loitering around or circling the school building. Elijah Khoda, Paula Hennig, and Andrew Little were doing their daily walk when they had nothing else to day but to wait for the bell to ring.

"You know what's getting close?" Andrew asked, with a little excitement in his voice.

"The end of the school year?" Paula guessed.

"X-Men!" he corrected.

Paula didn't reply, as she didn't feel like pretending the enthusiasm.

"When I was watching the cartoon, I started to think that it would be awesome if they made a movie of it, like with real people, you know? So it's like a dream come true. Hey Eli, maybe I'll go to the theatre with straws taped to my hands like Wolverine, eh?"

It took a brief moment for Elijah to answer, for that his mind was elsewhere.

"Oh...yeah, that-that'd be cool"

"Maybe we could find goggles for you that look like Cyclops" Andrew suggested, "It might not be as cool as his but..." he paused, trying to think of proper way to end his sentence.

"Better than nothing?" Paula added.

"Red!" Andrew replied, almost right away, "As long as its red and black. You wouldn't mind wearing swimming goggles, bud?"

Elijah could feel Paula and Andrew's eyes locking onto him. *Do they have to look at me?*

"Uh no, no, it's fine" Elijah finally answered.

Kids; they always talked about the possibilities that were impossible. Some of them even try to make it happen. It didn't always turn out great but at least they tried and they would have something to reflect on. It was their way of life but Elijah Khoda had put those days long behind him.

"Ooh, I'm looking forward to it" Andrew added, cheerfully. Andrew Little didn't seem to have changed a bit since Elijah met him back in the fourth grade. He was still humorous and upbeat, even after the mischiefs they got into. Elijah wondered how his best friend wasn't bothered too much by the punishments they faced. And there were times, Elijah secretly wished he was more like Andrew.

"You know what I'm looking forward to?" Paula asked.

Andrew waited for her to answer her own question.

"What?" he wondered.

"Silence" she told him, "Peacefulness, no sound whatsoever"

"What about your mom when she tells you supper is ready?"

"That's okay, as long as annoying classmates aren't coming to dinner"

"Maybe I'll give them an invitation with your address on it?" Andrew teased.

"Then we would move"

"With all your stuff? That would take forever. They would still catch you"

"We'll leave it all behind"

Normally, Elijah would step into their conversations or even arguments, just for the joy of it. But lately that didn't thrill him as much as it used to, maybe because it was getting too predictable. Having friends was nice but doing the same thing for two years was dull. The more Elijah thought about it, he began to think it was going to be like this for the rest of his life. At the same time, being with Paula and

Andrew was his only escape from reality. He had nothing against his friends but he felt like there could be more than that, whatever that may be and it didn't seem promising. Nothing did.

They continued walking. Just ahead of them, there was a group of girls standing in a circle, gossiping. They were familiar faces. One of them was Melissa Hartway, a red haired girl that was in the same class as Elijah. Before that, she shared a class with him and Andrew two years prior. They didn't exactly get along. Melissa was judgmental and more honest than any other classmate. She acted like a grownup most of the time, pointing out everyone's flaws and mistakes and just gives a lecture like she was the smartest person in class. Back then, Elijah and Andrew were younger and decided to give Melissa a piece of their minds by constantly teasing her until one day they went a little too far. Andrew came to his senses and moved on. Elijah however hadn't forgotten. To him, Melissa was an enemy that would appear on the radar. And after dealing with so much peer pressure over the years, Elijah would look at life from a different standpoint and realized just how annoying Melissa really was and became unfinished business.

As they were approaching, Elijah had his eye on Melissa, as she peered over her shoulder. He was getting the feeling they were being watched and talked about. Just as they were passing through, Elijah and Melissa met with each other's eye.

"What? What is it?" Elijah challenged, as he stopped.

Andrew and Paula froze, while Melissa's friends went silent.

"Do I have something on my face or do you just like to stare at people? It's not nice"

Melissa chuckled without humor. "I didn't even say anything and you're already trying to argue?"

"No, but you were staring like you always did, like I have some sort of problem" Elijah fired back.

"You do have a problem. You're trying to fight me when I actually didn't do anything. And for your information, I was 'staring' because I was being careful, because boys such as yourself are trouble".

Just like that, Melissa Hartway would think she could smarten Elijah up, but he wasn't giving up that easily.

"Elijah" Paula called, right away, hoping he would step back.

"Then how come I see you talking to Kyle? You were smiling and laughing when you did"

"Kyle is a friend" Melissa said, almost yelling, "But you're just like the other boys, so childish and immature"

Elijah was strongly offended as he was being schooled by a girl. He wanted to say more but was suddenly feeling weak. He'd rather not show it, not only Melissa, but anyone. Melissa started to laugh.

"Now who's staring?" she taunted.

Maturity; that was all Melissa cared about, acting her own age and insisted on everyone doing the same as if she was the ruler of the world. Life was weird sometimes. Being called immature by a person who then suddenly thought it was a good idea to make jokes. Not to mention it was the same person who had bitterness behind closed doors. Melissa could be bossy if she wanted to and probably felt so proud if she got her way. So Elijah imagined her laughing and taunting him on the inside. So he responded with harsh sarcasm.

"Yeah, well when someone looks in the dictionary for *mean, stupid,* and *funny looking,* they'll see your picture" Elijah snarled.

Melissa's jaw dropped. Elijah walked away immediately, followed by Andrew and Paula. He moved as fast as he could, thinking that Melissa could be looking for a supervisor in sight to tell on him. Secretly, Elijah hoped that she was hurt and learned her lesson from pretending like she was an adult.

"Elijah?" Paula called, as she was trying to catch up to him.

"Ah great" Elijah muttered. He still walked further with his eyes forward, hoping that Paula would give up.

"Eli!" Paula yelled, as she grabbed him by the shoulder.

Finally, he stopped and let out a sigh.

"Let go of me" Elijah insisted.

"I'll let go, only if you look at me and listen" Paula demanded.

Being lectured by a teacher, a parent, or even a classmate, was one thing. But Elijah thought Paula would've been different. He was hoping that she would be the one who understood. So avoiding her became a habit. Elijah finally turned around and Paula let go just like she said.

"Don't you think that was a little mean?" Paula asked, firmly but calm.

"I thought you don't like Melissa" Elijah replied, a little surprised.

"I don't. But what you just did was a little too far"

Elijah hesitated. Since he nothing to say for himself, he broke eye contact.

"I just never liked her" he mumbled.

Paula heard him loud and clear.

"Yes, you mentioned that before. But like she said, she didn't do anything this time and yet you were being mean to her. Look, it's not like I'm rooting her Melissa here, I'm just saying that was totally unnecessary"

Disappointed, Elijah continued to look away. He only glanced at Paula because she was his friend and felt obligated to, and he didn't feel like doing something that he was supposed to do. Paula waited and waited.

"Elijah" she called, impatiently, "Say something".

Things were getting too serious and that usually led to an argument. So much of them had happened for the past few years. Elijah just wanted them to stop. And they probably weren't going to stop, so he just looked for an excuse to get away from everything.

"Something" he responded, sarcastically, "I'm gonna play on the bars"

Elijah then stormed away before Paula would say anything else and he didn't look back. Paula sighed and looked at Andrew next to her.

"Why didn't *you* say anything?" she demanded.

Andrew exchanged a surprised look. "Me?"

"Yes!"

"I'm the funny one. I make Elijah laugh and tease you. That's what I do".

"Still, Elijah is your friend also. You should at least told him what he did was a bad idea or like what boys say 'uncool'"

"Well…" Andrew was trying to find an excuse.

Then Paula just put her hand up, thinking he was gonna try say something funny instead.

"You know what, don't bother. But seriously, you should try talking to him when he gets like this. Ever since his last fight with Brian, Elijah's been acting different"

"But he won. He got in trouble for it, but…"

"It's not the point" Paula added, abruptly, "He went after Brian and his friends to make himself feel better but I don't think it did. I'm scared that it might've made him worse"

Andrew had nothing else to add. He wanted to comfort Paula somehow, but he could see that she was too disappointed and worried. She glanced at Elijah was still climbing the monkey bars, pretending like his friends weren't there.

"What am I gonna do?" she said, in a low voice, "Every time I try talking to him, he just ignores me and walks away"

"I don't think E.K. likes to talk about anything serious"

"Then how is he gonna learn?" Paula asked, hopelessly.

"Summer is about to start" Andrew ventured, "Maybe two months of peacefulness will help"

Paula took her time. "Maybe", she hoped.

For the rest of the lunch break, Elijah didn't talk to Paula or Andrew.

Now it was time for the next obstacle, education. It was another pressure to deal with, just to get good grades to pass a course that Elijah didn't really care about. He was starting to think it was all pointless. If only there was a way to get out of it but really it was a dead end. Even if Elijah told his mom that he wanted to quit school, she would make him continue it somehow, whether it was homeschool or some other alternative. Somewhere along the way, Elijah would force himself to do schoolwork but most of the time he didn't even try. He'd just answer a simple question, right or wrong, Elijah just didn't want to deal with burden after facing so many. First bullies, overprotective friends and now strict teachers. Elijah's life became one big sinkhole and there was no hope on getting out of it.

Each time Elijah glanced at the clock, he hoped that it would be home time but they were still far from it. Sometimes it felt like it took a lifetime just for school to be over.

In gym class, they were about to play dodgeball. Mrs. Turner, Elijah's sixth grade teacher, divided the students into two teams. They all took their positions on the sides. But Elijah had no interest in taking part, like the other subjects. Physical Education was pointless, he thought. It wasn't like Elijah was going to pursue a basketball career. So sitting on the bench was the only thing he wanted to do.

"Elijah" his teacher called, "Come on, we're just about ready"

"Uh, Mrs. Turner, I kinda don't want to play" he told her, gently.

"I beg your pardon?" she replied, not as in she didn't hear but as in asking for an explanation.

"I don't really wanna play. Can't I just sit for this one?"

"If you sit, then everybody wants to sit. So no dice" Mrs. Turner told him, gently, "Now come on. I'm not going to say it a third time"

Elijah hesitated and gave a little sigh. "But I don't want to" he said, as calmly as he could. Then Elijah started walking towards the bench, hoping that his teacher would let him be but he could still feel her eyes watching him.

"Elijah!" she called again, this time a little more firmly.

There was definitely no promise of escape in this sinkhole. Elijah felt obligated to turn around. So he did.

"You can either participate or go to the office" she offered.

Mrs. Turner was smarter than she looked, as if she saw the argument coming a mile away. It would make sense because it wasn't the first time that Elijah Khoda refused to do any school activity. Just a few months ago, she had to force him into a group project and he replied with the words *kinda don't want to*. Just like he did then, Elijah gave in and joined in the gym class, although it was tempting just to sit in the office but he knew it would make things worse than they already were.

Elijah thought that was the end of it, until the day was drawing near. Something else required his attention. He was looking forward to going home and stay in his bedroom. It was the only place where Elijah felt safe. Just after looking at the clock and realizing it was almost 3pm, the teacher went up to Elijah's desk, "I need to speak to you after school" she told him.

No words came out, nothing that could get him out of it. And acknowledging it would be like admitting defeat. Elijah wasn't thrilled but then again he was only a kid. He had no power over the adults. Sometimes he wishes he did.

So once the school bell rang, everybody was excited to go home, but sadly, not for Elijah Khoda. He sat in his desk with Mrs. Turner keeping her eyes on him.

"Elijah" she spoke after the last student went out the door, "Come here"

He approached her and then she encouraged him to borrow one of the nearby chairs to sit across from her. It was too quiet. It was easy to tell that it wasn't a good thing. Mrs. Turner pulled a worksheet from underneath a pile of paper and placed it firmly in front of Elijah. It was his math test and the mark did not look good, 44 out of 100, it said. Things just keep getting worse and worse.

"You don't have to say anything" Mrs. Turner told him, "So allow me: you and I both know that this isn't good and neither of us can move on until it's done"

"Do I have to do it again?" Elijah asked, poorly.

"Take it home and re-do it" she rephrased, "So yes"

"Okay" he replied, quietly. Again, he let out another sigh; thinking that it displays some pity and it probably wasn't going to work but then there weren't many options.

"Elijah, I know it's hard" his teacher explained, strongly, "If it makes you feel any better, it's hard on me too because as your teacher it's my job to make sure you do good, to pass this grade, so you can move onto the future. That's how much I'm dedicated"

"Well, thanks" Elijah said, emotionlessly. He was about to get up from his seat.

"I didn't say you were dismissed, young man"

Oh great, what next?

"I want to talk to you about something" she added.

And it was dead serious. That was as far as attitude could go. So Elijah sat back in the seat and looked at his teacher in the eye.

"Today I asked you to take part in gym class and you said you didn't want to and that wasn't the first time you said those words. At the beginning of the year, you were just as ambitious as a regular student. Now it seems like you don't want to do anything but just to sit on the bench. So I want to ask you: why don't you want to do anything?"

Elijah took his time. Mrs. Turner waited patiently. He could've started anywhere but his mind was too blank to shape into focus. He sat there like a lifeless toy on a shelf.

"Because it's pointless, like everything else" he finally answered. He spoke like it was the first line of a statement.

"And?" his teacher replied.

"I just don't want to" Elijah added, shrugging his shoulders.

There was obviously more to the story but Mrs. Turner would rather not pressure him, as it would probably have a bad outcome.

"Well, I'm sorry to hear that. Elijah, sometimes you just have to face it because, well, it's life. You start off young and there's only one way to learn about the world, and it's through an adult. I'm here because I want to help and I know you can do better"

Elijah merely nodded. "Can I go now?" he asked, gently.

"There's one more thing" his teacher said, promptly. "To be honest, I've tried to be patient with you, Elijah. I thought maybe you would've learned by now. That's the other thing about life, you learn about the good and the bad, and what comes after bad, is consequence. I want you to write lines on the board"

Elijah couldn't say anything, even if he wanted to.

"Come, I'll get you started"

Mrs. Turner. She was firm but fair. At least she was good with names, unlike Elijah's fifth grade teacher Mr. McRay, who was too strict and frequently called Elijah by the name *Elias*. It was annoying for the longest time. Sometimes Elijah thought maybe he was doing it on purpose just to spite him. Thankfully, those days were over.

At the board, Elijah and Mrs. Turner stood as she wrote on top; *I will not talk back at the teacher.*

"You know what to do" she told him, as she handed Elijah the chalk. And so began the consequence. After the board was filled with lines, Mrs. Turner gave Elijah a note and finally dismissed him. The school grounds were empty. Everybody was long gone. It was probably a good thing. It meant that Elijah wouldn't have to deal with Paula or anybody, at least not for the next few minutes. So as Elijah walked home, he enjoyed the peace and quiet while he could.

Being at home after a day of school ought to be a nice way to recuperate. Elijah went about his routine, grabbing a snack and pop, go to his room and put on his TV, to escape reality. If only he could do it literally, he'd be very happy. It was nice while it lasted, but as Elijah sat on his bed, he kept glancing to his backpack, which was leaning against the closet door, just taunting him. He didn't show his mom the note after she and his dad got home after work. As usual, Elijah didn't say anything. It was the evening. He didn't give his poor test much thought. And once he was starting to feel the pressure, he decided just to get it over with.

With the test and note his hand, Elijah went to his mom, Madeline Khoda, who was sitting and reading on the bed while his dad was watching TV in the living room.

"Mom?" Elijah said, after clearing his throat.

Madeline lowered the book to give her attention to her son. Without saying anything, Elijah just handed her the papers. His mom read the teacher's note and did not look happy.

"Why didn't you show me this earlier?" she demanded.

Elijah opened his mouth but couldn't speak. There was too much hesitation. So he just gave up. Madeline sighed, "Come on, we better get this done. It's already getting late"

So for the rest of the evening, Madeline became her son's tutor. She looked over his failed math test and wasn't thrilled about how much they had to do. The test took them about an hour and counting. Madeline went through different parts with Elijah and even set a few examples. Even so, Elijah lacked the dedication. Half of the time, he sat there with his mind constantly wandering off.

"Elijah, I need you to pay attention!" his mom said, firmly.

"I am" he claimed.

"No, you're not"

"Well, I'm trying" Elijah told her.

"It doesn't seem like it" Madeline gave another sigh, "Eli, this isn't just a regular school assignment. It's a test, one of the things that will help pass the grade and I don't want you to fall behind. When I say try, I mean pick yourself up and just do it. No distractions, no hesitations"

Irritated, Elijah sighed, "Fine, I'll do that!"

He furiously grabbed the test and attempted to work on it himself.

"Hey!" his mom yelled, "Cut that out. I don't like it when you do that, especially when I'm trying to help you"

"By getting mad at me?"

"I have the right to get mad because you won't cooperate. You talk back to me and your teachers, and you cause trouble".

"I'm not causing trouble!" Elijah protested. He was starting to raise his voice.

"You're starting to now" his mom fired back.

Out of anger, Elijah grabbed his test and threw across the kitchen table. Madeline snapped and immediately grabbed her son's arm like he was about to cause more damage.

"Don't! Don't you start that now" his mom growled, as she gripped his arm, which weakened her son.

Anger consumed Elijah, but there was also hurt. Madeline then let go of Elijah's arm.

"Elijah, if you wanna be home schooled, I will quit my job and stop buying the things you like and teach you myself. But right now, we should be in bed. I am devoting a lot of my time, just to help because that is how much I care. And I expect the same thing from you, Elijah, or at least act like it. So you need to smarten up!"

So defeat finally got to his head. Elijah just nodded and said nothing.

"Go grab your paper" she told him, calmly, "You're not going to bed until you finish this"

It took a little while but Elijah finally re-did the test, with the help of his mom. After handing the test in and later on it was a relief to know that Elijah Khoda had passed the sixth grade. So for the last few weeks of school, things were okay or at least that was what he thought. Each day it was still the same, waking up and being with the usual friends, pretending that he was having just as much fun but really it was dull, predictable and uneventful.

One day, Elijah needed time alone. Paula respected his request because she knew that some space would do him good. But at the same time, she couldn't help but feel a little nervous because the last time Elijah wanted time alone; he went and antagonized Brian Kidman.

This time, he really was just pondering around in the silence. Elijah distanced himself from his friends and his peers. His mind was blank as he walked around WKE. The only thought he had was everything that happened that year, attending school and being controlled by everyone, including Paula. It was all probably going to happen again the next year, when Elijah would be in grade seven.

Nothing's ever going to change.

SABRINA

Life was made out of beauty and offered it in many forms, the warmth of the sun, the breeze of fresh air, and the comforts of home. All around, there was nature decorated with trees, water, and the blue sky. This was how Sabrina Clarin looked at life, as a beautiful life form.

She opened her eyes as she lied on the grass of her backyard and admired the blue sky above her. The sun warmed up the grass from the cold morning and that made it more comforting. She then raised her hand up as if she could touch the clouds in the sky. She then rolled on her side and felt the grass tickle against her hand. Looking in that direction, Sabrina spotted a white dandelion. It was only a few inches away, so she reached over, grabbed it, and pulled it out from the group. Sabrina sat up, admiring the dandelion. After a short moment, she began to blow the seeds off. Each of them flowed gracefully onto the grass.

It was probably time to go back inside and eat. So Sabrina got up to her feet, stretched her arms and began walking. Along the way, she felt the morning breeze and it lightened up her face with happiness. She just had the urge to dance and so she did.

Sabrina woke up early that morning, even before her family. Feeling well rested, she felt like she could do anything, even stepping outside in her t-shirt and pajama pants just to be with nature. It looked like it was going to be another beautiful day.

In Granisle, it was another day of school for the local kids. Everyone sat quietly as their teacher was lecturing them about their subject in history. They were learning about Alexander the Great. It was something they learned about for a little while. In the end, the teacher was testing the children's knowledge.

"Who can tell me how long Alexander had ruled half the world?" the teacher asked.

A few students raised their hand. The teacher picked the first student she made eye contact with.

"Seven?" the child guessed.

"No. Next?"

The other person to raise his hand was Zachery Epstad, for that it was one answer that he knew and he'd rather be the next person to get it right. He even raised his hand politely as he made eye contact with his teacher. She saw him and couldn't sworn she was about to pick him. Once the teacher gestured in his direction, he opened his mouth-

"Eight years" Sabrina Clarin answered.

"That's right!"

Disappointed and embarrassed, Zach realized who the teacher really gestured to, the girl sitting behind him. The teacher continued to ask questions to the rest of the class. Zach waited patiently until one question would catch his attention.

"Who did Alexander battle against?"

Almost all the students raised their hands.

"There's quite a few. How about one student gives one answer?"

"Egypt" one of the classmates called.

"Yes. Who else?"

She pointed to the next student.

"Greece"

"That's right"

Again she looked in Zach's direction. He could feel the excitement of being singled out.

"Sabrina?" she called.

"The Persian Empire"

She spoke like she already knew the answers before they even started talking about Alexander the Great. Zachery sighed as the session was over. From then on, whenever he looked at Sabrina Clarin or even heard her speak, he would imagine in his head that something bad would happen to her.

After the kids had their lunch, they all went outside to play. It was sunny and warm out. It was certainly a nice day. Sabrina Clarin walked along the schoolyard, letting the warmth of the sun consume her. She breathed in the fresh air and exhaled. She couldn't ask for a better kind of day. She walked around the perimeter, where kids were playing around. She saw her big brother Jonathan Clarin, playing alone on the teeter-totters, as he was running back and forth. Sabrina just ran up the wooden board before her brother put weight on the other side and lifted it up.

"Looks like you can use a friend" Sabrina told him, with a smile on her face.

"You're my sister" he corrected.

"So?"

"Brothers and sisters are family, not friends" Jonathan told her.

"I know, but we can still play".

Jonathan stepped off the teeter-totter. As he did, his sister quickly went in the middle to balance the whole thing, for the fun of it. She glanced at her brother, and noticed he didn't look exactly enthused.

"What's wrong? You don't wanna play with me?"

Jonathan hesitated, "Maybe at home…but not here" he admitted, trying to suppress the agitation in his voice.

"Why?"

Her peered around to make sure no one was near. He went up to Sabrina. "I just don't want them making fun of me for playing with my sister" Jonathan told her, in a low voice.

Sabrina chuckled. "Jonathan, there's nothing wrong with a brother and sister playing together on a playground"

Then she offered him her hand. Jonathan just looked at her funny.

"Okay, but I'm not holding her hand"

xxi

Sabrina wasn't offended but she let out a little giggle. "Alright" she replied.

Both Clarin siblings went on the teeter-totter. Instead of sitting down, like they ought to, they stood up and carefully sprinted back and forth. Together, they just enjoyed the excitement of being lifted into the air. After that, Sabrina and Jonathan stood at both ends, trying to straighten the wooden teeter- totter. Jonathan was rather focused, while his sister merely laughed, joyfully.

"What if I fall, would you hold my hand then?"

"Yes" Jonathan replied, almost right away.

After a moment of silent, Sabrina decided to jump on her end, just to see what would happen. As soon as she leaped, the teeter-totter went down on Jonathan's end rather swiftly. It surprised him. Sabrina just laughed.

"Not funny" Jonathan said, calmly.

She could tell he was just a little scared. But knowing that her brother was sensitive, she didn't bother teasing him about it. After the fun was over, Sabrina and Jonathan walked around the schoolyard, trying to find what to do next. Sabrina cupped her hand and held it up to her ear.

"I don't hear anyone making fun of you" she teased.

"Okay, so I was wrong" Jonathan admitted.

"See, there's nothing wrong with being friends with your sister"

"I guess"

Jonathan wasn't always that bashful. When they were younger, they were actually inseparable. But Sabrina knew that Jonathan was growing up and soon would rather do his own thing. Just like their mother, there was a part of Sabrina that didn't want him to.

"I need to use the bathroom" Jonathan told her, "I'll be right back".

Sabrina nodded and then her brother ran toward the school building. Once Sabrina was alone, she kept walking until she came across a hopscotch that was painted on the pavement. Without giving much thought, Sabrina decided to hop through it, with one foot and two in a pattern. She was having fun just from doing so little. As she continued walking, she even bent down, planted her hand on the ground and did a cartwheel and was back on her feet. Sabrina was a free spirit. But she didn't stop there. She wanted to try something different, and there she spotted the monkey bars shaped like a dome. There was already a few boys hanging around there, but she didn't care. Sabrina ran up and started climbing. One of the boys noticed and it was Zachary Epstad.

"Hey" he called, "What are you doing?"

"Climbing" Sabrina replied, kindly.

She didn't really get his firm tone. She thought it was just the way boys talked, trying to sound tough, especially for a boy like Zach. Sabrina barely knew him. To her, he was only a classmate. Zach had black hair. He was average height and wore casual clothes. He looked like any other student in the school. And just like other boys, he shows off, trying to impress everybody through his arrogance and his rather unwittingly humor. He was quite petty, the kind of student you wouldn't give much thought to. And Sabrina Clarin never thought she would come face to face with him, until this day.

"This is OUR monkey bars" Zach told her, strongly.

And there, Sabrina froze once all three boys were looking at her like she offended them.

"Well, it's not really yours. It's the schools" Sabrina explained. She was trying to be friendly, thinking that Zach was a child who was too shy to share.

"You can't climb here" he told her, practically yelling.

Now Sabrina was feeling the discomfort. The excitement she was feeling disappeared, like a kite that suddenly got caught in a hurricane. She climbed down from the monkey bars in shame.

"Sorry" she said, in irritation.

She began walking away, although Zach was far from finished. He started following her.

"Hey, if you're so smart, why don't you go to a different kind of school?"

Sabrina stopped and reluctantly looked back at the boy.

"What?"

"I saw you answering all those questions in class, just when I wanted to answer!"

Sabrina reacted skeptically. "You're mad at me just for answering honest questions? Do you want me to be sorry for that too? I mean, she picked me".

"Because you're so smart" Zach empathized, angrily, "You know there are two things I don't like: my parents making me eat food I don't like and kids who are so smart they think they can do anything. What are they gonna do for you next, build you a castle, you princess?!"

The hostility was making Sabrina more uncomfortable than being on the monkey bars. "Okay. I think you can leave me alone now"

Quickly, Sabrina turned around again and began walking without delay.

"I'll leave you alone once they send you to a different school. And if they do build you a castle, I hope it falls down on you, hits you in the head and knocks all that smart out of you!!"

Sabrina walked slowly after Zach was long gone, and trying to act normal as she was surrounded by her peers and hoped no one noticed her sadness. The mood changed. Sabrina tried to forget about it, but the power of Zach's words was echoing in her head. She thought just long enough for the burden to become heavy. Sabrina needed time to let it sink before giving herself confidence again. But Jonathan came back outside and he noticed right away that something was bothering her.

"Sabrina? What is it?" he asked.

The whole incident was still sinking in and it was pulling Sabrina away from the present.

"N-nothing, I'm fine" she claimed and then looked away.

Sabrina Clarin was always used to being happy and would've felt embarrassed if anyone saw her emotional.

"Well, you look a little sad. Come on…"

Her discomfort moment with Zach automatically replayed in her mind and finally struck her emotionally.

"It's…" she sighed. She was about to breakdown. While holding it together, she tried to find an excuse, but because of Zach's words haunting her, she couldn't think straight. Jonathan was waiting too long. She had to tell him something. "It's nothing".

That's something, alright.

"Do you wanna…" she added, hoping that her voice sounded casual, "Wanna go-keep playing?" Then she started walking towards the other parts of the playground, hoping that Jonathan would-

"Sabrina" her brother called. That was all he said and all he needed to say. By his firm tone, Sabrina knew that he really wanted to know and that he was willing to do something.

"It's Zach"

"Who?"

"Zach Epstad. He's in my class"

"What did he do?" Jonathan demanded. He was strongly offended as he saw the hurt in his sister's eyes.

Sabrina was about to tell him, but right then she feared the worse, thinking that maybe it wouldn't end well if her brother confronted her bully. She loved her family and would rather not see them hurt.

"Uh, y-you know what…" she muttered, "it's okay, just forget about it"

"No" her brother disagreed, "It's not okay. Just show me where he is"

She didn't answer. She was afraid to.

"Sabrina!" Jonathan urged.

His sister hesitated. "Okay-he's over at the monkey bars-but try not to fight"

She couldn't tell if her brother was listening, for that he was already walking ahead of her. It was too late. Sabrina couldn't help but regret telling him about Zach at all. It was tempting for her not to follow because she simply didn't want to deal with any bullies. But at the same time, she worried for her brother and couldn't help but feel something bad was about to happen. Sabrina finally started running to catch up with Jonathan.

Zach and his two friends were still hanging the monkey bars like it was their second home. They were minding their own business until they saw Jonathan Clarin storming towards them. As soon as Zach saw Sabrina, he just laughed.

"Who's this, your bodyguard?" he teased.

Jonathan stopped once he felt he was close enough. Sabrina kept her distance.

"I'm her brother" Jonathan warned.

Then Zach widened his eyes, but from his sarcastic tone he was only pretending to be intimidated.

"Ooh, I'm so scared…"

"What did you do to my sister?"

"I just told her to get lost. You should've seen her…she was crying like a little baby"

That was not true! Sabrina could've talked back at Zach, but she was too afraid. Jonathan froze as he was extremely offended that his sister was being picked on, much worse than he thought. Zach peered over at Sabrina.

"You wanna tissue, you wittle baby?" he taunted.

Boys will be boys. That's what some people would say. They would do or say anything they'd feel like for the fun of it. If Zach wasn't that cruel, Sabrina might've let it slip but as she noticed that he was looking directly at her, his words were like a punch in the face. Now she felt threatened.

Jonathan finally snapped and aggressively shoved Zach away. His friends were alerted and stepped forward to help their friend. Zach only lost his balance but once he regained control, he stormed after Jonathan. Sabrina immediately dashed to get between them.

"You take that back!" Jonathan yelled.

"You're gonna have to make me. Come on, do it!" Zach insisted.

It was only a matter of seconds until Jonathan would do something reckless. He tried to storm after Zach, but Sabrina blocked him, trying to prevent it.

"I'm gonna make YOU cry like a little baby!" Jonathan growled.

"Then do it. I'm waiting" Zach challenged.

"No! No, please!" Sabrina cried, in a low voice so nobody would hear. "Jonathan, it's okay. Just forget about it"

His sister's sweet and innocent voice prevented Jonathan from making another move. Zach didn't care if he didn't have to fight. Just seeing the Clarin siblings retreating was enough victory for him.

"Come on" Sabrina insisted.

Finally, the Clarin siblings turned their backs to the bullies, and just before they did, Zach stuck his tongue out at them. Jonathan noticed but his soft spot for his sister repressed his anger, even though it was a strong attempt. But in the end, Jonathan took his sister's advice and walked away.

Feeling defeated, Sabrina and Jonathan sat down at a bench, with their heads down, being further away from their peers mentally. After a silent moment, Sabrina finally exchanged looks with her brother since the incident. He was just as hurt as she was and that made her feel bad. She did not like seeing her own family down and it killed her inside. No words at that point could comfort them. So then Jonathan reached over and held Sabrina's hand.

It was that day that Sabrina Clarin realized that life wasn't always clear skies. There was a dark cloud, one that shadowed over her mind.

For the rest of the afternoon, Sabrina tried to move on like the incident didn't happen, but it continued to trouble her. It was more relieving once school was over for the day. The Clarins didn't live far from the school. After all, Granisle was a small town. They walked up the hill until they made it to their street. Jonathan finally took a moment to check on his sister, who still had her head down and was mentally miles away.

"Hey, are you all right?" he asked, gently.

It didn't take Sabrina long before she met her brother's eye.

"I'm fine" she replied, "I just don't wanna talk about it"

"Okay?"

She took a deep breath.

"I'm just glad you're okay, Jonathan"

"Yeah" he nodded, "I'm glad you're okay too"

Sabrina didn't sound as hurt and afraid as she did earlier. So that convinced Jonathan that she was going to be fine. They continued walking and soon they were home. Both Sabrina and Jonathan entered the front door of their home. They felt safer as they set foot inside.

"Sabrina, Jonathan?" a voice called.

It was their father.

"Hey" Jonathan replied, mildly.

"Hey dad" Sabrina said, acting and sounding normal.

Jonathan dropped his bag by the front door as he usually did, while Sabrina carried hers with her up the stairs. Once they reached the top, their father came around the corner to greet them. Michael Clarin was his name. He was in his early-thirties. His hair was black and short and looked pretty youthful.

"So how was it?" he asked, kindly.

"It was alright" Jonathan answered, promptly, "It's school, you know"

"Just another day" Sabrina added, sounding like one of those kids that were tired of school.

Sabrina met her dad's eyes and gave a soft smile, in which he returned the expression. That alone always brought comfort to Sabrina. Then their mother, Leah Clarin, came out from the hallway and met with her family.

"Oh good, we're all here" she said, "Now I don't need to worry about calling your names and one of you not responding"

"And by one of us, you mean me" Jonathan blurted out, sarcastically.

Leah ignored her son's remark. "Come on, all of us to the living room"

"We are in the living room" Jonathan told them,

"Good, now stay here, particularly on the couch" Leah replied, on the same sarcastic level. "You too, Sabrina"

"And no, you're not in trouble" Michael said.

"At least, not yet" Sabrina joked.

Michael then gently placed his hand on his daughter's collar bone.

"Don't push your luck, kiddo" he told her.

And then he playfully pinched Sabrina's lower neck, more than once.

"Ow!"

Sabrina and Jonathan did was they were told and sat on the couch side by side. Their mom sat on the chair next to them, while their dad stood in front of them.

xxviii

"So we have some news" Leah started.

Their children listened closely but didn't say anything.

"Remember when we talked about moving?" she asked.

"Yeah?" Sabrina was the only one that replied.

"Well, today that's become official" Michael added, "The relator called earlier...and...we got the house!"

Sabrina pretended to be fully excited. "Really?"

"Yes" Leah admitted, remaining modest "Yes, we did"

"So where are we moving to?" Jonathan asked.

Their parents exchanged looks with each other. The Clarin siblings were waiting with anticipation.

"Burns Lake" their dad finally answered.

PART ONE
Birth of Feelings

CHAPTER ONE

Day One of Hundreds

"Elijah, it's almost eight o'clock" Madeline called, as she gently knocked on his bedroom door.

It was just as Elijah predicted. Summer was over in a blink of an eye and before he knew it, it was another school year. Another set of ten months of having to wake up early, only to put up with other kids and grownups for eight hours. Even for the third grade, it was becoming dull. Surely there had to be at least a few good things in almost every day, but for the seventh grade, Elijah Khoda felt like those good things were being limited. Those thoughts flowed through his mind as he lied there in bed, not having the courage to get up. Looking at the clock and realizing it was only a matter of time before mom would lose her temper. So Elijah decided to get it over with and it was only because he was expected to.

After having his shower, Elijah took his time getting dressed. It was quarter after eight. There was still time to loiter. It was all he was interested in, a place where he could watch TV or play videogames, and not having to worry about the world coming out to get him. Just sitting there, Elijah was considering if he should just pretend to be sick like he did that one time during primary school. Would they fall for it? Probably not because Elijah wasn't a kid anymore. He was getting further away from childhood and beyond manhood. Being lost somewhere in between was confusing. Elijah wondered didn't what life meant anymore...yet he still got up from his bed and out his bedroom.

Elijah entered to kitchen, where his dad was making coffee.

"Hey Eli" Sam Khoda greeted.

"Hey" Elijah replied, trying to sound casual.

He poured himself cereal and started eating, and then the one thing he didn't want to happen-

"So how do you like taking a shower?" his dad asked.

Elijah couldn't even eat in peace. He swallowed the small portion of his cereal just to respond.

"It's good"

"If you like that, maybe you can try coffee next" Sam suggested.

"No, thanks"

Confusing indeed; first they said coffee wasn't really good for kids and now Elijah was being offered some. It was rather irritating like everything else. He then took another bite, hoping that his dad would see so he wouldn't ask any more questions. Sam Khoda sat next to his son at the table, with his coffee in front of him, and some toast.

"Well, it's September" Sam said, "You know what that means?"

Elijah didn't answer.

"Time to get some firewood and I might need your help"

After taking a few bites, Elijah slowly turned toward his dad.

"Yeah...sure"

He didn't sound certain. Even though Elijah didn't feel like doing anything, he just didn't have the strength to turn his dad away. Kindness was still something he had, whether he wanted it or not.

"Sooner or later, you'll have to learn" his dad added, "Because if I'm not here, you have to take charge, and not just the firewood"

There was no doubt that his dad was trying to say something. Elijah could only assume it was everything that he would have to take charge of, but his inner child told him it won't be for another lifetime. Therefore, he didn't think much of it.

"Okay" Elijah replied, gently.

It was almost eight-thirty, might as well be on time for the first day of school. Elijah finished his cereal and put his bowl away.

"Well, I gotta go"

"Okay, I'll see you later"

Elijah grabbed his backpack that was filled with binders, notebooks, writing utensils, and indoor shoes. He was already out the door and stepping off the porch, not even paying attention to the scenery around him. It was a nice sunny morning, something to enjoy before the season changes. But Elijah barely paid attention to little things like that.

"Elijah?" his mom called.

She opened the door, hoping to catch her son before he went any further, in which he was only halfway across the front lawn when he turned around.

"I just wanted to see you" his mom said, sincerely.

Sincerity was always a relief to hear in his mom's voice. It was a way to tell that Elijah didn't do anything wrong.

"Have a good first day" she encouraged. The words were comforting but the look in his mom's eyes said something else, like try not to get into trouble.

"Thanks" Elijah replied, gently.

He carried on and walked to school. He lived on upper reserve of Woyenne, in the town of Burns Lake. The elementary school wasn't far from where he lived. As Elijah got older, he learned to walk on his own, at least from that distance. So far, he only went straight from school to home, and vice versa, so his mom trusted him with walking.

The day had barely begun and everything was already dull and predictable. It was probably going to be the same like it was the year before, the same school, same classmates, and same walking distance from home to the school building. It was hard to think of anything else after living the same life for the past three years. The only big difference was that Elijah Khoda didn't have to deal with Brian Kidman because he was now in high school. So that was the bright side, having a little more peace.

But was that enough?

There had to be more, something that was worth getting out of bed in the morning and not just getting good grades and hanging out with the same people. It had to be something special, whatever that may be, and Elijah hoped that he would find it and perhaps having his own life where nobody had control over him. It seemed impossible but it was the only thing that kept him going.

Arriving at the turning point, the school was just around the corner. There were a few boulders on the trail, nearly blocking the path. Shortly, Elijah stepped off the gravel and onto the grass. There were trees on both sides and up ahead there was a hill. Just as he was reaching the top, Elijah could see the tip of the school building rising up and stepped onto the field. The sound of students talking could already be heard in the distance. There were several of them at the playground just on the other side. Elijah made his way to the end and stood at the top of the wooden steps, gazing down at his peers. He could already see familiar faces from that far. Nothing new, it was all the same.

The grade seven classes were on the left side of the school building, just down below from where Elijah walked down the wooden steps. The entrance was there with a roof being held by two pillars. The other students were hanging around there, talking to their own friends, students Elijah only knew by name. He didn't feel like looking for his friends. So he just leaned against the pillar and listen to life around him.

It wasn't long until Andrew Little arrived.

"E.K." Andrew greeted, cheerfully.

"Al" Elijah replied, trying to sound friendly as possible.

It was just from the year before Andrew started calling Elijah by his initials. In return, he did the same, only he called Andrew, "Al", as in Alan. The two boys reunited and gave each other a hug.

"How many months are in summer?" Andrew asked.

"Two" Elijah answered.

But then Andrew made a buzzing, like the kind you'd hear on a game show. "Wrong guess; the correct answer is one!" Then he showed Elijah a little card that had the number one.

Although the fun may be fading away and becoming repetitive, Andrew still had his moments, no matter how silly they turned out to be. It was just enough to make Elijah chuckle.

"I know eh. I miss summer already"

"I don't know. I think someone is secretly making time go by fast. Whoever it is, he or she probably doesn't like it when we're relaxing and having a good time. Damn that person!"

Elijah chuckled.

"What about you? How was the rest of your August? I haven't seen you since July"

"It was good, went to Old Fort like always"

"Ah, the great Fort I been hearing about. You'll have to take me one day. That'd be okay, right? I'm not gonna get chased out for the color of my skin?"

"Nah, it should be okay. We've actually had needos come visit a few times"

"Damn. I thought I would be the first"

The word "needo" was a Carrier word for white people. Elijah Khoda was First Nation, while Andrew was Caucasian. Sam and Madeline Khoda actually refer to Andrew as needo in a friendly way whenever he came to visit.

"Wanna go walk before the bell rings" Andrew suggested.

"Sure"

They began walking.

"Hey, if there's an Old Fort, is there a New Fort?" Andrew wondered.

They walked to the other side of the building where the younger students resided, both the fourth graders and the fifth graders. After reaching the end, they went around the corner that led them to the back of the school and there were basketball posts set up for students to play. Then shortly, they approached the monkey bars where the sixth grade students reside. Before they went any further, there were a few kids in the corner, hanging around and spotted Elijah and started approaching. Elijah wasn't particularly thrilled.

"Wassup?" the boy called.

His name was Quinton Malcolm, another First Nations student. He was a year younger than Elijah. He was one of those kids who tries to be funny and thinking he was tough. Quinton may have had his moments but there were times when he was short tempered. Elijah remembered him being kicked out of class for yelling at the teacher a couple of years back.

"Who, me?" Elijah said, hoping that Quinton really was talking to someone else.

"Yeah"

Oh great, not now.

Quinton had tried to befriend Elijah for a while, but Elijah didn't really feel comfortable around him, for that he recalled being manipulated by the kid when he first tried borrowing money off him.

"How's it going?" Elijah only said it to be nice. He was reluctant, thinking that the conversation was going to take a lifetime.

"Good. I just wanted to say hi and wassup"

"Hey, what about me?" Andrew asked, abruptly, but as a joke.

Quinton just looked at him funny.

"You ain't my friend" he said, calmly.

Andrew usually had high tolerance for his peers. "What about him?" he added, pointing to thin air on his left.

"What?" Quinton was confused.

"My imaginary friend!"

Quinton, still unsatisfied, shook his head in disapproval, "You're crazy"

"Come on, every kid had an imaginary friend at least once in their lives. Admit it; just hope that wasn't a ghost that later haunted your house"

"Yeah, well I grew up" Quinton said to Andrew, strongly. Then he turned his attention back to Elijah and spoke in a friendly tone, "Yo, Elijah, my man" he spoke in an urban manner, "We should definitely hang out with us. Hang out with your bros, you know"

And by us, Quinton was referring to his followers, Roscoe Lewis, Devon Welks, and June Disher. Elijah glanced at them, only one of them nodded. Then he happened to meet June's eye. June Disher was also a first nation's student. Just like Quinton, she was younger. She had black hair and lighter skin than the other natives. One time, Quinton had told Elijah that June liked him, which he didn't really believe, thinking that it was just Quinton's way of trying to initiate friendship.

June smiled and waved at Elijah, and he only waved back out of courtesy.

"I'll think about it" Elijah mumbled.

"Alright, man. Just let us know" Quinton encouraged.

Okay, good. He didn't try talking me into it.

Then Elijah continued walking.

"Hey, tell your imaginary friend I said hi" Andrew said to Quinton.

Supposedly Quinton Malcolm wasn't all bad, from the looks of it. He was being awfully nice. Elijah didn't really understand and had no intention to. From there on, he hoped that he wouldn't have to be friends with him.

Elijah and Andrew circled the school and made it back to the grade seven entrance, where they met Paula Hennig, waiting for them.

"Heeyyy Paulie!" Andrew greeted.

Paula opened her mouth, in the most cheerful way like she was about to respond in the same manner-

"Hey..." she replied, rather mildly.

Andrew noticed her sarcastic behavior and decided to tease her.

"Good to see you too, Andrew" he added, pretending to be her, "I missed you so much. Aw, you did? Come let me give you a hug"

Then Andrew opened his arms wide and dashed at Paula, who put her hand up firmly as she backed away.

"No!" she refused.

"Three years later and still no hug" Andrew said to Elijah.

Paula chuckled. "Does your life really depend on you getting a hug from me?"

"Of course; we're friends, right?"

"Well, some friends are not huggers. Let's just keep it at that"

Then Paula met Elijah's eye. For a while, they both stared at each other like they had something else to say other than speaking generally.

"But you, I will always hug, Elijah" she told him, kindly.

They hugged each other. And just like he did with Andrew, Elijah played it nice and friendly.

"So how was Vancouver?" he asked, casually.

"It was good, minus riding in the car with my sister. Even when I tried resting my eyes, she just wouldn't leave me alone"

"Did you bring me back something?" Andrew asked, abruptly.

"No" Paula answered, promptly.

"Did you bring *us* back something?"

"I already said no" she replied, slightly irritated.

"I know, but when I said 'us', I mean did you bring us something back for me and Eli"

Paula made a face at Andrew, a mocking smirk and lightly bopping her head. "Again, no"

"What was she supposed to bring us back, matching t-shirts?" Elijah asked.

"There you go! Now that's something" Andrew agreed.

"Yeah, well I spent all my money on clothes so I wouldn't be matching t-shirts with anybody" Paula told them.

The conversation was short-lived. Andrew couldn't think of anything else to say, while Elijah's mind was going on and off, as he kept thinking about the flaws of his life. So the three of them stood in silence and glanced around at their peers.

"Well, it's another school year-the last year of WKE to be precise" Paula said.

Then they turned around, facing the school building.

"Yup…last one" Elijah muttered.

"Good old Willy K." Andrew added. Then it was silent.

"What, you don't have anything funny to say?" Paula asked.

"Maybe I'm too sad to think because you didn't bring us matching t-shirts"

"Oh suck it up, loser" she replied, almost bitterly.

Last year of being in elementary school, like they said; that was the only thought in Elijah's mind. Just by looking at the school building, the first memories to emerge were all the bad times that Elijah suffered through, being bullied, lectured and getting suspended. Therefore, he couldn't think of anything nice to say that could add to his friends' conversation. One thing was for sure, Elijah couldn't wait to leave all that behind. That thought he kept to himself.

The bell went off and echoed through the school grounds. Then every student around them began to make way to their entrances.

"Well, I guess it's time" Paula said, "Good luck to all three of us"

"Thanks Paula" Elijah replied.

"Best of luck to you, my lady" Andrew said, giving a salute.

"Please don't call me that"

Just as Andrew and Paula left for their classes, Elijah joined his classmates as they lined up in the center as the other two groups were lined against the wall. Good luck, indeed.

The classroom was already crowded before Elijah could even set foot in the room. Even that was too much pressure. His classmates went to choose their lockers which were beside the desks. Because there were more than a few students, Elijah had to wait. He was hoping he'd get an upper locker but ended up with a lower locker, just like the year before.

He let out a sigh, *again.*

Elijah then put on his indoor shoes, grabbed his essential supplies and went to his desk. First thing he done was gazing at the clock. It was five to nine. Class was about to begin. It felt like forever for the day to be over, even though it was only half a day. So Elijah enjoyed the last minute of freedom and rested his head on his desk.

As tempting as it was, Elijah closed his eyes and was ready to sleep. Hopefully it would be the end of the day by the time he opened-

No, that was a silly thought, but if only it was that easy. He could hear his classmates' chatter echoing through his ear that was pressed against his cold desk. But then shortly, he felt a firm tap on his shoulder. Elijah opened his eyes and looked up.

"You'll have plenty of time to nap after school, young man" Mrs. Parker told him.

So Mrs. Parker was Elijah's grade seven teacher. He hoped that she would be alright. Just thinking about that made it more tiring, for that the teachers were usually the same every year, making you do things where you don't really want to. Elijah was counting on that. After she walked a few feet away, he gave a another little sigh. There was no choice but to give in. So Elijah sat up straight, trying to stay awake like a typical everyday student. First he glanced at the chalkboard, and then he slowly turned to scan his surroundings. Halfway through, he noticed something that caught his eye.

Like a lighthouse on a shore, there wasn't much for Elijah to do but to sit there and wait for a sign of life. That day, something-someone, had surfaced.

The student sitting next to him; it was a girl. But she didn't look any familiar to Elijah's eyes. She had long dark brown hair. That was all he could see, aside from the side of her face, still mysterious. For a moment, Elijah stared at her, trying to figure out if he had seen her before. He was starting to think no. Then suddenly he was thrown off focus once the girl turned to his direction. At first, Elijah thought maybe the girl was trying to turn to Mrs. Parker…But she wasn't…The girl soon met his eyes, while he found himself looking at hers. Suddenly, time and reality became distant and faded away as this moment between Elijah and the girl froze.

For years, Elijah Khoda seen many eyes look towards him, whether it was a teacher or a parent demanding a right answer or a fellow student looking at him, puzzled or weird because they saw him as a misfit. Each of those looks often pressured him to act like everyone else, even if it meant looking at them when spoken to and that was something Elijah once had a problem with because he was so shy to begin with.

But in this case, the eye contact just happened. And whoever this girl was, there was something about the way she stared. She wasn't waiting to hear a right answer. And no, she didn't look at him with discomfort or confusion. She was staring directly at him, blankly and perhaps intrigued. Elijah didn't know why he was looking at her for so long. They say it wasn't nice to stare. He was starting to feel awkward and he could've ended it any second just by looking away. Maybe it would've been rude in case the girl would've said something like a simple hello.

But that didn't happen. Neither of them spoke.

Yet, Elijah didn't and couldn't turn away. He was actually about to because the staring went for a little too long but before he realized it, the girl's features caught his attention.

Whoever this girl was, her dark brown hair was perfectly straight. Her eyes; there was something unique about them. They were wide open, not in the way he'd seen before. It was indescribable. But even so, it provided a warm feeling, like the sun on land. Her lips were pinkish colored. Not to mention her mouth was slightly open and that was somehow appealing. Her face was so clean that the lighting in the room shined off her, making her eyes, lips, and eyebrows standout. And the way she turned her head-it was tilted downwards until she lifted it up straight with her chin out-like one of those models in hair commercials.

Who is she? Elijah asked himself. Now the girl became a person of interest.

She was still silent when she could've said anything, even something bitter-sweet like *what are you looking at?* Like any other kid. It was a little surprising that she didn't and that was another thing that made Elijah Khoda wonder in silence. Finally, he was about to apologize out of kindness-

The girl slowly formed a smile, from ear to ear, and even showing a bit of teeth. That alone was rather astonishing and beautiful. It made Elijah stare much longer. He was actually about to smile back until their teacher came along.

"Hello there" Mrs. Parker greeted, as she approached the girl.

As the teacher and the new girl were getting acquainted, Elijah turned away, blankly, like he just woke up in a dream, no thinking, just a strange feeling in a familiar place, filled with great mystery and no way of telling what was going to happen. Just like any dream, it had to run its course until you would wake up.

Once that feeling sunk in, Elijah came to realize what just happen; he tried to process the weird experience from catching the girl's eye to finally turning away. But it was just the thought itself and no possible explanation to go along with it. That remained a mystery that needed to be solved.

It was just a second ago but thinking about it, it almost felt like that moment lasted an eternity. *Did that really happen?* That was the one question that floated in Elijah's mind. He mentally re-lived that scenario again and again, like a scientist trying to make a breakthrough. And the first image Elijah saw in his mind was her, the girl, looking back at him and smiled. Then there was a feeling inside of him. It was hard to tell but it made his heart lift. In a way, it was creating a rather excited feeling.

Weird, Elijah thought.

Suddenly he was right back into reality once the second bell went off, indicating that class was officially starting. Elijah scanned his surroundings-even overlooking the girl next to him as if she was just a regular student-and noticed a slight change of scenery. The rest of the students were all seated and Mrs. Parker was standing in front of the class, introducing herself and explaining on what to expect for the upcoming year. Elijah sat up straight and listened. As the teacher was still talking, he slowly turned to his right and noticed that girl was still sitting next to him.

She was still there!

Then that feeling of excitement started up again and it happened as Elijah laid his eyes on the girl as she was facing forward, probably didn't realize that she was being looked upon. Elijah almost couldn't believe it, knowing that she was there, as if that dream became a reality.

After the introduction, Mrs. Parker decided to acknowledge the new girl. "I know I recognize some of you. Speaking of which, there was someone in particular I honestly didn't recognize, only to realize that we have a new student to our school"

She gestured to the girl sitting next to Elijah, who became greatly curious once he was about to find out who the girl was. Nearly everyone in class looked in her direction, but that didn't seem to bother her, for that she turned and gave a friendly wave, followed by a gentle smile.

"Would you like to introduce yourself or should I?" she asked, kindly.

"I can" she insisted.

Elijah barely heard the girl's voice when she was first talking to the teacher, but once he heard it loud and clear, it sounded so beautiful.

It was light and smooth. She sounded like a regular girl, but there was something special about this one, like she had the voice of a singer and every word she spoke almost had a sense of rhythm that filtered the kindness of her tone.

She stood up in front of the class. Mrs. Parker even gave her space. The class was silent.

"My name is Sabrina Clarin" she told them, "I just moved here from Granisle, which is not too far from Burns Lake. Some of you may know Granisle. It's smaller than here but it's nice"

Sabrina's mouth was open, but didn't know what else to add. She quickly glanced at Mrs. Parker who was leaning on her desk.

"Uh, wanna tell us a little about yourself?"

"Sure" Sabrina nodded, "I...have one brother-big brother-he's just a year older than me"

There was a little pause.

"I guess that means we won't be seeing your brother here?" the teacher asked.

"Nope, he's in grade eight now, just starting high school" then she glanced at her classmates and spoke with false cheerfulness, "Next year, we'll be there!"

"That's right too" Mrs. Parker agreed, right away. That gave Sabrina relief, knowing that she avoided an awkward silence with her new classmates. Then Mrs. Parker concluded the introduction, "Anything else you'd like to add, Sabrina?"

"Uhh, not really, expect that I'm now here with you guys at WKE, and I look forward to learning with you"

"And we're glad to have you" Mrs. Parker added, cheerfully, "Thank you, Sabrina".

After that, Sabrina sat back down at her desk. From there, Mrs. Parker began giving her class the orientation of what they're about to do for the year, from subjects to classroom rules. Then she instructed the class that she expects them to be on best behavior and the consequences if they weren't. She was firm but polite. The students were already treating school like a second home. During the lecture, Elijah suddenly behaved like a good student as he sat there and listened, and did not give a second thought to anything else, almost like he was ready to learn.

Once time reached noon hour, the first day of school was over. Every student crowded the school grounds while vehicles and school buses were idling in the parking lot. Elijah acted casual as he waited for his friends. Paula was the first to step out.

"Oohhhh, that's a relief!" Paula called, as she approached Elijah.

"Yeah? Everything went good?" he asked.

"My teacher for this year seems alright"

"Oh yeah? What's her name again?"

"Ms. Bogue. She seems calm and polite. It's nice to know I can breathe in class"

Elijah only nodded. Neither of them said anything for a moment.

"What's your teacher like?" Paula asked.

"Mrs. Parker? Yeah, she's nice, I think" he answered, as he glanced at Paula, "Much better than the last two teachers. Well, Mrs. Turner from last year was okay"

"Well, that's good to hear; and how about the fact that you don't have to deal with Brian this year?"

"Oh, it's a very good thing. So glad I don't have to see him at all"

Then again, the first day of school was always easy because it was only a few hours long. Really, it was an introduction to what was yet to come, days and months of constant homework. The only thing that couldn't be predicted was the misery. And it was only a matter of time until the bad side of things would reveal itself. That was one of the things that Elijah learned about life, no matter of how much self-confidence that you could give to ones' self, there was always going to be bad days. For two years, Elijah Khoda had been on guard, like a knight on the wall that could see the danger beyond the horizon.

"Wonder where Andrew is?" Elijah said, only to make conversation.

"He's probably still trying to get his shoes on but too lazy to loosen the laces up" Paula replied.

And there Elijah saw Andrew appearing out of the crowd. He began to approach once he saw his friends.

"There he is. Your shoes still fit?"

"What?"

"Paula said you were lazy to put on your shoes"

"Oh yeah…" Andrew paused, "Least I'm not too lazy to finish my sentences"

Puzzled, Paula glanced over to Elijah. "Who are you referring to, exactly?"

"To you, Paulie" he then pointed at her, "My finger points at you. The finger never lies"

"Haha, you're cute"

"Anyways" Andrew said, after a little chuckle, "Now, the first day of school is over. Do I need to comfort anyone? Hugs?"

Andrew opened his arms to Paula like he did that morning. Paula just looked at him with dull eyes.

"If you're referring to the first day of grade six, for the last time, I just dropped my pencil case in front of the class. It's not like it scarred my life"

"But I'm sure some of them laughed at you"

"And I'm sure I walked it off."

"Fine, I'll hug myself" Andrew turned and wrapped his arms around his upper body, and then he started shaking. Once he started moaning, Paula couldn't help but feel a slight discomfort.

"Don't you have a bus to catch?" she asked.

Andrew ended his gag and turned back to his friends.

"I don't catch the bus, the bus catches me" he said, in a real sly voice.

Paula and Elijah just looked at him funny.

"That doesn't really make any sense" she told him.

"It doesn't have to. I'm Andrew!"

Then he started to sprint passed them to catch the school bus.

"See ya" Andrew called, as he waved his friends farewell.

Only Elijah waved back.

"Well, I think I just saw my mom in the parking lot" Paula said.

"Alright, so I'll see you tomorrow"

"Oh, you will"

Elijah was by himself after Paula left. He was starting to make his way towards the wooden steps that led to the soccer field in order to head home. Just as Elijah was passing by the entrance, Sabrina Clarin came walking out. Seeing her automatically made him watch her every move like a security guard eyeing a suspect that triggered his attention. Elijah walked slowly, as the new girl made her way towards the concrete staircase and there she stopped. She was probably waiting for her parents to pick her up.

Who is she? There was that question again. But he didn't give it much thought. So Elijah went about his business and started for home. Just after he walked passed the entrance, he again peered at the girl out of habit, and she was still standing on top of the staircase. This time, Elijah stared for more than a few seconds.

Over the school years, classmates were just faces, kids that had the same intention to become successful. Many of them either kept to themselves or had their own inner circle of friends. There was really no reason for Elijah to give much thought to. But with this girl, it was almost like following the main character from a favorite TV show and you couldn't help but wait and see what happened next. Only thing is, it wasn't a character, it was a real person standing several feet away.

For some odd reason, Elijah couldn't move. He stood there like a statue, with his eyes still on the new girl. It was almost like he was afraid, but afraid of what? The only thought that occurred was that the girl could turn around any second and then freak out once she realized she was being watched. Whatever it may be, there was that tingling feeling inside Elijah, that rather excited feeling and suddenly he wasn't so afraid anymore.

A new thought emerged: *go and say hi.*

As he approached closer, Elijah stopped completely as he realized what he was really doing. It was like that moment when you're about to jump off the diving board, only to realize how high above ground you were. *Do I really want to do this?* Elijah hesitated. The girl still had her eyes forward, unaware of who was behind her. After staring blankly, he finally tried getting her attention by clearing his throat, but it was rather silent. He did it again, but she didn't hear him. Elijah was already feeling embarrassed. So he turned his head slightly, getting ready to walk away.

But then he found the courage at the last minute. So in the end, Elijah reached out and tapped the girl on her shoulder gently...

Driving on the highway, the Clarin family was getting close to their new hometown. Mom and dad were upfront, while Sabrina and Jonathan sat in the backseat. The radio was the absence of silence. But for Sabrina, the world around her was a quiet place for that she was miles away in her mind and of course she was miles away from home. She sat back in her seat and watched the nature go by. It was easy to catch a glimpse of a single tree for just a few seconds before it passed. That was how it felt for Sabrina now that she thought about her home in Granisle, what should've been a lifetime felt like a few seconds and now suddenly it was all left behind almost as if they just packed up and ran away without anybody, even her grandparents, knowing about it.

Their parents gave Sabrina and her brother a talk before moving, that everything would be alright and that they just needed time to get adjusted to whole new scenery. Sometimes words weren't very helpful; at least that was what Sabrina Clarin thought, when it came to a situation where they was literally nothing you could do and the only choice was to wait it out, which at times felt forever; the joys of being a kid.

"Well, this is it" Michael Clarin spoke as soon as they entered their new hometown, "Burns Lake"

Sabrina gave a friendly nod, just to show that she was still there.

The Clarins went straight to their new home, which was located on top of one of the avenues, where dozens of residential homes resided. Sabrina and her family stepped out of the car to take it all in, the front yard that was filled with green grass, trees in different parts of the area. So that gave a sense of nature around them, and there were plenty of neighbors in that street, probably more than the ones they had back home. Their new house was just the same size as the one in Granisle, fairly big but not too small either. Together, the Clarin family entered the house. It was completely empty and lifeless. No furniture or appliances, for now at least.

"I don't know about you guys, but I'm kind of excited decorating this whole place" Leah Clarin said.

"I'm excited to get my bed into my new room" Jonathan added.

They all ignored his sarcasm.

"Well, since you two didn't see this whole place yet, let's show you around" Michael offered.

Both the parents gave their kids the tour of the house, from the bedrooms and the basement on the inside to the backyard on the outside. In the end, Sabrina chose her room. She walked in and put her bag down and stood in the middle. The sun was shining through the window. Then she went and looked in the empty closet. After examining everything, Sabrina sat down and leaned against the wall, staring blankly. She thought the change of scenery would improve but she couldn't help but feel that something was still missing, aside from leaving her grandparents in Granisle. She already started missing them before the move, but that couldn't be it. Whatever it was, it had to be something that could make her feel better, something special.

"Sabrina?" her mom called.

As soon as she heard her mom's voice, Sabrina quickly stood up and acted normal.

"In here, mom" Sabrina answered, hiding the sadness from her voice.

Leah walked in and glanced at her daughter and then her new room. "I see you chosen your bedroom" she assumed.

"Yeah, I think so" Sabrina agreed.

Leah entered and stood with Sabrina, proudly holding her close as they looked around.

"Looks nice and it will look better once we get everything in here, which is why I came to get you. The movers are here. Come on, it's time for teamwork"

After a week passed, the Clarins had settled into their new home. Before any of them knew it, the first day of school had started. That morning, Sabrina was already awake before her alarm went off. This time, she didn't go outside to enjoy nature. Instead, she just lied in bed with nothing but silence to comfort her.

The first thing Sabrina did after getting up was eating breakfast in the kitchen. Her dad made it as a way to start off the school year. Nearly the whole house had the scent of bacon and eggs. When both Michael and Leah began the pep talk-just as Sabrina predicted-she pretended to be excited.

It's your first day of school! Aren't you excited?

Remember, just be yourself.

It was the usual sayings, pretty much the same speeches being told through different layers, words that Sabrina heard over the school years, like knowing every single line in a movie. But in this case, she was starting to get a little irritated just enough to make her roll her eyes.

"Is Jonathan up, yet?" Leah asked, as she poured herself another cup of coffee.

"I don't think so" Michael replied. He was sitting opposite from Sabrina at the table, eating the breakfast he just made.

"Can you go check?"

"Already did, a few minutes ago. So it's your turn and I think I don't need to mention that I just sat down"

Leah just gave him a look, for that she sensed the attitude he was subtly giving. "Always looking for different ways to fight"

Michael just shrugged his shoulders. "Bound to happen sooner or later"

His wife just scowled at him, almost wanting to shake her head. Then she walked out of the kitchen, "Jonathan!" she called, "Come on, it's the first day of school. Time to get up"

"Now that's marriage for you" Michael muttered to Sabrina, who didn't say anything, "You take turns, even if one doesn't want to"

Sabrina just gave a chuckle.

When the time came, Sabrina was trying to choose what to wear on her first day of school. It was a natural instinct, to make a good impression and look presentable. While she was still in pajamas, Sabrina displayed two new shirts on her bed. One was a regular girl's t-shirt and the other was a white blouse with long sleeves. They both looked equally exquisite. As Sabrina took a long look at her clothing, she examined them thoroughly. The t-shirt was something simple but then she realized that it was...a little too ordinary. Suddenly, her interest began to diminish. Now studying the blouse, it was something fancier, something that would bring the beauty out of her. But was it too much to wear at school? Since she couldn't decide, Sabrina went to see her mom in the living room.

"Hey mom" she said and then she held up both shirts, "Which one do you think is better?"

Leah took a moment and examined both shirts, "The white one"

Sabrina was a little surprised. She glanced at the white blouse to see if there was anything special about it, "Really?" she replied, uncertainly.

"I think it looks nice" her mom added.

Nice? Sabrina was kind of hoping to hear something other than nice, something more lengthy than a compliment. She wanted to hear what was special about the blouse and how it would bring the best out of her. At the same time, she was also hoping to hear a comment about the t-shirt. She glanced back at her mom, hiding her mild disappointment. Sabrina opened her mouth, about to say something else like, how is it nice exactly? But ended up saying, "Well, if you think it's nice, I'll wear it"

Back in her bedroom, Sabrina was still undecided about her clothing. She imagined herself what she would look like if she wore one or the other.

The regular shirt was something simple and most likely other girls would be wearing the same kind as well. The white blouse seemed a little too formal. Maybe that was why Sabrina was a little skeptical about it. Putting on that blouse would make it look like she had a fancy dinner planned right after school. That thought tempted her to take the blouse out of the equation.

Sabrina sighed as the misery started again and that put her back into that emotional state. For a minute there, Sabrina had the confidence like a normal girl would right up until she laid her clothes out but now things didn't really feel normal for some reason. It was like there was a part of Sabrina that didn't really want to be herself. It was rather complicated. She ought to go criticize her mom for choosing the blouse but then she figured it would be pointless. Then Sabrina remembered that she already promised her mom that she would wear the blouse. So she put the t-shirt down.

Sabrina saw herself in the mirror after getting dressed and wasn't exactly thrilled. She only wore it just to avoid her mom questioning her about choosing the regular shirt. At that point, she didn't feel like explaining anything because she was afraid of someone judging her or making fun of her.

(Princess!)

As Sabrina gazed at reflection, she gave herself some advice: "Maybe no one will notice", she muttered.

"Okay before you guys go, I wanna get a quick picture of you" Leah insisted. The whole family was outside in their front yard. It was a last minute decision to take a photo before leaving, "Jonathan, Sabrina, maybe stand in front of the house".

The Clarin siblings did as she said and stood by each other in front of their new home. First they had to smile and ended up taking more than one photo. After they were finished, Sabrina and Jonathan went to the car, while their parents stood there, looking upon them.

"Wow" Leah said, "Grade seven and grade eight. Where has the time gone?"

"You know, I been wondering the same thing" Michael said.

After dropping off Jonathan at the local high school, Leah took Sabrina up to the elementary school. It was merely a few streets away from their home. Once they arrived, Leah parked the car for them to gaze at the school building in front of them.

"Well, this is our stop" Leah said, "Or your stop, I should say"
Sabrina didn't say anything as she took it all in.

"William Konkin Elementary School" her mom added, "Seems like a nice place. You got nature all around you and a suburban area right next door"

"Yeah, I'm sure it is" Sabrina agreed, trying to sound optimistic. There were dozens of students all around. Sabrina wondered if she would ever befriend any of them. Up until then, she never gave any thought to making new friends. Before, her brother Jonathan was the closest person she had to a best friend. They grew up together, played together and saw each other at their best and their worst. But now they were on different paths and about to pursue lives of their own. And being a new student, making friends seemed like a chore, debating if she would have to be the one to say something first or wait for the other person to,

"-just half a day today, so I'll be here to pick you up at lunch time" her mom was saying.

Sabrina was so deep in thought that she wasn't paying attention. She quickly wrapped her head around what her mom was telling her before responding, "Oh…yeah, sure". Then she was naturally about to get out of the car but just couldn't once she looked back at her peers again.

"Sabrina?" Leah said, calmly.

"Oh, I don't think I can pretend any longer" her daughter replied, finally releasing the distress went off in her voice.

"What's wrong?" Leah asked, worriedly.

It was time to admit it. Sabrina gave a little sigh. "I don't' really know" she said, hopelessly.

"Come on, think" her mom encouraged, "What's bothering you?"

"It's just…" Sabrina paused to find a possible explanation, "I don't really know. I thought maybe it was this whole moving thing that got me feeling a little sad but I feel like it's something else"

Leah tried to think of a way for her daughter to express herself, "Do you think you might be feeling nervous, being a new student and all?"

"Maybe" Sabrina replied, softly. She was about to add how making new friends suddenly required a lot of effort but then she wasn't sure if that was the problem. While she was having a private conversation with her mom, Sabrina then thought about bringing up her dilemma of what to wear but that was starting to feel insignificant at that point.

"Well, that feeling is mutual" her mom said, gently, "Today I'm sure you're not the only one" But that comment didn't comfort her daughter at all. So she gently combed her fingers through Sabrina's hair and held her head to comfort her. Sabrina met her mother's eyes, still feeling nothing but doubt.

"Honestly, I don't know what else to tell you" Leah said, "But I think your mind is a little too clouded that you can't think straight"

That brought a little sensibility to the conversation.

"You're probably just overthinking" her mom added, "One thought leads to another and then they start piling up. You just need to learn how to balance it"

"I guess that's what it is" Sabrina agreed.

"Can you think of anything else you want to say?"

"No, not really"

"That's all right. Sometimes when we can't think straight, we have a hard time expressing ourselves. I don't wanna make you late for school but just know that this is a new chapter for you. Take a deep breath and be yourself. I'm always here if you wanna talk"

"Sure. Oh, mom?"

"Yeah?"

"Do you think I'll make friends here?" Sabrina asked.

"Of course you will" her mom promised, "You're a wonderful person" She placed her hand on Sabrina's shoulder for comfort and then gently rubbed her cheek. "All it takes is for one person to see it".

Mother's words fed Sabrina confidence.

"Thanks, mom" Sabrina said, proudly.

The morning bell went off, putting an end to the mother and daughter moment. Sabrina became completely still once she realized that her first impression was being late. She turned around and noticed every student in sight was running towards different entrances. What am I still doing in the car?

"I guess I better go" Sabrina admitted, sounding like a regular student again.

"Okay, I'll be here to pick you up at noon" Leah spoke fast as if they only had a few seconds to spare. "Have a good first day, Sabrina"

Sabrina was already getting out of the car.

"Did you want me to take you to the entrance?" her mom called out.

"No, I should be okay" Sabrina said, as she stuck her head back in the car. Then she closed the passenger door and started making her way to the school. Sabrina stopped as soon as she noticed there were three different entrances. She went back and opened the car door, "Where am I supposed to go?"

Leah pointed ahead of them, "Over there beside the field. That's where the grade seven students lineup"

"Thank you. Love you" Sabrina said and then departed.

Her mom waved, even though Sabrina was several feet away. She relaxed after that little excitement. "I love you, too".

Just as Sabrina was approaching, the students were entering the building. She gazed at the school itself as she was still walking. "WKE" she whispered, "Nice to meet you".

Not knowing which lineup was hers, Sabrina just followed the students inside but she kept her distance because she thought it would be weird walking close, considering that she was new. Before moving any further, she took a deep breath just as her mother encouraged. Just be yourself. Got it.

No one noticed that Sabrina Clarin was one of them. They all did their morning routine, putting outside shoes on the rack in the boot room and headed towards class. Sabrina figured out which classroom was hers. The paper said Mrs. Parker's and the sign outside displayed that particular name.

In a weird way, Sabrina already felt like a part of the crowd already as she entered the classroom. She went un-noticed until after she got settled at her desk. There was a boy sitting next to her, a First Nations student. Just shortly after Sabrina sat down, she could feel his eyes watching her. Surprisingly, there wasn't any discomfort. Sabrina Clarin was too kind to rudely turn him away. That wasn't the kind of impression she'd give first. Besides, whoever this boy was, he didn't seem dangerous. He was probably just curious about her-the new student-in the same class. Sabrina realized once she made eye contact, the boy's eyes were warm and gentle. Then out of kindness, she gave a smile.

"Hello, there" her new teacher greeted, as she approached.

"Hi" Sabrina replied, kindly.

"You must be the new student I heard about"

"That's me" Sabrina said, like was trying to be clever. It only made her feel a little stupid.

"Well, I'm Mrs. Parker, your seventh grade teacher"

"Sabrina Clarin, your new student" she then looked away and nearly mouthed the words oh boy. Mrs. Parker already knew that she was a new student.

"Welcome to our class"

"Thank you"

Next thing Sabrina knew was that she was encouraged to introduce herself to the class, just as it was predicted. With more than a dozen of eyes staring, Sabrina was able to keep it together. She kept her introduction short and simple by mentioning her name and where she came from and a little family background. Luckily, it only lasted a few seconds.

Well, I guess that wasn't bad, Sabrina said to herself as she exited the building. The first day of school had come and gone. It was time to go home. The moment they were dismissed, Sabrina took her time leaving the classroom, expecting something else to happen. She didn't know what, either a classmate going up to her and ask questions as if she were a celebrity or perhaps someone offering friendship, anything as long as it didn't involve hostility, unlike a certain boy from Granisle. But nothing happened. She became invisible again as her peers walked passed her and didn't say a word. Sabrina stood on top of the stairs, looking for her mom, who hadn't arrived yet. Then suddenly she felt a tap on her shoulder.

….She responded casually as she turned around slowly. It was really happening. He saw the girl's eyes turning towards his direction. For a second there, Elijah acted like a regular student in a lineup and the girl in front of him only turned to look at something else. But no, the girl's eyes turned and locked directly onto him, like a spotlight as if he was on stage in front of hundreds of people. Just like in that scenario, Elijah froze, and his mind was blank and drifted into silence.

What was Elijah looking at? Into the eyes of a girl, yes, but yet it felt more than that. Being up close to her felt entirely different than being in class; her eyes had Elijah hypnotized. It was a mix of emotions, such as being watched by a strange entity from the shadows. He couldn't turn away and he couldn't speak. At the same time, it was just as normal because he was looking into the eyes of a human being. It was only natural. But in this case, those eyes-her eyes-were something else… something special. It was almost like Elijah had seen a magical gateway into another world. Maybe it was just that, in a way.

And her face, her face was another thing. It was clean white, like a doll and it made her shaded eyebrows and eyelashes standout. Her cheeks were slightly curved with a pointy chin on the bottom; a perfectly shaped oval face, and of course her hair, long dark brown, hanging down nice and straight on both sides. Elijah noticed them all right away as soon as their eyes met. It was rather amazing, nothing like he'd seen before.

Say something, he thought to himself. "Hi" Elijah finally spoke.

"Hi" the girl replied.

She acknowledged! That feeling inside Elijah was getting more exciting.

"I just...wanted to say hi" he added.

She looked at him a little funny, "You just did"

"Oh..."

Then came an awkward silence, but then the girl's chuckle made up for it. Elijah laughed a little, nervously. He didn't know what else to say. And he could do nothing but stare as he was studying her features over and over like he was admiring a great work of art. That was something about her that he couldn't turn away. Maybe it was kindness because Elijah thought it would've been rude if he turned around and walked away embarrassed. Or maybe it wasn't kindness. It was something else, something that Elijah couldn't tell.

This was much more than Sabrina Clarin expected, being gawked at by a classmate. Yet, there wasn't any discomfort, so there was no reason to protest or walk away. She didn't know who he was but she could tell that was just as normal as any other boy. He had dark skin and black hair that made him distinctive from the crowd. But skin color was no matter. Whoever this boy was, he seemed like the quiet type. So that gave Sabrina a safe breathing space. It also showed that there was probably more to him on the inside, such as kindness which was already displayed from the way he stared. Just like before, the boy's eyes were gentle and real, like he was actually looking at her instead of seeing what he wanted to see. It made her feel accepted on her first day at WKE. That's what she was waiting for.

"Did you just come here to have a staring contest?" Sabrina asked, in which she meant it as a joke. She hoped that her voice wasn't at all harsh.

Elijah was lost in her eyes. It took him a moment to answer.

"Huh? Oh, I just wanted to say…" *Don't say hi again,* "I'm in your class, Mrs. Parker's?" He was suddenly feeling both nervous and excited that it nearly drained the good vibe. He quickly took a deep breath and kept it together.

While for Sabrina, it didn't take long for her to remember him. "Right. I thought you looked familiar. You're the one sitting next to me"

"Yeah…I am" Elijah admitted, still feeling an ounce of nervousness.

Then the girl formed a friendly smile, which made things feel good. Elijah couldn't help but smile in return. Then shortly, he cleared his throat. *What else do people say when they're first meeting? Introduce themselves.*

"I'm Elijah…Elijah Khoda" he told her, as he extended his hand.

Sabrina glanced at his hand, quite relieved that this boy was well mannered. So she then extended hers. Things got more interesting once Elijah felt her hands mingling with his. It was soft and warm, that sent a certain vibe through his body. Now that nervous and exciting feeling faded away and was replaced by something that was indescribable. It was liberating for sure and it also lifted his spirits up higher than it ever did.

"Sabrina Clarin" she said.

Sabrina Clarin…That was a beautiful name, one that he didn't hear often; it was a great name for a girl. And the last name, pronounced as 'Clare-ring', was like the icing on the cake, it added to it and altogether it had a nice ring.

They shook hands and gazed into each other's eyes for a moment. There was that stare again. But this time, it somehow felt greater than before. Sabrina's features were still there, just as amazing as before. Then there was her smile, friendly and heartening. That was what made it extra special. A certain feeling struck Elijah, something he hadn't really experienced before. He was at the same school where he had been for a few years, a place that developed a dull routine. But that morning, meeting Sabrina Clarin was something out of the ordinary. After meeting those eyes and putting his hand in hers, he was taken to a better place, where there was no pressure from reality, just happiness.

A car honked in the distance. Sabrina turned and peered over her shoulder. "It's my mom. I gotta go" she said gently. Aside from trying to put his mind back in the right frame, Elijah didn't know what to add for that he felt the urge to say a funny or clever remark. "It was nice meeting you, Elijah" Sabrina told him, with a little smile.

"Nice meeting you too" he replied, sounding gently as he could, for that there was a little excitement in his voice.

After Sabrina bid farewell, she turned around and started walking towards the car. Absently, Elijah watched her leave until she was out of sight. Suddenly his day felt different. First, it started off with not wanting to do anything with school, but now something else had made it a little special. Elijah didn't give it much thought until he reached the field. He stopped and realized, *what just happened?*

That entire morning had stayed with Elijah, from laying his eyes on Sabrina in class to meeting her in person. As he was walking back home, he kept replaying those moments in his mind, recapping every detail; long dark brown hair and eyes so bright, a voice so girly and light, hands so soft and warm. They were amazing features, but yet Elijah could not figure out what it was that put that feeling inside of him. At the same time, it made him feel good and that interfered with the pressure of school. Maybe this year wouldn't be so bad, Elijah thought for a moment.

"Sabrina Clarin" he muttered repeatedly, as he was walking home. He couldn't get that name out of his head. It just sounded too extraordinary and the more he said it, the more he realized how it made it so. The first name, Sabrina, was a nice build up with three syllables, while the last name, Clarin, it was short and easy to pronounce. Each time Elijah said her name, he began to say it slowly just because he admired it like it was nicely written lyrics from a song. "Saa-briii-na… Clarrri-in".

Elijah had the house to himself for the rest of the afternoon, for that his parents were working. After he came home, he napped for a little while and then watched TV after he woke up. Eventually, both his parents came home. First thing Madeline did was going to see her son. She walked down the hallway and peeked into his room.

"Hey Eli" she greeted, kindly.

"Hey mom" he replied, glancing at her from the TV.

"So how was your first day?"

"It was good"

Elijah's response was casual, which was alright to hear.

"Good" his mom said. And then she left to her bedroom.

Just thinking about the first day of school in general brought back a particular moment he had with a certain girl. *I think I made a new friend*, Elijah thought as he looked away from the TV blankly.

CHAPTER TWO

Welcome the Fourth Member

The second day of school had begun. This time it was a full day. So Elijah had packed a lunch that morning. It was all ordinary like for any student, get up in the morning and get ready. That's how it was for Elijah Khoda, as he merely devoting his mind to the present and focused on one task after another, eat breakfast, shower, and get dressed. Elijah's mind didn't mentally wander off until he arrived at school and saw Sabrina Clarin. His first instinct was to go up and say hi like he did on the day before. Just as he was approaching her from behind, he stopped and opened his mouth-

That was it, nothing else. Almost right away, Elijah slowly turned around quietly and pretended that never happened. He stood there with his back turned, wondering what the problem was, because he was suddenly too nervous to talk to Sabrina.

What could it be? I talked to her yesterday and nothing was wrong. Why can't I do it again? What is it?

"What are we looking at?" Andrew whispered, as he was literally trying to see from his best friend's point of view. Elijah was nearly startled. And then there was Paula, joining in on the conversation.

"Oh, nothing" Elijah replied, a little nervously, "I-I thought I seen a…a spider"

"Hey, Paulie's right here" Andrew told him, gesturing towards Paula to their left, "Isn't the spider supposed to be on her?"

"You know, I gotta think of different responses because you're becoming too predictable, Andrew" Paula said.

"That's good, Paulo, because I'll probably be…"

Elijah paid no further attention to their conversation as he turned around and saw Sabrina, who was still waiting around for the bell to ring. He made no effort to introduce his friends to his new classmate, at least not yet. Why? It could be because Elijah was too nervous to even say a word around her. But he acted normal as he hung around with Paula and Andrew. Once the bell rang, the students lined up. Elijah was by himself with his classmates. He purposely waited for Sabrina to join in, so he would be right behind her. And that was it, just standing behind her like strangers in an elevator. There was some waiting time until their teacher came out to claim her students. During that wait, Elijah was slowly developing courage. He took small steps until he was close enough to Sabrina.

Talk to her like you did yesterday. How hard can it be?

So Elijah leaned closer and opened his mouth.

This was it.

"Hey Billy!" a voice behind interrupted.

Elijah was startled and now the courage disappeared. All that was left was agitation.

"Why are you in front of the line?" That voice was Jeff Tomly, quite a character that appealed to everyone but not to Elijah, "You're never in front of the line!"

Rolling his eyes, Elijah didn't pay any further attention to Jeff. And with the volume of his voice, there was really no point in talking at all.

Damn you, Jeff!

Class was about to begin. Elijah was at his desk. A few minutes alone eased his agitation. The day became a fresh start once Sabrina came and sat down across from him. Just by looking at her, he could feel her presence washing away the negativity. It was such a warm feeling and gave some breathing space. Now it was time for a second chance, as Elijah turned slowly and watched her from the corner of his eye. Sabrina was unaware. He didn't speak or even breathed, still unsure how to start a conversation. At one point, he thought Sabrina would've but she was quiet. Elijah was able to relax and turned his head all the way and saw Sabrina with her eyes down, fidgeting with her pen. *What are you waiting for?* Then finally, some courage was found.

"Hi Sabrina" Elijah greeted, kindly.

She heard him loud and clear as she turned her head towards him.

"Hi Elijah" she replied, in the same manner.

Smiling at each other, it was just the same as last time. It made the day feel good. But then Sabrina looked down again. *That's it?* That couldn't be it. There had to be more to say than just saying hello. Elijah stared in the new girl's direction, trying to think of what to say that could get them talking to each other. He noticed that Sabrina was still fidgeting with her pen. It looked like she was drawing little dots on her fingertips. That was something to talk about. So Elijah leaned over and again opened his mouth-

The second bell went off. It was time for class. *Next time,* Elijah thought, trying to stay positive as he sat back in his seat.

Something was different. The silence took over and suddenly it made Elijah feel awkward and more nervous. After staring for a little too long, he turned his eyes forward before she or even anybody else noticed. That was when Elijah Khoda realized that he wasn't really good at starting conversations. Before then, he'd only spoke if he was spoken to, whether it was Paula, Andrew, a parent, or a teacher. Usually one of them would start a small talk and Elijah would respond casually. So for the first part of the morning, Elijah didn't say a word to Sabrina.

It was a matter of seconds once the students of WKE stepped outside as they were dismissed for recess. Elijah was the first to exit. There was no sign of Paula or Andrew. But right away, he noticed Sabrina was pondering around, alone, just near the entrance. The thought of asking her to hang out was there but it took time for commitment, which made Elijah stand still in the middle of the crowd of students like a wolf in the bushes. Since neither of his best friends was outside yet, Elijah decided to mingle with the new girl like he meant to earlier.

As he approached, he was able to summon some courage but getting closer started to make him nervous, although there was some resistance. And as Sabrina's eyes met his, Elijah's mind just went blank and made him lost for words.

"Hey…" Elijah was able to greet to begin with.

"Hey" she replied, gently.

Think, Elijah, think!

"Hey" he repeated.

You idiot!

"I, uh, saw you earlier-when you were sitting right beside me, drawing on your hand?"

Sabrina looked rather puzzled. She didn't catch the last part. "I'm sorry?"

"Earlier, when you were sitting at your desk-before the bell rang, I saw you were drawing on yourself with a pen"

"Oh, you mean this" Sabrina showed him the little the blue ink that was dotted on each tip of her fingers. "I do that sometimes when I'm bored"

"Cool, that looks cool" Then Elijah just randomly raised his hand briefly, "Me, I don't have any"

Of course you don't, he thought to himself. Elijah was starting to feel silly. Just looking at Sabrina's eyes gave that exciting feeling and yet some great comfort. "So, uh, how do you like our new school?"

"It's…" Sabrina was about to answer but was interrupted by Elijah as he realized what he said.

"Sorry, I meant to say YOUR new school, not 'our' new school" Then he added a chuckle that sounded rather nervous. Oddly satisfied, Sabrina just laughed with him.

"It's-it's a nice place" she replied.

"Well, good. I'm glad you do, do think that"

Embarrassed, Elijah looked away because he realized that he couldn't even talk like a normal person. He looked back up and caught Sabrina's eye, along with her beautiful features. But it was too awkward to admire them again.

"So have you been going here for years?" Sabrina asked.

"Yeah, yes I have" Elijah replied, honestly.

She just nodded.

"Ever since grade four" he added, "I grew up here, in Burns"

"Really?"

"Yeah, its home"

Almost perfect, Elijah thought cheerfully. He was able to get a conversation going, despite that he was un-witted at first but Sabrina did her part and asked an honest question, to which Elijah gave a couple of facts about him. It was a start.

"There it is again!" Andrew's voice called from the distance. Elijah turned and saw him playfully chasing Paula out from the entrance, as he firmly clawed her back.

"Don't!" she whined.

"But the spider is still there. I see it"

"I already know it's your hand. So it's no use to repeating it over and over"

But Andrew didn't listen. He repeated the gag and Paula still reacted skeptically.

"It's my friends" Elijah explained to Sabrina, who just nodded, "They're pretty funny. I gotta go. I just wanted to see how you're doing"

"Oh, well, I'm doing good" Sabrina answered.

"Cool. Well, see ya"

"Bye"

If only Elijah kept the conversation going a little longer but then he couldn't think of what else to say. So maybe he was meant to meet with Paula and Andrew. As they went along, Elijah turned to glance at Sabrina, who was now alone. Now he couldn't help but feel bad. Perhaps there was something else he could've done.

When recess was over, Elijah caught up to Sabrina in class when they went to grab their indoor shoes from their lockers. "Hey" he called, as they were surrounded by their peers.

"Hi" Sabrina said, with a soft smile.

"Listen, I just wanted to say that I'm sorry…" Elijah meant to add more information but where they were standing; a few classmates were coming and going. So he had no choice but to step aside but not too far.

"Sorry for what?"

"For leaving you to go be with my friends"

"Oh no, you don't have to be sorry! Why would you be?"

"Uh, because you seemed a little…lonely?"

Sabrina just stared at him. *Maybe I am a little lonely,* she wanted to say. But she was mostly touched by how sincere and thoughtful he was; maybe a little naïve but she could tell that he meant well. "Don't be silly" she replied, pretending to be humorous while trying to think of something else to add but nothing came to mind. They both went back to their desks to put on their shoes. Elijah felt optimistic from their little small talk. So he made the best of it.

"Yeah, those were my friends. I've…We've known each other for a few years" he told her.

"Well, that's good"

With the little time that they had, Elijah was trying to think of what else to say. He was still dealing with the guilt of leaving her by herself. He was still feeling bad about it. Then Elijah thought maybe there was a way to make it right.

"Hey" he called.

Sabrina gave her attention as Elijah leaned over to speak.

"Would you like to meet them and maybe we could show you around the school?" he offered.

She considered his offer in silence, "Sure".

Once lunch break started, they both sat in silence and ate. Every few minutes, Elijah would turn and glance at her. Most of the time he was trying to think of what to say to her and not just one thing, but anything really, that could get them socializing for some time, maybe for the rest of their lives. Elijah liked that thought. And there was one possible solution, Andrew. His best friend was more sociable to the outside world, his peers and even the teachers. He could never forget those times in grade four when he often used humor whenever he interacted with their classmates with one-liners and comebacks, even though not all of them were clever but they were still funny in many ways. Andrew made that year memorable and he was always there to help Elijah.

After everyone finished eating, it was time for their second recess. Elijah reminded Sabrina and made sure that she was by his side when they both left the school building. They waited outside the entrance. Andrew was the first one that came out. Right away he saw Elijah in the distance and then walked excitedly to the sunlight and did a pose by lifting his head up and arms up like he was a singer on stage. Elijah chuckled while Sabrina seemed amused by Andrew's entrance. After having his fun, Andrew finally looked and realized the new face standing beside Elijah and became intrigued. Then he decided to acknowledge with a little humor.

"Elijah, don't look..." he said, directly to him, in a low voice like he didn't want the new girl to know, "But there's a strange girl standing next to you".

Sabrina clearly heard him but was quite entertained. She could tell right away that his witticism was unique. Not knowing how to respond, Elijah just simply said: "I know".

Andrew stood next to Elijah, "Since Pokedex isn't real, who is she?"

"I'll tell you when Paula gets here"

Then Andrew looked at Sabrina, "Who are you?"

She paused as she was about to answer honestly but then she decided respond with humor. "A Pokemon, apparently"

A little surprised, Elijah quickly turned his attention to her, for that she was familiar with that subject. "You watched Pokemon?"

Then Sabrina admitted, "Doesn't everyone?"

"Well, maybe not everyone" Andrew added, "Last time I checked, everybody was going crazy and not buying Pokemon cards! I mean one second it was the best thing in our lives next to food and now everyone just cares more about food."

They just paused. There were no words that could add to Andrew's energetic humor.

"I guess it's not as popular as it used to be" Elijah replied, promptly, and then he was eager to start a conversation with his new friend, "So Sabrina, you collected Pokemon cards, too?"

"Me and my brother did. But I haven't seen mine in a little while. And I just moved, so I think they might've been thrown out"

Then Andrew joined in on the topic, "I still have some! I got a few shiny ones. Phew. Even though nobody collects it anymore, I don't wanna throw mine away. It will remind me of awesome times"

"I think I only have a few but now I wish I kept some of the good ones..." Elijah began, conversationally. It was just how he expected it, having Andrew bring up a certain topic that would give him a chance to socialize with Sabrina. Suddenly, getting them acquainted didn't seem to matter because it already felt like she was part of the group. They talked about their own experiences with Pokemon. That gave Elijah the idea that Sabrina Clarin grown up watching the shows that he watched and that gave more opportunities to get to know her-

"Paula!" Elijah greeted.

As none of them realized, Paula was standing in front of them, listening to their conversation. Even before she approached them, she realized the new face that was among them and right away she knew that this girl was a new student. Paula did her best to ignore the delusion that her best friends were trying to replace her.

"Hey" she replied calmly, "What are you guys...doing?"

Paula hesitated only because she was trying to find the right words to say when trying to maintain focus after the thought of not being invited to the party.

"Oh, just talking" Elijah replied, casually, "Actually, we were waiting for you."

Once the gang was all together, Elijah went and stood beside his new friend. "Guys, this is Sabrina Clarin."

"Hi" she greeted, softly, like a shy kid meeting the outside world for the first time.

"Sabrina, these are my friends, Paula and Andrew, the ones I told you about earlier?"

"Hello there" Andrew greeted, kindly.

"Hi" Paula acknowledged.

"Nice to meet you" Sabrina said, "I'd introduce myself but I'm pretty sure you heard Elijah say my name".

"Sabrina is new to the school and to Burns Lake. She's in my class." Elijah added.

"That's me" Sabrina added, raising her hand. That was the exact same words she said to Mrs. Parker. This time it felt more genuine. This time, Elijah was feeling more confident, knowing where the conversation was going. Next he decided to tell Sabrina at least one thing about his best friends as he went to stand next to them shoulder to shoulder.

"Uh, Paula likes to read and Andrew likes to say something funny" Unwittingly, Elijah turned to Paula, "Say something funny, Andrew"

Then he realized who he really was talking to but it felt too late to correct it. Sabrina couldn't help but let out a little chuckle. Paula exchanged a quick glance, unsure if he did that on purpose just to be funny. Either way, she couldn't find it in herself to be offended from Elijah. Thankfully, Paula played along.

"Peanut-butter-pop-tarts" she replied.

Sabrina was expecting someone to say a little joke. She didn't think she would hear something random and that made her burst out in laughter but she kept in mild, thinking that they might've been sensitive. Elijah saw the joy in her eyes and that convinced him that their first impression went well.

"What?" Sabrina chuckled.

"It's..." Andrew was about to explain.

"It's something funny that Andrew and I came up with years ago" Elijah told her instead, "Peanut-butter-pop-tarts. It's something you say when you don't have anything else to say"

"This one day, I just felt like trying peanut butter on my pop tarts" Andrew added, "I told them about it and next thing I knew Elijah kept saying it like everyday"

"Peanut-butter-pop-tarts" Elijah added. There really was nothing else to say. So he could use that phrase for the rest of the day, "It's kind of cool to say it". Well maybe not cool. Funny probably would've been the best word to describe it.

"Huh, funny" Sabrina replied, modestly. Out of courtesy, she then decided to mingle with Paula Hennig, "So Paula, what do you like to read?"

"Mostly fiction. Every now and then, I enjoy reading about history" she answered, "It all started with my sister hogging the TV constantly. Had nothing else to do, so I just grabbed the dictionary. That's how bored I was."

"Hey" Elijah spoke, abruptly, "Sabrina has an older sibling too. Right?"

"Yes, I have a brother. He's one year older than me; just started high school."

"Hmm" Paula nodded, "My sister just started grade nine. Maybe they'll meet each other."

"Yeah, you never know."

Then Andrew began walking up to Sabrina. He looked like he was on a mission, from the way he studied her. "Sabrina" he said, "Like the Pokemon gym master?"

It took her a moment to catch up with him.

"Oh, that Sabrina" she replied, "Was she the one that used psychic ones?"

"That's right"

"Yup, just like her"

"Sweet; hey, it's not every day you meet someone with the same name as a character from a movie or TV show. Last one I met was George, as in George of the Jungle"

Only slightly amused, Sabrina forced herself to laugh.

"Haha, yeah, Andrew's pretty funny" Elijah told her.

"I can tell" she replied.

"If you think I'm funny" Andrew said, "You should meet Detective Andrew!" he pulled out a pair of sunglasses and then he quickly turned around to put them on as he was turning into another character. He stood up straight with his head up and showed an expressionless face. "Miss, are you Sabrina Clarin?" he asked, with authority in his voice.

"Yeah?" Sabrina replied.

"I'm Detective Little. Don't let the last name fool you. I'm still a cop"

"Okay"

"We gotten word that you're a new student at WKE and it's our job to inspect the newbies. Please come with me"

Then Andrew gently grabbed Sabrina by the shoulders and pulled her closer to Elijah and Paula. "You are to hang out with these students. They will be your chums. And they will decide if you're worthy to go to this school"

Sabrina started to laugh, "Okay.

Clever, Elijah thought. It was almost like Andrew read Elijah's mind, bringing Sabrina closer to him, humorously and naturally. Now most likely she would feel more comfortable with him and his company.

"Oh and if you hear rumors about us cops horsing around in our spare time, it's not true"

This time, Sabrina let out more laughs, "Okay".

"Settled" then Andrew turned around to pull off his sunglasses and went back to being himself. "Hey guys"

Elijah chuckled, "Hey, Andrew"

"Well, Sabrina. I hope you like jokes because I got plenty of them." Andrew said.

"Sure, I like jokes"

"They may involve your greatest fears" Paula warned. "He does that"

"Well, this should be fun" Sabrina added.

Elijah went in closer and stood in front of her. "Haha, yeah me and Andrew have been friends for years, best friends actually…"

"And before that?" Paula suggested.

"Oh yeah and Paula has been friends with me since Muriel Mould, which is just down the hill." Then Elijah redirected his attention back to Sabrina to finish the summary of his friendship with Andrew, "It was grade four when we both met and we been good friends since."

Andrew nodded, "Good and best" he replied, proudly, "That's kind of like..."

Elijah raised his hand up for a high five, which Andrew gave. In that moment, Elijah just wanted to express his respect for one of his best friends. After that, he then offered two high fives. Of course, Andrew complied to; Elijah felt genuinely excited. It was like they were putting on a show for Sabrina. Then he gave low fives. Elijah found himself improvising, as he then gave a thumbs up to Andrew, who did the same. Then awkwardly, he brought his thumbs up gesture closer. Elijah meant to do a fist bump but his mind was in a few places at once. Thankfully, Andrew went along and did their thumbs up-fist bump handshake. And finally, Elijah patted Andrew on the back. He felt both excited and a little silly as he realized that they showed off their bond a little too much.

"What was I gonna say?" Andrew said.

But at the same time, Elijah said, "So Sabrina, want us to show you around the school?"

Sabrina smiled and nodded. "I'd like that".

And so began the tour. Their first stop was the main office. Elijah gestured towards it but no explanation was needed. Aside from the lightness, the office was also a shaded place. Just thinking about made Elijah freeze for a moment once he recalled the times where he had to walk in and face the consequences. Sabrina didn't know that. She couldn't know. He was about to add that it was also a place where troublemakers go but that reminded him of the bad times of his past and it made him hesitate. Elijah was able to dismiss that thought and moved on. As the four of them walked along, Andrew decided to tell one his jokes:

"Wanna know where the 'behind entrance' is?" he asked, in the most emphasized way that it had Sabrina thinking it was probably a trick question.

Sabrina hesitated. "In the back?"

"You don't wanna know" he added, with a little smile.

42   PHILIP PATRICK

"Believe me, you'll wish he hadn't asked that" Paula said, "He used that joke on me. Took me a little while to get it and then I started to wish I was deaf"

Sabrina paused. "I see."

"Well, let's move onto the next." Elijah insisted.

Their next stop was the school library. The exterior was mostly covered in windows.

"This is our library from the outside."

"Looks nice" Sabrina said.

"And if you look closely, you can see Mr. Beck's glasses reflecting the light" Andrew added.

Then Andrew went up close to the windows to peer through. Then Sabrina played along and did the same, followed by Elijah. Paula was the only one that was waiting for them.

"I don't think anybody's in there" she told them.

Andrew glanced over his shoulder, "Shh" he replied, "Paulie, we talked about this, if you're right, keep it to yourself."

After the library, they showed Sabrina the computer room, which was right next to it. Then they came across the grade four entrance, which led to the tire swings on the other side of the school, the basketball poles that was in the back, and then the monkey bars that was at the end. The center of the monkey bars was formed into one straight line.

"This is the monkey bars" Elijah explained.

Sabrina was able to look at it.

(*This is OUR monkey bars*)

But only briefly.

"That's neat" she managed to say.

After the monkey bars, they went up the hill to where the playground was, and right behind that was a basketball court, and the entire field was right beside it.

"And this is the last part" Elijah said, "Playground, more basketball, and the field where we can play pretty much anything"

"Cool" Sabrina replied, "Well, thanks for showing me around. That was very nice of you. Now I won't get lost-haha"

"Yeah…" Elijah responded, promptly, "We should do it again, only this time we…do something…like more…playing."

Sabrina nodded, which was convincing enough. It showed that she was keen on spending more days with Elijah and his friends. And the fact that she started off with a good impression with Andrew and Paula meant that they were in for it for a long time. That seemed promising.

"That's another thing we haven't showed you" Elijah offered, after a moment of silence. It was something he thought of when he was brainstorming ideas.

"What's that?" Sabrina asked.

"The gully!"

She was intrigued but puzzled, "Where?"

"Well, we can't really go there, but it's close" Elijah promised, "Follow me"

That was a start. He led his friends to the end of the field, where they could get a view from the gully that was just a block away from the school. Elijah showed Sabrina as he pointed it out. There was a gap between the avenues. Some boulders were visible to keep any vehicle from entering and possibly falling in.

"Looks nice" Sabrina said.

"And it's even more cooler on the inside" Elijah added, "Well, if you like trees and rocks"

"Or wild animals" Andrew said, "Every now and then, there's a fox wondering around this area" Then he made claws with his hands and impersonated a growling sound.

"And sometimes a cougar" Paula said, "One time there was one near the school and we had to stay inside"

Finally, the conversations started and that got Elijah thinking of their time in primary school.

"Yeah, you know what, the same thing happened at MMPS" Elijah told Sabrina, "Years ago, there was a moose close to the school and we all had to run back in. It was quite scary"

"I remember that day" Paula admitted, "We were running back inside and I just couldn't help but imagine a wild moose charging right behind us"

"Wow" Sabrina replied, "That sounds pretty wild"

"Very wild" Elijah agreed.

"Hey, if you like wild" Andrew said, "This one time, a mouse tried to pick a fight with me."

Sabrina looked at him, funny, almost laughing.

"No I'm serious" he added, "I was just trying to be nice by offering cheese."

"Nice try, Andrew" Paula replied, "We all know you're making that up."

"Who said I was? Years ago on Halloween, my sister dressed up as a mouse."

Everyone paused as they came to a full realization.

"Yeah, if you love life, don't give her cheese."

Now that everyone was familiar and comfortable with each other, it was time to play together. They all went to the supervisor that was renting out sporting goods to students. The tether ball was their choice. Andrew exchanged a chocolate bar for a tether ball.

"Don't even think about eating it" Andrew said to the supervisor as a joke. Once he got it, he approached his friends and held the ball above his head. "As the weirdo of this group, I hereby declare this tether ball to be used for playing and maybe to hit Paulie in the head" he called.

"Bite me" Paula replied, with boredom in her voice.

Elijah and Sabrina just responded with laughter.

The pole for the tether ball was located on top of the hill, right next to the field. Luckily they were the first ones to use it. So they had it all to themselves. Andrew went up and hooked the tether on the chain. Then they decided to play in teams. Elijah deliberately paired Andrew with Sabrina, just to avoid showing his attachment to her. So it was Elijah and Paula against them. Out of courtesy, Andrew allowed Sabrina to start off the game since she was new to the school.

The four of them took a step back, just a few feet away from the pole. And then Sabrina served, as she hit the ball with her fist. The game had begun. The tether ball swung around until Elijah hit it back towards their opponents. But then Andrew reversed it. Shortly, Paula was able to jump in and pushed the ball back. From there, it swung back and forth until Andrew and Sabrina made the tether ball wrap around the pole rapidly. The chain was almost at its end. Elijah had a chance to reverse it, but as he got close to the ball, he hesitated and didn't bother in the end. Andrew and Sabrina won. Paula noticed that Elijah failed on purpose, but didn't say anything. In the end, they all celebrated the good game they just had.

They went back to return the tether ball, where Andrew reclaimed his chocolate bar. "Well, I'd say this victory deserves a bite of sweetness"

Andrew un-wrapped the chocolate bar, broke it half and gave a piece to his teammate. For a moment there, Elijah saw the way Andrew bonded with Sabrina, as they celebrated and even gave each other a high-five. It was all natural and genuine. It was like he didn't need to write a speech in his head to socialize. Elijah was almost jealous. How could he be that social, without hesitating and always know what to say?

"Hey…" Elijah called, as he glanced over in Sabrina's direction just to get her attention, "You guys know that movie Cruel Intentions? What if it was called 'Cool Intentions' and everyone was wearing sunglasses?"

It was a joke that Elijah thought of a year ago and didn't share it with anyone until now. Sadly, the only response he got was a chuckle out of Paula, while Andrew was too busy to respond, for that he was still eating.

"That's funny" Paula told him, sincerely.

"Haha, yeah" Elijah said, mildly.

That was most likely an obligated response. What Elijah was really hoping for was a burst out laughter from Sabrina. That joke probably would've been funnier if Andrew told it. To avoid the awkward silence, Elijah kept the conversation going.

"You haven't seen that movie, Sabrina?" he asked.

Sabrina shook her head. "I don't think we're allowed to see it because isn't it R-rated?"

"Yeah…"

"I've seen the Beavis and Butt-head movie and I was only ten!" Andrew interrupted.

"Really?" Sabrina replied. She seemed intrigued.

"Wait, I think I might've been nine at the time" Andrew said. Then he tried to recap in his mind and started counting with his fingers.

"Only because it was on TV" Elijah added, trying to sound gentle as he could because his emotions drowned in disappointment.

For the last moment before lunch recess was over, the conversation continued as Andrew was bragging about the movie, how much he enjoyed it and even started quoting lines from it. Elijah thought for sure it was the end of it but then Andrew began talking about how much it annoyed Paula back then, which became the next topic. And Elijah had many stories to share involving those two. He would've been more than happy to tell Sabrina about it, but she was too drawn into Andrew and Paula's bickering.

"…come on, Paulie, you like some of my mean jokes."

"I like any joke about people I barely know but that doesn't mean I enjoy all of them, especially your sick and weird ones."

"You sure? Because that one time I joked about the teachers getting together on N.I. days to see who acts like the best chicken. I'm pretty sure you were laughing like you had ants in your pants."

Sabrina just giggled. Yes, anything said by Andrew was funnier.

"Don't push your luck, Weirdo."

"So you admit it. You like my dirty jokes" Andrew said. Then he turned around to speak to a group of random students nearby, "Hey, she just admitted she likes dirty jokes!" he called out. At that point in their lives, Paula had gotten used to Andrew's crazy humor. She just glanced at Sabrina, who couldn't help but laugh a little, while Paula just smirked and shrugged her shoulders.

That moment of entertainment eased Elijah's disappointment. He couldn't raise his voice if he wanted to. But he was still feeling insignificant. Now Elijah's mind was too weary from all that negative energy and couldn't think straight. All he could do was walk it off. Soon recess was over. And finally, Andrew stopped talking as they started making their way back to class. By then, there was no courage to socialize.

Bringing Andrew and Paula into the circle should've been helpful but there was nothing left but disappointment. It was even tempting for Elijah to keep Sabrina away from them next time. The thought was there for a little while, but after a few hours of silence, the hard feelings wore off. But he did manage to speak to her afterwards, although it was only brief. Once school was over, Elijah did nothing but stood around to wait for his friends. And luckily, Sabrina was the first one to meet with him. He went up to her right away.

"Hey Sabrina" Elijah greeted.

"Hey" she replied, happily.

"Well, I hope you had a fun time with us" he told her.

"Yeah I did. And I appreciate you guys showing me around the school. That was very nice of you"

Elijah smiled, "Yeah, yeah, it was nice. It was a lot of fun...and nice" Repeating words over and over again seemed like all he had; *If Andrew was here he'd do a better job than me. Boy, I'm such an idiot...*He paused as he realized that Sabrina was waiting patiently. "So, I guess I'll see you tomorrow" he finally said, although it wasn't what he wanted to say.

"For sure"

"Alright, bye"

It didn't really make up for lost time but it was better than nothing, Elijah thought as he parted ways from his new friend. He didn't bother waiting for Paula or Andrew. Instead, Elijah went straight home. For the rest of the day, he turned off his thoughts of Sabrina like a light switch. The next day was another opportunity, despite how dull it was to begin with, it was always worth a try.

But that day was rather different. Elijah didn't feel like socializing. Even when all three of his friends were together, he ought to be happy but he wasn't a bit pleased. It was probably because Elijah felt like an outcast when Paula and Andrew were entertaining Sabrina. He stood there from a distance and saw them, mingling and laughing. They hit it off pretty good as if they were friends for a while. And Elijah himself could barely say one word to her. But even when he did after school, he couldn't think of what to say.

How do other boys do it? How do they talk to girls without messing up or saying the same thing over and over? It was like having nothing to study with and never finding out the answers. It was certainly a subject that Andrew knew very well. All Elijah could do was his best. So he finally approached his friends in front of the entrance. Only time Elijah spoke was when he said hi and they greeted him in return. That was something.

"...it was a lot more fun to scare my sister when she was little" Andrew said, "This one time I told her that I was gonna send the tape of her slipping on the ice to America's Funniest Home Videos"

Sabrina started to laugh. Paula did, too. Elijah wanted to join in but for some reason he just couldn't. Forcing a chuckle was the only thing he did.

"She was so scared, she started crying" Andrew added.

"You're mean" Sabrina told him.

"I'm mean because I care. But now she puts up with my jokes"

"Well, at least you're more friendly compared to my sister" Paula told him, "One time, Nathalie tried to push me into the swimming pool. She only made go as far as the ledge. But even so, I was so irritated"

Elijah was starting to feel left out because there was no story he could add in that topic since he was an only child. He in fact considered Paula and Andrew his siblings. There were plenty of stories he could share but they probably weren't as good as theirs.

"Yeah, I guess when you're a kid you're more easily scared" Sabrina added, "Like one time, I believed my brother when he said that bears come to eat little girls who annoy their big brothers. I remember thinking that a bear was going to come up to my window at night and try to snatch me out of my bed. I was too scared to sleep so I went to sleep in my parents' room"

"Now I know what I'm being for Halloween" Andrew said.

Sabrina looked at him, "A bear?"

"Yes"

She replied with laughter.

"Yeah, like I said: your greatest fears" Paula told her.

"Hmm, although that doesn't really scare me anymore"

"Oh, you'll be scared" Andrew promised, "Even if it's just at first". Then he turned around and pointed out towards the parking lot, "Hey, what's that?" While he was able to make the girls look away for a second, Andrew dashed towards the pillars behind them and then came around with the intent of startling Sabrina, "Heyyy!!" he growled.

But she wasn't startled at all, "Nice try" she chuckled, "I kinda knew you were going to do that"

"Just warming up" Andrew told her.

There were laughs, jokes, and bonding. Elijah couldn't help but feel-

He dismissed the thought quickly. Nonetheless, life was happening in front of him and he just wanted to be a part of it.

"Peanut-butter-pop-tarts" he finally spoke.

All three of his friend looked at him. Elijah had what he wanted but didn't know what to do with it. "Hi..." he added, casually and waved rather poorly.

"Hi" Paula replied.

And then Andrew said, "Hey"

Sabrina didn't say anything but she gave a little wave. It was a start.

"How are you, Elijah?" Paula asked.

"I'm fine" he replied, "You?"

"Good" Paula nodded.

It was just formal greetings, no jokes, nothing clever to say. Even Andrew didn't have any other funny stories to tell, at least nothing he could think of. Elijah felt like it was his turn to talk but couldn't think of anything. Little that he knew, his mind was mostly focused on Sabrina, just thinking about her in general. Most of the time, they just hung around in front of the school. They talked about little things, like asking Sabrina how she liked Burns Lake, which was probably something they already talked about.

Elijah couldn't think of a way to interact with Sabrina unless something or someone would set the whole vibe. So he had to create his own motivation. During class, while everyone was working on their given assignments, there was an idea to get Sabrina's attention. Elijah sat there, fidgeting with his pencil, waiting for the right moment...*Snap!*

"Aw man, I broke my pencil!" Elijah pretended to be upset. He spoke loud enough for anyone nearby to hear. So far, he only had Mrs. Parker's attention and probably a few students around him, which he didn't bother looking for in order to act natural. He could only hope that Sabrina was observing the small situation.

"Don't you have another?" Mrs. Parker asked, gently.

"You know what, I don't think I do, I think I might've broke them all" Elijah claimed, "I do that when I'm bored"

Elijah took Sabrina's quote from the day before but it didn't really land. And Sabrina herself didn't even look.

"Hmm" the teacher replied, "Does anyone have a pencil or pen that Elijah could borrow?"

Please be Sabrina, please be Sabrina!

The student in front of him responded first. "I do" she said and then she turned around and offered her spare pencil. Then all the hopes and dreams faded.

"Thanks, Stephanie" he said, as friendly as he could be.

As class continued, Elijah was still thinking of a way to get Sabrina's attention. It had to be something that would get her talking to him. So he then thought of something humorous and simple. Elijah began writing a small note on a sheet of paper. And when the right time came, he slowly and quietly placed the note on Sabrina's desk while she went up to. The note was labelled *I'm going to kill you scum*. It was gag that Elijah and Andrew pulled on each other back in fourth grade, where they playfully threatened each other.

Sabrina was returning to her desk. Elijah couldn't help but feel excited. She was halfway there. He glanced over to make sure the note was still on her desk, only to realize that he placed the paper slightly off the ledge, for that it slid off and flown to the floor. Sabrina sat down and didn't realize the paper underneath her feet. Elijah let out a little sigh as he just put his head down.

Once it was time for recess, Elijah decided to make another attempt to socialize. He thought of another simple idea. He crumbled that same sheet of paper he used. As he and the other students were heading outside, Sabrina was ahead of him. Elijah raised the crumbled paper and was going to throw it at her but then started losing interest, thinking that it was going to be another fail. It probably would've been. Now Sabrina was lost in the crowd. Elijah just changed his mind. So he then crumbled the paper even smaller and stuffed it in his pocket with the intent of throwing it away sooner or later. Outside, the three of his friends greeted each other and had small talk before their leader became the center of attention.

"Alrighty, so what should we do for this fine recess?" Andrew asked, looking at Elijah. Then the girls looked towards him as well.

Elijah didn't say anything as he glanced at each of them. He was rather surprised that it was his turn to talk. And of course Sabrina was there and listening. So it took him a moment to think.

"Well, we can always…" Paula spoke after a moment of silence.

But then Elijah finally responded, "Walk around"

"That's what I was just gonna say"

"Yeah, me too; so let's walk and maybe we'll find something to do or maybe something will find us" Elijah said, not that he was expecting a laugh. His humor then was rather mild. It was more like expressing his sarcastic nature, since there was no way he could compete with Andrew's wit. But it was always worth a try. "You guys don't mind walking around, right?" Suddenly the idea of walking didn't seemed that exciting, at least maybe not for the others.

"No, of course not" Paula replied.

"I don't mind at all" Sabrina added.

Then lastly Andrew said, "We all gotta exercise sometime. When you think about it, it's P.E. outdoors with the rest of the school. Some of us just don't know until we get bumped into"

So they did as their leader suggested and starting walking around the school clockwise. Elijah walked casually for a short period of time. Soon, Andrew began talking and that started a conversation between just him and Paula. So while they were discussing, Elijah stopped to pretend that something caught his eye just until his friends were far enough and he went to walk beside Sabrina. It was then he thought of how to interact with her. Elijah pulled out the crumbled paper, straightened it and showed it to her. Sabrina kindly took the note and read it.

"'I'm gonna kill you...scrum?'"

"Oh, it actually says 'scum'" Elijah told her, "It's, uh, something we played before". He gave a vague description by saying "we" instead of him and Andrew because for once Elijah wanted one moment alone with Sabrina. And if Andrew heard them talking about it, he probably would've joined in on the topic.

"Huh, that sounds entertaining" she replied. And then she returned the note. It probably wasn't the best way to start a conversation but at least Elijah had her attention.

"So, uh, if you were a Pokemon, what would you sound like?" he asked.

Sabrina gave a puzzled look, as she was trying to uncover the meaning behind the question. "I'm sorry?"

Elijah clearly didn't think that through. Now he had to reconstruct his words properly. "Uh, yeah, remember the day when you met Andrew and he called a Pokemon? You know?"

You mean yesterday, Sabrina almost said but she didn't want to offend him.

"Oh yeah, sure" she replied.

"Yeah, you know how Pokemon usually say their names or some of them just growled or roared, you know"

"Uh huh?"

"Which one would you sound like?"

Sabrina finally figured out what Elijah was trying to say. "Oh I see what you mean. Well, I'd probably feel a little silly saying my name over and over..."

"I wouldn't!" Elijah said. Then as he caught Sabrina's eyes looking towards him, he stopped. Those eyes were just simply beautiful, like her. Sabrina stopped as well to listen. "I mean, I wouldn't stop saying YOUR name"

Something did happen there. That feeling inside Elijah wrapped around his heart and made him burst out those words. He spoke like it was pre-determined thing. Maybe it was. After all, he cared about her, even if they only known each other for just a couple of days but there was something between them that Elijah could sense. Maybe he was dying for her to see it.

Sabrina was a little surprised and also flattered. There had to be more to this boy than the eye could see. Through his sincerity, Sabrina was convinced that Elijah cared about her like any friend would. But it was more than him than just being by her side. Creatively, he made her see herself through his eyes and that made her feel appreciated.

"Hey!" Andrew shouted as he jumped between Elijah and Sabrina, who weren't even close to being startled. Elijah however was irritated by the disruption. "Why did you guys stop? What if I turned around to ask one of you something and you weren't there?"

"We were just talking" Elijah said, casually.

"About being a Pokemon" Sabrina added.

"Hey, you know what, that actually reminds me of one of my nicknames…"

Elijah just drifted away emotionally as Andrew was socializing with Sabrina again. But this time, it was less disappointment than the last. Looking over that moment again in his mind, Elijah liked how Sabrina was intrigued by what he said, about not getting tired of saying her name over and over. And he wouldn't. So that short conversation they had was enough to build friendship.

The school day was going into its second phase after the first recess. Elijah took advantage of the one time he had Sabrina to himself when she sat next to him in class. He waited until she arrived at her desk.

"Hi, Sabrina" Elijah said, loud and clear, and in a friendly way.

She merely glanced as she was taking her seat. "Hi, Elijah" she replied, casually.

That was it; just a simple hello and things went silent as Sabrina had her head down, like she wasn't in the mood to talk. Elijah noticed and could only hope that he didn't annoy her. She could be just tired. There were still a few minutes until the second bell would go off. It was best to take advantage of the given time.

"Wonder what we're gonna learn in social studies today?" Elijah asked, but he didn't exactly look at Sabrina. There was no answer. He slowly peeked at the corner of his eye and she still had her head down, as she was fidgeting with her pencil and binder. She looked bored. Elijah was looking long enough for Sabrina to notice.

"Sorry, were you talking to me?" she asked.

"Yeah, I was"

"Oh, I heard you but I thought you were talking to someone else"

"That's okay. I was, uh, just...wondering what we were gonna learn in socials today" Saying that sentence with not much confidence created doubt. Elijah wasn't really sure if he was doing the right thing.

Sabrina stared him for a brief moment. "Probably the same as yesterday, just a different part" she replied, gently.

"Oh yeah...yeah" Elijah muttered.

The bell went off. Class was now in session. They went back to schooling for another couple of hours, until lunch break.

Elijah and Sabrina were eating their lunches, peacefully. No words were spoken. It was only silent between them, while some of their classmates were talking and mingling. After Elijah finished eating his sandwich, he thought of a funny way to get Sabrina's attention. He took the small saran wrap that was used for his sandwich, crushed it into a little ball. It was a gag that he often played with Paula and Andrew over the years. Elijah then threw it gently at Sabrina, hitting her shoulder softly. It got her attention right away. He was expecting her to throw it back in the same manner, but she only smiled briefly during the awkward silence.

"Haha" she said.

Then she went back to eating her lunch. Elijah frowned and turned away, pretending like it didn't happen. That moment stayed with him and built a heavy guilt that silenced him half the time. And the rest of the day turned to be uneventful.

CHAPTER THREE

Talk to Girls

So the fun was over? It sure seemed that way. Elijah and Sabrina had only been friends for few days and it was already becoming dull. He didn't want it to be that way, not with her. It was still nice that they were still hanging out and sitting beside each other in class, but Elijah felt like there could be more. Even when he did try to start a conversation, he literally had nothing to say, nothing but saying hello in the morning and goodbye in the afternoon.

That slight problem was the only thing in mind. So Elijah spent most of his time, trying to find a way to improve his predicament, a way to make things a little more fun. Being himself wasn't enough and he certainly wasn't as entertaining as Andrew. Other than that, nothing was coming to mind. Elijah let it go for the time being as he was enjoying the comfort of home.

It was halfway through the evening, Elijah began contemplating his social problem, only to recap the dull day that he had. It was hard for him to think outside the box. Soon, there was only one thought that finally came about, talking to girls the right way. Maybe there was something he didn't know. The answer had to come from someone who had to be experienced in life. So Elijah couldn't just ask his peers. In the end, only one person came to mind: his dad.

Elijah put on his sweater and stepped outside where Sam Khoda was chopping up wood in the backyard. "Hey, Eli" he greeted, as his son was approaching.

"Hey dad" Elijah replied, gently.

"As long as you're here, you wanna bring these woods to the shed after I chop them?" his dad asked.

Elijah didn't say anything and just started doing as he was suggested. After carrying a few logs into the wood shed, he approached his dad, he got straight to the point. "I...uh...need help with something"

"What's that?"

That was when Elijah realized what he was about to say to his dad, about girls. He hesitated, as for that he was expecting to get yelled at for even thinking about girls, considering the fact that Elijah was still a boy and was too young.

"Uh..." Elijah muttered, after a silent moment, "Do you think you can...tell me how...to talk to girls?"

"Talk to girls?" Sam repeated. It was a gentle and neutral manner. So that wasn't a bad sign.

"Yeah" Elijah admitted, as he was gaining the courage for the coming discussion. There was another silent moment. Sam put the axe down next the wooden stump he was using to chop wood on.

"Okay" his dad agreed.

It was a start, his dad being willing to help.

"So, uh, which part of talking to girls do you need help with?"

"Like I wanna talk to her, like regular friends. I don't wanna just say hello. I...wanna say more"

Sam nodded and took a moment to find an answer. "Alright...so if you wanna start a conversation with a girl, start with asking 'how's it going?', and she'll respond with the natural answer, she'll say 'good'. And that's your starting point"

Elijah nodded.

"And say whatever's on your mind; it can be almost anything, how your day went or how your evening went or a funny story. If she's nice enough, she'll join in on the conversation and there you got the girl's attention"

"Okay" Elijah replied, promptly, "And what if I don't have anything on my mind?"

That was the major issue he had been dealing with. And he was glad that his dad understood and gave an honest answer.

"Uh, then you'll have to find something to talk about. You can even look around and find at least one thing, like the weather, say something like 'oh, looks like it's going to be a nice day', just little things. For example, when I was out here starting to chop wood, I saw a squirrel running from our woodshed to the trees. Maybe she likes animals. Starting a conversation about almost anything is a nice way to get to know someone; you learn of what that person likes or doesn't like. And it's natural too"

Elijah nodded again.

"And as long as we're talking about this, you should know one important thing, girls are more sensitive than you think" his dad explained, in the most emphasized way, "Don't say anything like, your hair looks funny or your voice sounds funny. Don't call her fat, even when she's not. And don't make fun of her clothing, her friends, her family, or her background"

"Background?"

"Background, like if she's a native girl from another nation that's different from us, don't tease her or threaten her about it. And that leads us to our next lesson, if someone is different from you and everybody else, you can't bully them, period. And like I said, girls are strongly sensitive. If you make fun of her in any way, she'll never forget it and she'll be mad at you for a long time"

Sabrina Clarin wasn't a native girl. Elijah didn't really care about skin color. But he understood where his dad was coming from. And he would never do anything to hurt Sabrina. He cared about her too much.

"Anything else?" his dad asked.

There was something else and he didn't think of it until now.

"What if I wanted to talk to her, like in a serious way?"

"A serious conversation" Sam offered, "Well, those kinds of talk can be pretty deep, it can either be good or bad. Either way, if you really wanna talk to her in the most sincere way...You go up to her and ask gently, 'can I talk to you?' If she has enough respect for you, she'll hear you out. And in serious conversations, whatever you have to say, you have to mean it and it has to be honest, especially if you care about her. Don't joke, don't exaggerate, and don't lie. If you want to have a good friendship, she has to know the real you"

That put Elijah into deep thought. If Sabrina had to know the real Elijah Khoda, what would she think? He was aware of the troubles from his past but he decided to hide them when he started growing fond of Sabrina. It sounded like that Elijah would have to reveal it someday, perhaps sooner than later and that's what scared him.

"And Elijah, above all that, the most important thing: respect. When I say respect, I mean don't beat her up even when she's mad at you. If you care about her, be patient; think about her and what she might be going through because at some point she might need you"

"Okay" Elijah said, after a silent moment. He does care about Sabrina and would like to have a deep conversation with her someday. And there was no way that he could hurt her. There wasn't any intention. "I think I got it" he added, "Thanks dad"

"Yup; oh, Elijah, I forgot one thing" Sam admitted.

"What's that, dad?"

"Before you talk to a girl, there's a way to give yourself confidence: take a deep breath and put your chest out". His dad showed him an example, just the way he described it, taking a deep breath, putting his chest out, and standing straight and tall, like a man. "I know it sounds a little silly, but that's what men do" Sam Khoda approached closer to his son and told him: "Men were born to be brave".

Elijah repeated his dad's words to himself in silence. "Thanks dad, it means a lot to me" he replied. Then he turned around and went back in the house.

Meanwhile, Sam Khoda looked at the remaining chopped wood on the ground. "Okay, I guess I'll finish this myself".

His dad had giving him lots to think about and it kept Elijah awake past his bedtime.

In the morning, Elijah arrived at the school. When coming down the wooden steps, there was Sabrina, just her. Andrew and Paula were nowhere to be seen, which was alright. She was near the entrance, sitting on the bench. Elijah remained hidden at the corner, finding the confidence he needed. Then he took his dad's advice-

"Men were born to be brave" Elijah muttered. And there, he put out his chest and began walking towards Sabrina, undauntedly. "Hi, Sabrina" he greeted, boldly.

"Hi, Elijah" she replied, kindly.

"How's it going?" Elijah asked.

There he naturally made eye contact with her as she formed a smile on her face.

"Good. How about you?"

Elijah smiled back. "I'm good"

That was a start. Elijah had her attention and went from there. "Is it just you here?"

"Just me"

"Where are Andrew and Paula?"

"You know what, I haven't seen them yet" Sabrina admitted.

"Ah well, they'll be here, or maybe Andrew already is here and is looking to scare us"

"Yeah, I bet he would"

Now Elijah wasn't nervous like last time. The introduction worked better than he thought. Just by asking a simple question to start a conversation, it was pretty basic. Secretly, Elijah couldn't but feel a little dimwitted; thinking that talking to a girl was once a difficult task. But now those days were gone, Elijah took advantage of this new opportunity. And it all starts with a question.

"Mind if I sit next to you?" he asked, gently.

"Sure" Sabrina agreed.

They sat together and watched the world go by. At first, Elijah sat in silence, as he took it all in and even praised himself for properly socializing with Sabrina. *Good job,* he thought to himself as he looked away and smirked. After a moment, Elijah turned his attention back to Sabrina, not saying a word but just observing her presence, which brought warmth, comfort and joy altogether. While she wasn't looking, Elijah studied her, briefly, her dark brown hair and light skin. Just by gazing at her features tickled him with some excitement for reasons unknown. Maybe it was the thrill of her catching his gaze any second. Elijah would feel foolish if that happened. Or maybe he was just so astonished to see Sabrina was that beautiful up close. After befriending silence for too long, Elijah felt that it was time to start another small talk. Shortly, he noticed Sabrina had a bright grey backpack with blue colored zippers.

"Nice backpack" he told her.

"Thanks!"

So far, so good, he thought.

"Where'd you get it?"

"I got it in Prince George" she told him, "Just a few weeks ago before school started"

"Cool. I like the colors"

"Yeah, me too" Sabrina said, proudly.

Naturally, that led to their next topic. "What's your favorite color?"

"My favorite color?" Sabrina repeated. Then her mind wandered off for a few seconds. "I'm not really sure, to be honest"

"You don't have one?"

"Well, I do...I did. It changed a few times now that I think about it. I used to like pink when I was little, just like other girls. You know, girls get the pink color and boys get blue, right?"

"Yeah" Elijah nodded.

"I think it's because my parents got me a set of markers and I loved it just because it was so...colorful. So yeah, I guess I like all colors"

"That's neat"

"Mhm"

"I kinda like red" Elijah told her.

Sabrina nodded. "Red is nice"

"You ever get those markers that had a smell to it?"

"Yes!" Sabrina replied, with some excitement, "I loved those!"

"Those were awesome" Elijah agreed.

Sabrina chuckled. "I remember this one time; I spent like ten minutes maybe more just smelling each of them"

"Yeah, they smelled pretty nice"

So that was what having conversation with a girl felt like, bonding with one another, even in words. It was almost as fun as playing at the playground. It was definitely something to get used to. Elijah felt like he accomplished something. He took in the glory. And this was only the beginning. Just when class was about to begin, every student was at their locker. As he was getting his schoolwork, a certain memory came back to Elijah and decided to share it with his new friend.

"Did your textbook come out and hit you?" he asked, after they left the lockers.

Sabrina froze and looked at him, with a little disbelief. "Did my textbook come out and hit me?" she repeated.

"Yeah"

She could see he was trying not to smile and that brighten things up. "No? What do you mean?"

Elijah was about to tell the truth straight up but then he remembered how Andrew revealed the funny story about his sister. So just like him, Elijah decided to play around with the story. "One time in grade four, a kid opened his locker and the book slid out and hit him in the head"

"Ow! And you think that's funny?"

"The kid was me" Elijah admitted.

Sabrina got the gag and started laughing, mildly. Elijah continued to play along and just flicked himself in the forehead. "Ow".

And that got Sabrina giggling, genuinely. *I made her laugh!* Interestingly enough, Elijah didn't really plan on flicking at himself. It just came to him and he went for it and it turned out successful!

If talking to a girl was that simple, so many other conversation starters came to mind. *What's your favorite food? What's your favorite school subject? What's your least favorite subject? What restaurant do you like?* So many questions that Elijah could ask all day and there were too many to choose from. He spent half his morning contemplating on what to ask Sabrina next, anything to get to know her. Those thoughts turned on and off as he was focusing on his schoolwork. At one point, they were allowed to talk before moving onto the next subject. Before that Elijah was observing his surroundings and noticed the clouds outside.

The weather! As Elijah glanced out the window and remembered what his dad mentioned in their conversation, find something to talk about like the weather. So once they had free time to chat, he leaned over to his new friend: "Hey Sabrina?"

He got her attention.

"I can't tell if it's going to be sunny or rainy today. Can you?"

Sabrina looked outside to come up with an answer. "Well, if the sun has been hiding for too long, I think it will rain"

"Yeah, you might be right. As long as we're not outside when it happens"

"Yeah, unless you wanna play in the puddles, get wet and then get yelled at by your parents" Sabrina was implying that as a joke. Elijah could tell by the little excitement in her tone, which brought a smile to his face. "But as long as there's no thunderstorms" she added.

"Mhm, don't want that"

Their conversation had to be cut short because they had to get ready for their next subject, art. Mrs. Parker led her students to the art room. The room itself included four tables, big enough for all the students to sit. There were different kinds of artwork displayed around the room and a window to the outside of the school was at the back of the room. While the other students were choosing their seats, Elijah quickly sat beside Sabrina before anyone else did. He made it look casual so she wouldn't think that it was on purpose.

Art was something that Elijah was good at but not always. He had been drawing since he was a kid and since then his skills had been improved over the years. With that in mind, Elijah thought that could be his next conversation with Sabrina, to tell him one thing about himself, art.

Their assignment was learning to paint on canvas. The whole class spent their next half of their class, trying to capture an image from their minds. While Elijah was brainstorming ideas, he peered over and saw Sabrina drawing out her image. It appeared to be a flower and it looked nicely done.

"What is that, Sabrina?" he asked, "It looks cool"

"Oh, it's a flower" she picked it up and showed to him, which was only halfway done, "I've always liked flowers because they're so beautiful and colorful. I like them so much I even designed my own, like flowers that aren't real, just for the fun of it. This one picture, I drew flowers growing out of trees"

Since Sabrina told him something about herself, Elijah felt it was natural to tell her something about him. It didn't take long but an image came to mind and shortly it was on the canvas. "Hey, Sabrina" he whispered. He showed her the illustration of a ship with white sails on the ocean, "I've always liked ships. I don't know, they're just so big and cool"

"They are cool" Sabrina agreed, "The drawing looks nice, by the way"

"Thanks" Elijah replied, sincerely.

After art class had ended, the students were on their way back to the classroom. Elijah followed Sabrina like a stray dog. "So you're from Granisle?" he asked, as he walked behind her.

"Yes I am" Sabrina said.

"What's it like? Well, I had been through there before, but…" Elijah had been to Granisle many times. It was on route to Old Fort. He trailed off as he considered telling Sabrina about it but there wasn't really much time. "What's it like?" he repeated.

"It's nice, quiet, peaceful and it's close to a lake" Just explaining brought Sabrina back there, mentally. She could see the lake, the neighborhood, their old house and the old apartment they lived in before that. Suddenly Zach Epstad came to mind.

(*You can't climb here!*)

"I miss it" she added, after brief silence. Sabrina was able to bring herself back to the present before drowning into that one bad memory.

Their free time was limited for that they had to go back into class routine. Elijah made the best of it after sitting back at their desks. "Well, hopefully one day you'll get to go back to Granisle" he told her, gently.

"Oh, I'm sure I'll be visiting there at least every now and then. My grandparents still live there"

Now that Elijah had confidence in starting conversations, he felt like he could say anything and not having to wait for somebody to start one for him. When it was recess, the four of them walked around until they decided what to do. Andrew and Paula were occupied by their conversation, while Elijah walked beside Sabrina as they slowly fell behind. It was another perfect opportunity to get to know her, only it was hard to think of a question. But soon he thought maybe telling her something about himself. He went with the first idea that came to his mind.

"I can speak a second language" Elijah told her, as they kept walking.

Sabrina glanced over, "What?" She probably didn't mean what as she did not hear.

"I can speak another language"

"Really?"

She seemed a little intrigued.

"Carrier language" Elijah explained, "Well, I only know a few words"

Then they stopped as Sabrina came to a full realization. "You know what; I should've known that from the start. You are First Nations. Huh, I never had a First Nations friend before"

Sabrina froze, thinking that her comment might've been slightly offensive and that put her in silence, considering it was too late to take back her words. Elijah couldn't help but be a little surprised.

"So I'm the first" he replied, rather smoothly.

With that gentle response, Sabrina was able to breathe again and relaxed.

"Hadeeh" Elijah said.

Sabrina just looked at him, a little puzzled. Andrew and Paula were ahead of them. He realized how far behind the other two were. "What the heck are they doing?"

Paula couldn't tell but she noticed that Elijah and Sabrina were in their own world at the moment. "I don't know. But they'll catch up" she told him.

"That means 'hello'" Elijah explained.

"Oh...Ha-dee?"

"Close but there's an H at the end…"

"Right, right" Sabrina replied, "I'm usually a fast learner. So I don't know what happened there" She cleared her throat, "Hadeeh" she repeated, and even gave a little wave.

"Hadeeh" Elijah greeted, in the same manner, "Soh' eendzin? That means 'are you well today?'"

"Y-yeah I am. Thanks for asking" Sabrina laughed nervously. She didn't know why. Maybe she just felt a little silly responding to a foreign language with basic English or maybe learning a different language felt a little exciting for a moment. Elijah just felt the joy in her tone and laughed with her.

"There's also another word for 'yeah' and its 'M'ah'" he added.

"M'ah?" Sabrina repeated,

"M'ah Soh' ezdzin, means 'yes, I am well'"

It took Sabrina few tries but she got it. "Wow, that's pretty impressive, Elijah"

"Thank you. But I still have a lot to learn"

Elijah seemed different somehow. He wasn't just the boy in her class. He seemed more like a person, a friend, a leader. And most of all, real, a side to him that Sabrina had seen but yet there was probably more to him. And a part of her wanted to find out.

In that moment, Elijah stared at her for what seemed to be blankly. It didn't feel awkward. Something had improved and it couldn't just have been his social skills. There was something else. He could feel it inside. It was a mystery and Elijah was ambitious solve it.

After that, they stepped out of their own world and back into the real one and realizing that Paula and Andrew were long gone.

"Wanna race to Andrew and Paula?" Elijah challenged.

"Okay!" Sabrina agreed, without giving a second thought.

They both ran side by side. They made it to the back to their entrance where Andrew and Paula were waiting patiently. "We're back!" Elijah announced. All that excitement had him going and he just felt like sharing with the world.

"Welcome back!" Andrew replied,

"Elijah, Andrew won't stop teasing me" Paula complained.

"Don't confuse 'tease' with 'teach'" Andrew told her and then he faced the others to explain, "I was just teaching how to pronounce the word 'probably'. You should've heard her; she said 'proper-bly'"

"A teacher who likes to gossip, some educator you are"

Elijah and Sabrina exchanged looks as they were laughing under their breaths.

"Hey, I'm sure one of these teachers said something about us" Andrew claimed, "I don't see why they wouldn't. I was pretty funny in the fourth grade. I was coming in like the Titanic"

"How do you mean?" Sabrina asked, giving a weird look.

Andrew paused, "I don't know...I came in with big...jokes. Only in this case, people would laugh instead of scream"

Everyone laughed.

"Or cry" Elijah added.

"Yeah, that too" Sabrina agreed.

It was a proud moment for Elijah, for that he and Sabrina were bonding.

Then they continued walking together. While they still had some time, they wondered aimlessly to the monkey bars at the back of the school.

"Wanna climb the monkey bars?" Elijah offered, "I'll race ya"

At first, Sabrina was a little surprised, realizing that she was granted permission to go on the monkey bars after being forbidden. It was as if Zach Epstad's rule was broken and Sabrina felt like she was free.

"Sure" she agreed, almost right away, and then she added, "You're on!"

That was easy. Before at one point, Elijah used to think that all girls were afraid to be adventurous and would rather play with dolls and have their little tea parties. But this girl was different.

Andrew and Paula were left alone as their friend went to go entertain their guest. "Oh boy, looks like we got a monkey bar race in our hands" Andrew said, like he was a sports commentator, "its E.K. versus the new kid, all the way from Granny's isle!"

To him, it was like being at a sporting event. But in actuality, they were really just drawing unwanted attention to themselves, which made Paula feel a little awkward. "Would you stop?" she demanded, "You're making me want to punch you out"

"Coming up, we got a last minute boxing match!" Andrew added

Sabrina glanced at Elijah for a brief moment and then she already started running towards it. He ran to catch up with her. But she already beat him to the start of the race as she started swinging from one bar to the next. Sabrina was surprisingly fast and adventurous. Elijah was swinging behind her, trying to keep up. He was almost beside her. Soon they were halfway through. Elijah's arms were already getting tired, but he didn't give up. At the same time, they both reached the end but Sabrina was the first to let go and land on the ground.

"Woo!" she cheered.

"Yeah!" Elijah shouted.

Then they looked at each other as they were both catching their breaths.

"That was…great" he told her.

"Thanks. You weren't so bad yourself".

A compliment from Sabrina Clarin! Flattery had rained all over Elijah and made him smile proudly. That was fun! He was able to go on a little adventure with Sabrina on the same day he got to know her a little. And when he locked eyes with Sabrina, who returned the smile, Elijah could tell that it was quite an accomplishment.

"I'm sorry, who won?" Andrew asked, as soon as he rushed over to them, "I couldn't really see. Plus, I was too busy bugging Paulie"

"She did" Elijah answered, just the same time as Sabrina said "I did".

"Sabrina the New Kid wins the monkey bar race, making E.K. look like a turtle in gym class!"

If only Zach could see me now.

There was just too much excitement to waste. So Elijah made the best of it and clapped for Sabrina's victory. Sabrina herself grew shy from the attention she was getting and just gave a little wave. During the small celebration, Paula went up behind Andrew and punched him in the arm.

"Ha-ha-ow!" Andrew cried, "Where did that come from?"

"Last minute boxing match, your idea" Paula told him.

Just when Elijah thought he gained enough success that day, another opportunity came along. Afterwards, Mrs. Parker's class was in the gymnasium for P.E. lessons. Everyone got into their gym clothes and was ready. First thing they did was run laps around the perimeter. Halfway through the second lap, Elijah was already getting tired out. He managed to stay beside Sabrina. He was panting and so he took a deep breath before he spoke, "This sucks!" he complained.

"Yeah, maybe" Sabrina said, as she continued running, and then she glanced over at him, "Come on, Elijah, you can do this!" she encouraged.

"Alright, whatever you say" he replied, not knowing how to respond at first. So without giving a second thought, Elijah picked up the pace. He was able to keep up with Sabrina. The second lap was over and the third had begun. Elijah was getting more tired.

"Go Elijah go!" Sabrina cheered.

That sound of support gave him the courage he needed, especially coming from Sabrina. Next thing Elijah knew he developed more energy to finish the lap. Soon, they reached the end of line and the third lap was finished. Elijah was glad to have a moment of rest after that rush. Mrs. Parker gave her students time to catch their breaths while she set up for their next activity. Since they had free time, Elijah went up to Sabrina.

"Thanks" he said sincerely, "I needed that"

"You're welcome" she replied.

"Not really a fan of doing laps"

"Well, least you got some exercise"

Elijah paused, trying to think of what to say next. "You like P.E.?"

"Sure, I don't mind it. It can be fun"

The word fun brought back a certain memory from primary school that Elijah just had to share. "Hey, you know what I miss? That parachute that we all played..."

"Yeah, we did that as well back home." Sabrina told him.

"I loved that game"

"It was a blast!"

Mrs. Parker blew her whistle to call everyone's attention. Next thing they did was some warm up exercises for their next activity: soccer. She divided the class into two teams. The other half went to grab pinnies. Elijah was thrilled that he was on the same team as Sabrina. Once everyone was ready, they all got into position. Mrs. Parker placed the soccer ball in the center where two of her students stood waiting, while Elijah stood next to Sabrina in the corner.

"Ready, Sabrina?" he asked.

She looked over to him, "Sure am, are you?"

Before answering, he paused to think of something clever to say, but only the simple words came out, "Yes, ready".

The anticipation grew almost as if they were in a real soccer game. Mrs. Parker blew the whistle and the game had begun. The pinnies had the advantage as they took the ball. Elijah and Sabrina's team went to claim it. At first, he stayed by her side, thinking that it would help to achieve their goal but soon they got separated as both teams collided. The ball went from one player to another. Eventually it made it to Sabrina. She was able to kick it around for a moment but as she was running, her foot stepped on the ball, putting enough pressure on it for it to roll away and making her trip. Sabrina fell and landed on her back. Worriedly, Elijah went up to her right away and helped her up. Meanwhile their opponents ran off with the soccer ball.

"You're all right?" Elijah asked.

"I'm fine. Could've been worse" she told him, "Come on; let's do this"

Sabrina was a trooper.

They both continued playing. The teams were still aiming for their first score. Soon, Elijah had the ball. He kicked it towards their opponent's net. Quickly, he looked up for an opening. A few students in pinnies were starting to block him. Some of his teammates appeared next to his left and there he saw Sabrina and decided to act fast.

"Sabrina!" he called.

Just when he was about to kick the ball over to her, someone from the other team came along and took it. Elijah couldn't help but feel a little irritated but he wasn't giving up that easily. So he went and pursued their rival team. He caught up and kicked the ball away. Sabrina was still far from it. So instead one of their teammates claimed it and brought it back towards their target. That classmate was getting kicked the ball away once he was having no luck. The ball had come back to Sabrina. She took the advantage and moved incredibly fast. She made it to their opponent's net, kicked the ball and scored the first goal for the team! Almost everyone cheered. Elijah was amazed by Sabrina's energy.

"Well done, Sabrina" he told her, sincerely.

She smiled and replied, "Thank you but I couldn't have done it without you".

Elijah just smiled in return.

Soon the next round started. The other team had their moment of glory when they got their first score. After that, Elijah still wasn't giving up. Sabrina's comment gave him strength and he put all his focus on the game. He was always tempted to score a goal. Maybe it would impress Sabrina. But the other team was constantly taking away the ball before Elijah could achieve. Eventually they got their second point. The game was becoming more competitive. Once the next opportunity came, he had the ball but ended up passing it to his teammates and one of them scored their second point.

The game was tied.

For the next round, all the players were on one side, fighting over the ball. Someone kicked it out of the crowd and started rolling to the other side. Elijah went after it and claimed it. As he turned around, everyone was coming his way. He had to go back to other side to score another point. So he started making his way. Then he saw Sabrina out in the open and passed it to her. But her chances were thin, for that some of their opponents were advancing. So she kicked the ball to one of her teammates and made the same attempt but soon had the give up the ball, which was kicked away and came towards Elijah. He was alone and the net was on the other side of the crowd. It was a perfect opportunity. He just kicked the ball and it went flying over everyone but the ball hit the wall and made its way towards Sabrina. She took it, went in closer and scored!

Their team ended up winning the game since gym class was coming to an end. Mrs. Parker gave her students some time to rest. Elijah went up to Sabrina while they had free time.

"Well, we did it" he said.

"We sure did, thanks to you" Sabrina replied.

"Thanks, although I didn't make a score but…"

"You helped"

"Yeah…I guess I did"

"If it weren't for you, I wouldn't have caught the ball and scored. I'm sure the others feel that way, too, like when you passed the ball to them and made the second score"

Slowly, Elijah nodded with pride.

"See, you helped them and I think that's what matters" Sabrina added and she even patted him on the shoulder.

"Well, thanks again"

Sabrina just smiled.

"You did good yourself. You have good…energy, just the way you moved, it was…pretty…cool"

"You think so?" Sabrina was remaining modest.

"Yeah, I do" Elijah agreed, "We're lucky to have you on our team… and I'm…lucky to have you as my friend"

Sabrina's smile grew bigger. "Aww, why thank you. That means a lot"

There were no words to describe it. Elijah just smiled. During that time alone, he decided to raise his hand for a high five, which was Sabrina was more than happy to give.

Sabrina acknowledged by locking eyes with him. His eyes were gentle, just like the day they first met and since then Elijah Khoda had been nice to her. So they were now comfortable with each other. They were now friends and not just classmates.

Before either of them knew it, a connection had formed.

CHAPTER FOUR

Twelve Years and Counting

So that was it! Elijah Khoda got adjusted to society. He now felt a little more confident, knowing that he could interact with someone and give a piece of his mind. In this case, that someone was Sabrina Clarin. Each day he woke up smiling. After eating and showering, Elijah would pick up the pace as he was getting dressed. Once he was ready, he practically jumped out of the door and walked to school with great anticipation and smiled along the way. He even started running as he got closer to the school, running like he was about to miss the bus. For once in his life, Elijah was actually excited to go to school. After arriving, he always met with Andrew, Paula, and Sabrina. As time passed, Sabrina Clarin was no longer known as the 'new girl'. She was a friend and earned her place in Elijah's inner circle. Every school day, the four of them were inseparable. They played together and sometimes they sat in silence, and they always made the best of it.

While they were waiting for the bell to ring, Elijah, Sabrina, Paula, and Andrew, were loitering on the railings that were across from the main entrance. Since they already talked and caught up with their days, they had nothing else to do, just standing around. Shortly, Sabrina started tapping her foot on the pavement, rather repeatedly.

"What are you doing?" Elijah asked, casually.

"Oh, nothing" Sabrina claimed, "It's something else I do when I get bored, just tapping my foot"

She demonstrated by tapping again.

"You do it just for fun?"

Sabrina gave a little shrug, "Pretty much. I actually started doing this to my brother, after watching The Little Rascals, just to annoy him"

"Oh I think I know what you mean"

"You saw it too, right?"

"Yeah, a couple of times"

"So you know why it's become a habit" Sabrina told him, and then tapped her foot again.

Sabrina tapped again.

"Just tapping away" Elijah agreed, and then tapped his foot as well, to play along.

She kept on tapping and started creating her own rhythm as she was tapping faster.

"That's cool, almost sounds like you got a song going on" Elijah added.

"Hey, that looks like fun" Andrew said, "Let me try!"

With Andrew, he gave a little more than expected. Instead of one foot, he tapped with both of his feet. Paula started to laugh, genuinely, "You kinda sound like a horse galloping"

"Maybe I am" Andrew replied, jokingly.

They kept on tapping their foot. Soon Paula was encouraged to join them. So all four of them were doing the same thing and enjoyed themselves. And then the bell rang. So it was time to start schoolwork. Being together as a group was always fun but Elijah's favorite part of the day was when it was just him and Sabrina in class. And every day there was always an opportunity to connect. And the more Elijah talked to her, the more he got attached to her.

Few hours later, it was lunch break. Once they were dismissed, Elijah got up to his locker and pulled out his lunch, along with the rest of the class. He sat back down, across from Sabrina, who was unpacking her lunch. While the other students were eating and chatting, Elijah and Sabrina were in their own little world. He took the time to build up a little confidence and just said the first thing that came to his mind.

"…I packed my own lunch" Elijah told her. It caught Sabrina's attention. The sound of silence went off as soon as he realized what he said, and he almost regretted it. It probably wasn't the best way to start a conversation-

"Did you sneak in come candy?" Sabrina asked.

Elijah paused and redirected his attention towards her. "Uh no, never thought of it".

"My mom wouldn't let us take candy for lunch"

So that embarrassment led somewhere after all. "My mom won't let me take pop to school" he added, "Which is fine".

"Makes sense" Sabrina replied, "It's nice to have a soft drink, but not all the time".

Just from socializing with her, Elijah wasn't sure if he was saying the right thing, but it certainly didn't feel wrong. He looked towards Sabrina and noticed she was eating a sandwich as well. "What kind of sandwich are you having?" he asked.

"Turkey, lettuce and mayo" she answered, honestly, "What about you?"

"Uh, just plain ham" Elijah said, reluctantly, "It's not much, but I like it".

"That's alright" she told him, "My brother Jonathan is just like you, sort of"

"Really?"

"Yeah, he likes his sandwiches plain, such as plain jam, plain peanut butter or just plain ham as well. One time I made him try peanut butter and jelly sandwich, he didn't like it"

"Really?"

"Yeah, I felt bad but it was kinda funny at the same time. It looked like he was about to puke; just the face he made, had me laughing"

They both broke into laugher after she told the story. Then they took a moment to eat their lunches. "Oh" Sabrina muttered, "I just remembered, he actually made me promise not to tell anyone. So if you ever meet him, don't say a word"

"Oh, don't worry" Elijah promised, "I won't"

"And I probably shouldn't have said the word puke"

"Why?"

"Because we're eating right now"

Elijah had no comment. After finishing most of his lunch, Elijah opened a small tray that small cookies and a chocolate dip inside. "Want some?" he offered, as he held it out towards Sabrina.

"Dunk-a-Roos, sure!" she replied, "I haven't had those in a while"

She then helped herself to one cookie and dipped it into the chocolate. "Thanks Elijah!"

Elijah didn't say anything because he didn't feel the need to, just knowing that he just made Sabrina's day was enough. But in the end, he did give a flattering smile. And since then, they had been sharing Dunk-a-Roos almost every day.

That same day, the gang met together for lunch recess. Everyone was in a good mood. So every opportunity to bond with each other just appealed to them and brought laughter as they played on the playground. Afterwards, they took it easy and sat on the field, enjoying the comforting silence after all that fun.

"Sabrina!" Elijah called, "You sound like you watch movies, since we were talking about Little Rascals earlier. What movie is your favorite?"

"Uh, Edward Scissorhands, I LOVE that one! And I also like Adventures in Babysitting, The Lion King, Parent Trap…Those are my favorites"

There was one other film that Sabrina liked, but didn't mention. It was a rather guilty pleasure that she didn't share. Sabrina continued the conversation, "What are your favorites?" she asked.

"Independence Day, Batman" Elijah told her, "Jurassic Park, I kinda like dinosaurs"

"Cool" Sabrina added.

"Back to the Future; that brings back memories. Same with Star Wars"

Sabrina nodded. "Awesome"

"I like Ghostbusters" Andrew said, abruptly, "And I also like Terminator, Star Wars, and Jurassic Park as well. Me and Eli pretty much like the same stuff"

Sabrina nodded. Then she peered over at Paula, who was sitting at the end. "How about you, Paula?"

"I don't think I have a favorite" Paula admitted, "But I kinda like Forrest Gump. Oh and Mulan"

"Mulan was a great one!" Sabrina agreed.

Paula nodded. "One time, my sister made me watch Sixth Sense with her; big mistake. I couldn't sleep that night"

Andrew responded with laughter. "I watched Arachnophobia and you know how many hours of sleep I lost? None! Because it was during the day!

"Good for you" Paula replied.

So both Elijah and Sabrina liked to watch films. Right away, he imagined that maybe one day they would all get together and watch a movie, or maybe just him and Sabrina. For Elijah that would be a perfect date!

For their last part of the recess, the four of them waited patiently outside the entrance. Feeling tired out from all the fun, they leaned against the railing in silence. Even Elijah didn't mind the silence at that point. Then he just felt the urge to say something meaningful to their new friend.

"Well, Sabrina today has been fun" he told her.

"It sure has" she agreed.

"Yeah…in fact pretty much every day has been fun" *with you here,* "I couldn't ask for better…friends"

"Aww" Sabrina replied.

Elijah smiled rather bashfully.

"Yeah and you know what?" Andrew said, turning to Sabrina, "Since you've been hanging out with us a lot lately, I'd now like to make you a member of…never mind. But you get the idea"

"Member of never mind?" Sabrina replied, playfully.

"Oh, it's just…I was gonna say the name I picked out for our group last year but E.K. said it was too silly"

Sabrina looked at Elijah, who showed nothing but guilt followed by an apologetic expression. "Why? What was the name?"

"I called us…" Andrew started.

"E-three" Elijah finally said, "Because there's three of us"

"And you can probably guess what the E stands for" Andrew added.

"Elijah?" Sabrina answered.

"Yes, indeed"

"Well…" Elijah began. It was the sixth grade when Andrew came up with the name of their little group. But at that time Elijah, who wasn't feeling exactly the greatest, thought it sounded too kid-like. By then, he wanted to abandon his childhood. "…I, uh, did think it was a little silly at that time. B-but, uh, now I see it can be a…cool name because Andrew came up with it and there are three-four of us now. You guys are my friends. So…"

"Cool!" Andrew cheered, "We are now…E-Four!"

Both he and Elijah said it at the same time.

"E-Four" Sabrina repeated.

"E-Four" Paula replied.

Feeling more proud of it now, Elijah raised four fingers to acknowledge the group's name. Andrew liked that gesture, so he did the same.

"Hey, this would be like our salute" he said, now raising his four fingers.

The girls did the same gesture.

"E-Four!" they all said.

It was the second week of September. Elijah Khoda's birthday was getting close. This time it was on a weekend instead of a weekday. Most likely it would be the same as the year before, have a dinner or a barbeque and have his friends over. Sabrina Clarin was a friend. Elijah wondered if she would come over. It would mean so much if she did. Would she? What if she'd say no?

The thought was floating in his mind all week. Elijah kept telling himself, you never know unless you ask her. He even practiced at home asking the question as if she was standing in front of him.

Sabrina, we're having a birthday dinner, would you like to come?

Hey, Sabrina, I hope you like parties because you're invited to one!

I'm having a birthday party and since you're a friend, I'd like for you to come.

Some confidence came to him whenever he was at home. But at school, it was nothing but hesitation. Elijah just stared like he usually did when she wasn't looking. Ask her. It was simple, but what was Elijah so afraid of? It took some time but he built up some courage to ask Sabrina and he decided to ask her while they were in the company of Andrew and Paula. Maybe they could talk her into it somehow. So the question came up while the gang stood outside together.

"Hey Sabrina" Elijah said.

She looked directly at him.

"M-my, my, uh, birthday is coming up, this weekend on Sunday..." he paused.

"Oh?" she replied.

"We're having a dinner, at my place" he added, "Paula and Andrew will be there. Maybe you would like to join us?" Just like what Elijah did when he first met Sabrina, he tried to find ways to kill the silence, "Will you like to join us?" he repeated, nervously but calmly. That didn't go as well as he imagined but now the words had been spoken.

"Aww, I'd love to" Sabrina's response was sweet and casual, but from the way she sounded, she was about to add an answer that Elijah prepared himself for, "But I don't think I can"

That was it. Little sadness poured into Elijah's heart but he was able to keep it together.

"I mean, it's not like I don't want to" she explained, "It's just me and my family are still in the middle of moving..."

"Oh no, that's fine" Elijah replied right away, "I understand. I mean, there's always next year, right?" He then glanced at Paula and Andrew to acknowledge.

"Oh yeah, of course" Paula agreed, looking at Sabrina, "There's always next time"

"And just a heads up" Andrew spoke, "The leftovers belong to me"

"Haha" Sabrina chuckled, "Okay, got it"

"So when is your birthday, Sabrina?" Elijah asked, conversationally.
"November fourth"
He spent the next moment, trying to think of what to say.
"Nice…November is nice"

So the day came when Elijah Khoda turned twelve years old. There they were, all four of them sitting at the table, at Elijah's home. His parents serving them food, and later Elijah would open his presents from three of his friends. Wonder what Sabrina would've gotten for Elijah. That would've been extra special, next to having her by his side.

But in reality, it was only Andrew and Paula at Elijah's house. Sometimes, they would invite family over for his birthday. But Sam and Madeline would let their son decide how he would like to celebrate since he was getting older.

The three of them did the same thing as usual. Elijah and Andrew would play videogames, while Paula watched them. Later it was time to eat. Sam and Madeline made steaks just for them. Elijah barely got any gifts that year, only something from his parents, and Paula made him a tray of cookies just for Elijah. Once it was time for cake, Sam lit up the candles and they all sang happy birthday to Elijah.

"Make a wish, Eli" Paula encouraged.

Was it too silly for a twelve year old boy to make a wish?

Elijah sat there looking at the flames of his candles, shining above the cake. Make a wish, right?

I wish that me and Sabrina Clarin will be friends forever.

Now all twelve candles were blown out.

After a few weeks of unpacking, cleaning and rearranging, the Clarin family was finally settling into their new home in Burns Lake. Sabrina and Jonathan had set up their rooms the way they wanted it. So they celebrated by ordering pizza. After supper, they were all laying back and enjoying the comfort of their new house. Jonathan was sitting on the couch, as he was hogging the TV to play his videogames. Sabrina was admiring her new room while the parents were resting in their own room.

Sabrina sat on her bed, just thinking about how her life had been for past weeks. And she realized that she wasn't sad like before. She owed that to her new friends for keeping her entertained and taking her mind off things. She did not think she would make a friend that quickly. But even so, it was a good thing. Maybe moving wasn't so bad after all.

"Sabrina" her dad called.

She looked up and saw her dad entering the doorway of her bedroom.

"We're thinking of going for a drive, just to see more of the town" he told her.

"Do you want me to come?" Sabrina asked, with a smile.

Michael Clarin didn't answer. He just gave a chuckle, which also meant yes.

"Better get ready" he told her. Then Michael turned around and walked down the hallway, "Hey, Jonathan…"

The Clarin family was driving in their car, coming down from one of the avenues and into the main street of Burns Lake, and went from there. As they drove down, they were looking at every building on each side, from businesses to residential homes.

"I hear everyone in town knows each other" Michael explained, as he was driving.

"Oh, good, now we're gonna feel like outsiders" Leah joked, "We'll be fine, I know"

"We're doing good so far, I think. See anything interesting, Sabrina? Jonathan?"

"I see their theater is still here" Sabrina replied, with a little excitement.

"I see nothing but buildings" Jonathan answered, without emotion, "Can we go home now? I don't think I'll be going into any of these places"

"You will, Jonathan" his mom warned, "Believe me"

"How will you know I'm gonna need a pair of shoes?"

"Because you won't stop growing"

"Then we'll buy the shoes for you" Sabrina teased, "How about nice pink ones?"

Jonathan peered at his sister, who was grinning from ear to ear. "Then I'll just color it"

"Then I'll hide the markers" Sabrina added.

"Then I'll use dad's paint" Jonathan promised.

"Oh no, you're not going anywhere near my paint" Michael told him.

Jonathan just sat back into his seat, with boredom consuming him. Then he glanced at his sister who was waiting to be noticed. Once their eyes met, Sabrina stuck her tongue out briefly to taunt him. Jonathan didn't feel like playing, so he just gave a dismissing wave.

After touring Burns Lake, Michael pulled into the convenient store downtown. "I don't remember saying let's stop at the gas station" Leah said.

"I'm feeling snacky" Michael told her.

"We just had pizza and now you want junk food?"

"Hey, maybe I'm getting you something"

Leah rolled her eyes, "Please, last time you said that, I ended up changing my shirt"

"That's why you gotta be careful when you're eating a creamsicle"

Leah Clarin just scoffed and her husband then stepped out of the car.

"I'll come" Jonathan insisted.

"Well as long as we're here, I might as well buy myself a bottle of water" Leah said.

"I'm gonna wonder around" Sabrina told her.

Everyone was out of the car. Sabrina and her mom were approaching the entrance way. Just before her mom went in, she grabbed her youngest by the shoulder, gently but firmly.

"Hey" she called. The mother and daughter looked eye to eye, "Stay around here".

"Okay" Sabrina promised.

Once she was on her own, Sabrina went to the perimeter of the gas station. She went up to where the sign was, just at the corner of the parking lot and gazed at the view before her. There was highway 16, the hardware store and the bank across from each other. The weather was nice and warm, yet cool air flowed through the town. It was a beautiful evening.

A new home, in a small town, new friends, and a loving family on her side, it made Sabrina feel happy and proud. It gave her enough energy to play around. There were cement bumpers on the perimeter, where she hopped on and started walking carefully. As she got used to it, she began to walk a little faster from one to another, until she reached the end, and there she jumped to the ground. Sabrina then decided to step back on the cement bumpers, only to jump off for the fun of it.

Sabrina stopped playing once her eye caught something in the distance. Behind the gas station there was a backstreet of Burns Lake. A couple, a boy and a girl were walking the opposite direction. They looked a little older than Sabrina. They had to be teenagers. And Sabrina noticed that they were holding hands as they were standing close to each other. After a short moment, the couple stopped just to talk. Sabrina had never seen a young couple in real life. The only couple Sabrina ever saw intimate was her parents. But seeing a couple that were just a few years older than her felt quite extraordinary after watching them in movies.

Only one thought went through Sabrina's mind: *If they're in love at that age, would it be too early for me?*

CHAPTER FIVE

Definition Perfection

October.

A month ago, Elijah Khoda started off the school year thinking that it was going to be dull. But to his surprise, it evolved in a way he did not expect and it all happened by simply saying hello to a girl name Sabrina Clarin. At the end of the day Elijah thought that the school year wouldn't as good as it was now if he hadn't approached her. Since his social skills had improved, each day Elijah got ready in the morning and took the time to maintain confidence. During that moment, he always thought about that first day as a reminder that he is a good person. He kept thinking proudly to himself, *I'm glad I stopped and said hi to Sabrina.*

When he was being so thankful for what he had, Elijah realized that he hadn't once lost his temper since he met Sabrina. No grownups yelling at him or telling him to go to the office. That was when Elijah was convinced to change himself for the better. And it all happened with barely any effort. He liked to think that Sabrina Clarin changed him from the moment they looked eye to eye on that first day of school-

(That was another moment Elijah kept thinking about, when he met Sabrina the first time. Looking back at it now, he noticed how it changed his life in a major way. Each time he thought of it, it touched his heart. It made him happy. She started off as a classmate who had a vibe that triggered Elijah's senses and developed a feeling inside that urged him to step out of his comfort zone and say hi to someone he didn't know. And now that someone was his close friend.)

-And that moment made Elijah forget all his bad memories from the past, being picked on and losing hope in his own life. This school year was a chance to start fresh and make new memories. Elijah couldn't ask for better people to spend it with.

"Paula, Andrew" Elijah greeted, with a smile "Hello!"

It was a new day at school. It was a perfect day already. All three of his friends were together.

"Yo!" Andrew replied.

"Hey Sabrina"

"Hey Elijah"

"Morning" Paula greeted, "You seem to be in a good mood"

"Yeah, I know" Elijah admitted, gently, "Why wouldn't I be? I got you guys"

"Well…" Paula started, trying to think of something meaningful instead of just saying *that's good,* "We got you, too".

Elijah acknowledged by giving a smile. "So did I miss anything?"

"We were actually just talking about what words sound funny to us" Andrew explained.

"Oh and which ones do you guys find funny?"

"Pants!" Andrew answered, promptly.

"Inappropriate" Sabrina said.

"Guacamole" Paula added, "It's not really ha-ha funny but yet it's oddly appealing"

"Yeah, it kinda sounds like 'whack a mole'" Andrew told them, "Whack! Whack-quack-ahh-moly; holy moly"

Sabrina giggled.

"Cheese" Elijah added, "I think that sounds kind of funny"

"Cheese-Louise" Sabrina joked,

"Ah, cheese off"

"Well, you guys are feeling cheesy" Andrew told them.

"Say cheese" Paula added.

The laughter went on. Soon the bell rang. Elijah walked side by side with Sabrina as they went to join their classmates. "Hey, Sabrina?" he called, as he stood behind her.

"What's up?" she replied, as she turned her head back to meet his eye.

"Uh, how is 'inappropriate' funny?"

"Well, it kinda sounds funny when you say it over and over. I never really thought of it until one of my old classmates back home mentioned it. I guess it just depends how you say it or who says it"

During class, Mrs. Parker was in the middle of a lesson. All the students sat and listened. Elijah's mind was wandering back and forth as he was thinking about Sabrina. In the past month, he learned to take every opportunity to make conversation with her, even if that meant passing a note with a simple question. Elijah wrote on a piece paper and held it out to Sabrina while he had the chance. Luckily she saw it and took the paper before anyone noticed.

Goosebumps or Are You Afraid of The Dark? Sabrina read. She kept it hidden until she had the chance to write down her answer. Elijah received the paper back. He unfolded it and saw the checkmark beside the second choice, *Afraid of the Dark.* Elijah glanced over at Sabrina and just gave a nod.

The lesson was interrupted when one of the students abruptly broke out in laughter. A couple of boys on the other side were horsing around. Mrs. Parker wasn't particularly happy, which led her to giving a little speech about how it was 'inappropriate'. That word itself just being said out loud made Elijah froze briefly and then couldn't help but turn to Sabrina, who happened to look in his direction. Smiles were formed on their faces and they giggled in silence.

"That was funny" Elijah said, in a low voice. They had a minute of free time while they were getting ready for the next subject.

"Inappropriate?" Sabrina replied and laughed a little, "I honestly wasn't expecting that"

"Me neither. Yeah, I guess it does depend on how you say it" Elijah just cleared his throat and had to give it a try, "Inappropriate!" he said, in an agitated tone.

"Inappropriate" Sabrina repeated, bitterly.

They kept saying over and over, just for laughs until Mrs. Parker heard them. Next thing they knew, she was staring directly at them. Elijah and Sabrina couldn't help but feel a little guilty. They were rather speechless. But their teacher didn't say a word and continued on.

Later, in the school library, the class browsed the book shelves for their assignment. A few sounds of students chatting were on and off, but most of the time it was quiet. As Elijah was searching for a book, he noticed Sabrina on the other side of the shelf, doing the same thing. He took a moment just to admire her, from all the moments they spent together for the past month. By the time, Elijah's mind came back to reality, he caught Sabrina's eye-she finally noticed him! Before more guilt struck him, he managed to avoid the awkwardness and just acted normal.

"Hey" he said, gently.

"Hey" Sabrina replied.

There was nothing else to add, even when Elijah wanted to, nothing was coming to mind. Sabrina continued looking through the books. After glancing at a few titles, Elijah couldn't help but looking back at Sabrina as if he was waiting for something to happen. Only thing is, he didn't know what, perhaps waiting for her to start a serious conversation, one that they didn't have before, something that would truly connect them. After all, they had been friends for a month. It ought to happen someday.

(Now what kind of serious conversation would Elijah Khoda and Sabrina Clarin have? It made him wonder. He could only paint the scenarios in his mind; imagination. This particular conversation should have meaning, words from the heart that would strengthen their friendship. Maybe Sabrina would open up to Elijah about something that troubles her and he would be there to comfort her and/or vice versa. In the end, they would be drawn closer than before. Either way, Elijah imagined that he would see Sabrina Clarin for who she is on the inside, beautiful. It made him more curious just thinking about it. But it's not the kind of thing where he could just ask for a serious conversation. So there was no choice but to wait and make the best of the time that's given.)

Once Sabrina caught Elijah's eyes again, he made a rather funny face, as if he just ate something sour. She thought it was silly and just had to giggle. Elijah couldn't think of anything to say. So he just improvised and played around. The best part was, Sabrina responded in the same manner, making her own face at him. Elijah leaned in closer but went in a little far and too quick that he bumped his head on the book shelf. Both he and Sabrina tried not to break out in laughter because they were in the library.

During recess, Elijah, Sabrina, Andrew, and Paula, were walking around the school side by side. After a short period of time of being silent, Elijah decided to play around. While Sabrina wasn't looking, he gently and deliberately bumped into her.

"I slipped" Elijah teased.

Sabrina noticed as she met his eye. Giving a sly smirk, she returned the favor and bumped back in the same manner.

"Whoops" she said.

It was a little challenge that Elijah took advantage of. So he did it again, only this time he bumped into her slightly harder.

"Did it again"

"Not so hard, you're gonna make me bump into Andrew" Sabrina told him. Then she glanced over and winked at Elijah. That gave him the courage to bump again, hard enough to push Sabrina over. He did it a little harder than he intended to and she did end up bumping into Andrew. Sabrina began to laugh.

"Oh, so that's how it is" Andrew said, playfully.

The four of them stopped once Andrew was preparing to bump back by bending his legs like he was about to dash any moment. He was looking at Sabrina, but then he took a step backwards, nearly falling, just to bump into Paula.

"Whoops, I slipped too" Andrew taunted at Paula.

"Well, four can play at this game" Paula replied, in a sly voice.

Then Paula pulled the same stunt on Andrew and bumped into him. And then Andrew passed it along to Sabrina, and then her to Elijah, and repeated. They were all laughing. Soon, it was getting slightly rough as they started pushing each other, just for the fun of it.

"Alright, that's it!" Andrew spoke in a deep voice, like he was trying to impersonate a character from TV.

Andrew ran from them briefly, only to get a running distance.

"Oh, I don't like looks of this" Elijah said.

Elijah and the two girls waited to see what Andrew had in store for them. And there he began to charge at them.

"Run!" Sabrina told them.

Then she, Elijah, and Paula began running away from Andrew, who gave out a battle cry as he was running. They were behind the school. Andrew chased them as far as the tire swings on the side of the school, where they all stopped, panting, and laughing.

"That was fun, Elijah" Sabrina said, "Thank you"

Elijah just smiled. Bringing joy and pleasure to his friends was always a good feeling.

The next day, the four of them were throwing the Frisbee around on the field. It was boys against girls. They stood far apart from each other so there was enough space to run around. After a moment, Sabrina threw the Frisbee a little too high. It was flying towards Andrew, but he was gladly to jump high as he could, but the Frisbee flew past him.

"Damn! I almost had it" Andrew said, "It's your fault, Paulie"

"Oh yeah, just like it was my fault when they cancelled sport's day last year, but it was actually because of the rain!"

"I have to blame somebody"

"Just go get the Frisbee" Paula insisted.

Andrew did as she said and went to reclaim the Frisbee that landed several feet away from them. Since they were taking a little break, Elijah decided to spend it with Sabrina.

"Nice throw" he told her.

"Thanks"

It was tempting to add something else. Elijah wanted to but it was one of those moments where he couldn't think and only observe. While they were still waiting for Andrew, Elijah couldn't help but look at Sabrina. She finally caught his stare. Luckily he didn't feel awkward around her anymore. And she then responded casually.

"What?" Sabrina replied.

That was when he learned that sometimes words are not enough.

"Uh…I'm trying to distract you" Elijah claimed. Then he raised his hand, expecting Andrew to throw the Frisbee but he was still too far off, "Why's he taking so long?"

"He spent most of his time, fidgeting with the Frisbee" Paula said.

Andrew came back with the Frisbee. Without warning, he decided to throw the Frisbee towards Elijah and Sabrina's direction. "I dare someone to catch it!" he challenged.

So they started running for it. The Frisbee was flying lower and lower. Elijah and Sabrina were running beside each other. "I got it" he called.

"Not if I get it first" she warned.

They both reached for it. Before Elijah knew it, Sabrina's hand caught the Frisbee. They both stopped to catch their breaths. All proud of herself, Sabrina showed him the Frisbee. "See?"

"Any girl who catches the Frisbee last has to put carrots in her mouth"

"Carrots in my mouth?" Sabrina repeated.

It was the first joke from the top of the head. Maybe it wasn't all that funny but it was the only thing Elijah could think of. On the upside, it provided some advantage. While Sabrina was distracted by the nonsense, Elijah grabbed the Frisbee. "You've been distracted!"

"How clever" Sabrina replied.

As the game continued, Elijah ran back towards Paula and Andrew. Sabrina went after him. Once she was able to catch up, Sabrina quickly reclaimed the Frisbee.

"Thank you" she called.

"Hey!" Elijah called back.

Sabrina threw the Frisbee towards Andrew and Paula, who were getting ready to catch it. Again, the Frisbee flew passed them. Paula saw it coming and went to get it first before Andrew even turned around.

"Woo!" Sabrina cheered, mildly, "Girl power". Then she went up and gave Paula a high five.

Each day, memories were being made, with every activity and conversation alike. There was always something to take away and remember for the longest time. And each of them was engraved in the mind and the heart.

The next day at school, something changed the way Elijah looked at Sabrina. They were in gym class. Everyone was wearing their attire for physical education. Sabrina was wearing shorts. During one moment before they started another activity, Elijah was behind her, staying close but keeping his distance. Then he noticed that his shoelaces were coming loose. So he knelt down to tie them. After they were tied, Elijah looked up and stayed where he was to catch his breath. Then something caught his attention and most of all his interest, Sabrina's legs. His mind turned off and he stayed perfectly still. Before he knew it, Elijah was staring longer than he should have. The way the light shined on Sabrina's legs, showed how clean white they were, just like her skin. And the way she was standing, one leg straight and the other was bent behind it, like a ballerina that was getting ready to twirl. It was quite appealing.

"Alright class, let's get started" Mrs. Parker's voice pulled Elijah out of his mental state.

So he got back to his feet as they continued with their education. But since then, he couldn't stop thinking about Sabrina's legs. They were just one thing. Before Elijah knew it, he found himself looking at Sabrina in a way he didn't before. He was attracted to her, physically.

Elijah knew there was something appealing about Sabrina. Of course, it was her charm and humor. He'd shown her the same kindness as hers and they had since developed mutual respect for each other. After that day in gym class, something else attracted him to her, her beauty on the outside. It was more astonishing than he imagined. Now each time Elijah looked at her, he found himself eyeing at her features, her neck, her chest, her breasts, her buttocks, and anywhere there was bare skin-

No matter how many times Elijah dismissed that thought; it came back to him like a recurring dream. Deep down, he knew it wasn't right to think of a girl that way but he couldn't help himself. Sabrina Clarin was just too beautiful! Whenever he saw her, Elijah could only think about her on the outside. One day, something different happened.

It was in the morning when the students were arriving at school. Elijah kept an eye out for only Sabrina. He didn't think about Andrew or Paula. And so he kept his distance as he wanted his own space. Elijah didn't know why but he just felt like talking to Sabrina Clarin alone. Once she came, his heart started beating with excitement like it never had before. And that feeling started to overcome and Elijah just lost control as he was sprinted towards Sabrina. She was just coming up the stairs outside the grade seven entrance while Elijah ran on the soil grass. At that point, he didn't really care just as long as he got close to her. Just as Sabrina noticed him, Elijah decided at the last minute to slow down. She was halfway through the staircase and he was on the other side of the railing. All that excitement was draining and it had Elijah panting as if he just did a number of laps.

"Hi Sabrina" Elijah managed to say smoothly between breaths.

"Hey Elijah"

"You're…looking…fine today"

Those words just slipped out. Elijah wasn't thinking before speaking. And it just so happened that he was looking directly at her when he said it. It was probably because of the fact that he had been thinking about her, so intimately that it created a claustrophobic feeling that needed to get out. Meanwhile, Sabrina suddenly froze. She had never been complimented like that before, especially from a boy her age. It was odd for her, surprising even, but yet she couldn't turn away from Elijah.

"Thank you?" she replied, after a moment of silence.

"Yeah…" Elijah nodded. He was speechless.

It was starting to become awkward that Sabrina just had to say something to break the silence, "And you're…looking…" she was about to say something casual like the word nice but something else came out, "Handsome".

Where did that come from? She wondered. Maybe it was because he complimented her with the word fine and she felt obligated to say something familiar for his benefit.

As they continued gazing at each other, Elijah did his best not to look at Sabrina's features. Finally, he went and climbed over the railing to meet with Sabrina.

"You made it!" he told her, only then he meant it to make conversation.

"Of course I did" she responded.

"Wouldn't know how to start the day without you"

Sabrina heard him clearly but she could tell Elijah was trying to imply something.

"Huh?"

"I mean…" Elijah tried to redefine his words, "Things wouldn't be the same without you" He still wasn't sure what he was saying but the way he spoke, it sounded like he meant it, "I would be…upset?"

Sabrina made a face. She was puzzled but also flattered in a way.

"Well I wouldn't be too upset-I know because you're so…"

Think of a word to describe her!

"Strong…"

Another compliment: it made Sabrina want to smile.

"…and…" Elijah hesitated and then he started to look away as he whispered quietly,

"…beautiful"

"Strong and what?" Sabrina asked.

Elijah started to feel embarrassed and almost changed the subject, but looking at Sabrina's eyes pulled him back in. So he then cleared his throat, "Beautiful?"

There was no comment. Sabrina just stared at him and was actually starting to become awe-

"HEY!" Andrew yelled, rather abruptly.

The moment was ruined, just when Elijah and Sabrina's conversation was going to a place where it never gone before! Andrew had to sneak up behind them and startle the both of them. Elijah only pretended to enjoy the little scare but he was mostly focused on his conversation with Sabrina. The gag should've been short-lived; at least that was how Elijah wanted it to be. But unfortunately, Sabrina started a new conversation with Andrew.

"Okay, you got me this time but now I'm gonna have to get you back someday" Sabrina warned, playfully.

Elijah was trying to be patient. *Okay, Andrew, that's enough. Now leave us alone!*

"Good luck" Andrew taunted, "You'll never see this Little Man coming. I can squeeze myself into your locker just to give a little scare. I'd be like 'Hello, Sabrina!' Wait, that sounds too normal. It should be a little scarier" Then he spoke a deep and haunting voice, "Hello, Sabrina"

She just nodded.

"Or should I try a little high pitch, like an old lady?"

Andrew repeated the line, this time in a high and raspy voice like he suggested.

"That's funny" Sabrina said, "That actually reminds me of what my dad did to my mom…"

Well, it looked like Elijah wasn't going to finish his conversation with Sabrina, for that she started one with Andrew and it sounded like it was going to go on and on. Neither of them noticed Elijah afterwards, like he was wiped from existence. Feeling neglected, Elijah sighed and went to take refuge with Paula, who stood by the entrance, reading a book. She and Andrew must've been walking around the school, if only that would've lasted long enough for Elijah to connect with Sabrina on a different level.

"Hey" Paula greeted.

"Hey, Paula" Elijah replied, with a little disappointment in his voice. He acted normal the best he could as he stood beside Paula. Sabrina and Andrew were still talking.

"Are you all right?" Paula asked, once she noticed Elijah's sour face. That wasn't the first time she saw that face.

"Yeah, I'm fine" he replied, gently.

They paused.

"Are you sure?"

Now came one of those irritating moments when Paula knew something was wrong or she thinks something was wrong and tries to encourage-more like pressure it out of Elijah. Next thing, he would escape those cliché questions.

"Yeah, I'm fine" Elijah assured, more firmly.

"Okay, I'm just checking" Paula told him, calmly.

That was the first time in Elijah's life that he was annoyed at Andrew.

For the rest of the afternoon, Elijah wandered aimlessly into silence, waiting to find the confidence or something to find him, more like SOMONE to find him.

The other thing that Elijah couldn't stop thinking about was when he practically snapped at Paula earlier. It was a rather painful thought and he hated himself for it; if only Paula wasn't so worried about him. *I'm not a little boy anymore. I can take care of myself.*

Being mad at Paula was one thing, but thinking about all the bad things he did before was probably worse. Elijah tried to forget about it and move on. And that was something that Sabrina could never know. He was scared that if she did, she might not want to be friends anymore.

After school was over, there was another opportunity to mingle with Sabrina, even if it was just to say bye. Elijah thought about continuing that conversation with her but he still had hard feelings towards Andrew and that's what was holding him back. And most likely, Andrew would interrupt them again. Plus it would probably be tricky to try and restart that conversation. It wouldn't be as natural as before.

"Well, I'll see you tomorrow, Sabrina" Elijah said.

"For sure" she promised.

Sabrina gave Elijah a smile before she left.

It just had to be a short interaction. It was something but it wasn't enough. Elijah wanted more, more than just saying hello and goodbye. He not only wanted to finish that conversation, he wanted to talk about a lot more. He wanted to be with Sabrina Clarin, with no one else around. Elijah wanted them to have their own life, their own world. It would be the best one yet.

CHAPTER SIX

End of an Era

Fall had officially begun, with the days getting shorter and leaves on the trees were nearly gone. Elijah grew more attached to Sabrina. He was thinking about her constantly, every day, from waking up in the morning until going to bed at night. She was someone that he could bond with. There was something about her that just made things special. He was even giving more attention to her than Paula and Andrew. As days went by, Elijah had practically forgotten about them. But in even one month, time has its way of changing things.

It was gym time for Mrs. Parker's class. They were playing volleyball. The class was split into two teams. Elijah and Sabrina were playing against each other. The volleyball itself was flying back and forth. It was coming into Sabrina's team. The ball was almost out of line, but Sabrina was the only courageous enough to run quickly and hit the ball before it even touched the floor. Half of the class was impressed. The volleyball came back to Sabrina. She had her hands together and hit the ball, but it happened to bounce indirectly for that it didn't go forward. The volleyball was in the air for what it felt like forever. It happened a little too fast for Sabrina to think of a strategy, and of course it was out of her reach. But behind her, Carly Dawson was able to hit the volleyball with her wrist that launched back to Elijah's team surprisingly fast, no one was able to hit it back. The ball rolled away from their opponents, who won the game.

Sabrina's team cheered. As they were waiting for the next round to start, the students went back to being themselves as they were panting and catching their breaths. Sabrina's teammates admired her athletic abilities, especially Carly Dawson, who went up to her.

"Hey" Carly called.

And that was when Sabrina Clarin and Carly Dawson made eye contact for the first time.

"Thanks for handing me the ball" Carly said, kindly.

"Hey, thanks for winning the game" Sabrina replied, in the same manner.

Carly nodded. "Anytime"

Before Sabrina knew it, the compliment led to a conversation.

"That was cool, by the way" Carly added, "The way you hit the ball before it even touched the floor"

"Thanks, but I try" Sabrina admitted, in a modest way, "I guess I got lucky"

"Either way, you did good"

Sabrina smiled and nodded, as she took the compliment. The next round was about to begin. Both teams got back into positions.

"I'm Carly" she said to Sabrina,

"Sabrina; but you probably knew that already"

"I did, actually"

Carly Dawson was a blonde haired girl, with a light girly voice, a little shy but can be a good teammate. She was into almost any kind of sport. Once she saw Sabrina Clarin's stunt, she thought it was probably someone she could bond with.

Elijah however wasn't much for sports, at least not as much as he used to. When he was little, he would play basketball or hockey, but that was only because of the sport movies he once watched. During the next game, things weren't really going well for Elijah's team. They were falling behind. At one point, Elijah thought he could turn things around but he was trying a little too hard. Each time he missed the ball or failed to score, he'd start getting frustrated. And of course, he was thinking about Sabrina Clarin. So his mind wasn't really in the right frame.

The volleyball was coming towards his direction. Elijah ran to it, but before he knew it, he accidently bumped into one of his classmates, Jeff Tomly, who attempted to hit the ball, but because of their sudden encounter, the ball went passed them and landed on their side. Once again, they lost. While Sabrina's team was celebrating, Elijah's teammates were pondering in defeat. Gym class was nearly over. So it was time to pack things up.

"Excuse you, Elijah" Jeff said, rather strongly.

Elijah only scowled at him and then walked away. He wasn't particularly fond of Jeff, for that he found him annoying. He first came to WKE in grade four but he and Elijah didn't meet until they were in the same class in grade five. Jeff was a little taller, and had red hair. Normally a nice young man, funny in his own way, but he was often talkative. Everyone was so easily amused by Jeff. That was one thing Elijah couldn't stand about him and had no desire to interact with him whatsoever.

In the boys change room, Elijah quietly got dressed back into his casual clothes, as well as the others. They were all chatting and teasing each other. It was a crowd Elijah barely knew and would rather leave the change room immediately. Half of them were already done and went to regroup with the rest of the class. There was only a few left in the change room, and Jeff Tomly was one of them. He noticed Elijah across from him.

"Hey, Elijah" he called, gently.

But Elijah didn't answer.

"Aren't you gonna say sorry?" Jeff wondered.

He just had to ask in front of the other boys. Elijah gave the same look he did before.

"Normally, when you bump into someone like that, you're supposed to say sorry or at least say excuse me"

Hogging all the attention from everyone in class was one thing, now he was teaching Elijah manners. Jeff was waiting patiently. Elijah was finally ready and hurried out of the change room.

"Don't tell me what to do" Elijah finally spoke, in a snarling way. And then he stormed out of there.

That minor dispute had ruined Elijah's day. He tried not to think about it and hopefully that was the last time he interacted with Jeff. As he met with his classmates, Elijah noticed that Sabrina wasn't there. She must've been in the girls change room still. So he waited patiently and even glanced over at the door, hoping to see her come out, but only saw the other girls. Finally, she stepped out and she was walking side by side with Carly. By that time, everyone was together and Mrs. Parker began leading her students back to class. They all exited the gymnasium at the same time. It was difficult for Elijah to keep up with Sabrina because there were too many of their peers between them. Once he did catch up with her, he couldn't get a word in because she was talking with Carly Dawson.

"Did your wrist hurt at all when you hit the ball?" Sabrina asked.

"A little, but I'm used to it" Carly admitted.

Elijah opened his mouth-

"Do you play sports, normally?" Carly added.

"Sure, although not normally, but sometimes"

"What kind?" Carly spoke like she was dying to find out.

Sabrina paused for a moment. There was Elijah's chance.

"Hey Sabrina" Elijah called, as he was walking behind her.

She glanced over her shoulder, but not for long.

"Yeah?" she replied, casually.

"Good game back there" he tried to start a conversation.

"Oh, thanks" Sabrina told him and then she turned her attention back to Carly.

Elijah frowned. Alright, maybe it was just one time she would talk to Carly Dawson.

At first, the girls were talking about sports. One question led to another and soon, Sabrina shared how her previous school was different. Carly listened to every word and there was even a little humor in the mix. That was when they won affection from each other. From those topics that they discussed, Carly felt the urge to share her stories and experiences. So they talked up until their next school subject commenced.

At lunchtime, Sabrina and Carly were still talking. For once, Sabrina wasn't sitting across from Elijah; she was sitting beside Carly's desk, having lunch together. Elijah didn't want to bother her, so he stayed where he was and ate his meal silently. After they finished eating, Elijah met up with his friends and decided on an activity. Elijah and Paula waited outside the entrance, while Andrew went to go get the sporting product. Once Sabrina came out, Elijah went up to her right away. He could see Carly right beside her, but he assumed that they were done getting acquainted.

"Sabrina, hey, we're heading up to the field. We're gonna throw the Frisbee around" Elijah told her.

Sabrina paused. It was a rather awkward silence. She then exchanged a quick glance at Carly, who was patiently waiting, and then met with Elijah's eyes, with a guilty face.

"Uh, I think I'm gonna hang out with Carly today" Sabrina replied, gently.

Elijah said nothing, even though it was tempting to say no.

"Is that okay?" she asked, innocently.

Elijah could've refused, he wanted to, but there was too much respect he had for Sabrina.

"Yeah…sure" Elijah finally agreed.

"Thank you" Sabrina added, kindly, "And I'm sorry, maybe some other time we'll play"

Elijah gave a weak smile, secretly hoping she would see his pain and change her mind out of pity. But instead, she and Carly turned their backs almost right away.

"Maybe tomorrow?" Elijah suggested, but unfortunately he didn't speak loud enough. By that time, the girls were already further away. Sabrina was out of Elijah's reach. And deep down, that made him a little sad.

Carly led Sabrina to the path in front of the main entrance, and there was another girl waiting for them. She had long black hair, with bangs, skin that was clean white. "Sabrina, this is my friend, Melanie Peyton" Carly introduced, gesturing towards Mel, "Melanie, this is Sabrina Clarin, the new girl that I mentioned last month?"

"Thee Sabrina Clarin?!" Melanie replied. She was quite surprised, as she looked directly at her, "You're prettier than I thought!" she blurted out, almost loud enough for the school to hear.

Sabrina paused. She wasn't expecting such a compliment, especially if it was on her appearance. She chuckled casually. "Thank you"

"You're welcome!" Melanie replied, kindly. And then another feature caught Mel's attention, "Ooo, I love your hair"

Before Sabrina could say anything, Melanie ran up to her promptly and started combing her fingers through Sabrina's hair. "It's lovely, soft and comforting! Go on, Carly, feel it"

Reluctantly, Carly raised her hand but then stopped herself for a moment. "Um, if it's okay with you?" she asked, gently.

For a brief moment, Sabrina was feeling a little bashful, just being the center of the attention. She never thought she would get a social life like this. It was a little exciting, almost made Sabrina laugh but tried not to.

"Sure, it's fine" Sabrina finally answered, followed by a little giggle.

Then Carly interlocked her fingers through Sabrina's hair and Melanie wasn't lying. "It is nice" she said.

"I know, right?" Melanie strongly agreed. She even rested her head on Sabrina's hair as if it was a pillow. Sabrina thought that was cute.

"It smells nice too" Carly added.

"Well, thanks for noticing" Sabrina replied, with flattery. Then Carly and Melanie stopped what they were doing.

"Me and Sabrina started talking in gym class after a volleyball game. She's quite good at it" Carly said to Mel, who replied: "I bet!"

"Yeah; we talked more after that and now I asked if she wanted to hang out with us"

"That's fine by me" Melanie said, "We can always use some nice hair to rest on"

Melanie Peyton had a pre-existing relationship with Carly. They had been friends for a few years. They were in separate class for the seventh grade, but still maintained their connection. Melanie would be easily amused and wasn't afraid to show it. She had energy and a sense of humor that appealed to Sabrina Clarin and they both simply enjoyed life. So therefore they became friends instantly.

On the field, Elijah, Paula, and Andrew, had to play without Sabrina. After she went off with Carly and Mel, Elijah pretended everything was okay as he explained to Paula, telling her that he understood. But he could only act normal for as long as he could. While they were throwing the Frisbee to each other, Elijah's mind would wander on and off. He looked to where the wooden steps, hoping that a certain someone would catch up to them, but she was nowhere in sight. Then the Frisbee flew passed Elijah and landed a few feet behind him.

"Whoops" Elijah said, trying to sound casual as possible.

"Ha! The Frisbee's like...'How dare you miss me, I had such high hopes for you" Andrew teased, in a high pitched voice.

Elijah responded with a late chuckle. Once he reclaimed the Frisbee, he then threw it to Paula, who could tell that her best friend was distracted. Paula had the Frisbee and then passed it to Andrew, who then held it for a moment.

"Hey, E.K., wanna have Paulie throw the Frisbee like a football? Just like what we did last time?" Andrew offered.

"Ahh" Elijah hesitated, "No, maybe not today"

"Oh well, it's the fun that matters" Andrew said. Then he passed the Frisbee back to Paula, "You know what to do, Paulie"

"Throw it farther and farther, and make you look like an idiot?" Paula replied, sarcastically.

"Idiots were born to have fun"

"That's a way to put it" Paula said.

Then she threw the Frisbee as hard as she could, and Andrew started running across the field, hoping to catch it when it reaches the ground. As the Frisbee was falling closer, Andrew had his arm stretched out, but didn't see where he was going and accidently tackled a fellow student.

"Well, at least I'm not the only one who bumped into someone today" Elijah muttered.

When lunch was over, Elijah went to meet his classmates, and realized Sabrina was still mingling with her new friends. There was no point in saying hello because he felt like he was bothering them. He stood in line, while Sabrina and Carly were talking to Melanie as she was lining up with her classmates. There were already a few students standing behind Elijah. So there was no chance of her standing behind him. Finally, Sabrina and Carly joined their class, in which they were way behind. He never felt so invisible.

Reality had struck Elijah, whether he knew it or not. He kept thinking that Sabrina was going to come back to him, Andrew, and Paula, only because that she promised that they would play another day. When the next day came, Elijah and Sabrina only said hi to each other once. She was still sitting across from him. He was expecting her to explain her absence, but there was nothing but silence. The last thing Elijah wanted was putting pressure on the person he truly cared about. So he let Sabrina have her space.

The day after that, Sabrina was giving most of her attention to Carly and Melanie. She and Elijah barely spoke.

He continued to wait, but nothing happened.

It was the end of the week. Elijah had decided to say something before the weekend started. He knew it was going to bother him if he didn't. As soon as recess had begun, Elijah excused himself from Paula and Andrew just to catch up with Sabrina once she and her girlfriends were in plain sight.

"Sabrina" Elijah called, but it wasn't loud enough.

He went up closer.

"Sabrina" he repeated.

He finally had her attention. She stopped and turned her attention towards him, Elijah opened his mouth, but no words were coming out. They were looking eye to eye and suddenly he didn't know what he wanted to say. At first, he thought of letting it all out in the pettiest way, just so Sabrina would feel bad. But now Elijah was questioning his own motive, wondering if he really wanted to do it. What would happen if he did? Would she really feel bad...or...would she get uncomfortable and look the other way?

"I…" Elijah tried to speak, but then his mind wrapped around the fact they were in awkward silence for too long. Even Melanie and Carly were waiting. They were probably getting impatient, "just wanted to say hi" he finally said, poorly.

Sabrina forced a smile, definitely not the same smile he seen before where it was natural and beautiful. "Hi" she said, without emotion. Then she and the other two girls turned around to continue walking.

That tone of voice was telling Elijah something, that maybe he and Sabrina suddenly became strangers. That scared him. He finally turned around and started to walk back where he came from. *Was there something I did wrong?* That was one question Elijah kept repeating in his head. Sabrina Clarin was his friend and now it didn't feel like it anymore. He was walking slowly, thinking it would freeze time and would get the answers sooner or later. If only it was that easy. There was nothing and that was all Elijah Khoda had.

No more fun, no more excitement, nothing to look forward to. The only thing Elijah did was wake up in the morning, go to school, come home, and sleep. It was already repetitive as it was, and Sabrina was the only one that made it different. Andrew and Paula weren't very helpful either, considering they were the only two faces he saw each day. But that was no surprise; he was actually getting bored with them before grade six was over. Elijah realized how much he liked Sabrina, even within that month; he thought of just having her by his side and face the world together. He finally had something to call his own, until Carly Dawson and Melanie Peyton took it away from him!

As Elijah kept dragging his feet to school and back, he was getting more depressed, but his kindness forced him to hide it. Whenever someone noticed, like his mom did that one night, Elijah would just make an excuse and it was mostly him being tired. But he also didn't want to talk about it, so there were some days he acted normal the best he could, but sadly, the culprit of his sadness happened to be in the same class as him. Those days were challenging.

And to make things even worse, Mrs. Parker decided that her students would rearrange their desks around. Instead of having them in rows, they put them in groups. Each of them had six students put together. In the end, there were a total of four groups. Sadly, Sabrina wasn't sitting across from Elijah anymore. That broke his heart.

It bothered Elijah for the rest of the morning that he was no longer sitting across from his special friend. He tried not to think about it. But it was already taking him further away from reality.

"For Halloween this year, I think we all should dress up like we did in grade four" Andrew suggested, as he, Elijah, and Paula were hanging around the pathway.

"Sure, as long it's essential and not an excuse just to make fun of me" Paula said.

"Relax; if I wanted to do that, we'd be dressing up as ourselves" Andrew teased, "Elijah, what do you think?"

Elijah had no interest in celebrating Halloween. Ever since his friend was taking away, it felt pointless to do anything "Yeah, maybe, but I'm not sure if I wanna dress up this year"

"Why not?" Andrew asked, skeptically.

"I don't know, I guess I just haven't thought about it that much. Maybe this year is not as fun as it used to be. Kids are no longer collecting Pokemon cards. I think everyone is growing up"

"It's not fun unless we make it fun" Andrew offered.

Elijah was really saying that he was hoping that his new friend would be by his side during the festivities. But obviously that wasn't going to happen. Talking about it was starting make Elijah a little emotional.

"Yeah, maybe" he said, hopelessly, "Hey, uh, listen I'm gonna go for a walk around the school, alone"

"Okay, we'll be here" Paula replied, in a friendly way.

Then almost right away, Elijah left to clear his mind. Paula merely watched him leave. She could only imagine what he was going through. It was actually bothering her for a while, knowing that her best friend had been dealing with issues from the year before, but she couldn't help but feel something else was troubling him, something different.

"Hey Andrew, do you notice anything different about Elijah?" she asked.

Andrew paused to think of a possible answer. "I noticed that he hasn't been angry or gotten into trouble"

"I picked up on that too. And it's probably a good thing. But I think there's something else"

"Yeah? Did you notice anything?"

"I notice everything. Elijah has been awfully quiet, for a little too long"

"I guess a little summer break didn't really do any good" Andrew added.

"I guess not"

Paula's mind trailed off. Andrew noticed the worried look on her face. "You're alright, Paulie?" he asked, gently.

"Yeah, I'm okay, it's just…I think I know what's bothering him"

"And?"

Paula looked at Andrew and leaned in closer. "Sabrina…" she answered, "I think Elijah likes her"

"Really? Huh, how can you tell?"

"Ever since Sabrina stopped hanging out with us, Elijah seemed pretty distracted. Before that, I noticed he was being so polite to her. In fact, I had never seen him so upbeat and sociable. He was almost happy. And I remember at one point, he didn't want anything to do with people and there he was, mingling with a new classmate"

"And I don't think he liked girls before or even talked about them" Andrew added.

"Except for those days when you guys were badmouthing Melissa Hartway"

"Oh right"

"The other thing I noticed that Elijah let you and Sabrina win at tether ball. Remember that day? You guys were almost winning. He was about to prevent that but he changed his mind at the last minute"

"Right; that makes sense"

"And let's not forget when you brought up the name for the group. Last year, he didn't really like it but now he was okay with it because Sabrina was part of the group"

"Huh" Andrew paused, "I guess he won't like it again now".

"Yeah, he definitely wasn't like this at the beginning of the year."

"What do you mean? He seemed fine to me"

"Just because he's fine on the outside, doesn't mean he's fine on the inside. I can see it in his eyes and hear it in his voice. I don't think he changed a bit since last year. I guess meeting Sabrina was a good thing because she brought out the best in him. But now she's made new friends and I don't think he likes that. He's back to his quiet self and I'm scared that having feelings for a girl might destroy him even more"

"How do you know?"

"My mom once told me that love challenges you. And I know there's good in Elijah. Deep down he's a caring person. But what if he cares too much that he becomes obsessive? That probably won't end well. That's what scares me".

"So what do you think we should do?" Andrew asked, "Should we try and get Sabrina hanging out with us again?"

"Maybe or I don't know" Paula said, uncertainly, "I'd like to help… but…it's just…" she trailed off as she was trying to think straight but she couldn't and ended with a sigh. Paula turned away and leaned on the railing. Worriedly, Andrew went up and stood beside her.

"Paulie? What's wrong?"

Paula breathed in and out before she answered. "Elijah can be complicated sometimes". The distress in her voice went up and tampered with her emotions. "And I feel bad for saying that because I shouldn't be talking about him behind his back like this. But he obviously needs guidance and yet he doesn't want it. As his best friend, I decided to trust him but I don't think he even trusts himself"

Andrew didn't know what to say. He never handled a serious discussion before. "I guess the only person he trusts is Sabrina but she's not with us-or hanging out with us anymore. So…I don't know"

Paula gave it some thought before she spoke. "I guess that's not an option. The last thing I want is to put Sabrina in a bad spot. And besides, we don't know how bad things are until it happens"

Unfortunately, Paula thought. Nowadays, they had to learn things the hard way.

"You know, when we were kids, a lot younger than we are now, we just wanted to have fun and be happy. And then we grow up. Growing up is never easy. Sometimes it takes away the best of us. I think all Elijah wants is just to be happy again".

Elijah was expecting some sort of miracle to happen every time he came to school, but always found himself sitting in silence that went on for too long. The fact that Sabrina Clarin didn't really look at him anymore made him sadder by the day. And he was afraid to speak up, thinking that Sabrina didn't really care. Talking to someone about it wasn't something Elijah had in mind. The last thing he wanted was being told what to do, and he didn't want anyone to know that he liked a girl in his class, fearing that he would be told to let her go. Elijah didn't want Sabrina to go. Why did she have to make friends with other girls?

One day in class, Elijah unwillingly worked on his assignments, which was basically his only purpose, endless homework. He didn't want to but he had to. Before he knew it, things went back to the way they were before, looking at the clock constantly, putting up with the outside world until the afternoon, for that the only thing he had to look forward to would be going home. Elijah sighed quietly and tried to get his work done.

He looked at the corner of his eye and noticed Sabrina got up from her seat and went to the back of the room to use the pencil sharpener.

I know this is probably going to be embarrassing but I'm sure they won't mind a little noise, Sabrina thought as she placed her pencil in the sharpener. It was the electric type, so it let out a fairly loud rusty noise. After holding the pencil in for a few seconds, she pulled it out; still wasn't sharp enough. She tried again. After the noise died down, Sabrina heard someone's voice behind her.

"Don't you hate it when they're too loud sometimes?"

A little surprised, Sabrina turned around and realized a fellow classmate was standing behind her. It was the one with ginger hair.

"I'm sorry?" she replied.

"Pencil sharpener can be a little loud sometimes" he rephrased, "Almost makes you want the manual one back, eh?"

"Oh, y-yeah; wouldn't that be nice"

"It would be" then the ginger kid started impersonating the sound of the pencil sharpener and motioned with his hands as if he was using it for real.

After a moment, Elijah couldn't help but look back at Sabrina, just to see her, but saw something else that aggravated him. Jeff Tomly and Sabrina Clarin were talking to each other by the pencil sharpener. He didn't know what they were saying because they were speaking in a low voice. The longer Elijah stared, the more hatred was filling his heart. It was bad enough that Carly and Melaine took his new friend away, but why did Jeff have to talk to her? Doesn't he get enough attention from everybody else?!

Jeff ended his impersonation, "Hey?"

Sabrina just forced herself to laugh, considering that she didn't really know this ginger kid. "Haha, well I think this is sharp enough. It's all yours now"

"Why, thank you" he replied, kindly.

Finally, school was over for the day. Elijah went home immediately, and didn't even bother saying goodbye to Paula or Andrew. He didn't want to be there when Sabrina came out, because seeing her talking to someone else just made him sick. Everything was changing. Elijah didn't like it. And when his emotions were starting to get adjusted to the new predicament, something else happened. One day, in class, Mrs. Parker had decided to rearrange the desks. Now Sabrina was no longer sitting across from Elijah. When the new arrangement was done, he found himself with classmates he barely knew or didn't care for. And Sabrina was sitting ten feet from him. There was no way of saying hi. What was the world coming to?

Carly Dawson, Melanie Peyton, and Jeff Tomly, those were the names that Elijah had stuck in his head, and they were haunting him as time went by. He blamed them for his problems for having Sabrina who was supposed to be Elijah's friend. He met her way before they did. But sadly, it's been almost two weeks since they last spoke.

During the first recess on the next day, Elijah was avoiding his best friends, as he stormed away, trying to create a long distance between them. But Paula was trying to catch up to him.

"Elijah" she called, "Can we talk for a minute?"

Paula was being rather demanding. Elijah peered over his shoulder.

"Not right now" he refused, turning his head away.

"Yes, now!" she insisted.

Elijah glanced back at her, angrily. "No!" he yelled.

After that intense moment, Elijah didn't talk to Paula or Andrew for the rest of the day. He didn't want to talk to anyone. If he had the power, he would turn back time and try to find a way to keep things from changing. But he couldn't. Elijah was just a boy and that was all he'd ever be.

For the rest of the week, Elijah kept his mind blank. Maybe schoolwork would take his mind off his problems. Mrs. Parker was giving them instructions on their next assignment until she gotten a phone call that excused her from the class. And Elijah wasn't surprised of the person she chose to be in charge.

"Jeff Tomly, would you like to be in charge?" she asked,

"Why, Mrs. Parker, I'm flattered. Of course, I'll be in charge"

Then half of the class laughed by his response; Elijah just rolled his eyes. As soon as Mrs. Parker left the room, Jeff quickly got up and pretended to be their teacher. He even started writing his last name on the board. A few classmates already started giggling.

"Hello, class. I'm Mr. Tomly" he announced.

Another laughter emerged.

"Oh great" Elijah said, silently.

"Hi, Mr. Tomly" some of the classmates responded.

Seriously? Elijah shook his head.

"Now today we're gonna learn about…" Jeff paused briefly. Then he glanced at his own desk and picked a random object, "The eraser!"

There was more laughter. Jeff sure could make someone's day without even trying.

"The eraser comes in all shapes and sizes. Now they say there's more to it than just erasing mistakes. You can use this and four push pins and make…a little pet. Allow me to demonstrate"

Jeff looked around. "Do we even have push pins around here?"

And there he saw some next on the bulletin board next to the chalkboard, and grabbed unused push pins. Now Elijah really wanted to go home. Once Jeff was done, he held the eraser above his head, showing it to the class. Like always, everybody was satisfied with Jeff, no matter what he said, he evidently made it special. Elijah peered over his shoulder and saw a certain someone smiling away. It was Sabrina and it looked like she was just enjoying Jeff's humor as much as the others… Was this really happening? That was the same girl that he genuinely liked from the moment they met, the same one that sat across from him in the beginning of the school year. Now she was Jeff Tomly's best friend!

The stare turned into a scowl as Elijah slowly turned towards Jeff was still in front of the class, entertaining the class and gaining more friends. The smile and all the laughter had darkened Elijah's heart. The pressure was getting to him. There was no strength to fight it. Everything was taking away from him, his friend, hopes, and dreams. Finally, Elijah snapped. It was time to fight!

"Alright!" he yelled, slamming his hand on the desk firmly. The laughter had died down as the whole class fell silent and turned to Elijah. "That's enough! You sure like the attention, don't you Jeff! I think we all get that, but when is it enough? It's probably never enough for you! So please…stop…tak-"

Stop taking my friend. That was what Elijah was about to say. As soon as he realized, he fell silent like the others. And then Sabrina Clarin's name popped into his head. Sabrina. He glanced in her direction and noticed right away the surprise look on her face. It also had worry written all over it…Elijah had scared her. It was bad enough that he came close to embarrassing her in front of the class and that's what stopped his rant.

There were no words to that could fix what just happened. Elijah was speechless and he felt like he didn't have the right to speak at all, maybe not anymore. So he just sat back in his seat, with his head down.

Don't cry. Boys do not cry.

After that ugly scene was over, Mrs. Parker came back. Elijah was expecting Jeff or somebody to tell what happened, but surprisingly… nobody did. They carried on like everything was alright. Elijah however was still in that moment. The only thing he could think about was how much he might've hurt Sabrina. He didn't mean to and there was no chance to patch up the wound. And the worse, Sabrina Clarin may never speak to him again. That was merely one thing. People would talk and soon the whole school could find out what happened. Elijah could hear the gossip already…

God, what is his problem?

Did you hear what he did to Jeff?

I heard they got into a fight right in front of the class.

Elijah Khoda? I heard that kid has problems. You should've seen what he did to Brian Kidman.

That kid's crazy. They should put him where crazy people go.

Then what would Paula and Andrew think?

That's it. I really can't take it anymore. Elijah won't listen and I don't think he wants to be friends anymore.

Dude, what did we ever do to you?

And it makes me sad because we been friends since grade three. I always saw you as a brother.

And then Sabrina…

Elijah, what you did to Jeff was so rude! I don't think we can be friends.

The bell rang…School was over…Everyone started packing up and headed for home. Elijah was a little surprised that he was still in the classroom, for that he was expecting something to happen. It didn't have to be Sabrina, but he felt like he should be in the office being punished. Had Elijah gone crazy? He actually wanted to go to the office, which was always the last place he wanted to be in. Now he was starting to regret ranting out at Jeff. He didn't mean to make everyone uncomfortable. All Elijah wanted was to be friends with Sabrina again.

The whole world had gone quiet. In fact, it was more like fading away. Elijah had destroyed it and there was nothing he could do. He tried patience, thinking that maybe Sabrina would make up for everything, but the wait had gone on too long. So now Elijah considered just letting her go, which was extremely painful, because he didn't want to.

It was almost the end of the week. Since that day of the incident in front of the class, Elijah was thinking long and hard. He didn't talk to Paula, Andrew, or anybody, not even his mom. If his mom had found out, Elijah feared of what might happen, being pulled out of school and just end up being home schooled. That was actually something that almost did back in grade five because of what happened between him and Brian. But there was always a soft spot for Paula and Andrew. It seemed like that was the case, being home schooled and never had to deal with the outside world anymore, and maybe leave his best friends forever, until...Elijah had discovered an alternative.

Once recess started, Elijah was walking alone. He was behind the school building, minding his own business. Just as Elijah was coming near the grade six area, he saw Quinton Malcolm, playing with his friends, and June Disher was there with them. Then Elijah remembered Quinton encouraging him to join his inner circle. That was something to consider. After all, Elijah had wanted a change of scenery and since Sabrina was taking away from him, there was another way. And Elijah was aware that it involved a different crowd. Maybe that's what he needed.

Elijah went back to the front of the school to look for Paula and Andrew. Luckily they were there, loitering around. They hadn't been doing much since Elijah was neglecting them for a short period of time.

"I need to talk to you" Elijah said. His voice was strong and firm, "Both of you"

His friends didn't say anything. Paula was rather eager because she had wanted to interact with Elijah for a while. First thing they did, was finding a private place. The three of them went to the sidewalk that was right beside the pathway. There were barely any students, so they had the privacy that they needed. Paula got straight to the point.

"Elijah, what is with you?!" she demanded, "You been avoiding us more than usual. I know you need your own space but do you ever think that I'm dying on the inside just wanting to talk to you?"

"Yeah, bud" Andrew agreed, gently, "I mean…we miss you, a lot! It's been…pretty quiet without you"

Andrew never had a serious discussion with Elijah before. So he didn't have much to say, but he spoke as gently as he could.

"Elijah, talk to us. Just please talk to us!" Paula insisted.

"I've had a lot on my mind" he admitted, in a slightly cold voice.

"Obviously" Paula said, with irritation.

There was a lot that had to be talked about, but Elijah never thought of how to say it. He was actually about to say how Sabrina Clarin was the culprit of his emotions. But he didn't want his best friends to find out. Why? Maybe he didn't want them to know because Sabrina was supposed to be his special friend and no one else.

"Look, I'm just getting tired of this" Elijah told them.

Paula waited.

"Being talked to and being asked if I'm okay" he was trembling, now that the truth was coming out. It was unbearable but it had to be done.

"But you're not!" Paula nearly yelled, "That's the problem"

Anger rose. "You think I'm…" and then Elijah stopped. His emotions made more fragile than angry. It was probably because he was thinking of someone.

"Listen, I can't do this anymore" he told them.

Paula was getting more annoyed, as she was hoping for a specific explanation. "Can't do what anymore?" she snarled.

"This" Elijah added, pointing to both her and Andrew. *This and a whole lot of other things, like Sabrina being taking away from me!*

It was really happening. And he didn't give it much thought.

"Not sure if I like the sound of that" Andrew muttered, as he turned away.

"Look I just want something of my own" Elijah said.

"And what's that?" Paula asked.

"My own life"

"But you have one, don't you see?"

"I know but I don't really want it because I can't have any fun when people keep telling me to do this and that, you, my mom, and the teachers!"

Paula flinched like a cold wind flowed through her body. Her eyes widened as she heard harsh words from the boy she befriended back in primary school.

"So you're mad at me for looking out for you?" Paula said, mostly hurt than offended.

Elijah hesitated, "Y-yeah, well, sort of, I..."

Slowly, Paula looked down from Elijah, "I'll take that as a yes"

Now Elijah started feeling bad. "No, Paula, I didn't mean..."

"Well, what do you mean?!" she snapped.

"I just want things to be different. And I...can't do it with you guys"

Paula didn't even breathe as she realized where he was coming from. "Are you serious?"

There was nothing left in this world. That was the only thing on his mind. Elijah really wanted things to be different, but he lost that chance.

"Look, we been friends for a few years..." Elijah said, gently, "It-it was good and then..."

"What are you saying, Eli? That we're not good enough for you?" Paula asked, trying to stay strong.

"Maybe, I don't know"

"What does that mean?"

Andrew could tell the discussion was already not doing any good. "Come on, bud. It can't be all that bad" he explained, "We're your friends, you know. And I know you have problems once in a while, but…friends were made for listening"

The words sunk into Elijah. He was already in too deep. "I can't" he said, after a paused moment.

Paula was trying to convince herself not to go there, the conclusion that Elijah was ending their friendship. But the silence had already consumed them. And since Paula didn't get the answer she was hoping for…Maybe Elijah was serious. Tears were starting burst from her eyes. Her best friend probably noticed but chose not to say anything.

"Okay…" Paula said, emotionally, "You know what, it's okay. You don't have to explain. I get it. You don't want us to be friends anymore"

Those words floated in Elijah's mind, but it sounded different once he heard it from Paula.

"Paula, I…" he tried to explain, out of pity-

"Just go!" Paula blurted out, as she turned his back on him.

That was it. Elijah had made his choice official. There was no turning back. He glanced at Andrew, noticing the worried look. So Elijah turned his back and started walking away and tried to keep his mind blank, and didn't look back. As he was talking away, he heard Andrew saying one last thing.

"At least think about it"

Before going to the back of the school, Elijah had to take moment to shake off all that feeling that was bothering him, the loneliness, the sadness, and the guilt. It was time to start a new chapter. Elijah went to find Quinton Malcolm. Luckily, he was still in the same area as he was before. Quinton noticed him approaching.

"Hey Quinton" Elijah greeted, and he meant it.

Quinton smiled, as he could easily tell that Elijah had finally accepted his friendship.

"Hey, man" he replied, smiling.

CHAPTER SEVEN

Clarin, Dawson, and Peyton

Sabrina had hit it off with Carly and Mel pretty good. Each conversation they had, they got to know each other a little better. Since then, the girls had been inseparable. It was only the early days of their friendship but it was starting to feel like they've known each other for a while. Sabrina did not expect to befriend girls her age, who were just down to earth as she was. So they certainly gave positive vibes. Every day was a breath of fresh air. Sabrina was looking forward to seeing what life had in store for her.

One day, after meeting outside for recess, Carly was staring at her reflection on the window, repeatedly planting her finger on her cheek, confused and uncertain, while Sabrina and Melanie were behind her waiting patiently.

"For the eleventh time, you don't have anything on her face" Mel claimed.

"Yeah, I heard you" Carly admitted, calmly, "It's just I could've sworn I saw something this morning"

"Yeah, I heard YOU" Mel emphasized, "Sabrina, would you please tell her that there's nothing wrong with her face?"

"I already did" Sabrina told her, "When we were in the girls' room"

"Twice, when I was looking in the mirror in my locker" Carly added.

116

"Now she's relying on a window" Melanie teased.

Carly wasn't getting slightly annoyed. "I can see myself, can I? And this isn't a joke"

"Nobody's laughing" Sabrina promised.

Melanie gave a sly look to Sabrina, "Not yet" then she leaned in and started tickling her new friend. Sabrina burst out laughing. Carly scowled at the girls. The laughter died down. That was one thing about Carly, she was quite sensitive. Sabrina felt a little bad and went to comfort her.

"Carly, seriously, there's nothing wrong with your face. You're pretty and purdy"

It took a moment for Carly to reply, "Thanks".

They finally moved on, after standing outside the library. They continued walking forward. The cold October weather was getting to them.

"Brrr!" Melanie muttered, "I can smell the snowflakes already"

"Don't say that" Carly whined, "Not a fan of the cold weather"

"Relax, you got two friends to keep you warm" Mel promised.

"How can you smell snowflakes?" Sabrina wondered.

"Why not?" Melanie said. As they were walking, she added, "It's gonna snow" she muttered. And then her voice rose a bit, "It's gonna snow" she was more sly, and then spoke up, "It's gonna sssnnoww!"

Carly sighed, "Who am I kidding, it's gonna come whether I want it or not"

As they were walking, Sabrina and Melanie linked arms with Carly. "That was kinda cool, what you said back there, Sabrina" Mel told her.

Sabrina turned her attention towards Peyton, trying to catch up with her.

"Pretty and purdy" Mel reminded.

"Yeah, I liked the way it sounded" Carly admitted.

"Oh right, yeah when I was little I used to pronounce 'pretty' as purdy. The one day, I kept saying both words and came up with that combination"

Another nice thing about Mel and Carly, they were good listeners. Since day one of their friendship, they were hanging on every word that Sabrina had to say, like she was the leader.

"Just like me actually. When I was little, I kept saying 'whoops' a lot" Melanie told her, "I kept on saying it and then the same word turned into three, whoops, whoops, whoops!"

"It's true" Carly said, casually, "She says that a lot".

Pretty and purdy; Sabrina thought it was a little too silly at times. So she was quite relieved that it led to Melanie's story. And now funny sayings were their common interests.

"Whoops, whoops, whoops" Sabrina repeated.

"Oh, looks like you got Sabrina saying it now" Carly joked.

"Yes!" Melanie cheered, raising her hand in triumph, "A new addition to Annoyance"

"I don't think it's annoying" Sabrina told her.

"My little brother does. Carly did, too, onetime"

So now both Sabrina and Melanie looked at her. Carly just threw her hands up.

"I was having a bad day. Honestly, the whole 'whoops' saying didn't bother me anymore after that"

"I don't know" Melanie replied, as she glanced at Sabrina, "We should probably test it"

Then Mel went up to Carly and started poking her repeatedly, "whoops, whoops, whoops!"

Carly was giggling as she tried to back away. She begged Melanie to stop but it was unlikely. Sabrina just stood there, watching them in amusement.

After school, Sabrina, Carly, and Melanie were waiting together outside. That day their friendship was taking another step because the girls were about to visit their new friend for the first time. It was decided when they needed some help with homework. Since Sabrina was good with numbers, she offered to help them with math. Also it was probably the best way to start their visitation as friends for years to come. Sabrina was a little nervous but mostly excited because before she hadn't brought any friends over. At one point she was worried that her family would start off with bad impressions but she trusted Carly and Melanie.

"Well, today's the day you're about to visit the Clarin residence" Sabrina said to her friends.

"Yay! Field trip" Melanie cheered, "Come on, Car, get excited",

"Yeah but we're about to do homework" Carly replied.

"So?"

"So I probably shouldn't"

"Gotta do something before homework"

Soon, Leah Clarin pulled over with the car. Then all three girls jumped in. Sabrina was sitting in the front while the other two girls were seated in the backseat.

"Hey mom, this is Carly and Melanie"

Leah glanced over her shoulder. "Hi!" she said, kindly.

"Mrs. Clarin" Melanie greeted.

"Hi" Carly said, as she gave a little wave.

"Sabrina was telling me about you, girls. Nice to meet you finally" Leah added.

"You too" Carly said.

Then Leah put the car into drive and drove away from the school grounds.

"So you're Sabrina's mom?" Mel asked.

"Yeah?"

"Wow, she looks just like you!" Melanie added, strongly impressed.

Sabrina and her mom exchanged a quick glance and smiled. "Thank you" her mom said, chuckling. Carly and Melanie were on their way to visit Sabrina at her place. When they arrived at the Clarin residence, the three of them were settled in after Leah encouraged the guests to make themselves at home.

"Uh, Mrs. Clarin" Carly called, politely, "Can I use your phone so my mom knows I'm here?"

"Absolutely" Leah replied, kindly.

"Thank you"

Carly excused herself to use the phone like she requested.

"I'm probably gonna have to do the same" Mel said, putting her hand up.

"Sure. And if you girls want something to snack, I actually baked some macadamia cookies"

"It's a favorite in this house" Sabrina explained, as she was looking at Mel.

"Don't mind if we do!"

Sabrina was showing her friends her room. It was carpeted and surrounded by white walls, nice and tidy all around. Sabrina had posters of her favorite music artists and had photos of one section on her wall. And there was a dresser with a stereo displayed on top, with CD's on the side. Her friends admired the bedroom, while Sabrina sat on her bed.

"Your room is nice" Carly told her.

"Thank you"

"Can I check out your CD's, Sabrina?" Mel asked, "I'm standing here and I can hear them calling my name"

"Of course"

Just as Melanie wished, she walked up to her friend's dresser and started browsing her CD collection, while Carly was sitting with Sabrina at the bed, where she couldn't help but lie down. "Your bed is so soft"

"Right?" Sabrina agreed. Then she lied down beside Carly. After that, it became silent as both girls were resting their eyes after a day of school.

"Hey!" Mel's voice was right in Sabrina's ear, which startled her. Once she opened her eyes, she realized Mel was practically right in her face.

"You like Spice Girls?" Melanie asked, almost like she was testing her.

"Yes?" Sabrina reluctantly admitted.

"Me too!"

Sabrina felt a little relief, "Oh, well another thing we have in common"

"Mhm"

"Mhm" Sabrina mocked.

Then Mel lied down beside her new friend and rested her head. Sabrina was tempted to doze off. As she rested her eyes, she couldn't help but form a little smile, as she was thinking how her life had progressed since the beginning of the school year.

"You seem so happy" Mel acknowledged.

"I am" Sabrina proudly admitted, "You know, I was a little sad about moving because I felt like we were just abandoning my grandparents back in Granisle. Before I used to think that we had it all, even for a town smaller than Burns, but…I was happy, because it was home, our life. But right now, things turned out a little better than I expected. I got you girls"

Melanie smiled. "Aww, you're sweet"

There was one little detail that Sabrina had left out. She hadn't forgotten about that encounter she had with Zachery Epstad and how uncomfortable it made her, thinking that her brother Jonathan was about to get hurt. It was one reason she was feeling nervous about enrolling at WKE. But then she learned that there was still some good in the world.

"Hey" Melanie called.

Sabrina opened her eyes and paid attention to Mel.

"You know what else is nice? Me and Carly are now visiting. So how about we make the best of things?"

"How so?"

"I'm about to fidget with your stereo. So please don't hate me!"

"Of course not"

Melanie then looked over at Carly, lying down at the end of the bed. Her eyes were still closed. "Hey Car" she said. Then she reached her hand over and started tickling her on her stomach; that woken Carly as she giggled.

"Stop that!" she laughed, "You sure have a way of waking up people"

"That should make our sleepovers more exciting" Melanie added, as she got up from the bed. Then she went up to the stereo on the dresser, put in the CD, and pressed play. Almost right away, the music started. The volume was quite high. Sabrina forgot about the volume level. But it didn't bother them that much, for that Mel was already dancing along with the rhythm of the song. Sabrina and Carly sat up and watched her. Smiles were all over the faces as the music was building momentum.

And that feel-good feeling was getting to Sabrina that she got up and joined her friend as they danced together.

"Come on, Car" Mel called, over the music, and offered her hand.

Carly hesitated, "Uhh, I'm kinda of a horrible dancer".

"Don't worry; this is what bedrooms are for, to be yourself!"

Then she went and grabbed Carly by the hand and pulled her firmly. Soon, Sabrina, Mel, and Carly, were all dancing. Shortly, it got more exciting, and then Mel stepped onto Sabrina's bed and started jumping. Sabrina herself just grinned as she was having fun.

The next day at school, Sabrina, Melanie, and Carly were sitting together on the bench. As they were waiting patiently for the bell to ring, they reminisced about their first visit at Sabrina's and how much fun they had. After their little party, they worked on their schoolwork. But altogether there were laughs and a lot of bonding. And the girls made a great impression on the Clarin family, which was a good thing.

The waiting continued. Just after their conversation, it was rather quiet between them as they sat there with eyes forward. Melanie even started making a clock sound effect with her tongue. The other two heard it but didn't say anything. The silence went on a little too long.

"I guess we talked about all the things there was to talk about" Carly said.

"Yeah, I guess so" Sabrina admitted.

"Doesn't mean there never will be" Melanie promised, "Think of this as a coffee break"

"We can't drink coffee" Carly replied, "Well I can't, I don't know about you guys"

"Alright, then this is a bench break"

"Sitting out in the cold break" Sabrina added, as a joke.

"Pretty much"

Once it was quiet, Melanie pulled out a magazine out from her sleeve. Sabrina noticed right away. "You tucked that in your sleeve?" she asked.

"Yeah, I left my top hat at home. Thought I'd try this out. Since now that we're friends, I wanted to show you something"

"What's that?"

"Her boyfriend?" Carly suggested.

"Haha. I guess you can say that" Mel replied. What she had was a teen magazine. "I know what you guys are thinking. 'Oh, look at that, Melanie's too young to read that kind of magazine', 'she must've gone crazy'".

Sabrina and Carly just looked at her funny.

"Hey, if you girls aren't going to say it, who else?" Mel added.

She then opened the magazine and started flipping through pages until she found the one she was looking for. "This handsome fella!" she said. The page showed a photo of a young male teenager, dark hair and good looking. "I like him".

"I'm pretty sure she means love" Carly muttered.

"Yeah, more like love" Melanie admitted, "He's cute, right?"

"Or handsome like you said" Sabrina agreed.

"Indeed!"

As Melanie held the magazine up, the left page flopped over and the poster inside rolled out.

"Whoops, whoops, whoops" she replied, "I think God is trying to take my magazine away. It's what I get for sneaking it to school. Nobody needs to know about this"

Sabrina happened to glance at the poster and then suddenly became intrigued. "Who's that?" she asked, almost right away.

"Oh, him? Tyler Bryce" Mel answered.

"Why does that name sound made up?"

"Who cares? It makes him sound more handsome"

Sabrina shrugged her shoulders, "I don't hate it". Then she looked back at the poster with interest. Melanie noticed immediately.

"Handsome, isn't he?"

"Is he ever".

Sabrina was daydreaming. The idea of love came back to her. She remembered the couple she saw behind the gas station downtown. Now seeing a poster of a young man gave her an idea of what kind of boy she wanted to meet, someone who was handsome. Sabrina gazed at the poster longer than she realized.

"Do you want it?" Mel offered.

The daydreaming ended. Sabrina looked back at her friend. "The poster?" she asked.

"No, my lunch; yes the poster"

"Oh" Sabrina was uncertain, "No, I probably shouldn't" she replied, only out of courtesy because it was her friend's belonging, "Unless you don't need it".

Then Melanie gently tore the poster out of the magazine and offered it to Sabrina. "I'm spoken for" she told her, and then gave a wink.

After inheriting the poster, Sabrina hung up on her wall later that evening. It was now hanging just above her bed. Since she was alone, she could daydream for as long as she wanted, about love. It was the end of the day and she lied in her bed with her discman. The music carried her away and far from reality, for that she imagined what it was like to be in love, the passion and the comfort. Sabrina could feel it already as she kept looking at her Tyler Bryce poster. That was how her daydream started, constructing the perfect boy. He'd be just as young, dark haired, smart, brave, handsome, and one of a kind.

If only dreams became real just as you thought of them.

Each time Sabrina came back to the real world, she only realized how dull it was. It had her wishing more than ever. After a short period of time, Sabrina just felt the need to express herself without telling anybody. Only one idea came to mind, writing it down. So she leaned over her bed to grab a flashlight underneath. She didn't want to turn her bedroom lights on in case one of her parents might suddenly wake up. With the flashlight guiding her, Sabrina carefully went across her room to get pen and paper out of her backpack. Now back on her bed, the supplies sat in front of her, with the flashlight lying next to them. By following her instincts, Sabrina wrote the first words that came to mind.

Here I am, she then paused to think of another set of words, something that had to be heartfelt, *waiting for you, wherever you may be.*

That was all she could think of that night.

CHAPTER EIGHT

A Day with June

It was almost a week since Elijah spoke to Andrew and Paula. He lived up to his decision and was hanging out with Quinton Malcolm and his followers. Every day, Elijah met up with them near the monkey bars. So far, things had been going good for Elijah. He got new friends who were different in many ways, and it included one girl that he got to socialize with regularly.

"Wassup?!" Quinton greeted.

"Sup" Elijah replied, and they both shook hands in a real urban style.

The others soon came out and met with them.

Devon Welks, he was the shortest one in the group but had a sense of humor and got along with everybody. Roscoe Lewis, he was athletic, and a little taller than Elijah and Quinton.

And June Disher, the only girl in the group; she was playful and quite mysterious.

They were all First Nations and Elijah Khoda was just a year older than them.

"Hey guys" Elijah greeted. Roscoe merely smiled and gave an up nod.

"Yo-yo-yo!" Devon replied, practically shouting.

125

"Hey you" June said, smiling at Elijah, like she meant it.

Elijah had gotten adjusted to his new friends rather quickly. They already treated him like he was one of their own. It was a good start. Next thing he knew, he was playing basketball with them. It was two against two, Elijah and Quinton versus Roscoe and Devon, while June was a bystander, watching them play.

"Yeah, baby!" Roscoe cheered, after scoring a goal.

"Lucky shot" Quinton said.

Both Roscoe and Devon high-fived each other.

"Don't worry, bro, we'll bounce back" Quinton promised Elijah.

"I'm not worried"

"That's the spirit! And if I call you bro, you call me bro"

"Okay, bro"

"Okay!"

The boys were getting ready for another round. Elijah glanced over and happened to lock eyes with June. "You don't wanna play, June?" he asked.

June smiled and shook her head, "I would beat you guys, easily"

"She's just afraid" Roscoe teased.

"I'd go easy on you" Quinton added.

"I'm waiting for my moment" June assured.

The boys went back to playing ball. They went on long enough and near the end June finally jumped in and stole the basketball and scored.

"That's my moment!" June cheered.

Everyone laughed and praised her. Elijah had only been with his new friends for more than a few days and they were already inseparable. Every day the five of them hung out from beginning of the day to the end. But that day was a little different because Elijah was about to visit Quinton's place for the first time.

Together, the five of them walked after school. Elijah quickly dropped off his backpack at home and met up with his friends to have a different kind of fun. As soon as they arrived at Quinton's, they all gathered around in the backyard, where there was a wooden stump and soon a baseball bat and a case of empty beer bottles. Each of them took turns hitting the glass bottles, aiming it on the painted target on the fence. The gang praised each other along the way. Finally, Elijah got his turn. He walked up, with bat in hand, felt like he was on the baseball field. Just as the others did, Elijah raised the bat, glanced at the bottle before he swung and made it fly, and then hit right on the target.

"Woo! That's my bro!" Quinton cheered.

Devon and Roscoe shouted words like *yeah* and *way to go*, like teammates. Elijah noticed June's smile as she clapped. That convinced him that he found his place in life. They loved him so much; even Quinton encouraged their newest member to have another shot. Elijah hit another bottle and gained another successful hit!

"Damn, you got skills, bro!" Quinton praised. He was quite amused, "A basketball player AND a baseball player"

The compliments were like a throne and Elijah Khoda was the heir.

"What else can you do?" Devon asked.

Everyone stopped breathing just to hear an answer. The long silence meant that they were serious. Each of them was kind enough to wait. Initially, Elijah was about to give an honest answer about himself, like one of his hobbies perhaps. Wait…that was the OLD Elijah thinking.

"He likes to be quiet" Roscoe joked.

After taking a dramatic pause, Elijah stood in front of all of them, "Fight!" he finally answered.

They seemed more intrigued and were dying to hear more.

"Last year, I fought some white boys. I won by throwing them in mud!"

"Ooohhhh" Quinton replied, amusingly, "Three things in one!"

There was another pause.

"Maybe there's more" Elijah added, grimly.

All eyes were on him.

"I wanna do more than just play sports and fight…"

There was another thing he was about to add but it was hard to put female companionship into words. So he left that part out.

"I wanna do that and more. Whatever that is and I wanna find out. And I want you by my side, all of you"

"And we'll be glad to" Quinton promised.

"I think it's happy, not glad" Roscoe told him.

But Quinton didn't reply.

"Anyways, Elijah-bro, you're one of us now. Enjoy it. It should be fun"

Quinton approached his new friend, patted him on his back. Elijah smiled as his initiation was granted. They shook hands, in an urban style. Then the others went up and did the same.

"Alright, let's celebrate by smashing bottles!" Quinton insisted.

So he went up and grabbed the bat from Elijah and then set up a single bottle on the stump. Quinton swung the bat but missed. The gang responded with laughter. Even Elijah couldn't help himself.

"Shut up" Quinton said, sourly, without looking at any of them.

"Can't shut up; it's too funny" Devon explained.

"Whatever"

They played for a little while longer, until June and Roscoe had to go. The others were out front to bid them farewell.

"See you, guys" Roscoe said, as they were leaving.

"See ya, suckers" June added, with a smile.

"Why are you calling us suckers?" Elijah asked, "We weren't playing against each other, did we?"

June cocked her head back just to see Elijah, "I know"

Elijah wasn't sure what that meant but it was still amusing since June gave a smile, like she usually did. After they were gone, it was just Elijah, Quinton, and Devon.

"Come on, bros. I wanna show you something" Quinton insisted.

They followed Quinton to his bedroom, which was a little messy. There were clothes lying on the floor, empty plate with crumbs on it and candy wrappers all around, to which Elijah had no comment. Quinton grabbed a magazine from his closet and showed it to his friends.

Elijah was expecting a gaming magazine or sports. How wrong he was. The front cover had an image of a young woman in a bathing suit-half naked even! For a moment, it stunned Elijah and made him speechless. Of course, he got the impression that Quinton Malcolm did his own thing but didn't think that he could do everything he wanted, even getting his own copy of an adult magazine.

The three of them gathered together on the bed as they looked through the magazine together and admired dozens of photos of women wearing bikinis and showing a lot of skin.

"Damn, she's hot" Quinton said.

"Yeah, but not as hot as her" Devon said, as he pointed to another photo that he found more appealing to his liking.

That magazine was supposed to be for grownups only. Elijah could only imagine how his new friend was able to get away with it. And he couldn't question him about it, for that the photos drew his attention away.

Women, beautiful women, nothing like Elijah had seen before, from their eyes, lips, and perfect fit bodies. It was a new definition of beautiful. These women had to be more than ten years older than the girls at school-

Sabrina!

Suddenly, Sabrina Clarin came to mind.

What if...? Just imagine...

No! Don't think about it! Don't even go there!

"What's wrong, Elijah?" Devon teased, "Too hot for you"

"What?" Elijah was playing dumb.

"Leave him alone, man" Quinton told him, "But you gotta admit really hot, right?"

Hot? That was the first time Elijah heard any of his peers describe a female as hot. Even Andrew once used the word *pretty* before.

"Oh yeah, real hot" Elijah replied, casually.

Quinton nodded and turned back to the magazine.

"Man, I'd like to grab her boobs" he admitted. Then he placed his hands on the one photo of the women, pretending he was touching her breasts. Both he and Devon burst out laughing. Elijah just played along and only gave a mild chuckle.

The next day at school, the gang was hanging around the monkey bars. Elijah was on his own at one point for that he was climbing different parts of the structure. He then took a moment to appreciate what he had, new friends that were willing to do things differently, in a mischief sort of way and one girl who caught Elijah's attention. As he stood there, he realized how much he thought about June. And not just because that Quinton claimed that she liked Elijah but also there might be more to her, something that ought to be discovered. So after a moment of silence, Elijah boldly approached June, who was watching her friends play around. "Hey, June" he greeted, "What's up?"

"Hanging out with losers" she joked, "You?"

Elijah laughed at her remark.

"Hanging out with you and the losers"

June laughed. It seemed like June Disher was always happy and made the best of the time she had. That was one appealing trait about her. "So you're in grade seven, right?" she asked.

"Yes" Elijah admitted, "I am"

"So you'll be in high school next year"

"Oh, I will be, should be fun"

"You gonna get drunk, stay out late?"

Elijah shook his head, "No, not at all"

"Gonna cause some trouble?"

"No"

June raised an eyebrow, "And you said you like to fight?"

Elijah hesitated. "Well, I don't fight all the time, only if I have to"

Brief silence. "You're kinda cute" June told him. That was a surprise response. Elijah was expecting some judgment or more questioning. *How am I cute?*

"Yeah?"

"Oh yeah!"

Then June ended the conversation with a wink. Elijah couldn't help but watch her in awe as she walked away. What kind of conversation was that? He wondered. It was like June was joking around but also was up to something. But yet it didn't feel all bad. It was also kind of satisfying. One thing was for sure, Elijah looked forward to their next interaction.

Later, Elijah was hanging out with Quinton after playing around.

"That was fun" Elijah said.

"Oh yeah" Quinton agreed, "Fun, fun, fun! Everything is fun"

They gave each other a high five. Roscoe and Devon were near. They were horsing around by the play-fighting. Devon pretended to throw punches and Roscoe just shoved him away, playfully. Then he was able to grab both of Devon's hands. Devon tried to break free. They laughed.

"Ah, look, they're dancing!" Quinton yelled, jokingly.

They laughter grew. Elijah joined in. Then Devon tripped and Roscoe just happened to catch him in his arms easily because Devon was short. Roscoe made the best of it and picked up Devon like a baby.

"Anyone have a bottle of milk?" Roscoe said.

June continued laughing, hysterically. Devon was back on his feet and chased Roscoe around the monkey bars. For the fun of it, June went after them.

"Hey bro" Quinton said, once he and Elijah were along, "I was wondering if you could do me a favor?"

"Okay" Elijah already agreed, not giving any second thought to his kindness.

"Do you think you can do my social studies homework for me?"

Elijah didn't say anything.

"I would do it but I have to go to church tonight and it's due tomorrow. Please, it would help me a lot"

"Sure"

"Cool! Thanks bro, I owe you one"

"Anytime" Elijah said.

Then the sound of clanging went off. All three boys stopped and looked. It was June banging a rock on the monkey bars. "Hey! No running around" she said to Devon and Roscoe. She jumped to the ground and approached them, "You boys are so bad, I'm putting you on timeout" June pointed at both of them and then she set her finger towards Roscoe, "Just you". Roscoe just smiled, as he was amused by June's playful humor. And then she looked at Devon, "But you can go because you're so short and cute!" June even grabbed Devon's cheeks and squeezed them.

Everyone laughed. "Haha whatever" Devon replied.

Once school was over, the gang took their time walking home. And they did because they felt like it. Elijah was feeling rebellious. After making it further down on Sus Avenue, they turned right to explore the gravel area, where there was nothing but dirt and rocks.

"See anything interesting yet?" Devon asked.

"It's the rez" Quinton said, "Nothing is ever interesting"

"Well, if you don't find anything interesting soon, I'm gonna fall asleep. You don't want me to get my clothes dirty, do you? So hurry and find something interesting, okay?"

Quinton ignored him. Elijah giggled under his breath. He found Devon quite amusing, calm and funny, without even trying.

"Found something!" June yelled, as she picked up an empty beer bottle, "Is this yours?" she joked.

"Whatever, I don't make a mess like everyone else" Quinton claimed.

"Like your bedroom?" Roscoe taunted.

"It's my bedroom; I do whatever I want with it. I mean out here, where people make a mess"

"Uh, are you guys done arguing?" June asked, "Because I want all of YOU to watch ME"

All the boys watched June just as she demanded. She placed her left hand on her hip, stood nice and tall, and then pretended to drink out of the empty beer bottle.

Nobody said anything.

Then June looked straight at them and narrowed her eyes. She started walking towards them with her hand still on her hip. It was both playful and appealing, the way her shoulders moved up and down. June stopped as she was close enough and then whipped her hair for dramatic effect.

"Hey boys, how you doing?"

She smiled and then gave a wink. They boys were struck with awe. None of them commented until Elijah did.

"That was very cool" he told her.

"Why, thank you" June gave a bow like she was on stage.

Then out of courtesy, Elijah even clapped, which brought nothing but funny looks.

"Haha!" Roscoe laughed, "He's clapping"

Elijah suddenly froze, "What's wrong with that?" Normally, people clap after being entertained. Apparently these boys thought it was funny. Nobody answered. And Elijah just let it slip his mind.

"Let's see that" Roscoe insisted, extending his hand. He wanted the empty beer bottle, which June happily gave to him. Everyone was expecting Roscoe to do something similar but he actually threw it into the air.

"Run!" he shouted.

With fear and excitement, the others quickly dashed forward, expecting the bottle to fall on them but they were out of reach once the glass bottle hit and shattered on the ground. They all laughed and cheered.

Afterwards, two of them went home. Elijah walked Quinton home and there he gave Elijah his schoolwork. Quinton thanked him and parted ways until the next day. Now it was just Elijah and June.

"You're doing Quinton's homework?" she asked.

"Yeah, he said he has to go to church tonight. So that's why"

"Did you believe him?"

"Yeah" Elijah replied, casually.

Then he stopped and looked at June. Was she trying to say that Quinton was lying? He thought June would've explained further that maybe Quinton Malcolm had a history of being a liar. But instead, Elijah only got weird looks from June. Maybe she was waiting for him to explain or maybe it was just her way of messing around. Finally, the silence was broken by June's laugh and then she began to walk. Elijah followed her, aimlessly.

"Nice green sweater" Elijah said.

"Why, thank you"

"Where'd you get it?"

"Kamloops" she answered, "Do you want one?"

"Haha, no"

"I can give you mine" June teased.

"Uhh" Elijah hesitated, "I think it would be too small on me"

June laughed.

"You're smart"

No comment from Elijah. They just continued to walk. As they did, Elijah found himself staring at June, until she glanced over and met his eye. He quickly acted normal and hoped that she wouldn't say anything, at least not about him staring.

"You liked that, didn't you?" June asked.

Oh boy

"What's that?" Elijah said.

"When I did my little drunk talk"

Elijah paused. He didn't answer right away because he was suddenly brought back to that moment when she was entertaining him and the other boys, with the empty beer bottle in her hand.

"My drunk walk" she added.

They were in too deep in that subject. There was no turning back.

"Maybe a little" Elijah admitted.

Then June stopped, not taking her eyes off Elijah.

"You thought it was sexy"

Now Elijah stopped and just couldn't take a step further. Never before that had he heard one of his peers would use such a word. The grin on June's face clearly stated that she meant what she said and that she was waiting for something to happen-more like a courtesy response. But what was there to say?

"I, uh, didn't say that" Elijah told her.

"Say what?"

June knew what she was doing and she was doing it on purpose. She then approached Elijah slowly. That feeling inside him picked up again, although it felt a little different. It made Elijah feel like he was getting into trouble but not the kind that would send him to the office and that sparked his curiosity.

"Say what?" June repeated.

June's voice was calling out to Elijah as if there was a dark hole in front of him and something or someone mysterious was waiting on the other side. June was a lot closer to Elijah now, more physically than he'd ever been to a girl. Her eyes locked onto his. She was so close that Elijah could feel her body nearly touching his.

"Sexy?" Elijah finally said.

Amused, June's eyebrows went up and a smile formed on her face. Elijah was expecting her to laugh but she didn't. She only stared at him, casually but also with interest. That feeling went away once June continued to walk. Still puzzled and curious, Elijah stared blankly. He couldn't help but feel that moment was leading somewhere. And he also wondered if he would ever find out.

The next day, Quinton thanked Elijah at school, like a normal person, for doing his homework. When recess started, Elijah was hanging out with Devon, talking and joking around. Then a girl came along that caught Devon's attention for a moment. She was a blonde but only a stranger to Elijah.

"See her?" Devon asked.

Elijah nodded.

"She's in my class. Her name's Ryan. I like her"

No comment.

"If I could, I would ask her out and make her my girlfriend"

Elijah just gave another nod.

"Do you think she'll marry me one day?"

There was a pause. Before Elijah could answer, he noticed the grin on Devon's face. Then they laughed. So it turned out that he was just messing around.

"Is there any girl you like, Elijah?"

Sabrina was the one that came to mind. Elijah liked her. He actually came close to admitting it but then wasn't sure if he wanted his new friends to know. He could've chosen a random girl from his own grade but someone else emerged into his thoughts.

"June" Elijah told him.

"June Disher?" Devon said.

Another paused moment.

"Yeah"

Devon just nodded.

CHAPTER NINE

Bad Vibes

At first, Elijah treated his new friends like any other kids, with mutual respect. He also saw them as every other kid, normal and fun. But Elijah learned that there were different sides to people and it all started with this group. Together, the gang walked around aimlessly around the school, talking casually. Elijah brought up a certain subject of what led to a reaction he didn't expect.

"Hey, so are you guys gonna dress up for Halloween?" he asked.

Quinton just looked at him and scoffed and the other boys just started laughing. Elijah stood there as he couldn't help but feel a little embarrassed. *What? What did I say?*

"Halloween? Are you serious?" Quinton replied.

"What's wrong with Halloween?" Elijah said, calmly.

"It's for kids, bro!"

Elijah was speechless as he was being mocked. Then Roscoe leaned in to Quinton and Devon. Suddenly it became a private conversation but they could still be heard.

"Just see him..." Roscoe told them, as he knelt down, "Trick or treat!"

By "him", they were probably talking about Elijah.

"I can hear you" he told them.

But the other boys only glanced at him, briefly, and still laughing. They didn't seem to be aware that they might've offended one of their own or they probably did and just didn't care. They continued walking ahead. Elijah walked slowly, trying not to let the pressure get to him. June was just up ahead. So he took comfort with her company.

"I guess they don't celebrate Halloween?" Elijah said.

"I know Quinton stopped celebrating a while ago. I'm sure the other two are just getting out of it" Elijah didn't say anything. June turned her head to him, "I dressed up last year"

"You did? What did you dress up as?"

"Little Red Riding Hood"

Right away, he couldn't help but create that image in mind, of June Disher carrying a basket and wearing a red hood. It was rather appealing, probably because Elijah liked the color red and it mixed well with June's black hair and light brown skin.

"That's cool. I was a cowboy last year"

As they were catching up with the boys, June looked directly at Elijah and put her finger over her lip, hinting him to keep their conversation secret. Maybe because June didn't want them to know that she still celebrated Halloween. So Elijah didn't expect to get a mockery response but at least he had one honest conversation with June about the topic. And the fact that they were keeping it from the others convinced Elijah that he and June had their own world.

(Once Halloween did come, Elijah observed the Halloween costumes around him. It looked like those kids were having fun. Suddenly a part of him missed it. So his new friends didn't celebrate Halloween because they say it was for kids, even though they were clearly in that same category. It made Elijah wonder about them, as if they simply didn't want to take part or there was a part of themselves they were hiding, or maybe they were too embarrassed to admit it. What was wrong with being a kid and having a little fun?)

November.

The weather was changing. The days were getting colder. It was only a matter of time until the snow would come. The gang decided to enjoy it while they could. So they rented a basketball and played two against three, Elijah and Quinton facing June, Roscoe, and Devon. Somehow it was a little more fun with June playing the game and she was a natural. They took a break at one point, where Elijah just couldn't help but hang out with June.

"Hey, you did good" he told her, as he approached.

"You did great! How about when I showed Quinton who was boss?"

"That was good, or great, I mean".

June laughed like she normally did. But Elijah had nothing against it. That was probably one of the things he liked about her. And June thought that their new friend was very kid-like but yet strong and he was different from the other boys, not too serious and had some decency. And Elijah didn't bad mouth anyone or even curse. June knew that Quinton and the other boys often said swear words for fun but compared to them, Elijah Khoda was quiet. In secret, she was glad to have him part of their group.

"You said great already..." Elijah managed to say, "I said good and didn't want to..."

"Say it again?" June suggested.

"Uh, yeah" Elijah nodded. Instead of saying anything further, he just raised his hand up, offering her a high five, in which she obliged to. June clapped Elijah's hand with hers, a little too hard. He even felt the pain inflicted on the palm of his hand. While trying to hide it, he shook it off but June already noticed.

"Haha! Did I hit too hard?"

Elijah was about to deny it, just to avoid embarrassment, "Maybe a little" he admitted, "But I'm fine. I still got my hand" He then held it up, just to show her. June saw the opening and pretended that she was going to high five again. For a second, Elijah feared the worse and quickly backed away.

"Got'cha" June mocked.

Since she was being playful, Elijah just had the urge to do the same. June didn't have her hand up like he did. So he had to think of something. So he went up to her, grabbed her hand gently, lifted it up and high fived her a little more firmly.

"Got you back" Elijah replied, grimly.

Suddenly, June raised both her hands, bended them like they were claws, "Rawrrr!" Elijah didn't even flinch but he gave a little smirk.

"Bro" Quinton called, "She's playing against us and you're high-fiving her?"

Elijah couldn't think of something clever to say to impress June. So he only grinned at her and they all went back to their basketball game. During that interaction, Roscoe watched them with caution.

Elijah spent the late afternoon with the gang like it was an after school special. Over the weeks, they had plenty of laughs and did their own thing. Most of them time, without any permission from parents, like just going out when they felt like it. One evening, they were all hanging out at Quinton's place, watching TV in his bedroom. For a short period of time, it was nothing but silence.

"You got yourself a belly going on" Roscoe teased, as he was poking Devon's stomach.

Devon scoffed, "Not even".

Then Quinton leaned over and tickled Devon on his stomach, which made him giggle.

"Just a little wider and then he'd take off like those air balloons"

"You mean hot air balloons" June corrected.

"Whatever" Quinton replied, slightly irritated.

They went back to their seating positions-back in silence. Then June leaned towards Devon while he wasn't looking. Next thing the boys heard was laughter as Devon was being tickled by June. Elijah and the others watched in amusement, for that Devon was just laughing like a baby. June didn't plan on stopping and the laughter grew.

Afterwards, they were drawn into professional wrestling that was being broadcasted live. Quinton and his gang were avid fans. Elijah watched a few shows with them and slowly became a fan of it.

"That guy's awesome" Quinton said, "He could take on anyone"

"Yeah, unless he's fighting a bigger guy" Roscoe added.

"Still, he's pretty tough"

"And quite hot, too" June said.

"Yeah" Quinton muttered.

"Did you just say that he was 'hot'?" Roscoe spoke, after brief silence.

Skeptical, Quinton exchanged a quick glance, "What? No!"

"We just heard you say 'yeah'" June pointed out, although she meant no offense.

Quinton was speechless, embarrassed even.

"Sounds like Quinton has a boy crush" Devon joked.

"I didn't say he was hot!" Quinton yelled.

The hospitality was becoming hostility, which brought discomfort to Elijah.

"I think he's cool. That's it!"

"Wait, which guy we're talking about again?" Devon wondered. It was hard tell if he said that to irritate Quinton any further.

"The guy with the yellow hair" Quinton explained, as calmly as he could. That was some decency right there.

"Yellow hair" Roscoe repeated, "You mean blonde. You never heard of the word blonde before?"

Quinton was ready to yell again, but he just couldn't. June saw the hurt in his eyes.

"Quinton, we're just joking around" she said, sincerely, "Just relax and watch some wrestling"

The only response was a sigh.

"Whatever" Quinton muttered and got up and left the room.

Elijah didn't bother asking why Quinton was so sensitive, thinking that it might've been a personal thing. So they let him have his space. But after Quinton was gone for more than a few minutes, Elijah decided to check on him. Quinton was outside in his backyard, hitting his baseball bat on the wooden stump and the fence. It was his way of taking out anger. Elijah went out to meet him. And Quinton noticed.

"Getting sick and tired of being treated like I'm stupid" Quinton snarled.

Elijah said nothing.

"I knew what blonde meant! I just forgot, is all! Stupid Roscoe and stupid June; damn them!"

Quinton spoke like his own friends had been hurting him for a while. He could've been just upset and probably didn't mean what he was saying. Elijah had been there before.

"They're stupid!" he added. At the final point of his rant, Quinton firmly slammed the bat against the ground and let it go.

"I'm glad you're here, bro"

The anger was fading.

"You don't make fun of me, not like them"

Elijah finally went up to Quinton.

"Anytime, bro" he told him.

After a moment of silence, Quinton said, "You know what we should do one day? Get our own place! I mean a place where we can hang out and maybe live in it. No grownups bossing us around. Think about it, we're not little kids anymore. We could take care of ourselves, since you know how to fight. What do you think?"

Kids always talking about the impossible, except with Quinton it almost sounded promising. Elijah actually didn't hate the idea. "I think that would be great".

After that conversation, Elijah just let Quinton have his space and went back inside. He noticed right away that Devon was in the kitchen, looking for something to snack on. Elijah went back to Quinton's bedroom and the first thing he noticed that Roscoe and June were having a rather intimate moment. They were holding each other, not in a way that friends would hug. And whenever friends hugged, it was because one of them was emotionally hurt. But that wasn't the case.

Nobody was hurt. It was nothing but silence. They held each other for a long moment. Once Roscoe noticed, Elijah quickly turned around and left the room, feeling embarrassed.

Were Roscoe and June boyfriend and girlfriend?

They would have to be the first peers that were a couple. Over the school years, Elijah only heard rumors on his classmates liking him or her. A normal person would think that it was cute, but when Elijah walked in on June and Roscoe, he suddenly felt intimidated. It might've been because he told Devon that he liked June.

(November 4ᵗʰ.

It was a rather special day because it was Sabrina Clarin's birthday! Elijah hadn't forgotten. Just remembering her birthday made him think about the beginning of the school year where he and Sabrina were the best of friends; the simpler days. Elijah lied there in his bed, wondering how she was doing. He wondered if she missed him back or even thought about him briefly. While he couldn't sleep, Elijah even tried to think of what he would've got her for a birthday gift, a nice necklace maybe. *Girls like jewelry, right?* Maybe a movie that Elijah liked and she hadn't seen before. That would've been kind a cool way to get to know each other by showing her his taste in films and how it reflected his vision of life. But everything seemed impossible.

If only Elijah could write Sabrina a letter. If he knew her address, he would've told her how much he missed her and perhaps why they stopped talking, because of Carly and Melanie. *Damn them!* And most likely, he would brag about himself for a bit, about the videogames he played, the movies that he'd seen and the ones he would like to see-anything that he hadn't told her yet. Then he imagined what she would say if she wrote him back:

Hi Elijah! I'm doing great. I'm sorry that I hadn't talked to you for the past month. I hope we're still friends.

He even tried to imagine those words in her voice. Writing a letter was just a way to cope with the emptiness on the inside. In actuality, he wanted to talk to Sabrina for real; in person, eye to eye, like how they used to. Elijah just sighed. She was only a few feet away during school days and he couldn't even talk to her. Maybe someday they would talk again.

"Happy birthday, Sabrina" he whispered.

Elijah missed her, a lot.)

It was a rather dull day at school. The gang wasn't feeling ambitious to do anything. But that didn't bother Elijah, for that he thought about Sabrina on and off. They were loitering in the corner while the other students enjoyed their free time. Elijah stood next to June as he was drawing in his notebook.

"Hey, check this out" Elijah said, to June.

So she looked and saw the drawing of a wild moose standing on a hill.

"That's pretty cool" she said, "I couldn't draw to save my life"

"Yeah, not everybody can"

June nodded.

"Well, I'm glad you can"

The compliment was greater than expected. Elijah was flattered and wasn't afraid to show it by smiling at June. While the others were talking amongst themselves, Elijah wondered off into his own world, his mind, where it was isolated. As he recalled that night when he was thinking about Sabrina and how badly he wanted to talk to her somehow. So he started writing out her name on a blank page in his notebook. It was rather aimless. He didn't have a vision in his head, only the need to express himself. First he thought of making his own birthday card to Sabrina-a late birthday card, to be precise. But then another idea-something different-came to mind, a card that simply says *I miss you*. That's something that Elijah hadn't seen in a card section before.

Sabrina

That's how it started, again and again. Elijah wrote her name on a new page. As an artist, styles can be a big deal. Each time he wrote Sabrina's name, the font styles were different, for that he tried to decide which one would work-which was half the fun when it comes to art.

"What are ya writing?" Quinton's voice pulled Elijah back to reality.

Elijah was so deep in thought; he forgot that his friends were even there. He reacted like he was caught doing something illegal. Not to mention Elijah couldn't help but be a little disappointed because he was actually just about to write a heartfelt message, something that he would say to Sabrina. Elijah quickly turned the pages back a few because he'd rather keep it a secret.

"Not writing, drawing" he was able to answer casually.

"Oh yeah? Let me check it out" Quinton said.

Elijah hesitated.

"I thought you said you don't like art"

"I know but I wanna to see yours"

With all the kindness that Quinton Malcolm had shown, Elijah felt like he had no choice but still there was hesitation. By the time Elijah put his notebook in someone else's hands, it was too late to say no. Quinton looked through the pages of illustrations. Naturally, Elijah was expecting a compliment but Quinton seemed rather puzzled.

"What's that?" he asked.

"Don't you ever watch Digimon?" Elijah said, gently.

"Nah, I don't watch those kid's shows"

But we are kids, Elijah wanted to say. Quinton turned the page and glanced at another drawing.

"That's just weird"

Weird? That didn't sound like a compliment and didn't want to ask why.

"Well, that's pretty much it" Elijah concluded, as he reached his hand out.

"Wait, I see more"

Now you wanna see more after criticizing? What's wrong with you?!

"No, that's it!" Elijah claimed. Fearing the worse, he just snatched the notebook out of Quinton's hand, "That's all I have, okay?" he added, innocently.

"Don't lie" Quinton said, "I saw more pages"

Now he was trying to reclaim the notebook, without even asking. That was just rude! Elijah kept backing away as far as he could.

"I said no"

"Come on, don't be like that"

Quinton just wouldn't stop, even after Elijah tried to be polite. How inconsiderate!

"Quinton, just leave it alone" June practically yelled.

Finally, Quinton gave up. "Alright, geez" he cursed.

A bad vibe went off and effected Elijah, for that Quinton glanced a serious look, almost like he was about to throw a punch. Elijah remained still until his friend walked away. It was safe to breathe again. After that, Elijah never had his drawings around Quinton or his friends ever again.

Once school was over, Elijah went straight to the back of the school to meet with the gang. Quinton didn't seem mad but didn't seem happy either. Elijah wouldn't be surprised if Quinton was still upset about not seeing the other drawings. Elijah was expecting him to snap any minute. But he didn't.

However, someone else did practically snap.

As the gang was walking back to the reserve, Roscoe deliberately walked slowly just to have a word with Elijah.

"Hey, I need to talk to ya" he insisted.

"Sure" Elijah replied, gently.

They both stopped, standing face to face.

"June is with me" Roscoe spoke, strongly, "Not with you. Understand?"

Nervously, Elijah couldn't speak. He only nodded. Roscoe said no more but he did scowl at Elijah for a moment. He was serious. After intimidating silence, Roscoe continued to walk. Did Devon tell Roscoe that Elijah liked June? It was the only logical explanation. Why would he do such a thing? Here, Elijah thought he wouldn't say anything. After all, it seemed like a secretive conversation when they were talking about which girls they liked. Either Devon might've said it by accident or he had allegiance for Roscoe from day one. Elijah never found out why and he was too afraid to ask. So this time, Elijah kept his distance from his new friends as they walked. Nobody didn't even look back to acknowledge him. Quinton didn't seem to notice or even cared. If he was the leader of the group, he ought to check on his friends every now and then. Instead, Elijah was left alone with shame. He just decided to go straight home and not spend time with his new friends.

Since then, the new comfort zone wasn't all comfortable. Some days it was quiet and intimidating, like it was hard to tell if any of his new friends was having a bad day or not. The thought of them snapping out of nowhere always came first. There were a few good days, where they would laugh and of course some days where they bored out of their minds. But even then, Elijah kept mostly to himself and only spoke when spoken to. The one day, the five of them leaned against the wall, all quiet and none of them moved a muscle.

"Wanna play on the monkey bars?" Elijah said, since no one else bothered to kill the boredom.

"Nah" Quinton refused, "Played on it so many times"

"How about building a snowman?" Elijah meant that one as a joke.

Quinton reacted like he was offended, "What am I, five?"

So much for lightening the mood; it appeared that most of the gang barely had sense of humor after all. They would make fun of someone but wouldn't laugh at something simple.

"Peanut-butter-pop-tarts" Elijah blurted out.

The only response he got was questioning instead of laughter.

"What?" Devon was uncertain and confused. That was odd because Elijah thought Devon liked to joke around.

It's something you say when you don't have anything else to say.

"Nothing" Elijah replied, mildly.

Maybe he wasn't trying to lighten the mood, but maybe because a part of him missed hanging out with Andrew and Paula.

That was a big letdown, being friends with kids who lack imagination and have a sense of humor that could only go so far. So that made Elijah feel alienated. He didn't think that Quinton and his friends were that different. Changing them was unlikely and not all of them were really keen on learning. That was just one thing. Elijah felt like that he hadn't resolved the issues with Devon, Roscoe, and Quinton. Therefore, he kept his distance from June because it felt like Roscoe was watching him like a vulture flying from above. And he hadn't being really open with both Devon and Quinton because after what happened. Neither one of them came forward to patch things up. Trust issues could go a long way. Elijah knew it and for a brief moment, it was tempting to leave the group.

It was the weekend. Elijah decided to have some alone time. It felt nice to sleep in on a Saturday. So he made himself cereal and watched a movie in his bedroom. About an hour later, his dad came to the room and told Elijah that someone was at the door for him.

Elijah had a feeling of who it might be. Maybe it wouldn't take long, he thought to himself. And just as he suspected, he arrived at the door and it was Quinton!

"Hey, bro!" he greeted. Quinton seemed to be in a good mood all of a sudden.

"Hey…bro" Elijah replied, hoping his voice was friendly enough, "What's up?"

"We came to see what you're up to"

We? So it was more than just someone. Elijah looked around the corner and saw June, Roscoe, and Devon waiting patiently. They too seemed all happy. That was quite odd. Elijah thought that Roscoe wouldn't speak to him again.

"Hey guys" Elijah greeted, emotionlessly. He hoped that they would sense impatience or agitation in his voice so they could sense that they were being a burden and leave him alone. Unfortunately, none of them were observant. "I'm not doing much…" he added.

"Mind if we visit?" Quinton asked.

Elijah didn't say anything. Sadly, the awkward silence didn't convince them that he wasn't interested. He wanted to say no but then his kindness interfered.

"Sure"

None of them seemed to realize that Elijah was uncomfortable. They all came in at once. Elijah reluctantly led them to his room. His mom was just coming down the hallway and noticed the new faces that her son was hanging out with and she couldn't help but be surprised. Elijah just looked at her, awkwardly, hoping that she would protest the unexpected visit. But no, Elijah ended up entertaining his guests longer than expected.

"What are you watching?" Quinton asked,

"Rush Hour" Elijah told him.

"How old"

Elijah looked at him, slightly offended, "It's still good"

"Still old; come on, let's play some games"

How insulting! Quinton and his friends invite themselves over and acted like they own the place. It was difficult time to play nice for Elijah.

After hanging out for more than an hour, they went down to the gas bar that was on the reserve. The snow was now taking over all of the north, especially Burns Lake. It was already getting quite cold, so cold that it was mandatory to stay inside and relax. Once they got to the gas bar, Quinton asked Elijah for money, claiming that he forgot his wallet at home.

Yeah, right.

Again, his kindness showed again and bought the snacks for Quinton, who bought a few which was a lot. They left the gas bar and just wondered around, aimlessly, while they enjoyed their junk food. There were some laughs. But still, Elijah was hoping to have a day to himself. What was more irritating, was that Quinton and his followers just happened to be up for a good time after Elijah tried to make things fun but none of them was interested then. For what was meant to be a quiet day ended up being filled with laughs and insults.

Elijah didn't get home until late afternoon. He would've been home sooner if Devon hadn't put him on the guilt trip. It was just after they walked around the reserve, Quinton, June, and Roscoe went home. Elijah and Devon were by themselves. He only stayed out of courtesy. Then Elijah was going to make an excuse to go home-.

"Let's go find those moose tracks" Devon insisted.

Please be joking.

Apparently, there was a moose spotted that morning. It's what they were talking about before Quinton and the others went home.

"But I really need to get home" Elijah claimed, hoping to sound desperate enough.

"Come on" Devon urged, "It'll be fun"

Really?

"It's just moose tracks"

Why would Devon get excited over footprints?

"But I want to see if it's true"

Seriously? Devon Welks wouldn't get excited over something random, like saying *peanut-butter-pop-tarts* but he would go crazy over a wild animal that may or may not have been spotted in the area?

"Come on" Devon repeated.

Just walk away.

"I really need a friend" he added, rather innocently.

Now Elijah felt bad but also irritated by just how inconsiderate Devon was being.

"Okay, let's go" Elijah reluctantly agreed.

Thankfully, Sunday was a quiet day. No unexpected visits happened.

The following school week didn't feel always fun. It felt like going to the doctor's office, not really exciting but trying to be strong and hope to get good results. But being with this new crowd, it seemed like it was always bad results. Elijah didn't like the fact that he couldn't really do much, like even just saying hi to June might put him in a bad spot because of her apparent boyfriend Roscoe. Elijah didn't bother starting any conversations with Quinton because he was too moody and Devon wasn't really trust worthy. These rules were much worse than the time Elijah was in fifth grade.

Growing up meant that things change-a lot of things-like the way you think. When Elijah Khoda was a little kid, he used to think that all kids were the same, polite, well mannered, and playful. How wrong he was. Over the years, Elijah had seen more than just one side to one person, like a teacher whose normally nice, suddenly yells. That was the same way he saw Quinton. Elijah remembered from a few years ago that Quinton lost his temper by yelling in class. We ought to learn from our mistakes but Quinton Malcolm seemed like he was still stuck in that moment and hadn't moved an inch.

During the week, Elijah just remained silent as usual and before he knew it, he was getting bored with the way things were. Finally, someone in the gang noticed his silence but it didn't play out as he hoped. They were all walking around the field. That was pretty much all they done recently.

"Wassup with you, bro?" Quinton asked.

Elijah turned around, showing his straight face.

"What?" he replied.

"You been pretty quiet a lot"

That was sad. Nobody even asked him if something was wrong.

"I know"

Elijah was waiting for this moment to happen. The only thing he hoped was that they would do the talking, like admitting their mistakes for one thing.

"Why so quiet?"

Maybe because I'm not allowed to talk or I can't even talk to you at all!

"Just don't feel like talking" Elijah said, shrugging his shoulders.

Not all kids were very observant, especially not these kids. They didn't see the hurt in Elijah's eyes or maybe they didn't like to talk about anything serious. Maybe that was why they often made fun of each other.

"Hey, I know what will cheer you up" Quinton said.

Curious, Elijah stood there as his friend walked up to him, expecting to tell him a joke or even offering him some candy would've been alright. But there was none of that. Next thing Elijah knew, Quinton's hands firmly grabbed his chest, particularly where his nipples would be. Now he and the other boys started laughing. Surprised and offended, Elijah pushed Quinton's hands away.

"It's not funny" he protested, gently, for that he tried not to give it much thought but Quinton's mischievous behavior put Elijah back into that emotional state, only deeper. He kept on doing it. Then Devon came up and flipped Elijah's peck muscle upwards.

"Pick up your mo'h" Devon joked.

Now Quinton was doing the same thing and saying the same phrase over and over. Elijah looked at Roscoe as he stood there, laughing at him with mockery. For a moment, Elijah stood there with defeat, for that he was the laughing stock.

"Okay, that's enough, you guys" June said.

She was probably the only one in the group that had a conscience. But even so, it didn't stop the boys from teasing, teasing merely for fun. Finally, Elijah let out an aggravated sigh and stormed away. His eyes were forward as he was practically running. It was silent at first and then he heard his name being called.

"Elijah!" It was Quinton but he couldn't really be trusted, "Bro, come back!"

But Elijah had no intention to do what he said, no matter how comforting it was, not from those kids in particular. Some alone time was much needed. Sadly, there was nowhere to go. Most of the grade seven students were occupying the whole area and snow covered almost everywhere so there was no place to sit. The only place there was, was the pillar just outside the entrance. Elijah just leaned against it and enjoyed every second of being alone. After a moment of being mentally absent, Elijah looked around trying to get back into the real world. As he scanned the area, he saw June Disher coming down the wooden steps. It appeared to be just her, no sign of the boys, which was a good thing.

"Hey" she greeted, gently, as she approached Elijah, "Are you all right?"

Still speechless, Elijah just shook his head. The pain was stronger than he thought. It actually almost made him cry for some reason. But he kept it together, while June decided to wait patiently.

"Is it even okay for you to talk to me?" Elijah asked, trying to sound calm after thinking about that day he was practically being antagonized by Roscoe.

"Of course" June promised.

"You know, Roscoe told me not to talk to you" Elijah told her. He knew that wasn't exactly what Roscoe said but he was implying it. June gave a disappointed sigh, which brought a little comfort knowing that she had support for Elijah.

"I knew he was gonna do something like that" she said.

"Are you guys…?" Elijah was about to ask but he suddenly didn't feel comfortable saying the word.

"Dating?" June finished. Elijah didn't say anything. In fact, there was a pause. "Sort of" she answered. It was just as Elijah suspected. Hearing the truth actually cleared his mind. Oddly, it didn't affect him as much as he thought it would. But still, he had no comment. He just looked away, aimlessly. "Elijah, it's okay. You can still talk to me all you like". After a short pause, he turned back to June, with determination.

"You know what, I don't care what Roscoe says" Elijah replied, strongly, "I'll still talk to you". June didn't seem offended by his tone, for that it made him sound more than just a boy. "So why do they do that? Why do they make fun of me all the time?"

June was trying to think of what to say, "I don't really know. I guess they just enjoy it too much and got hooked on it. It's not just you but they tease each other all the time as well". But yet they don't care about someone who was sensitive? That part was still a mystery. "I guess you guys just have a different sense of humor?"

That was the only explanation that Elijah could accept, "I guess so" he replied, "So they make fun of me, or each other, whatever, but then they start acting serious. That's why I been quiet a lot because I can't talk or joke around with them. They're just so serious all the time!"

"I actually like it when you're quiet" June told him. Elijah looked at her, a little surprised, for that compliment struck him as odd, "I mean, that's one of the things I like about you, Elijah. You don't make fun of people or talk bad about them. But at the same time, you're... something...else?"

Elijah was both intrigued and puzzled. It almost sounded like he was getting another compliment from June, "Something else?" he asked, gently.

"Something good" she told him, "And a little bad, but in a good way"

It was starting to make sense. June was probably trying to say that she kind of liked his bad side. At least that was the impression that he was getting.

She wanted to say more but wasn't sure how. It was comforting, either way. Not to mention June didn't laugh constantly for once, not that it was a problem but it showed that had some kindness in her and that made their conversation deep and meaningful.

"Thanks?" Elijah said, still feeling uncertain. June merely nodded.

"Come on" she said, patting him softly on the shoulder, "Don't let them ruin your day. They're just being stupid is all" Those words were just enough to keep Elijah around. "If it makes you feel any better, we can just hang out for the rest of lunch, you and me" she offered.

Without giving a second thought, Elijah just agreed, "Okay, wanna walk around the school?" he replied.

"Sure".

Elijah and June circled the school perimeter until they reached the monkey bars in the back. He noticed Quinton, Roscoe, and Devon hanging around. This time, Elijah wasn't going to let them get on his nerves. In fact, after his conversation with June and her company by his side, Elijah was feeling tall and strong, almost like he was on a higher level than the other boys. From there, he was hooked on his pride and even had to shout a sarcastic remark.

"Hey pipsqueaks" Elijah called out, as he and June were approaching them.

"Pipsqueaks?" Quinton said. He was a little surprised.

"I am a year older than you"

"If anyone's gonna be it, it should be Devon, he's shorter" Quinton added.

"Pfft, not even" Devon replied.

"But I'm taller than you" Roscoe said, as he came in closer to Elijah, "So who are you calling pipsqueak?"

Elijah studied Roscoe's tone. It sounded like he was mostly threatening than joking. And of course there was a smirk on his face. So it was hard to tell. Elijah's next words floated around in his head and then came out of his mouth, just like that.

"Yeah but you're not the tallest in the world, Ross. I'm sure Bigfoot would say the same thing"

Quinton just laughed with amusement. At the same time, everyone was on edge because it was starting to feel like that Elijah and Roscoe were about to fight for dominance. But even then, Roscoe didn't say anything. He actually looked impressed by Elijah's sass. Perhaps there was some respect that he had, something he just couldn't express. Since Elijah didn't feel any hostel vibes, he decided to make best of his time.

"Hey June, I'll race you on the monkey bars" Elijah said.

"Uh, sure" June replied, almost right away.

Elijah was actually proving something to Roscoe, that he didn't care about what he said and that he was still friends with June Disher. They both went up to the center of the monkey bars and started swinging across. At first, Elijah didn't realize how fast he was going because he was still thinking about how he might've beaten the other boys at their own game of wits. But as Elijah was halfway through, he glanced behind only to realize that June was back on the ground.

"Sorry but I'm not really good at this" June explained, innocently.

So now the fun was over. Elijah didn't bother going any further. So he just dropped to the ground as well. "Oh, well that's fine".

But secretly, he was disappointed. He thought June would've been a little bolder. Elijah didn't realize at the time but he was pretending that June Disher was Sabrina Clarin.

After that day, Elijah kept on hanging out with the gang only because June comforted him. There were some good days. Elijah only interacted out of courtesy. The boys didn't tease him as much, which was a good thing. But even with all that, Elijah still found himself on autopilot during most of the days. It could be because that he was different from Quinton and his friends or maybe he couldn't stop thinking about the times they annoyed him in the past month. And it could also be that June failed to live up to Elijah's expectations when it came to having fun. She wasn't as ambitious as he thought. June was mostly laidback. She was nothing like Sabrina. Whatever it was, Elijah still continued being distant. After all, it was just another day of loitering.

"So I was watching Dragonball Z last night, so good!" Quinton said.

That caught Elijah's attention right away.

"I thought you said you don't watch cartoons, Quinton" Elijah said.

Quinton just stared at him for a moment.

"I said I don't watch kid's shows"

"Dragonball Z is for kids, isn't it?

"I know"

It was a little annoying because Quinton spent most of his time pretending to be tough and grownup and suddenly he was into cartoons after he clearly said he didn't watch them. Elijah didn't say anything else. He thought he would've taught Quinton a lesson that it was okay to be a kid. It was only natural at that age. Although not all of them saw it that way.

Once school was over, Elijah went to the back of the school to meet with the gang, only because he was expected to. Once they met, Quinton pulled Elijah aside for a private conversation and in the end Elijah regretted going to the back to see them.

"Hey, bro" Quinton said, afterwards, "Hey, I got this math work that's a little too hard. Do you think you can help me?"

Why was Elijah not surprised?

"You mean you want me to do homework for you again?"

"Yeah" Quinton replied, promptly.

He didn't even deny it. Elijah didn't answer right away. He just stared at Quinton, hoping that he would see an answer in his eyes, like a simple no or the fact that he wasn't interested in being part of the gang anymore.

"Come on, I thought we were bros" Quinton begged.

Elijah had never felt more used and manipulated.

"Yeah, okay" he said, reluctantly.

Later that night, *this homework is so easy, even a fourth grader could do it.*

The next day, Elijah returned the finish work to Quinton and just walked away and that was it. No greetings or hanging out. Again, they noticed that Elijah was being distant but didn't say anything, probably because Elijah practically told them not to on the day when they teased him more than they should've. Afterwards, during recess, the gang decided to plan a get together for Friday.

"We should hang out on Friday night, all of us!" Quinton insisted, "Devon, we should have a gaming night at your place"

Devon nodded, "It should be good. I don't have anything planned, except for sleeping and dreaming that I'm kissing the most beautiful girl"

Half the gang laughed. Considering the topic, Elijah avoided eye contact with June and Roscoe.

"That's funny, man" Quinton said, after he finished laughing, "Hey, how about we meet at the gas bar? Buy some snacks for the night?"

They all agreed. Even to Elijah, it sounded like fun. And they seemed excited and did it out of heart.

Friday evening had come. The gang decided to meet at the gas bar at 7pm. Elijah arrived early. But no one was there, except a few customers coming and going. He figured his friends were running late. So Elijah waited, patiently.

It was almost seven. Nobody came.

Ten after seven. No sign of Quinton.

Elijah waited another ten minutes, in the cold.

In the end, there was nobody but him. Not even Devon or June came. Elijah waited around a little longer because he thought maybe one of them would at least call the gas bar to ask for Elijah or anyone to tell them that plans were cancelled. But unfortunately, none of his friends did that, like they don't really do anything that friends should do. Disappointed, Elijah gave up and went home.

The first thing that Elijah did after the weekend, was talking to his friends, firmly. He was ready to yell at Quinton, Devon, Roscoe, and June, all of them, for not showing up that Friday evening. Even a part of Elijah hoped that he had gotten sick from standing out in the winter weather, just to make them feel bad. Elijah went to the back of the school and found Quinton almost right away.

"Hey, where were you guys?!" Elijah snapped, throwing his hands in the air, "I waited for you at the gas bar and nobody showed up"

Quinton just smiled nervously. It was disappointing that the anger in Elijah's voice was overseen.

"Sorry, bro, but I had to babysit at the last minute"

Babysit who? Quinton didn't have any siblings and he rarely spoke about his family.

"I was going to…" he explained.

But then Elijah's mind went miles away. It wasn't worth using it on Quinton.

"Maybe some other time, for sure" Quinton promised.

I don't believe you.

Quinton Malcolm's excuse wasn't convincing enough. So later on, Elijah decided to ask Devon just to see from another standpoint.

"Is it true that Quinton had to babysit?" Elijah said, gently, "Is that why nobody showed up at the gas bar?"

"What?" Devon replied.

Seriously? Elijah hoped that Devon was playing dumb because that wasn't the response he wanted to hear.

"On Friday!" Elijah was getting irritated, "We're were supposed to meet at the gas bar and go to your house but nobody showed up"

"I was waiting for you guys but nobody showed up there, either"

I thought you were supposed to meet at the gas bar, too.

"Okay then"

Devon didn't really answer Elijah's question about whether or not Quinton was lying. But what Elijah heard was convincing enough. The only theory he had was that maybe the whole thing was a set up for a lousy gag. Why else would Quinton be smiling nervously? Elijah could've asked June but after a while, the problem was starting to wear thin and he didn't think much of it.

Paula and Andrew would never do something like that. Even if they did, they would be thoughtful enough to give an honest answer.

Elijah didn't know what to believe in, anymore.

The whole gang was hanging out in Quinton's room, Elijah, June, Roscoe, and Devon. Half of them were sitting on the bed, while the others had to sit on the floor. They were playing video games for the evening. The boys were taking turns playing, for that Quinton only had two controllers. June was merely watching them and being entertained by their comebacks and insults whenever they teased each other.

Once their mind was being worn out from all that gaming, they took it easy and relaxed. They began talking about school, their families, and other stories. Quinton was probably making up most of those stories. Elijah didn't believe a single word. He knew that Quinton had lied about choosing church over homework and planning that get together that one Friday. The others probably knew but just won't do anything. There was no decency among them. And apparently they were fine with that. Elijah just didn't bother because it was pointless. He'd rather be at home right now. So he just sat there, daydreaming about the simpler days.

"Hey" Devon called, "So you got the stuff?"

"Yeah" Quinton answered, proudly.

Their little conversation caught Elijah's attention. Quinton told his friends to put on some music. So June volunteered and put on the CD and the music commenced. The sound and the rhythm went off and filled the entire home. It was rap music. Quinton was digging in his closet until he found what he was looking for. Elijah was expecting it to be either junk food, magazines with mature content, but it wasn't.

It was cigarettes!

Elijah had to look twice as Quinton was handing each of his friends a cigarette. They were kids, nearly his age and they smoked?! Elijah had seen it on TV before but didn't think he would see kids in real life to start such a habit that soon! He looked at each of them, still surprised as they put the cigarette in their mouths. Still in denial, Elijah was expecting it to be revealed as a joke, but once Devon pulled out a lighter, it was true. Quinton even offered one to him, like he just naturally assumed that he was a smoker, which he wasn't!

"No" Elijah said, shaking his head.

"Okay" Quinton replied.

Even June was a smoker! Elijah thought for sure that she was better than that. Once they each lit their cigarette, it was more real than ever. What was this world coming to? Normally kids at that age ought to be playing tag in the field, riding bikes together, getting stuck doing homework, or causing mischief. Elijah suddenly felt like an outsider, as he sat in the middle, with smoke fumes filling the air. The scent of tobacco was filling his nostrils. Elijah even put his head down for a brief moment, just to make sure it didn't get into his body somehow. The gang relaxed and danced to the song's rhythm. Elijah however sat there awkwardly, keeping his eyes forward.

"So how come you don't smoke, bro?" Quinton asked.

Elijah slowly cocked his head towards him. "I just don't"

"You should; we're Indians!"

That was no excuse to smoke! Growing up, Elijah had always been told that it was a bad habit and promised himself that he wouldn't get into such a thing, not just for himself, but for his parents. It was hard to imagine what they would do if they found out Elijah was even hanging with kids that were smokers. He could only hope that his new friends would be thoughtful enough not to force him. The more he thought what was going on around him, the more it started to scare him.

"Hey, Eli, you're all right?" Devon asked.

They sure picked a bad time to be considerate when they should've been sooner. But now that was hardly important. Elijah turned his attention toward him, trying to decide how to answer, whether to lie and say he was okay or say something and maybe talk some sense into them, but would they listen? The last thing Elijah wanted was to start a fight.

"Yeah, I'm fine, it's just...I didn't think you guys smoked"

Quinton laughed, which Elijah found insulting. "Come on, everyone does it". Yeah, like every student at school was a smoker. Was Quinton really that stupid? Elijah tried not to imagine his own peers with cigarettes in their mouths, but surely Quentin only wished that everyone did.

Since that evening, Elijah didn't look at his friends the same way again. Right up to that point, every kid in the real world seemed normal, but it turned out there are some that were more different in an unimaginable way. Growing up faster than anyone was one thing, but developing bad habits was something else, as it could probably lead to something worse and it was only a matter of time. But it was something Elijah didn't want to think about. It was all too much for him, that he needed to be alone even just for a little while. He excused himself from the gang.

"Hey, I'm gonna go for a little walk" Elijah told them, as he was leaving. But just when he thought his quiet time had started, he heard footsteps running behind him. It was Devon. Elijah just looked at him, puzzled and mostly irritated.

"I'll keep you company, okay?"

Fine! Elijah walked in silence with Devon by his side, who bragged about his daily life. Elijah only nodded but didn't say much. After a short moment, Devon was finally quiet. They were in front of the school. As Elijah was getting closer to where his peers were, he happened to look over to different crowds and there he saw an old friend, Sabrina Clarin. It felt like forever since he last saw her. She still looked the same, dark brown hair and beautiful in and out. It was quite extraordinary, almost like he saw her for the first time. There was a mix of excitement and sadness that sank in, which distracted Elijah from looking forward. If only he could talk to her again. Instead he could only daydream about her, nothing more.

Elijah kept looking back and forth just to see her face. Devon noticed and wondered what he was staring at.

The next day after school, the gang went to the gas bar. Again, Elijah had to buy food for Quinton, who claimed that he didn't have enough. Once they were done shopping, they started making their way to Quinton's home.

They were halfway through to their destination when there were two older kids coming towards their direction. They looked quite young but not exactly adults. They had to be teenagers. Elijah didn't recognize them but Quinton did, and he didn't sound happy.

"Oh great" Quinton cursed, "It's Henry"

It was easy to tell that he had issues with some other kids. Elijah was a little afraid to find out.

"Hey Quin!" Henry called.

Quinton led his friends, trying to ignore them, but then the older kid already caught up to him and blocked him from going any further.

"What do you want?" Quinton asked, furiously.

"You still owe me money" Henry said, with strong confidence.

"So?"

"So what's the hold up?"

"I don't have any on me. I been too broke"

"Don't lie. I see you got snacks with you. You gotta give me something"

Already angry, Quinton gave Henry the middle finger, "How about this?!"

Then Henry quickly grabbed Quinton by the hand, lifted it above his head and started going through his pockets.

"Hey! Back off!"

The rest of the gang was too afraid to stand up to the older kids.

"See, you got lots of stuff in here" Henry said. Then he found what he was looking for, a few dollar bills and some change. Elijah looked at them in surprise. That money seemed more than what any average kid would carry around. He couldn't help but imagine that Quinton might've had a hundred dollars on him. And yet Quinton asked Elijah to pay for his food. What else was he hiding?

"You see, this is what happens when you don't pay up!" Henry explained, firmly, as he held the money to Quinton's face.

The confrontation was over. Henry walked away with his friend. "See ya kiddies" he taunted.

After the older kids left, they all looked at Quinton who was angry and tried his best not to cry. Boys don't cry. Being gawked at was the last thing he wanted to see. "What are you guys looking at?!" he yelled.

And then he turned around and continued walking, while the others followed slowly.

That was a real eye opener. Almost no one had suspected that Quinton was quite weak, emotionally. The tension took some time to ease, but a little too slow for Elijah, for that he was uncomfortable with the dispute that took place in front of them. Going home was the only thing on his mind. If Quinton had problems with everyone on the reserve, he didn't want to be part of it.

They went straight to Quinton's room once they arrived at his place. Their host was in no mood to have fun after being robbed from those older kids. They just sat in silence and ate their food, with the music turned on loud. Quinton had a hard time eating and enjoying the company. So there was only one way to ease the tension, cigarettes. He left the room for moment to get some off his dad and came back with a handful and offered one to each of his friends. Just like the last visit, all four of them were smoking away except for Elijah, who was just sitting between them with the tobacco fumes filling the air.

"Frickin' hate that guy!" Quinton said, with great anger, "Can't get things himself, so he has to steal from me!" Then he scoffed and continued smoking.

Nobody had any comment on what he was going through.

"Bro" Quinton called.

Elijah didn't want to, but he turned his attention towards his new friend.

"I was kinda hoping you would've stood up for me back there" he explained.

Now he was putting Elijah on a guilt trip. That didn't sound good.

"He could've beaten me to death, you know. I would've done the same if someone was threatening you"

That was a little hard to believe.

"I thought you were better than this"

Elijah just stared at him, as he took the criticism.

"Hey, it wasn't his fault" Devon tried explaining.

"Shut up!" Quinton warned, without taking his eyes off Elijah, "Since you didn't do anything back there, you now owe me"

It was only getting worse from there and Elijah didn't like it. Quinton was offering him his cigarette. He wanted him to take a puff. He couldn't be serious.

"Go on, smoke it up"

There was a side of Elijah that felt bad for Quinton, but wasn't sure if he was ready to do such a thing.

"You owe me and you gotta do your part" he added.

Elijah said nothing; he only glanced at the cigarette and back at Quinton. The others waited in silence. It was a rather big decision to make, win someone's respect by doing something he never swore to do like smoking or do what was right. The waiting continued. Quinton was scowling at Elijah. He meant it; he really wanted him to smoke.

"Come on, don't be like that" Quinton urged.

After a moment of silence, Elijah had a decision of his own and he was thinking about his parents when he made the call.

"No" Elijah Khoda refused.

Quinton wasn't giving up that easily. He was still offering him the smoke. "Don't be like that" he repeated.

Was that what friends really did, force them to live up to their expectations? Elijah had experienced a singular friendship and it wasn't with Quinton Malcolm!

"No" he said to him.

"Hey, I said you owe me! Now come on, take the smoke"

"No" Elijah repeated, more firmly.

And then the voices grew louder.

"Come on!"

And finally, Elijah made a move. He stood up from the floor, furiously. "I said NO!" Then he immediately stormed out of Quinton's room and out of his house, without looking back. It actually felt nice to yell at him.

Disappointed and angry, Elijah left as fast as he could, hoping that none of them would come after him. What he just experienced would not be forgotten, that his friends weren't really who Elijah thought they were and they were different in so many ways. Quinton Malcolm was arrogant and nothing but bad news. Now that Elijah knew, he was more than willing to end their friendship the next time he would see them.

Elijah had never felt safer as he walked through the front door of his home. He could hear his dad watching TV in the living room. It was quite peaceful and isolated, which was something that Elijah needed, was to be alone. He spent the rest of the evening in his room, watching a movie and took his mind off things. Eventually, the tension had finally gone away, but Elijah still didn't want anything to do with Quinton or any of his followers. Fortunately, he never came to the house begging for forgiveness. Even if he did, Elijah doubted that he would change for the better. Later that night, there was no sleep at first. Elijah laid awake, staring at the ceiling, determined that he was not going to change himself just to win respect from people who he thought were his friends. Not now, not ever.

Elijah later fell asleep.

The night passed.

The sun rose in the morning.

Elijah lived to see another day.

For once, he was actually looking forward to doing some schoolwork after what happened. It was a way took take his mind off things. So for that morning, Elijah didn't worry about having friends or being somewhere at a certain time. He dedicated his mind and effort into his education like he never did before. Perhaps it was a way of making up for it, since dealing with bullies a few years prior. It seemed only right since there were times where Elijah took his schooling for granted.

For the next few days, Elijah avoided Quinton and his friends. It was a rather good feeling.

CHAPTER TEN

Like the Good Old Days

Elijah went back to living an uneventful life, but it was alright. Maybe he needed the space and the silence to get back in the routine. He hadn't talked to Quinton or the others. His days were mostly schoolwork, no social life. After a while that was one thing he was starting to miss, his old friends. Misery called for company, but would Paula and Andrew take Elijah back? At that point, it was the only thing he feared, thinking that they were mad at him for ending their friendship. Then he remembered what Andrew said that day, "At least think about it". So they might be willing to start over, but it still remained uncertain. It would require a lot of courage.

At the end of the week, Elijah decided to get out more instead of being isolated in his room, which was all he been doing for a while. It actually felt nice stepping outdoors and breathed in the fresh air, almost as if Elijah was hibernating. Both he and his mom went to town to buy some food at the local grocery store. As they pulled into Lakeview Mall, there were dozens of vehicles parked outside. Many of them were coming and going every few minutes. It was a busy time, for that Christmas was around the corner.

The store itself had people shopping for their needs. There were many voices talking all around, aisles crowded with locals. Elijah seen a few of his peers shopping with their parents, but no one he knew

167

personally. He spent most of his time helping his mom picking out food. After the cart was half full, Madeline was having trouble finding a particular product.

"Did you want anything, Eli?" she asked, "Like for a snack?"

"Maybe a bag of chips"

"Okay, you can go grab it. I still trying to decide what to make with the ground beef"

"Kay" Elijah replied.

So he departed from his mom and began searching each aisle for what he was looking for. Once he found it, Elijah walked down and searched the wide selection. After a moment, he finally decided what he wanted and grabbed it, then he went to exit the aisle, but there was a few other customers crowding the area, so he had to go in the opposite direction. Elijah was almost at the end and just as he turned the corner, he saw a face he did not expect to see…

"Hi, Elijah!" Sabrina Clarin said.

Elijah stopped, like completely stopped as if he was immobilized. His mind went blank and did not breathe one bit of air, as he realized that Sabrina Clarin was looking directly at him. Elijah even looked behind him to make sure she wasn't talking to someone else, but there was nobody around. It was an unexpected surprise. This had to be a dream.

"Hi…Sabrina" Elijah finally responded, trying to sound calm.

"How are you?" she asked.

It was definitely her! The same girl that sat across from him back in September; she was still just as down to earth as she was then.

"Ah, good-good" Elijah was still surprised. He had a little trouble keeping up with the small talk. "Uhh, how are you?"

"I'm good, thanks" she replied honestly.

This was the most real conversation Elijah had since October, honest and sincere. There were so many things Elijah wanted to say, like how good it was to see her and how much he missed her. Those thoughts were in his mind for a month but he didn't expect to bump into her at the store. Now it all disappeared from his mind once Elijah saw Sabrina in person. It sure felt like a dream but it was reality. It was a miracle! He wanted to ask her something while he had her attention.

"So…how-I…I haven't seen you in a while" Elijah told her. It wasn't exactly a question, but he wasn't sure how else to say it.

"Yeah!" Sabrina agreed, "It's been like a month?"

It felt longer than that. "Yeah, about a month" Elijah said.

"So what are you up to? I mean aside from the obvious reason of being a grocery store" Then she chuckled. Elijah sure missed the sound of her laughter.

"Just shopping, by myself…"

Sabrina nodded. She was nice enough to listen.

"I mean, for now. I'm just grabbing my chips and gonna catch up with my mom"

"Cool. I'm shopping with my mom too, although I kinda wandered off"

Elijah just gave a little chuckle, "Yeah?" He was still overwhelmed that Sabrina even said his name.

Their conversation ended up being short, since Elijah was lost for words. They both looked at each other. Elijah couldn't help but give a little smile and of course Sabrina smiled in return. It was nice to see that again. Then the silence went on for a little too long.

"Well, I should probably let you catch up to your mom" Sabrina told him.

"Okay…Well, see you Sabrina"

"See you"

Sabrina left as she made her way to the opposite direction. Elijah casually walked away, but then he stopped as he started thinking about Sabrina in general. He turned around to see if she was still there, but she already walked around the corner, going down the last aisle. Elijah did not think she was going to talk to him again, especially after giving that outburst in class. He thought Sabrina might've been upset with him for ranting out at Jeff, but she didn't seem mad at all. She spoke to him like nothing had changed. It was a great relief, knowing that she hadn't forgotten about him.

There was so much in one little moment that could stop you from moving with the rest of the world. Elijah was about to go catch up with his mom, but he kept thinking about Sabrina and how much he missed her. Only a minute had passed, maybe Sabrina was still in the store. That conversation didn't have to be the last and Elijah certainly didn't want it to. So he decided to turn around.

Following Sabrina's footsteps, Elijah peeked in every aisle. There were at least a few people but no sign of her. That old exciting feeling was back, the same one Elijah felt waking up every morning and knowing that he was going to see Sabrina. A few people were coming towards him, a couple of customers and grocery store clerk pushing a cart filled with fresh bread. Elijah quickly but gently dodged each of them as he passed through. Finally arriving at the last aisle, she wasn't there anymore. But Elijah wasn't giving up.

He sprinted down that aisle, which led him to the front of the store. The place was getting busier by the minute. Elijah kept moving forward. As he got closer towards the tills, he saw a girl, long dark brown hair. It had to be her! But there were other customers blocking the way, so Elijah thought quickly and took a little detour by crawling under the produce tables and came out the other side. Elijah did the same thing with one more table and finally he was close. And there she was!

"Hey, Sabrina" Elijah called.

She turned around and was just a little surprised to see him.

"Hey, again" she replied, "What's up?"

There still weren't many words to keep her attention, he just wanted to see her, but felt the need to say something. "Sabrina, I..." Elijah started, but couldn't finish. There were two main things he wanted to say, that he missed her so much and how much that he was sorry for what he did in class a month ago. The words floated in his mind. Sabrina was waiting patiently.

"I thought maybe...we can hang out for a bit?" he suggested, "You know, like the old days?

Yes, a serious conversation was his first intent but then again Elijah dealt with enough seriousness in the past month. It's been a while since he had a REAL conversation with someone who didn't pretend to be anything, someone who wasn't moody, and someone who simply loved life.

"Sure" Sabrina agreed, "I probably won't have much time, but I can spare a minute or two"

Elijah nodded, "Okay".

So there wasn't much time and Elijah wouldn't want to take up too much of it. In the end, their conversation started with something simple. "So you're looking forward to Christmas?" he asked.

"Yeah, definitely; both of my grandparents are coming to town and they're gonna stay with us. I'm so excited to see them!"

"Well, that's good"

"Mhm. What do you got planned for Christmas?"

"Nothing" Elijah answered right away, "I mean, nothing much. We'll probably just stay home, have dinner, and have some family over"

Sabrina nodded. "That's great"

That was almost the end of it, but Elijah wanted it to keep going. Luckily, Sabrina decided to show the displays she was looking at. "I think I know why I wandered off. I wanted to check out the Christmas stuff!"

The way she said it, she sounded so excited. It was the one thing Elijah was looking for, someone who acknowledges small things. And there was something about her voice that made it sound special.

"Check out this one" Sabrina said, as she grabbed one decoration. It was a little model tree, all white colored.

"It looks nice" Elijah told her, "I wonder if it lights up"

"I think it does, but I also think it needs batteries"

"Darn"

Sabrina laughed, "I know. I was kinda hoping to see some Christmas lights light up". Then she placed the product back on the shelf, "We haven't put up our tree yet...or...I guess it's too soon. It's not even December yet"

"You like Christmas?" Elijah asked, casually.

"I love Christmas!"

"I do, too"

"Yeah, it's kind of a nice way to bring everyone together" Sabrina added.

"Yeah, family and friends" Elijah turned her attention on her when he said the last part, "Something about it just makes it extra special"

"I think so, too" Sabrina agreed.

Then she looked at the clock that was hung up above the store entrance. "But I think I been gone a little too long. I should probably go find my mom before I get left behind"

"Okay, yeah I better go find mine too" Elijah said.

"Well, it was nice seeing you, Elijah"

"Nice seeing you"

Then Sabrina turned around and took her leave, but she glanced over her shoulder, "Bye".

Elijah merely waved as she went around the corner. That was nice, he thought, knowing that he still had at least one friend and it couldn't be anyone more special than Sabrina Clarin. One conversation was better than nothing, and definitely made up for the long silence within the last month. For the first time since then, Elijah was feeling more hopeful, that there was still something to look forward to. And it all it took was one word, when Sabrina said hi just when Elijah came around the corner.

That was one moment Elijah kept to himself. He moved on like things were normal. Soon, he found his mom, put his snack in the shopping cart and continued on with their evening. As they walked along, Elijah kept looking over his shoulder, thinking about that certain someone and how nice it would be if he would see her again.

"What's wrong?" his mom asked.

"Nothing" Elijah answered like any other kid that didn't really want to explain to his parent.

CHAPTER ELEVEN

Adult Situations

For a little while, Elijah thought for sure that he was done hanging out with troubled kids. He even started considering putting things back the way it used to be, the simpler days. Elijah realized the wrong that he did and was willing to make it right. Just when he started feeling ambitious about it, Quinton Malcolm walked back into his life.

After avoiding his former friends for less than a week, Elijah didn't want to accept the fact that he would have to associate with them somehow. But whatever reality had in store for him, it didn't seem good, not with someone like Quinton, who walked to the front of the school just to see Elijah. There was no sign of June, Devon, or Roscoe. Elijah was leaning against the railing when he made eye contact with Quinton. He looked rather guilty than intimidating

Might as well get this over with.

"Hey, bro" Quinton greeted, gently.

He was being awfully nice.

Elijah didn't say anything.

"Look, I'm sorry about what happened last time, okay? I was mad at Henry and not you"

There was still no comment from Elijah.

"So me and the others were talking and decided that if you don't want to smoke, you don't have to"

At that point, Elijah wished that Quinton could read his mind, so he could hear every rant, especially after all the times that they irritated him and made him uncomfortable, and ultimately not wanting to be friends with them ever again!

"Alright…" Elijah finally spoke after a moment of silence.

"Alright what? You accept my apology?"

Elijah wouldn't have let him off the hook that easily. But since his kindness scrambled all his hateful words, he only responded out of courtesy.

"Yeah but…"

"That's good" Quinton replied, promptly. Then he extended his hand out for a handshake but Elijah just stared at him, coldly.

During that time, Paula was beside the entrance, reading a book. Andrew comes along, blowing into his cupped hands.

"Paulie, do you have any mitts I could borrow?" Andrew asked, kindly.

"I do but I'm already using them"

"You don't have a spare?" Andrew teased.

Paula took her eyes off her book to answer.

"Me? You should be asking yourself that. You're the one that's always losing things"

"I try to buy spares of everything but I always end up buying something else"

"Then why are we having this conversation? If anything, go check the lost and found box. Maybe you'll find the pair you lost back in grade four"

"If anything, just tuck her hands into your sleeves"

"Then how would I turn the pages?"

"Use your nose"

"My-no way!"

"Let's try it out, at least. If it works, too bad for you"

Andrew leaned over to try and snatch Paula's book or at least pretend to. Paula then closed her book without realizing. Just as she turned away from Andrew, she noticed Elijah by the railings, talking to Quinton Malcolm. It caught her attention and filled her with worry, for that her best friend didn't look very happy.

"Why did you do that?" Elijah finally spoke.

Quinton put his hand down.

"Do what?"

"All those things, you lied to me and used me"

"I..."

"That's not what friends do, you know!"

"I know..." Quinton stopped himself from making an excuse.

You knew? Whatever, Quinton.

Ranting out was the first choice but then Elijah thought of something else while he had Quinton's attention.

"Listen, bro, there's something I need help with"

"I'm not doing any more of your homework, Quinton" Elijah said, promptly, "You do it yourself!"

"It's NOT homework, okay?"

"What is it?"

First, Quinton took a deep breath before answering. Whatever he had in mind, it was something different. "Meet me at my place tonight and I'll tell you"

"You're not gonna make me wait in the cold like you did last time?"

"No, not this time, I promise"

"Don't say that, Quinton"

"Say what?"

"Promise"

Quinton sighed.

"Okay, fine. But I still need your help, tonight. But for now, let's go hangout a bit"

"No" Elijah refused, "I'd rather be alone"

There was another sigh.

"Fine, okay, but just meet me at my place tonight"

Then after that, you and I won't be friends anymore.

It was tempting not to show up. If Elijah had to wait and nobody shows up, it ought to happen to Quinton as well. But it was likely that Quinton wouldn't stop bothering Elijah. Whatever he wanted, it was best to get it out of the way and finally move on.

Elijah arrived at Quinton's. It was only early in the evening and it was already dark out. As an addition to the evening, the snow was floating down from the clouded sky. Elijah cleared his mind, for that he was ready for anything. He knocked at the door. Quinton's mom answered. He gently asked for Quinton, who soon came around the corner and grabbed his winter coat. What do you know; he was actually ready and ambitious for once.

They walked to the end of the reserve. Neither of them spoke. Elijah had no desire to start any conversations with Quinton. They later stopped once they were getting close to their destination.

"Alright, listen" Quinton said, "This is where Henry lives…"

Henry, the guy who robbed Quinton of his money not too long ago; just hearing that name made Elijah a little edgy.

"I'm gonna talk to him and try to get my money back. You make sure that his brother or any of his friends try to fight me"

What?

"Fight?! You want me to fight? Are you serious?"

"No"

Quinton just sounded so calm! He probably didn't understand what the word fear meant, or feelings, or the word wrong!

"No" Quinton repeated, "Just make sure that I don't get beat up"

"It sounds like a fight to me"

"It's easy, just shove them away"

Yeah, like that's going to scare them.

"Quinton, why don't you just forget it?" Elijah said, angrily, "I can't do this anymore"

"Shhh, listen, bro, if you do this for me, I'll always have your back; you can borrow my games for as long as you want. I'll even let you boss me around, how's that?"

Quinton was trying to win Elijah's friendship back. It probably wasn't going to happen-no it was never going to happen.

"What do you need the money for, anyway?" Elijah asked.

"I wanted to save it and buy myself something"

"And what about the money that you owe ME?"

"That's another reason why we're doing this, so I can pay you back"

Elijah didn't say anything.

"Listen, bro, we can do this ourselves. We big kids now, we don't need grownups to tell us what to do. If we face these guys, we can face anything. Imagine that, we'd be strong and tough just like those tag team wrestlers, right?"

Still silent.

"Come on, man, if you do this for me, I'll make it up to you. I swear"

The burden of this new crowd had been heavy for too long. Elijah knew that and had to put a stop to it. Yes, it was tempting to argue with Quinton just to get all that anger out. But there was a part of Elijah that wanted to humiliate his former friend if his plan didn't go well. Elijah could see himself rubbing it in Quinton's face. So they went along with the plan.

The boys approached the house. Some of the lights inside were on. But the porch lights were off and kept them in the dark. So Quinton knocked on the door. Elijah stayed out of sight. After a minute or two, someone answered the door. Only Quinton spoke.

"Hey, is Henry home?" he asked.

It was silent again. Elijah continued to wait.

"What the hell you want?" a voice said.

Elijah looked back at the porch and noticed that Henry just appeared right in front of Quinton.

"You know what I want, I want my money back!"

Henry scoffed.

"Geez, kid, you just don't get it, do you? I gave you a lot of free smokes, A LOT. No way I was going to let you live off me"

"So?"

"So nothing. Now beat it, it's probably passed your bedtime"

Then Quinton suddenly went after Henry and started throwing punches. Elijah just couldn't move. Then Henry shoved Quinton off the porch and into the snow. Suddenly, another teenage First Nations boy came out. That had to be the brother, who then stormed after Quinton. Fear finally struck Elijah and softened him once Henry's brother grabbed Quinton by the coat.

"Hey, what do you think you're doing, messing with my brother?" he said.

"This is none of your business, asshole!" Quinton snapped. Then he looked over at Elijah, "Hey, come on, this is where I need you"

But Elijah didn't do anything. He couldn't. The other boys saw him and that's when the new level of fear started.

"What are you, his bodyguard?" Henry said.

"Come on, bro, do something!" Quinton begged.

Elijah hesitated. And once Henry started walking towards him, all courage had faded. When Elijah met the teenager's eyes, he couldn't breathe. Quinton waited, thinking that maybe his friend had a trick up his sleeve.

"What are you gonna do?" Henry said, "You want to fight me? Go ahead"

That's what Quinton wanted but not Elijah.

"I just wanna get out of here" Elijah finally admitted.

Henry looked at him for a moment, realizing the fear in his eyes.

"Then go" he told him.

Without any delay, Elijah turned around and ran.

"What? Hey!" Quinton shouted.

"Shut up" the brother said.

Elijah ran as far as he could and never looked back. Once he was halfway home, he stopped for a moment just to catch his breath. In that silence, he listened out for any disturbance but there was nothing. Elijah imagined that Quinton might've got beaten up by those older boys. A part of him felt a little bad but was it wrong to think that maybe Quinton deserved it? Elijah didn't give it a second thought. After all, deep down, he didn't really want to be friends with Quinton Malcolm anymore.

Elijah re-lived that night every waking moment. Witnessing violence in real life was much different than watching them in movies. It was like a nightmare that he couldn't wake up from. It was vivid and dramatic. Yet fear wouldn't let him turn away. At the same time, it opened Elijah's eyes to the kind of life that he had been living, someone who was driven by hatred and acted out in violence. It was almost as if he saw himself

180   PHILIP PATRICK

and that put him in guilt, just thinking how his friends and family might've thought of him. Becoming a bully yourself felt worse than facing one. It was wrong to befriend Quinton Malcolm. Elijah had regretted it and wanted things to go back to the way they were.

The next day, Quinton wasn't at school. Elijah thought maybe that was a good thing. Surely, it gave some peace and quiet, but at one point he wondered if Quinton had gotten in trouble for what he did and was imprisoned at home by his parents. It was either that or something worse. Suddenly, guilt came upon Elijah, for that he realized he could've helped Quinton somehow. Why was he feeling bad for his former friend? It was the same kid that used him and manipulated him. Maybe Quinton Malcolm got what he deserved. The thought pulled Elijah away from reality for the time being. That was one of the hard things about being a kid; trying to find answers but feel like you would never find them.

With all the privacy and quiet time, Elijah had a chance to recuperate and put his mind back to focus. That whole day, he didn't think about his problems. During recess, Elijah was on the curb, leaning against the cement wall just below the railings. Most of the time, students didn't hang around there. So it gave Elijah the alone time that he needed. He had his notebook with him. It was the first time he had it with him since that day with Quinton. Sometimes when Elijah didn't know what to draw, he would draw the scenery in front of him. In this case, it was the parking lot, the trees in the distance. It was his way to take his mind off things. Turing the page to start a fresh one, the writing of Sabrina's name was still there. Even after running into her at the store, Elijah still missed her. He began to think about that evening and how much it impacted him. Right up until that night, Elijah thought that Sabrina Clarin was mad at him but he was wrong. If she spoke to him like she did, maybe that meant Paula and Andrew would be the same way. Elijah just realized that he was standing in the same spot where he ended their friendship a month ago. It couldn't be a coincidence just when he started thinking about his best friends as he was standing there. So he gave it some thought and decided that it wouldn't hurt to at least apologize to them.

Elijah knew for sure that was more to life than long silence and troubled kids, after his most unexpected encounter with Sabrina that night at the store. Just hearing her saying hello was enough to bring Elijah back on his feet and to put his mind in the right place. Since that evening, it got him thinking about all that he had done and how he wanted to make things right. Paula and Andrew were his first priority, for that support was one thing he needed. And his best friends had never let him down.

Paula and Andrew would never make Elijah do things he wouldn't want to do. They always respected him and accepted him for who he was, especially Paula because she had been a friend for years, and most importantly when Elijah was an outsider in primary school. She was the only one that cared for him. Andrew, on the other hand, always made Elijah laugh and they trusted each other since they met in grade four. This was what Elijah Khoda had taken for granted and he felt bad about it.

The other thing that needed to be done was to apologize to Jeff Tomly, for lashing out at him in front of the class. If Jeff and Sabrina were friends, Elijah would trust her and respect her own world by admitting his faults, and then maybe that would win back Sabrina Clarin's friendship. These were the two things that Elijah determined himself to do. Once the next day came along, he spent the first recess walking around, gathering the courage to face his fears. Elijah hoped that it wasn't too late.

Breathing in and breathing out. That was a way to build confidence and keeping emotions balanced. That's what Elijah did as he walked around the perimeter of the school, keeping his eyes forward and his mind blank, for that he was about to right his wrongs. He couldn't help but feel a little nervous, hoping that Andrew and Paula weren't too mad at him.

Then suddenly, his walk was interrupted once Elijah saw Quinton coming towards him.

Oh great.

Quinton Malcolm blocked Elijah's path, as he scowled at him, not looking happy at all.

"What do you want, Quinton?" Elijah reluctantly asked, not wanting to deal with him whatsoever. During that moment, he studied Quinton's face. There was no sign of any bruises. It looked like things didn't get too rough with those older boys from the other night.

"I wanna say something to your face!" his former friend snarled.

This couldn't be happening. Elijah sensed a threat. He once had the guts to say something if he felt any discomfort, but now he'd rather avoid it and choose to live life like a normal kid.

"Not now" Elijah fired back.

"What are you, a pussy?"

"I just don't wanna deal with you! Now get lost!"

Elijah tried to ignore the hostility and stepped aside to continue to walk, but Quinton followed.

"You were my friend!" Quinton was starting to raise his voice. It was only a matter of time before it caught every student's attention. "I let you visit me, hit some bottles, and you couldn't even stand up for me!"

There wasn't much tolerance left, but Elijah tried to talk Quinton out of the conflict. "Maybe I didn't want to!" he growled, "Because I don't trust you"

The confrontation was completely unexpected. There was no time to think of kind words to someone who had problems of his own. Quinton continued to scowl, as more anger erupted within him.

"You listen to me" Elijah insisted, "Friends don't use each other. They don't make each other smoke or borrow money and don't pay back or do their homework…"

"I told you!" Quinton interrupted, "I wasn't really good at it"

"Well, that's not my problem! I can't do your homework forever, Quinton, or give you money, or smoke a cigarette. Not everyone can be like you and how dare you try to change me!" Quinton didn't say anything.

"And another thing…" Elijah started, "You lie! You didn't have church to go to that night. You just didn't wanna do your homework. So that's why you ask me to do it. And you act all grown up, saying you don't watch kid's shows but then you say you like Dragonball Z, but still you don't want to celebrate Halloween and such. I lend you money and you never paid me back. Maybe that's why I didn't stand up for you, because you deserved it! Now, Leave. Me. Alone!"

Furiously, Elijah turned around and walked away. Unfortunately, just when he walked around the corner, Quinton came running.

"You know what?" he called.

Elijah glanced over his shoulder, and gave out a heavy sigh, just when he hoped it was over.

"I would've stood up for you if you were in trouble"

"No, you wouldn't. Now leave me alone!"

Then suddenly Elijah felt a hand gripping tight on his shoulder. Next thing he knew, he was facing Quinton in the eye. "Look at me when I'm talking to you!!" he snarled. Those were rather big words for a boy nearly Elijah's age. It sounds like something Quinton learned from his dad. That could explain a whole lot of Quinton Malcolm's behavior.

"Because of you, June, Devon, and Roscoe don't wanna hang out with me anymore"

That seemed unlikely. He was probably lying. Before responding with words, Elijah violently removed Quinton's hand and pushed him away. There were a few students passing through, trying to ignore the conflict. Elijah glared at his former friend.

"Geez, I just told you that I don't want to be friends with you, anymore. Don't make me say it a second time!"

"You think you're so tough?" Quinton challenged.

There was a pause.

"At least I'm not stupid"

Quinton didn't say anything.

"I'm not the one who doesn't know what blonde means" Elijah snarled.

184   PHILIP PATRICK

Quinton's eyes were filled with hurt and anger.

"You said you won against those white boys. You think you can win against me?" he yelled.

Elijah said nothing.

"Go on, try. I dare you!"

It was tempting to teach Quinton a lesson. But for some reason, Elijah just didn't have it in him to fight, unlike his old self. Instead of feeling the urge to throw a punch, there was guilt, but guilty for what? It couldn't be for Quinton or maybe it was because Elijah thought about his friends and everything he done. Right then, Elijah really just wanted to walk away, but then his former friend began pushing him.

"Come on, what are you waiting for?" Quinton growled, "You're too scared to fight me?"

"Hey!" A voiced called from behind.

Then tension eased for a brief moment, as Elijah looked behind him. It was Paula! And right behind her was Andrew!

"What do you think you're doing?" she demanded, as she undauntedly looked Quinton Malcolm in the eye and stood beside Elijah, who felt a greater relief.

Quinton scoffed, "What does it look…?"

"Being stupid and trying to fight for no one but yourself!" Paula interrupted.

It's been a while since Elijah saw Paula taking a strong stand, not since she stood up to Brian Kidman for picking on her best friend. He remembered when Paula threw her fist deep into his stomach. After that, Brian was too embarrassed and didn't pick on Elijah as much as he used to. And it looked like Quinton was just as humiliated, as he was being singled out by a girl.

"Hey…" Quinton tried to talk back to Paula, until someone else joined the confrontation.

"Hey!" Andrew shouted, putting his hand up at Quinton.

Andrew Little; it was great to see him again! He was even wearing his shades for whenever he pretended to be an interrogating cop. Andrew stood tall and fearless.

"What seems to be the problem, boy?" he demanded, with authority in his voice, "And don't bother saying 'nothing' because I already see the problem and it's too late for you to sweep it under the rug"

Quinton just looked at him funny, like he always did. "None of your damn busi…"

Andrew cleared his throat loud and clear, "Do you see me standing here? I may have glasses on but I'm not blind. It's already my business and allow me to close the deal. You don't lay a hand on this gentleman" he then pointed to Elijah, "Then I won't make up a story to the principal that you're an alien in disguise who likes to steal peoples' pants, deal?"

There was no answer. So Andrew took it as a yes.

"Deal!" he concluded.

It was hardly important to fight with words after the humor that Andrew had displayed. Elijah couldn't help but smile, for that the conflict was surprisingly entertaining and it mostly revolved around Andrew's wit. Friends who stand by you during rough times were real friends, even after your faults and the mistakes you made. And Elijah was lucky to have two people that looked out for him. So then Andrew met with Elijah and Paula, and the three of them started walking away.

As Elijah was walking between his best friends, he patiently waited to get as far away from Quinton as he could. It was then he realized that trouble didn't always disappear; it had a way of coming back. Before Elijah knew it, he felt himself falling to the ground. The front of his body was suddenly cold and wet from all the snow. Quinton Malcolm had run up to him and angrily pushed his former friend to the ground.

"Hey…!" Andrew tried standing up to Quinton, but then he got shoved back. Paula was rather startled. Before she could say anything, Elijah already got up and tackled Quinton and the fight broke out. It only took one of the nearby students to notice a fight and shortly half the school realized. Elijah and Quinton were throwing punches at each other. They were on foot until Elijah was knocked down and they began wrestling in the snow. An agitated Quinton was growling with anger as he was hitting his victim in the stomach. Elijah had to withstand a few hits and then he felt the bully's palms pounding into his face.

186 PHILIP PATRICK

More students were watching from both sides.

At that time, Sabrina was loitering with her girlfriends near the entrance. "And that's how I got my first haircut" Melanie concluded.

Sabrina nodded, "Well, at least you have a story to tell"

"True. Oh, you should hear the story of how I lost my first tooth. It actually should be a Carly story because it involved sports…"

"Fight!" one of their fellow students shouted, most likely trying to get help. It caught the girls' attention as they noticed more of their peers were heading in that direction.

"A fight?" Carly said, almost worriedly.

At first, Sabrina was hesitant but she couldn't help but join the other students. So without saying anything, she went around the corner where there was a fairly large crowd. In the distance, she saw two figures wrestling each other. There were too many students in the way, so Sabrina went in for a closer look. Carly and Melanie however kept their distance. Once Sabrina got closer to the commotion, she finally recognized one of the boy's faces.

Is that Elijah?!

Elijah was temporally immobilized, but luckily support came just when he needed it. Andrew grabbed a handful of snow and threw it at Quinton's head, which caused a distraction. Once the chance came along, Elijah fists his hands and punched Quinton in the face. Then the anger took a whole of him. He didn't want to stop there. Elijah turned the tables and pinned his bully to the ground, and then returned a favor by pounding his face.

"I told you!!" Elijah shouted, "Leave! Me! Alone!"

The pounding stopped just so he could say something to Quinton's face, which was red, wet, and teary eyed. "And you leave me friends alone!" he growled. Elijah raised his fist, getting ready for another hit. But Paula immediately ran in and grabbed her best friend by the hand before it would get worse.

"Elijah!" she called but he didn't respond in any way. "That's enough"

Paula's voice pulled Elijah back into the real world, as he realized what he was doing, becoming just like a bully, someone who was lost and took his problems out on everyone. One thought led to another as Elijah Khoda had saw what he had become in the last few months, someone who pushed his friends away and did it for all the selfish reasons. That clouded his mind as he backed away from Quinton.

The fight was over. Supervisors on duty quickly approached the area once they heard about the incident. Elijah's heart was heavy and soon he began to shake as the tension mixed with the cold air and caused a great discomfort. Next thing he knew, there were groups of his peers looking back at him. Then Elijah started to imagine what they would be thinking, about the monster he truly was and that struck fear into his heart. Even worse, Sabrina was probably somewhere in the crowd. So Elijah just kept his head down. He'd rather not see the horror on Sabrina Clarin's face. Ranting in front of the class was one thing, but getting into a fight and showing his bad side was probably too far.

Both boys were escorted to the office, along with Paula since she was found on the scene, but they only needed her for questioning. Luckily, Quinton was kept separated as he was sitting in the office, while Elijah and Paula were sitting outside the office. He could still feel the pain on his face. The tension was gone. Now it was mostly fear. Paula could sense it. No words could comfort him at that point. The only thing she could was just wrap her arm around him. Through the windows of the office, they saw the supervisor and the principal approaching the door. It was time to face reality.

"Paula Hennig" the principal called, "I like to see you first"

Paula did as she was told, without questioning. She felt bad for leaving her best friend behind after that dramatic episode. But she accepted the fact that there was nothing she could do to fix it. She got up and glanced at Elijah for a moment before she went into the office.

Now he was alone.

It wasn't the first time he was sent to the office. The first time was in primary school when he got into a dispute with some kids and the supervisor. Second time was after he met Brian Kidman in the fifth grade. And the third time was Brian again, when Elijah antagonized him and Brian's friends. All those times, Elijah didn't give much thought because then all he cared about was himself getting out of there. Even a few times could be too much to handle. As trouble continued to come around the corner, the thought of being home schooled was tempting, but Elijah wasn't sure why he didn't go for it. Now he might realize why, because there was more out there than just trouble waiting for him. There was some good, there was life. There was...beauty. Then an image of Sabrina came to life in his mind. As Elijah sat there alone, he began contemplating that he did not want to be sent to the office anymore.

Paula was relieved from the principal's office. She was escorted out personally. Elijah didn't say anything, thinking that he wasn't allowed to. He and Paula only exchanged glances. It was hard to tell if it was good or bad, for that she looked at him with pity, and at the same time, there was a look of defeat. Elijah was expecting her to sit beside him again, but instead, she put her coat back on and went back outside.

"Don't go anywhere, young man" the principal warned, "I still need to talk to you".

Quinton was the next person to see the principal. Elijah saw him walking behind the principal until they were both out of sight. The waiting continued. The longer it went on, the bad feeling went deeper.

The time had come when the principal escorted Quinton out of the office. It wasn't revealed on whether Quinton was in trouble or he was let go. But Elijah got up once the principal gestured for him to follow.

Elijah remained calm as he set foot in the principal's office. He waited until he was allowed to sit. Once he sat across from the principal, that was when he began to feel nervous, like he was about to get a life sentence.

"Elijah Khoda" the principal spoke, "We meet again. With that being said, I don't need to remind you about why you're here. So I'll get right to the point; I was just questioning both Paula Hennig and

Quinton Malcolm about the incident that took place ten minutes ago. They told me about what happened from their perspective. And you're about to do the same. So it's pretty simple"

Then he leaned in closer. "I'm listening". That was the cue to start talking.

It took a little time, for that Elijah was about to do things a little differently. Before he wouldn't tell the whole truth and tried to make himself look like the victim, only to take the easy way out. But after the fight, Elijah felt like it mattered that he knew what everyone thought of him and how he saw himself. Something told him that he deserved to be punished.

"Quinton wouldn't leave me alone..." Elijah finally said. He didn't bother giving the full story about him and Quinton. It didn't feel necessary. "Me, Paula, and Andrew were just walking away...and then Quinton came up behind and pushed me down. And then I got up and fought him".

Elijah told the truth honestly and didn't make anything up or play any part.

"So YOU started the fight?" the principal asked.

There was a pause.

"Yes" Elijah admitted.

The principal raised an eyebrow, "That's not what Paula told me"

It was no surprise that Paula was trying to get Elijah out of trouble. It was noble but Elijah thought it wasn't entirely right. And he already told the truth. There was no turning back.

"Anything else?" the principal asked.

"I shouted at Quinton to leave me and my friends alone. Paula stopped me from fighting. And then the supervisors came"

There was silence.

"So what you just told me is what really happened?"

Elijah couldn't go back and fix the past. He nodded to his principal and that was it.

Suspended for three days.

The principal was convinced that Elijah Khoda was the one who started the fight and gave him his comeuppance. Elijah could only imagine what Quinton told the principal. He probably displayed himself as the victim. It would explain why he didn't get a suspension or any punishment. But nothing could be done about it. Elijah had accepted his fault and had to pay his debt to society.

Even though, the conflict was over but Elijah wasn't out of the woods yet. The principal had called Elijah's mom, told her about what happened and that his suspension was affected immediately and therefore he was dismissed for the rest of the day. Elijah knew his mom did not like walking into the office, only to see her son was in trouble. But just like his discussion with the principal, he had no choice but to face it.

Recess was over while Elijah remained in the office. He sat there and heard the bell go off and saw every student running to class. Shortly the outside world was empty and became silent again. Madeline Khoda arrived at the school and kept her emotions under wrapped. They both walked out of the office. Elijah was expecting his mom to yell at him any moment.

"Come, we better go get your stuff from-from...your class" Madeline said, absently. She sounded bored, like she was used to her son getting into trouble.

Elijah did as he was told. They were almost entering the hallway until a certain thought hit him, walking into the classroom with his mom would be a little embarrassing, especially when everyone heard about the fight, and he didn't want Sabrina to see him, not like that.

"M-m-mom" Elijah spoke, nervously.

"What?" she replied, with irritation. The anger was there and it was only a matter of time until it would come out in words.

"Can I...I can-I can go in alone...to get my stuff. I'll come right back"

His mom could tell there was something different about him, but it was hard to tell what and whether it was good or bad. There was already so much on Madeline's mind and didn't have time to argue.

"Okay" she agreed, calmly, "Get your stuff and come straight back. And don't forget to give your teacher the principal's...that thing"

"The note" Elijah corrected.

"Yes, now go!" she snarled.

Getting suspended was only the first step. The next one was getting punished by a parent, in which Elijah feared because the troubles had been going on for too long. He was worried about what was going to happen next. Elijah hurried down the hall, went to the classroom, and gave Mrs. Parker the note explaining the situation. Then she dismissed him.

Sabrina was sitting at her desk when Elijah entered the classroom. The initial shock of seeing him getting into a fight had passed. Now she only felt pity for him. Like some students, she wondered how that incident started. It was hard to see someone nice like Elijah would start a fight. *I'm sure he didn't mean to,* she thought to herself. There was no way of telling for sure. Once she saw Elijah going to his locker and getting ready to leave, she thought about getting up to give him a hug. But then she thought that would probably embarrass him and he been through enough. So as much as she wanted to, Sabrina remained seated.

As Elijah went to his locker, he could feel all the eyes in the room watching him. So he kept his head down, avoiding eye contact with anyone. They were all probably thinking the same thing, how messed up their classmate was. Elijah could only hope that Sabrina was any different.

The car ride was silent. Elijah kept his eyes forward, still waiting for an argument to break out. Once they arrived home, Madeline ordered her son to sit down in the living room. Elijah continued doing as she said and sat on the couch. She paced around in front of him, still didn't know what exactly to say.

"Eli, I don't know what goes on in that head of yours" she emphasized, as she was already raising her voice. "Frankly, I don't want to know, but yet I still wonder what it is at the same time."

That was only a few words and his mom was already getting emotional.

"And it's pointless to ask because I know you don't wanna tell me. You don't tell me anything about what's going on! Not to mention that you'll get mad at me for invading on your life, WHICH I GAVE. If you don't wanna tell me anything, that's fine! But the least you can do is pretend that you're grateful because we do so much for you! We gave you a home, clothes, and food. Sometimes I feel like that's not enough"

Normally at that point, Elijah would try to give his perspective but giving so little information, like claiming that he learned his lesson and promise it wouldn't happen again. But to his mom, it was called talking back, which would extend the fight a little longer and they both would fire words at each other. Since Elijah saw himself for what he'd become, he chose not to say anything.

"What do you have to say for yourself?" his mom demanded.

Elijah took the courage to look his mom in the eye. "I'm…I'm sorry" he kept telling her, as he was starting to break down, but tried to hold it together.

But that was all he could say.

Madeline actually expected a little more. And she was a little surprised of how quiet her son was and could only imagined what it meant. Madeline needed the time to take it all in, but after all trouble; she felt that she shouldn't let Elijah off the hook that easily.

"You're grounded, Eli" she told him, "For a week. No watching TV, no playing outside, no having friends over, and no allowance! Do I make myself clear?"

Right away, Elijah nodded.

"I have to go back to work" his mom added, "Although I'd rather stay home but…" she was about to say something else, but chose not to, "Just don't anything reckless while we're gone".

Elijah nodded again. Then his mom left. The door slam echoed through the quiet house. After a moment of waiting for something else to happen, Elijah finally lied back against the couch and started breathing again it had been forever since he breathed in air. The dramatic effect still had Elijah shaking. Tears were slowing flowing out.

Don't cry, he kept telling himself. *Boys don't cry.*

After sitting in silence for about ten minutes, Elijah finally got up and slowly walked to his bedroom. The fight with Quinton replayed in his head; it went from that to all the irritation and discomfort that Quinton AND his friends caused.

He was halfway to his bedroom.

Then Elijah remembered ending his friendship with Paula and Andrew. Only now he imagined how they felt, most likely heartbroken, this was something Elijah was feeling now.

He was entering the doorway.

Jeff Tomly; that moment came back to him when he yelled at him in class.

Elijah then walked toward his bed.

Probably the most painful memory, when Sabrina had left when she made new friends. She must've thought what everyone else was thinking, that Elijah Khoda was too troubled to be any one's friend. He may have lost her for good, just after they spoke to each other at the store.

Elijah slammed his door closed like the whole world was after him. He leaned his head against the door and cried his eyes out for the first time in a while.

CHAPTER TWELVE

Elijah has a Heart

Things felt different after a nap. All the tension that built for a while finally eased. Maybe a good cry was what Elijah needed, since he had been holding everything in since the end of grade six, where it all started, when he only wanted something to call his own. In the end, it didn't feel as disappointing as it was before. It felt more like a fresh start. Maybe all that trouble wasn't all for nothing. Maybe life was trying to say something; perhaps that Elijah already had what he was looking for. Everything happens for a reason. And Elijah could only figure that out for himself.

Day one of suspension, Elijah's mom didn't seem as angry as she was before. Whenever, she spoke to him, it was as if she pretended their argument didn't happen. Without giving any thought, Elijah kept quiet, acted normal, and did what his mom told him to. He had supper with both his parents at the table. After that, Elijah stayed away from his TV, for that he wasn't allowed to watch it. Since there was nothing else to do, Elijah decided to clean his room.

At the end of the first day, Madeline came into her son's room. Elijah stopped what he was doing, as he could tell his mom had something to say. "Eli" she said, gently, "I think it's probably best that you start talking to a counselor again. I can tell there's something on your mind and if you won't tell me, you need to talk to someone"

Elijah said nothing.

"I'll call Ken and ask him if he can meet you next week at the school"

There was no protest. Elijah just nodded and agreed that he would talk to someone about all that had been going on. During the weekend, Elijah helped around with the house, doing one chore after another and even helped his dad with the firewood. Before that, he volunteered to wash the dishes for his mom. It was then, the silence between them had broken when she went up to him and gave him a hug. Doubt had been replaced with confidence. Living in fear wasn't an issue. Elijah Khoda felt like himself again, in a different way. As the suspension was almost over, it gave him enough time to think about what he had to do to make things right.

The first day back to school; the first thing Elijah did was to track down his old friends. He was rather eager to talk with them and didn't give a second thought. Luckily, Paula and Andrew were waiting together, like they were expecting him. They were waiting by the entrance. Elijah hid his excitement as he approached them.

"Hey, Paula, Andrew" Elijah greeted, gently.

They looked at him casually, like how they used to before.

"Welcome back" Andrew said, in a friendly tone.

"Thanks" then Elijah met Paula's eye, "I wanna talk to you guys"

"So do we" Paula said.

The three of them walked away from the entrance to talk somewhere a little more private. So they went near the pathway, where there were hardly any students.

"I was actually gonna come talk to you guys last Thursday, but Quinton just had to start a fight" Elijah explained.

"Yeah, you know what?" Andrew said, "We need to have some kind of signal or a code word, just in case he comes around"

"I hope he doesn't" Elijah replied, in a serious tone.

"Which is why we need a signal or a code word; what do you think is better, tapping a body part like they do in baseball or shout something like 'red pants-blue pants'?"

Elijah couldn't help but laugh. "That's funny"

"So pants it is!" Andrew agreed. Then another thought came to mind. "Or how about a sound effect? I can do the t-rex roar from Jurassic Park"

Andrew then tries to impersonate the roar, in a rather poorly way. It was hard not to laugh even at any failed jokes from Andrew Little, for that Elijah stood there, forming a smile on his face. "I kinda like it" Elijah proudly admitted, "It just seems…you".

"Hey, if you like that, you should hear the donkey sound I use to annoy my sister…"

"Can you guys hurry it up so we can talk before the bell rings?" Paula insisted, impatiently. She turned away for a second and then looked back at the boys, "But I'm glad to see you guys are talking again"

Elijah and Andrew exchanged looks, followed by a proud smile.

"Okay" Paula started, "It's been too long since we last spoke. And to be honest, I wasn't sure if we were still friends. So I'm dead serious when I say this, Eli…talk to us!"

There were already words written in Elijah's mind. He took his time before speaking. "Listen…the reason why I left you is because I wanted something else, something where nobody would tell me what to do. At least it's what I thought. But after a while, I realized I was wrong. Quinton and his friends are bad! They're…they're not like you guys"

Paula and Andrew continued to listen.

"I ended up hurting myself, and most of all, hurting you guys. I'm sorry…I really am. If you guys don't wanna be friends with me, I'll understand"

"Eli" Paula replied, gently, "If we didn't wanna be your friends, we wouldn't be standing here right now. While we're talking, I wanna ask because this has been bothering me. What about those things you said, about us not being good enough? Did you really mean that?"

That was one painful memory that Elijah hadn't forgotten. Now this was his chance to take back what he said. "No. I…I didn't mean it."

"So what did we do that made you so mad?" Paula said, right away, "Ever since grade six, you been very distant, like emotionally."

The conversation went a little deeper than Elijah thought. Paula was so sincere that she tried to prevent herself from breaking down.

"I was just upset. I was getting tired of things being the same. I... wanted something different, a life of my own maybe. I was getting tired of being treated like a little kid and everyone worrying about me, even when I just want to be left alone"

"Well, if you wanna be left alone, you just have to say it but say it nicely" Paula added, "And as your best friends, we'll understand. As our friend, you should understand that we look out for you because we care about you. We don't want you to destroy others or yourself because you're mad about something else. Sometimes you don't realize it and that's why we're here"

"Okay" Elijah replied, calmly.

"But I think the one thing that hurts me the most is when you don't say anything at all" Paula told him, "Because when we first became friends, Elijah, I told you that you can talk to me about anything, especially if it's something that's bothering you. But lately, I feel like that you don't wanna talk to me at all, like I did something wrong."

There was no blaming her.

Elijah paused to gather some thoughts. "I'm sorry, about everything. I don't mean to be like this, to you guys. I know now that I shouldn't. It's just...I been through a lot of bad things and sometimes I feel like they wouldn't leave me alone, even after it happened. I don't wanna be like this anymore. I really don't. And..." He then trailed off. There wasn't yet much wisdom for a twelve year old boy.

What he said made up for the long silence since they last spoke. It reduced Paula's worries and frustration. She went up to comfort him. "Eli, I think those things are still bothering you because you are letting them. It's all in your head. Don't let it get the best of you"

"Yeah, I guess" he said, sincerely, "That must be it"

"And Eli, what if the life you want is right in front of you and you just have to make the best of it?"

That was a new perspective.

"Yeah, remember what I said?" Andrew asked, "It's not fun unless we make it fun"

Elijah nodded, "Yeah, I can do that"

"And don't beat yourself up too much. I know things have been bad but think of them as lessons. Learn from them." Paula told him.

Elijah didn't say anything. He just gave a meaningful look.

"How are you feeling now?" she asked.

"I'm starting to feel a lot better" Elijah said.

Paula gave a soft smile.

"You know when I was with Quinton and them" Elijah started, "They weren't like you guys. They weren't really friends. They didn't have a sense of humor like Andrew. And they weren't really caring like you, Paula. All they did was just used me and teased me. They didn't really wanna be kids. I guess that was why I wanted to hang out with them. They wanted to do things on their own. But I realized that hanging out with Quinton and his friends are not as fun as hanging out with you guys. That's another reason I wanna hang out...with you guys again"

As Paula had her hand on Elijah's shoulder, she saw the relief in his eyes. It was a sign that she had gotten through to him. "We missed you, badly" she said, "Andrew, do you have anything to say?" she asked.

Andrew hesitated as his friends were waiting for him. "Yyyes" he replied, "I do. I just haven't thought of it yet" He cleared his throat and started approaching Elijah, "Please remember that I'm usually not good at these things. I'm too used to the funny stuff, you know. E.K, you're my bud, always have been. You're like...Agent J and I'm K. We're like Tommy and Chuckie. We fight together, play together. Without you, I would just be Andrew on my own show. That show would suck because you AND Paulie are not in it. So I'd rather keep this going. You know what I mean, right?"

"Yeah" Elijah replied, almost in a chuckle, "I think I do. And I'll be happy to keep the show going"

Then Andrew placed his hand on Elijah's other shoulder. Paula glanced over at Andrew. "Well, I think I speak for the both of us when I say...it's good to have you back!"

Elijah smiled, as his best friends came in closer to give him a hug.

"Yeaaaahhhhh!" Andrew cheered, and then went and wrapped his arms around Elijah and Paula, and started jumping up and down. It was silly but also a great moment. They were being who they were, kids. Elijah Khoda wouldn't have it any other way. After the little celebration, Paula went up and gave her best friend a hug, for that they reunited.

"Hey, now let's all hug ourselves" Andrew suggested.

In that moment, all three of them just felt so happy that they had to act a little silly. So then Elijah, Paula, and Andrew, wrapped their arms around themselves tightly and shook gently. They all laughed.

The bell rang. It was time for another day of school. So the three best friends walked proudly to the entrance, with their arms around each other.

Reconciling with Paula and Andrew was the first step. The next thing Elijah contemplated on was talking to Sabrina Clarin. He may not have been on his best behavior around her, especially if he cared so much. Soon he was about to find out if they were still friends.

Once the first recess had begun, Elijah went up to his friends right away and explained in a mature way that he needed to be excused and that he needed the space. It was probably best to talk to Sabrina alone. After all the grade seven students were outside, the entrance wasn't as crowded. She was starting to walk with her friends. Elijah took a deep breath.

"Men were born to be brave" he muttered.

Then he started making his way to Sabrina. And he recalled the conversation he had with his dad, if you want to have a serious conversation you have to mean what you say and it all starts with a simple question.

"Sabrina" Elijah called, gently, as he approached her. Just like that, he had her attention. "Can I talk to you?"

"Sure" she agreed. Then she glanced at both of her girlfriends, "I'll be right back".

The two girls waited as Sabrina went with Elijah. He wanted to have a private conversation, so he led her to the pathway where there was hardly anybody around. Elijah turned and faced Sabrina. He thought about it all morning about what he had to say.

"Sabrina...I just wanted to say that I'm sorry" he started.

"Sorry for what?" she wondered.

"For all the bad things I have done. I-I yelled at Jeff in front of the class and I started a fight the other day and got suspended. I, uh..."

He trailed off for a moment as he looked into Sabrina's eyes. It had been a while since he saw those beautiful eyes. It felt like sitting across from her in class again. Elijah missed those days.

"I'm not really a good kid, Sabrina" Elijah admitted. It was the moment of truth. "I have a temper and I even was sent to the principal's office a few times..."

A familiar feeling was coming back to him, the same one he felt when he first saw her. It made their conversation emotional. Elijah wasn't expecting that. It took him a moment to hold it together.

"But I...I'm trying not to be like that anymore. Sabrina, I think you're a great...girl...friend" Elijah never once had a serious conversation with a girl. He wasn't exactly sure what to say. Calling her girl would've probably offended her, which was why he ended up saying friend instead.

"You're a great friend" Elijah rephrased, "And I don't wanna ruin everything. So if you're mad at me, I'll understand"

That was all Elijah had to say. Then he bowed his head in shame. He looked at the ground and only saw Sabrina's feet.

"Why would I be mad?" Sabrina said.

A nice feeling of relief struck Elijah. He was left speechless as he slowly looked back and met Sabrina's eyes.

"What, you're not..." he tried to speak.

"No, of course not" she answered right away.

Elijah was strongly surprised. It seemed too good to be true.

"But I yelled at Jeff in front of class...I thought...I thought he was your friend".

Then Sabrina looked a little puzzled. "Jeff and I aren't friends".

Just hearing that lifted more weight off Elijah's shoulders.

"Really?" Elijah was still uncertain, "But I saw you guys laughing and talking, back in October-last month"

Sabrina seemed confused. She looked away, blankly, trying to remember.

"You guys were by the pencil sharpener and I saw him talking to you"

Sabrina's mind finally came back to the present. "Oh, right! I remember now. That was nothing, really. I just got up to sharpen my pencil and then Jeff did the same thing. He was just talking about how pencil sharpeners can be tough. I just listened"

So the thought of Jeff Tomly replacing Elijah as Sabrina's friend was all a hoax!

"So you and Jeff are NOT friends?" Elijah asked, like his life depended on it.

"Not at all" Sabrina admitted, "We didn't talk anymore after that".

Staring absently, Elijah's jaw dropped and his eyes were blinking. The whole issue with Jeff was no longer a problem. But there was another issue they needed to discuss. "Uh, w-what about when I got suspended?" he asked, "You didn't think I was...a troublemaker?"

"Well, I admit, I was a little surprised when I saw the fight" Sabrina told him, "And after you got suspended, I was like 'oh I hope Elijah is okay'. But yeah, I just felt bad for you and I'm glad you're okay".

Surprised and greatly relieved. It was much better than Elijah expected. And the fact that Sabrina was concerned about him brought comfort.

"So you have a few flaws" she continued, "That doesn't mean you're a bad person"

"Flaws?" Elijah replied.

"It means you're not perfect, like you have a bad temper but your friends still like you for who you are, if that makes any sense"

Elijah was thinking about what she just said. "I think it does"

"And I know that you're not a bad person" Sabrina added, "I know because I saw the good side of you. And you admit all your faults. Not a lot of people do that"

To her eyes, Elijah felt like he was one of a kind and that flattered him.

"Well, thanks" At that point, Elijah didn't know what else to say, for that he still repeated Sabrina's words in his mind.

Sabrina looked at him sincerely and then went up to him and gave him a hug. That was one thing Elijah did not expect. In that moment, all of Elijah's problems went away as he felt Sabrina's arm wrapped around him, bringing comfort and warmth. Then he decided to take advantage of the moment and returned the hug. They held each other for a moment. In the end, they let each other go.

"Is there anything else you wanna say?" Sabrina asked, nicely.

There was something actually.

"I miss you, Sabrina" Elijah said, sincerely. He was actually about to cry but he tried not to. It was a lot to take in while trying to have a heart to heart conversation. "I miss sitting beside you in class. And most of all, I miss hanging out with you"

"Aww, I miss you too" she replied.

Talking to Sabrina again and reconnecting was merely a fresh start. Elijah felt like there could be more and so he asked her for a request.

"Sabrina, do you wanna walk around the school like old times?" he asked, gently.

First thing Sabrina did was glancing back at her girlfriends, who were still near the entrance. "I would like to, but just let me check with my friends, okay?"

"Okay" he agreed.

Then Sabrina went back to consult with Carly and Melanie. Elijah waited patiently. That exciting feeling was starting to come back as well, just thinking that he was about to hang out with Sabrina Clarin again. It had been too long. After a short moment, she came back to Elijah, who was still on the pathway.

"The girls are okay with it" Sabrina told him, "Shall we walk?"

Yes! Elijah thought. One of the best things about life is when you have moments that you hadn't planned on, but just happens. And Elijah didn't think he would spend recess alone with that one special person.

So Elijah and Sabrina walked side by side as they left the pathway and began walking. They passed the exterior of the library and soon came across the area where the grade four students resided.

"The good thing about walking is that keeps you warm in a weather like this" Sabrina explained.

"Really?"

"Yeah, once you move your body a lot, it warms your body up" she added.

"Huh, I guess I should've known"

They passed by the younger students, who were hanging around while some were playing in the snow. Elijah and Sabrina soon passed the exterior of the classrooms, where the windows were un-blinded. As they reached the end, Elijah peeked into the one window of the one classroom that was once his. There he saw nothing but empty desks and the lights were turned off.

"You know, this is where me and Andrew first met" Elijah explained.

"Yeah?"

"We were in grade four. Andrew moved here from Edmonton and we been friends since"

"Cool"

"Yeah; he was the first person that made me laugh"

"He is pretty funny" Sabrina agreed, "We all need to laugh sometimes. It's what my mom always said. So you're lucky to have a friend like Andrew"

Elijah realized how lucky he was, like he just realized it for the first time. Not only Andrew gave him something to laugh about but he was brave enough to help Elijah to get out of the conflict with Quinton. No other person could've done what Andrew did.

"Come on, let's keep going" Elijah said.

They both made it to the other side of the school building. There was a clear path from the snow, the same area where the tire swings were, just up ahead.

"So were you born in Burns Lake?" Sabrina asked, as they walked. Elijah felt like he was meeting Sabrina all over again. Only this time, he knew what to say. It was quite extraordinary.

"Yeah, I grew up here" Elijah answered, honestly, "Not many people like it, but I kinda do, because...well its home"

"I think that's what matters, how you think and if it feels like home...then its home"

"Yeah" Elijah agreed, "Where were you born?"

"Smithers Hospital, but I grew up in Granisle, as you already know"

Elijah and Sabrina entered the back of the school, just beside the grade five entrance. "I see you made new friends" he acknowledged. He didn't think he would mention Sabrina's girlfriends, after secretly being mad at them for taking her away from him.

"Melanie and Carly? They're pretty cool. I like them"

As they were walking, Sabrina turned around and started walking backwards as she was facing Elijah. "I never really had friends like them before, like with other girls I mean. So it's kinda nice"

"Be careful or you'll slip" Elijah warned, ignoring her story.

Then they stopped. Sabrina glanced to the ground and back to Elijah. "I know. YOU be careful"

That sounded like a challenge. Elijah tried not to smile, as he wasn't sure if she was joking or not. He continued walking but Sabrina was still walking backwards, like she did it for sport. Then Elijah slowed down as he realized that his new friend was being playful. Sabrina walked in the same manner as he did, slow and then casual.

"What are you doing?" he asked. For a brief moment, Elijah thought maybe Sabrina was trying to prove a point.

"Having a little fun, what are you doing?" she replied, with a little proud smile.

"Just walking" Elijah said, casually.

"How about this, we take three steps and then we switch places but without stopping?" Sabrina challenged.

Elijah didn't give it much thought. "Okay" he agreed. Like so, they continued walking. Elijah kept going forward, while Sabrina walked backwards. After three steps, they quickly but gently switched places; now Elijah had to walk while facing the opposite direction, while Sabrina walked forward.

They took three steps again.

Then they switched.

Sabrina was laughing just a little and it brought a smile to Elijah's face. He looked ahead and saw a few students coming their way.

"What if you bump into someone?" he asked.

"Then tell me which way to step" she told him.

Their peers were getting closer.

"This way" Elijah called, pointing to his right.

Sabrina did as he said and took a step in that direction. The other students had passed them.

"One, two, three" Sabrina said. Then they changed places.

As their little game continued, there were a group of students up ahead of them. They changed places again after three steps, and again. It was Sabrina's turn to say which way to go.

"To your right" she called.

But Elijah stepped the wrong way. He was already getting close to the group of kids.

"The other way" Sabrina warned.

Then he finally stepped to his right and avoided the other students. After that, Elijah and Sabrina stopped.

"I could've crashed into them like bowling pins" Elijah joked.

Sabrina chuckled, "You did fine though".

Elijah nodded. "That was fun"

Then he led the way and they both approached the monkey bars, where some students were playing around. From there, Elijah's mind went blank, just taking in the fact that he still had his friends, even after all the trouble that he caused. They walked in silence until they reached the field. Together they both gazed at the snowy environment. Sabrina stood beside him and could tell something was maybe bothering him.

"What's wrong?" Sabrina asked.

"Oh, uh, nothing" he claimed, as he glanced over to her, "I was just thinking"

"About?"

Everything was alright at that point. But then Elijah looked at Sabrina, like really looked into her eyes and just felt a connection that felt greater than before. And then Elijah remembered the one issue he tried to forget about a month ago.

"You know, I thought you might've forgotten about me, Sabrina" he told her, sincerely.

"What makes you say that?"

He recalled that one particular moment he tried saying hi to Sabrina, but she was busy talking to her friends and barely said anything to him.

"Well, I'm not sure if you remember, but that one day I tried talking to you but you were already talking with your friends. You only said hi and that was it. I thought maybe I was bothering you"

"Aww, Elijah, I didn't mean to give you that impression!" Sabrina said, "It's just that Carly was in the middle of telling me something serious and I didn't wanna be rude. But I guess I was being rude to you and for that I'm sorry"

He looked into her eyes and saw the sincerity. "It's alright"

"Yeah, I got nothing against you at all" she added, "You're a good apple"

Elijah then looked at her a little funny. "Apple?" he repeated.

"It's an expression. You know how some people say, 'oh he's a bad apple'. It's a way of saying that person is bad"

"Oh okay, I see what you mean" Elijah said, promptly, "Yeah, kinda like that one Aaron Carter song?"

Sabrina looked at him surprised, "You listen to Aaron Carter?"

There was a paused moment, "Yeah?"

"Well, that's good. It's just I thought all boys didn't listen to pop music"

"I listen to some. I listen to pretty much any kind of music" Elijah told her.

"Me too!"

Music; that was another thing that they had in common!

"Well, you're a good apple too" Elijah said.

The compliment put a smile on Sabrina's face, "Thank you"

Elijah felt a little silly that he just had to giggle, which brightened up the moment with laughter.

"So are we good now?" Sabrina asked, "You're not mad at me or anything?"

"No, I think we're good. But I just wanna ask, is it okay that we can hang out sometimes?"

Sabrina nodded, "Yeah, for sure! It depends what me and the girls are doing, but I think they'll be okay with it"

So Elijah didn't lose Sabrina at all. It was almost as if she was right by his side the whole time. And he was thankful for that. Just when he thought he needed a change of scenery, Elijah realized that he already had what he needed. It was overthinking that caused him to go through a reckless phase, only because there were problems that weren't even there. And Elijah felt lucky that hadn't lost his way, for that he still had her in his life.

"Oh, Sabrina" Elijah said. Something else had come back to him.

"Yeah?"

"Happy birthday" he told her, "I know it was a few weeks ago. It's just I never got to say it to you in person"

Sabrina was surprised and flattered that he remembered her birthday.

"Aww, thank you" she replied, kindly.

They stared at each other. After patching things up, everything felt normal again, but in a better way somehow and definitely more than Elijah expected. The bond between him and Sabrina felt more singular. And Paula and Andrew were still by his side like always. Elijah wouldn't have it any other way.

After a moment of silence, a few snowflakes came between them. Elijah and Sabrina looked up to the sky, only to realize that it was snowing! There was a little touch of cold spread on their face as more snow was flowing down on them.

"It's snowing" Elijah pointed out.

"I know" Sabrina said.

As they were gazing to the white sky, Elijah slowly looked back at Sabrina. Their eyes met. And then Sabrina stuck her tongue out just to catch some snowflakes. A little happiness lit up inside Elijah and came out in laughter. Then Sabrina laughed with him. Elijah did the same and started catching snowflakes with his tongue. But that was only the beginning, for that they both paced around to wherever the snow was falling, trying to catch more, almost like they were competing against each other. Elijah couldn't be happier that he reunited with his friends just before the holiday season, where everyone would come together and celebrate, Christmas!

Once recess was over, they both went back to the front of the school to meet up with their classmates. They were in the lineup. Elijah was right behind Sabrina.

"Hey, Sabrina" Elijah called.

She looked over her shoulder and met his eyes.

"I'm glad we're still friends" he told her.

Sabrina gave a warming smile. Her smile was always nice to see.

"We'll always be friends" Sabrina promised.

All the students were back in class just after they finally got all the snow off their hair and coats. Elijah put his coat away and put on his indoor shoes. Just as he was making his way back to his desk, he noticed Jeff Tomly was at his desk, alone. Elijah knew the next thing he had to do. With courage, he went up to his classmate.

"Hey Jeff" Elijah greeted, gently.

Tomly turned around and saw Elijah standing next to him.

"Hey, I just wanna say that I'm sorry, for yelling at you in class last month" Elijah had no excuse; even if he wanted to explain his reasons but just didn't how to put it. So he waited patiently for Jeff's response.

"You know, this whole time I thought there was something wrong with you" Jeff said, after a moment of silence, "But now I'm convinced, you're all right. So apology accepted"

Elijah merely nodded. He felt that he did his part and that no further words were necessary. After that, both boys moved on.

CHAPTER THIRTEEN

Dream Girl

After about an hour into class, there was a knock on the door. Everyone turned to see who it was, a young man, who wore glasses and dressed nicely. Elijah recognized him right away. Ken Peterson. Mrs. Parker went and answered the door and spoke to each other in low voices. It was a brief interaction. Then Mrs. Parker turned around.

"Elijah" she called, gently, "Ken Peterson would like to see you"

He looked and saw Ken standing in the doorway with a friendly smile on his face. Elijah did as he was told, got up from his desk and met with the counselor.

"Elijah" Ken greeted.

"Hi, Ken"

The counselor turned towards the teacher, "I'll have him back soon as possible".

Once the classroom door closed, Elijah and Ken began catching up. "So how you been, Elijah? It's been a while since we last saw each other"

"Yeah, I haven't seen you since grade six"

"And now you're in grade seven. Where has the time gone?"

"Ha-ha, I don't know" Elijah added.

"Who knows, right?" Ken agreed with a polite smile, "Well, let's talk somewhere a little more private, shall we?"

209

There was a room just outside the classrooms. It was a small room, where they often held Language Arts sessions or any other studies. The room included a table with four chairs, followed by extra stacked up against the wall. And there was a white board. Elijah and Ken sat across from each other.

"So Elijah" Ken started, "As you probably already knew, your mom called me and asked me to see you, and here we are; I trust that you remember how our little meetings work?"

"Anything I say is just between us"

"That's right, completely confidential" Ken promised.

Elijah liked Ken. He was friendly, patient, smart, and a good listener. They first started seeing each other since Elijah's first conflict with Brian Kidman back in fifth grade. Ken was probably the only grownup that Elijah felt comfortable around and that he could tell him anything, not just about his problems but also a friendly conversation about his daily life.

"So...I know this is a few months late, but how was your summer?" Ken asked, nicely.

"It was good. We went to Old Fort, but that was about it"

"Right, I remember you telling me about Old Fort last time. Was it just as nice?"

"Yeah, nice and sunny, sometimes too hot" Elijah told him.

Then Ken shared his story about his summer, travelling out of town to see family. After that topic, they began talking about Elijah's schooling, just all the general things, a different teacher, and the fact that Elijah was almost finished elementary school. And then home was the next topic, which had no problems there. That was usually how their meetings start, by talking about the casual life until they had to start talking about the problems.

"So Elijah, is there anything you wanna talk about?" Ken offered, "Anything that might be bothering you"

Completely confidential, just like Ken said; so Elijah wasn't afraid to talk about the trouble he had got into lately.

"Start anywhere, take your time" he encouraged.

First Elijah gathered some thoughts before speaking. Then he started with the fight he had with Quinton Malcolm and he explained the reason for the fight. Talking about it didn't hurt that much, unlike the confrontation with Brian Kidman, which startled him for a little while. Before Elijah realized it, his strength had grown a little stronger.

"So how are you feeling now?" Ken asked, gently.

"I'm feeling okay. After my suspension, I reunited with my friends, my REAL friends, Paula and Andrew"

Elijah almost mentioned Sabrina but since he kept it to himself for a while, he automatically stopped before he said anything further.

"Well, that's good" Ken said.

And that led to the next topic. Elijah explained the time when he left Paula and Andrew to join Quinton and his gang, in which he was fully honest about. Naturally, that led him to talking about how he wanted a change of scenery.

"And you wanted a change because…?" Ken wondered.

"Because I was tired of things being the same; ever since grade six, things were pretty much the same, getting up every morning, coming to school, seeing Paula and Andrew, all that was getting kinda boring after a while. But that was the old me"

Ken nodded. "So after that fight, you had been feeling refreshed, more like a different person?"

That would make sense because Elijah felt that something was different, considering he faced his own problems and tried not to get away with his faults. And the one major difference was when Elijah actually saw himself through everyone's eyes after yelling at Jeff in class and after fighting Quinton. Most likely something did change and Elijah was finally starting to see the answer.

There was a paused moment, for that there wasn't any mention of Jeff Tomly. Elijah's mind wandered off as he revisited that issue in class and that pointed to one person, Sabrina Clarin. Just thinking about her brought back that one feeling that's been there since the first day of school. Ken noticed Elijah's mental absence.

"Elijah?" he said, gently, "Are you okay?"

Shaking his head slightly, Elijah put his mind back in the right frame.

"It kinda looked like you were miles away there" Ken mentioned.

"Oh yeah, I'm fine, I was…just thinking"

"About what, if you don't mind my asking?"

Those words were similar to that one conversation Elijah had with Sabrina and that brought him back to early that morning. It projected in his head like the silver screen. There was Sabrina, with her perfect long dark brown hair and beautiful eyes. Snowflakes came down and they both started catching them with their tongues. Elijah started to smile a little.

"Whatever it is, it's certainly put you in a good mood" Ken said.

The smile disappeared. Ken could tell that he was witnessing a different behavior.

"So are you okay, Elijah?" he repeated.

When they first spoke two years ago, Elijah did the exact same thing, only that there was anger and sadness written all over his face. This time, it was quite mysterious, staring blankly for a long moment and then suddenly smiling again. Ken would rather not put any pressure on Elijah. So he remained patient.

"I'm fine" There was another pause, "I think".

Now it was getting confusing. Elijah convinced himself that he was fine but that feeling inside of him still floated around. It was hard to tell if it was good or bad. Even when he first left his friends, that feeling got the best of him and flustered his emotions. Maybe that was the reason for his behavior.

"You think?" Ken replied, gently.

Elijah had the option to mention Sabrina or not. Ever since that day in September, he didn't want anyone to know that he liked her, not even his own parents, all because of the fact that she was a girl and maybe his mom would forbid him from having a relationship just for being too young. Talking about his other problems didn't really bother Elijah that much. The only thing that was taking its toll on him was that one feeling. And maybe Ken was the only person he could talk to about it.

"Well…" Elijah spoke, "Ever since the first day of school, I've had this feeling inside of me"

Ken didn't say a word.

"I don't know what it is but I just feel it"

It was something he couldn't put into a speech. The thoughts were just piled on top of each other.

"I made a new friend, Ken. I met her on the first day of school. Her name is Sabrina, Sabrina Clarin. She sat beside me in class and when I looked at her, that's when I started feeling it. And it's been like that since"

That was the first time Elijah mentioned Sabrina's name to anyone other than his friends. He looked at Ken, like he was waiting for an explanation. There was a look in Ken's eye, like he already knew the answer. Then he sat back into his seat, glanced away briefly and then turned his attention back to his student.

"Well, Elijah…"

A moment of truth.

"…it sounds like you're in love"

Elijah just stared blankly and didn't say another word.

In love; so that was it.

Love; so that's what it was the whole time. Ever since hearing that word, Elijah looked at all the things that happened, differently. It would explain that feeling inside him when he first laid eyes on Sabrina Clarin. That's what he was running from when he left Paula and Andrew. That was the reason why he yelled at Jeff Tomly in class, it was because he was jealous that Jeff even spoke to Sabrina. That was also probably why Elijah had an interest in June Disher, since he felt like he couldn't have Sabrina and pretended that June was Sabrina. Elijah recapped the last three months with his jaw dropped, for that he realized how much his life had really changed. That feeling didn't just help him feel love but it also made him want to be different, perhaps in a better way.

Elijah's meeting with Ken had to wrap up because it was time to go back to class. Just approaching the door gave that feeling of excitement, just knowing that one special person was about to appear. Elijah knocked on the door. As he was waiting for his teacher to let him in, he peered at Sabrina, who was sitting with her group. Mrs. Parker let Elijah in, who still hadn't taking his eyes off Sabrina. This time there was something different about looking at her. That feeling inside started to spread and touched his heart like he never felt it before.

The thought of love was running through Elijah's mind for the rest of the day. He was able to turn it on and off whenever he mingled with reality. Every now and then, he would look over at Sabrina, just to see her. Peering from a distance was one thing, but when Elijah approached her up close, he realized how she truly embodied that beauty, long dark brown hair, clean white skin, pink lips, with a down to earth personality filled with strength and kindness. Sabrina Clarin was more than just a girl in the same class, she was a beautiful soul! And Elijah Khoda was in love with her!

Love, girls, feelings; those are the three things Elijah never gave any thought to. Normally, boys wouldn't give any thought to such a thing. Boys would usually ride bikes, play videogames, go on adventures and tell different versions of that adventure. And girls were merely children that boys would have to share the world with, but not all of them couldn't be friends.

Up until grade seven, there were only two girls that defined that gender, Melissa Hartway, who gave Elijah the impression that girls were mean and could be natural enemies to boys. And then there was Paula Hennig, who showed that some girls were caring companions, considering she had been friends with Elijah since primary school, but Paula was more like a sister. Now there's Sabrina Clarin who defined girls could be more than just friends. They were symbols of beauty, passion, and love. Their smiles were as bright as the sun and their inner beauty shined like stars in the night sky.

The more Elijah thought about Sabrina, the crazier he was about her. Not only he wanted to see her but he wanted to be with her. Every morning he'd arrive at school on time, just to see her and say hi. During the day, Elijah would look over his shoulder to gaze at Sabrina without her knowing. And after school, Elijah wouldn't leave without saying goodbye to her.

Time went on and the thoughts went deeper, and that feeling inside of Elijah had him in a harness, for that love had consumed him. Whenever Elijah was at home, he started to feel isolated because of the distance between him and Sabrina Clarin. Soon he was missing her and wondered if she thought about him. After a while, it was getting rather lonely that Elijah started to daydream about Sabrina sitting right beside him. There was no talking, just the two of them, enjoying each other's company.

Daydreaming was one thing. Love was the other. Before love was something that was only between grownups, the kind that involved passion and intimacy. It would be forbidden to any child's eye. But eventually, everyone grows up. And Elijah was at that age where the term love had him wondering about such thing and wanted to explore it somehow. The first thing he turned to was TV, particularly the music channel, recalling the times when he came across music videos that were about love. And there, Elijah saw love through the artist's eyes and expressed one's feelings towards another in a profound and artistic way, yet it was quite deep that made Elijah want to feel the same way about Sabrina.

It wasn't enough. Elijah felt that he had to see love almost from every standpoint. After music, the next was films. During one weekend, Elijah and his dad took a trip to the local video store. Searching the place, he found the drama selection that included many romance movies, several of them were mature themed. Elijah knew he had to find something decent. After examining different titles, he came across one called Picture You. The front cover of the movie included a boy and a girl, just a little older than Elijah. It was close to his predicament, so he went and chose that.

Elijah watched the movie later that evening.

Picture You was about a boy who met a girl and developed a close relationship. Soon they both became more than friends, for that they fell in love. And the boy had artistic skills. He could draw pictures simply with a pencil. Together, he and the girl drew one picture from each day they spent together and eventually they would draw the full picture. The movie was deep and yet it had a lot of heart that soon it connected with Elijah, for that he was thinking about the one girl he liked. Throughout the film, there were many intimate moments that caught the eye. There was love and passion, unlike anything Elijah had seen before.

That movie had changed the way Elijah thought about Sabrina. Before he would think about her with heart and kindness, but now love had colored his thoughts into something else. It became more erotic and desirable.

The following night came. Elijah was lying on his bed with his eyes to the ceiling. He was able to clear his mind after fantasizing about Sabrina Clarin. Was it wrong to think about her or any other girl like that? Elijah couldn't help but feel a little bad as if somebody read his mind. So then he took deep breaths, exhaled, and relaxed. Things were calm again. Elijah rested his head on his pillow. His mind was blank and then he went back to the beginning.

It was the first day of school, with nothing to look forward to, but homework.

Stepping into class like the previous years.

Sabrina...

Then sitting at the desk.

Long dark brown hair...

All it took was one peer over the shoulder.

Eyes so clear that you can see reflection of the world around you...

And there she was...Sabrina Clarin!

Sabrina, Sabrina, Sabrina Clarin, a five syllable name-just like Elijah Khoda-had permanently imprinted into his mind. The name itself was just a starting point, soon her face appeared and then her eyes opened. From the moment, her eyes met Elijah's, it felt like he was not just looking at a person, it was more like…life…was looking back at him, a life that has taking a beautiful form and it just happened to move to Elijah's hometown of Burns Lake. Since then, it silenced all of Elijah's problems and showed him a whole new side to life, a place that he didn't know existed, a place where love lived upon. Maybe someday, he and Sabrina could go there together.

Elijah Khoda could not have been born into a better generation. What if he was born into a different era? Would he have met someone different, if so would he have felt the same way? What if Elijah lived in another province, another country? There was no way that he could've met someone like Sabrina Clarin! She was young, in fact the same age as Elijah. They both liked music and movies. She was the kind of girl that simply enjoyed life and brought out a new side to Elijah that he didn't know that he had. If there was one thing he didn't know about girls, he certainly didn't expect one that made him want to be a better person. All these thoughts made him realize how lucky he was!

Elijah then closed his eyes and began to dream.

He imagined a world where it was just the two of them, together, inseparable, talking, laughing, and seeing themselves through each other's eyes. They would be watching movies together, listening to music and going for walks. It was just a world with the two of them, no school, no grownups, no responsibilities, just enjoying life. Elijah and Sabrina would design it by painting every detail and background with their heart. It was a world where time was infinite and they would be young forever.

"Eliijahhhh" a voice called.
The clouds in the sky faded and there the sun shined down, where the trees and grass grew.
"Eliijahhh" the voice repeated, in a gentle and graceful way.

Elijah finally opened his eyes. Then he got up and looked around. His name was being called by that same voice. He followed it to see where it was coming from. After walking up hills, there he saw someone standing the distance. It had to be her that was calling. Elijah began to run. It still seemed pretty far, even with every step he took. As the wind picked up again, he was suddenly running faster, almost like he was flying! He finally caught up to that person.

It was Sabrina!

She turned around and their eyes met.

"There you are!" she sounded greatly relieved to see him, "Here I thought you were a thousand miles away"

Elijah chuckled, "I was close. I'll always be close"

"And not just you and me standing here, but close in our hearts?"

"Yeah" Elijah admitted.

There was nothing but silence, as they gazed at each other.

"You didn't just run all the way here to have a starring contest, did you?" she asked.

Elijah thought for a moment. "Maybe I did" he said with confidence.

"Oh" Sabrina replied, gently, "Okay then"

She stepped in closer, with her eyes widening a little. Elijah played along and did the same. Finally, Sabrina stuck her tongue out and they both broke into laughter. Elijah played along and stuck his tongue out to the corner of his mouth and crossed his eyes. Then Sabrina strongly lowered her eyebrows, showed her teeth, like she was trying to impersonate a monster. Once the laughter faded, Elijah and Sabrina looked at each other.

"Well, what are we waiting for?" Sabrina said, "Let's go see the world!"

"Right behind you" Elijah promised.

"I'm sure you wouldn't let me win that easily" she challenged.

"Haha, we'll see"

Then they both started running, both ran as fast as they could. Just when Elijah was ahead, he saw Sabrina at the corner of his eye. She was catching up. They were halfway across the field. Soon, they were reaching the hillside. They were focusing harder than ever. As the end approached, none of them gave a single thought once they leaped off the top of the hill. *The wind blew hard enough for them to glide. Together they were off ground and it felt like the world below them was getting smaller. Sabrina was giggling. Elijah was speechless but still maintained the heart and excitement. It got even more exciting as they were gliding to the ground.*

"Woooo!" Elijah cheered.

Sabrina seconds the motion as she let out a louder cheer.

The ground was closer. They both lowered their feet. Once they made contact with the earth, they were running but they shortly tripped and rolled in the grass. To their surprise, they ended up laughing. As they lied there, Elijah and Sabrina looked over at each other.

"Haha, that was fun!" she said.

"It sure was" he agreed, with a smile.

Then Elijah looked up and saw small town, except it wasn't really a town. There were only a few buildings of their interest and they were all lined up as if it were a main street. And it was decorated with trees all around. Outside that little town was a sign entitled…OUR WORLD.

"Come on, Sabrina" Elijah insisted, "Catch me if you can"

He got up and started running with Sabrina chasing after him.

"Oh no, you don't" she replied, playfully.

As they were getting closer to their world, Sabrina caught up to Elijah and jumped on his back. To his surprise, he just started to laugh and she did as well.

"You've been caught!" Sabrina said.

"Haha you got me"

She then stood back on her feet and they stopped to look at each other for a moment.

"I know" she said, proudly.

So now they both stepped into their world. The street was wide and paved smoothly with cement. Their first stop was the ice cream stand; nobody in there but them, and the ice cream was all free. They each got their own dessert and continued walking down the street.

Next they were playing videogames at one of the buildings, in which the entire space was one gaming room. It had shelves of the games that Elijah ever played and the ones he always wanted. Sabrina was a fast learner.

220 PHILIP PATRICK

Together they both played games with each other and then against each other.

They continued on by walking down the street. Just like what they did in reality, Elijah walked forwards while Sabrina was walking backwards. After three steps, they switched places. After just taking a couple of steps, Elijah tripped and fell.

"Whoa!" he said, rather calmly.

Sabrina giggled, mildly, "Did you do that on purpose?"

He was actually just about to admit it but decided to play at the last minute. Elijah then looked over at his elbow and pretended to groan painfully. Nearly convinced, Sabrina went over to attend him. By the time she realized his elbow was fine, she felt a little kiss on her cheek. Sabrina looked at him, not saying anything. Then she leaned in and returned the kiss on his cheek.

The next thing Elijah imagined was them at a movie theater, one date that he would just love to have with his dream girl. In this auditorium, there were only two seats just for them. The lights dimmed down and they were drawn into the movie world.

After that, music became the next priority. There was a dance floor in their world where the music started once setting foot on it and above it, had rigs of lights to flash all around. The music was loud and gave it out a great vibe. Elijah was dancing his heart out and then offered his hand to Sabrina, which she gracefully accepted and joined him. The song was fast paced and made them in move in exaggerated ways. In the end, a slow song started to play. Elijah and Sabrina looked at each other, intimately. They moved closer and put their arms around each other and moved slowly to the music.

Once that part was over, they made it to a tree in the middle of their world. It was in the center of a fountain. "Look, Sabrina" Elijah encouraged. As they both gazed at the tree, some flowers emerged out of the branches, just like in Sabrina's drawing. Astonished, her jaw dropped. Then Elijah went to step on the fountain to grab a flower and gave it to Sabrina, who was grateful. She thanked him by giving him a hug. Since then, they become intimately close, for that they started to hold hands. They walked, peacefully.

At their last destination, they arrived at the ocean where they were a sandy beach and waves stretching out to shore. Elijah and Sabrina sat together and admired the view, where the sunset reflected off the water. They both looked at each other, meaningfully. Soon, they leaned in for a kiss, not on the cheek but on the lips.

No school, no responsibilities, no grownups; just them, in their perfect world.

In the end, Elijah was lying down with Sabrina by his side. They gazed towards the night sky that helmed many stars.

Opening his eyes, Elijah was in his bedroom, looking to the ceiling. His mind went blank again.

"Sabrina".

All it took was one name to put Elijah into an emotional state. That feeling inside would grow bigger and set off all kinds of emotions, excitement, love, passion, yet there was sadness. Why did it make Elijah sad? He did not know; maybe because he missed her, even when they were separated until the next school day. There was nothing else he could think of that could explain that emptiness inside of him.

At the same time, just thinking about Sabrina made Elijah a little excited, knowing that he someone special to see every day and to build their friendship and maybe someday, a beautiful relationship. It also made Elijah feel ambitious, like he would do anything for Sabrina, buy her almost any gift she wanted, dream big and someday make it happen, a journey for only the two of them, and most of all, to better himself just to be with her.

The school year started off rather dull, but now Elijah Khoda had found something that made his life meaningful. It gave him a purpose and the possibilities of adventures, while having someone special by his side. It was unexpected, but then again, life was full of surprises. There was certainly more than school, being disciplined, and doing chores.

There was beauty, love, another life waiting to meet another. And it all started when a boy and a girl looked at each other in class. From there, there were feelings from within that formed life in a beautiful way. And love had taking a part in the boy's life just when he found a new female companionship. Elijah Khoda had finally accepted the truth, he had a crush on Sabrina Clarin and he wanted her to be his girlfriend.

CHAPTER FOURTEEN

Holiday Spirits

December.

Christmas was getting closer by each day. The decorations everywhere was giving that feel-good vibe and the thought of bringing everyone together made it special, especially when having friends and family you cared about. Elijah was feeling blessed. Since reuniting with Andrew, Paula, and Sabrina, he was enjoying every minute of it and made up for lost times.

"I always try to make a snowball, like the ones you see in cartoons?" Andrew said, as he was shaping a chunk of snow with his hands. "All round and not a single bump"

"Yeah, I tried doing the same thing too" Elijah told him, as he was trying to make the perfect snowball with his hands.

"Out of all the things that can't be real, why can't this one be in the real world?" Andrew added. Then he glanced over at Paula, who was standing there watching them. "Paulie, why don't you try to help me to make my dreams come true?"

She just chuckled. "Last time your dream was to have your own secret laboratory"

"And now it's to make the perfect snowball" Andrew replied promptly. Then he leaned over to Elijah. "E.K, you think this is good enough?" he asking, showing him the little snowball he made.

"Uh, it's got little bit of bumps" Elijah replied.

Then Andrew gripped the snowball with his hand, "Ah well, doesn't matter", and there he threw it at Paula, which flew passed her head.

"Ha, you missed" Paula called.

"That's alright. There's snow everywhere, I got millions of chances!"

Paula gave a sigh, "Well, I can tell you this, it won't be as fun as grade four because I stopped pretending to be scare-"

Then another snowball came and hit Paula on the shoulder. This time it didn't come from Andrew. It came from Elijah.

"You got plenty of chances to fight back, Paula" Elijah advised, "What are you waiting for?"

Paula then formed a grimly smile and gathered some snow from around her, while Elijah and Andrew did the same. And the snowball fight began. First it was the boys against the girl. Then shortly, the three of them started throwing snowballs at each other.

They were inseparable like before. And this time, Elijah was thinking about how much his presence mattered to Andrew and Paula, as he devoted his mind and heart to the present and not worrying too much about Sabrina Clarin. After letting Sabrina have her space, one day Elijah decided to say hi to her. She was near the entrance, hanging out with Carly and Melanie. He stood by and watched them walking in the snow.

"Um, what are you doing, Mel?" Carly asked.

"I'm marking the snow with my feet!" Melanie claimed.

"That's it?"

"Well, there's nothing else to do. We walked around the school like twice and since we didn't bring any crazy carpets of our own, I'm just gonna see how deep this snow is"

Followed by Sabrina, Melanie took big steps into the snow. Each step buried deeper into the now. Finally, Carly decided to join them.

Soon the girls were moving carefully once they felt the snow reach closer to their knees.

"Watch this" Sabrina insisted. Then she leaped out of the snow, landing just a few inches in front of Melanie.

"Well, that looks fun!" Melanie said, "Good idea, Sabrina!"

Then Melanie started doing the same thing and leaped out of the deep snow. "Come on, Carly, your turn". Carly hesitated and once she jumped it wasn't as successful as the other girls. She barely moved from where she was.

"A little higher" Sabrina encouraged, "Don't think, just do it"

Taking her time, Carly leaped again, this time a little higher and almost caught up with the other girls. Melanie cheered and then all three of them started leaping from one spot to another. They were laughing with joy and excitement. It even brought a smile to Elijah's face.

"Race you guys back to the pavement?" Sabrina suggested.

Melanie immediately took a head start and made her back to the corner of the school. Sabrina and Carly were catching up. As Melanie approached closer, the snow was becoming less deep. Soon she was able to run. Carly made another leap, but then her feet slipped once it hit the snow and fell forward, accidently tackling Sabrina. In the end both girls fell to the ground.

"Whoa!" Sabrina called, just before her fall ended.

As Melanie turned around, the other girls were already on the ground and she just burst out laughing. Elijah chuckled as he saw the whole incident.

"Oh god, Sabrina I'm so sorry!" Carly panicked, as they were slowly getting back up. Then she went towards her friend to help her up. She thought maybe that Sabrina was slightly hurt, but she was actually laughing.

"Carly, it's alright" she told her, "There's much worse things to land on"

"Yeah, be glad it wasn't mud!" Mel added.

"That probably would've been much worse" Carly agreed.

"Yeah, we got winter coats. If only they made something that would protect us from mud"

"They did, it's called regular clothes! I know because I used to play in the mud a lot when I was little"

"Well, that must've been messy" Carly said.

"My parents thought the same, too".

Melanie regrouped with the girls, as they were rubbing the snow off their upper and lower body. That was when Elijah approached them just to say hi to Sabrina.

"Having fun?" Elijah called out, gently.

Not only had he got Sabrina's attention, but also Carly and Melanie's.

"Always" Sabrina answered.

"Haha that was funny, the way you guys fell" Elijah said.

"Ha, of course; we probably looked like idiots" Sabrina added, followed by a laugh.

Once the laughter was over, Elijah cleared his throat and spoke gently. "Yeah, I just wanted to come by and say hi"

"HI" Sabrina said, with her hand up.

"HI there"

During their little greeting, Elijah could feel two other pairs of eyes looking towards him. He decided to be polite and acknowledge Sabrina's friends. First, Elijah slowly turned towards Melanie. She just smiled from ear to ear once their eyes met.

"Hello, you must be Sabrina's friend" Elijah said.

"Yes sir, I am" Mel replied.

That had to be the first time Elijah and Melanie spoke to each other. They were actually in the same primary school years ago. "Melanie Peyton?" he said.

"Yes"

"I think we were both in Mrs. Evans' class together"

There was no uncertainty. Melanie remembered being the same class as Elijah Khoda.

"Yeah, you do look like the one kid in one of my old class photos" Mel told him.

"Oh, so you guys know each other?" Sabrina said, casually.

"Not exactly" Elijah told her, "We're…one of those kids that know each other by name and face"

Melanie chuckled, thinking that remark was a little cute. "Yeah, I do remember you. I don't think I ever heard you talk"

Elijah spared the embarrassment and used the comment to make conversation. "I was pretty quiet back then" he admitted.

Since Elijah and Mel got acquainted, he then turned to Carly.

"And you're Carly?" he asked.

Carly was a little shy to begin with, "Yeah" she said, gently.

"We're in the same class" Elijah added.

"Right"

He never thought he would be talking to Melanie and Carly. Not only he didn't know them but once despised them for taking Sabrina away. But things had changed for the better. Now he was willing to support her and the ones in her life. "I heard you like sports" Elijah said. That was an assumption, since he didn't really know Carly that well.

"I do like sports" Carly replied, proudly, "Thanks for noticing" Then she gave a slight smile, almost like there could be a possible friendship with her and Melanie.

"Your friends are cute" Elijah said, as he redirected his eyes towards Sabrina.

"Cute like puppies" Sabrina added, as a joke.

Melanie then stuck her tongue and started breathing. She was impersonating a dog and then added a little bark. They broke into laughter.

"Or cute like a kitten" Carly suggested, "I like cats"

"Yeah-hey, you know what, I call Carly kitten!" Melanie said, "I almost forgot"

Carly broke eye contact and looked away shyly, hoping that everyone wasn't staring. Melanie approached her and gently started scratching her neck. "Aw, little kitten" she praised, "Come on, give us a meow"

"Meow?" Carly said, after a moment of hesitation. Sabrina just formed a smile and then looked at Elijah.

"Like a kitten" she agreed.

Meanwhile, Paula and Andrew were by the entrance, watching Elijah mingling with the girls. They saw the smile on his face. This time Paula was getting a positive vibe from it, unlike the last time. "He looks happy" Paula said, "I don't think I ever saw him in this kind of mood before"

"Yeah" Andrew agreed, "I guess all the times he smiled, he was really just laughing at my jokes. But this time, it doesn't looks like he needs it"

Paula was leaning against the pillar, staring blankly. Andrew noticed that her mind was far off. So then he went in closer and waved his hand in front of Paula's face. She didn't even flinch. So he decided to do a different approach and punched Paula in the arm.

"Ow!" she reacted skeptically. Then she returned the favor and punched Andrew back.

"Just making sure you're still here" Andrew explained, trying not to laugh.

"I am. It's just…" Paula trialed off; she looked back at Elijah, who was still in a good as he was talking with Sabrina and her friends. Andrew was at the corner of her eye and feared the worse. "Don't!" she warned him.

Andrew looked at her a little funny, "Don't what?"

"Don't punch me again"

"I wasn't gonna"

"Yeah, right"

"Alright, no jokes this time" Andrew promised, "Tell me what's wrong"

"Nothing, I…just still can't believe that's the same boy I grew up with" Paula explained, sincerely, "I remember when Elijah was scared to go off on his own during recess. He wouldn't move until I was with him"

Andrew nodded. "Our little Elijah has grown up"

Paula casually glanced at Andrew, only to realize there was a little smile on his face. "Don't even think about it" she warned him.

Puzzled, Andrew tried to look at Paula, who then turned around and started walking away. "Think about what?" He tried to catch up to Paula. "How do you know I was thinking?"

"I just do" Paula admitted. Then she stopped once they were far enough from Elijah.

"What was I thinking anyway?" Andrew asked, feeling uncertain.

"That you and I are playing house" she told him, "When you said 'our little Elijah has grownup', you said it like we were married"

There was a short pause. Then Andrew started laughing. "I didn't mean like that" he tried to explain.

"I saw the smile on your face" Paula told him.

"Hey, maybe I was thinking about something else that was funny, like the time I put the child safety lock on and my sister couldn't get out"

To Paula, it seemed like Andrew would treat almost anything as a joke. There was enough tolerance for his mischievous side. Sometimes she would play hardball just to test him.

"Please, if Elijah is getting into girls, it wouldn't be long until you'd do the same"

Andrew stared at her for a moment. "Maybe you're right"

Paula still didn't feel comfortable, as she rolled her eyes. "You just had to look at me when you said that"

"Aww, you look stressed Paulie. Here maybe a little shoulder rub will relax you" Andrew went up to her and began rubbing her shoulders gently. "See, aside from the banana flavored cough syrup, this is the best medicine"

Paula didn't say anything. She just hoped that Andrew would leave her alone shortly.

"See, a little relaxation is the best meds. Relax! RE-LAX" And then for fun, he started shaking her firmly as he still had his hands on her shoulders. Paula broke free.

"Alright, you, walk in front of me. We're going for a walk" she told him.

"Walk in front of you?"

"So I can drop a chunk of snow in your shirt"

230   PHILIP PATRICK

Andrew walked backwards, away from Paula. "You know what, this isn't working out. I want a divorce"

Paula looked at him firmly and then quickly grabbed a handful of snow and threw it at Andrew. But he dodged it.

"Ha! Close, but no goodbye-kiss" Andrew taunted. Paula didn't give up and started chasing after Andrew, who was laughing along the way.

The last week of school before Christmas break was drawing to an end. Every class in the school was celebrating the holidays. They were having parties, giving out baked treats, playing games and watching Christmas movies. It was the one day of the year where the students didn't have to worry about schoolwork. They get to be themselves and enjoy the company of their friends, and have a good time.

Before the last day, Elijah thought about giving gifts to his friends. Especially after the trouble he been through, it was probably best to show his appreciation. He wanted to get something special to Sabrina, but didn't know what and he didn't have the money for it. There was nothing, but he wanted to give her something. So Elijah had to go with what he had, the little things. From the night before, there were plenty of candy canes on their Christmas tree at home. So Elijah took three of them.

Once the class had their free time, Elijah stepped out of the room and went to Andrew's class next door. They were having a party of their own. The students were talking amongst themselves. Elijah went up to Andrew and gave him the candy cane.

"My friend" was all that Elijah said. Andrew nodded with a proud smile. Then they both gave each other the thumbs up-fist bump, which was starting to become a regular thing.

After that, Elijah went across the hall and into Paula's class. This time, he stood in the doorway and asked the teacher for Paula, who got up from her desk to meet him. "For you, Paula" Elijah said, as he offered her the candy cane, "I'm glad to have you in my life"

Paula gave a little smile as she accepted the little gift, "Same to you, Eli". She then gave him a hug.

There was only one person left, the one who meant most to Elijah. He returned to class and went straight to Sabrina, who was sitting beside Carly, talking and eating baked treats.

"Hey Sabrina" Elijah said gently, as he approached her. Every time their eyes met, it was so profound that it would throw Elijah off guard, just seeing how beautiful she was, "Can I...see you...for a minute?"

"Sure" she agreed.

Sabrina got up from her desk and followed Elijah to the back of the room, where they had a little space to themselves. As Elijah leaned against the counter, he took a deep breath of confidence before meeting Sabrina's eye.

"Hey, so I got you something" he explained.

"Oh?" she replied, with interest.

"It's not much, but I wanted to give you something for Christmas. I didn't know what and I didn't really have any money. So...this is from our Christmas tree at home"

Elijah revealed the candy cane to her. Then something caught his eye, the candy cane was broken in half. "What the...?" he replied, skeptically, "Oh great!" He panicked, as the one moment he was waiting for was ruined and his heart just slowly dropped. Sabrina looked at him, awkwardly.

"It wasn't like this before!" Elijah explained, "I didn't know..."

"Oh, Elijah..." Sabrina replied, pitifully.

"I'm sorry, I..."

"Elijah" she called, in a calm manner, "It's okay, really. It's still pretty thoughtful of you"

"Yeah? Okay...Merry Christmas"

Sabrina gracefully accepted the candy cane, "Thank you" she said, kindly.

It brought a smile to Elijah's face. Sabrina glanced at the candy and then back at Elijah. "You know what; I know how to make this work". Then she gently pulled one half of the candy cane until the plastic broke in half. Sabrina offered it to Elijah.

"Merry Christmas" she said, with a beautiful smile.

Elijah certainly wasn't expecting that, a thoughtful gesture from Sabrina Clarin, especially when the moment almost went downhill. Elijah, more than willing, accepted the other half of the candy cane.

"Thanks!" he replied, "Now you're being thoughtful"

Sabrina smiled and broke eye contact for a brief moment. "Ho-ho-ho" she replied.

They both laughed. Then there was another surprise. Sabrina gave Elijah a hug, and of course he returned the hug.

"Merry Christmas, Elijah"

"Merry Christmas, Sabrina"

PART TWO
Dark Clouds

CHAPTER FIFTEEN

The Brave and the Girl

January 2001.

It was a new year and a time for new beginnings in which Elijah gave a lot of thought to. He decided that he wanted to make Sabrina Clarin his girlfriend. Not knowing how or when, Elijah took it one day at a time and waited for the right moment. It was all he dreamed about day and night and each moment after another, he hoped for the best.

The grade seven classes were on a field trip to Smithers B.C. It was their annual event of going skiing and snowboarding on the mountains. Every student was sitting comfortably on the bus. Many of them tried to keep warm, for that the cold air had made the north its home. Elijah was sitting beside one of his classmates, while Paula and Andrew were travelling with their classes on separate buses.

Elijah spent half his time holding his Polaroid camera that he got for Christmas. He'd already take a few random pictures before leaving the school. Then he lifted it up and took a quick photo of his classmates on the bus. Elijah got up from his seat and went down to see Sabrina Clarin. First thing he did was showing her the photo he just took.

"Picture of the class" Elijah explained.

"That's pretty cool, Elijah" Sabrina told him.

"Thanks"

After that, he showed her the previous photos he took, such as the one of the grade seven classes boarding the bus. Sabrina admired it and even showed it to Carly, who was sitting beside her.

"I think I can see you" Sabrina told her.

"Oh great, do I look ridiculous?" Carly sighed.

"It's just the back of your head. And don't you say that, you do not look ridiculous!"

"Please, every picture I'm in, I look ridiculously nervous"

"Car, if I had photos of you, I would never throw them away"

Carly gave a slight smile. Then she rested her head on her friend's shoulder. Sabrina then gave the photo back to Elijah.

"These are good pictures, Elijah" she told him.

"Yeah, I love my Christmas present. It's from my mom"

"Nice. Can I see?"

Elijah kindly gave her the camera. She examined it for a moment. Then she aimed it at Elijah and took his photo. Automatically, Elijah hesitated. The flash was the only thing he thought of and tried to blind himself from it before it even went off. Sabrina laughed.

"Haha, funny" Elijah said, "I look forward to seeing that one"

Sabrina gave the camera back. The bus suddenly stopped and Elijah quickly lost balance and then fell to the floor. Sabrina flinched.

"Elijah…?"

"I'm fine" he replied, promptly, "The camera's fine. I'm fine. Everything's fine"

Elijah got back up to his feet. Surely, there were quite a few classmates staring.

"I better sit back down" he said.

By the time Elijah got back to his seat, the picture just finished developing. It was the photo of himself that Sabrina took, where he smiled nervously but it turned out alright. Elijah couldn't help but give a little smile.

The students arrived at Smithers and then made their way to the mountain lodge, where they assembled both snowboard and ski equipment. Elijah exited the bus and went to take a picture of the mountain. Once the picture printed, Elijah put the camera away in his backpack and went to regroup with Paula and Andrew, who were just getting off their buses.

"Elijah!" Paula greeted, "We're in the mountains! Aren't you excited?" It was often cute whenever she was mildly excited since most of the time her humor was dry.

"Yeah" Elijah agreed, "I mean, it's my first time being up here. Why wouldn't I be excited?" Then he added a little chuckle just so that Paula knew that his reaction was genuine.

"You have every reason to be" she replied, with a smirk, "I never had been on a mountain before either".

"Hey, me too!" Andrew added, "I only looked at the mountains in Alberta. This one time, I tricked my little sister into thinking that we could cause an avalanche by clapping from where we stood. You should've seen her. She wouldn't leave until it would actually happen. She was even more disappointed when my dad told her how impossible it was. She never spoke to me for a day after that"

Nobody said anything. But Paula looked at him like he was up to something.

"Oh, I know that look" Andrew said, "It's the 'I know what you're thinking-look'"

There was no reply. Elijah just stood between them in amusement.

"What am I thinking?" he then asked.

"I'm not saying it" Paula told him.

"Why not?"

"Because you're gonna get ideas"

"Ah-ha! But the ideas are already in my head. They just need to be woken up by you"

Elijah laughed, admirably.

"I get it, you're fluent in smart talking" Paula added.

As most of their classmates were making their way to the lodge, Paula left, casually, assuming that the boys were about to do the same thing. In the end, it was one of those moments where Andrew would add a surprise gag.

"Avalanche!" he shouted and then he clapped his hands fairly loud.

Some of the students looked back at him. Some of them were amused; others thought that he was crazy, just like how Paula stared at him. One of the teachers called out to him, telling him to settle down. Then Elijah decided to join in on the fun.

"He's just excited about the trip" he explained, like a parent making excuses for his child's inadvertent mischief. Then Elijah clapped at the end. He just couldn't help himself. The excitement fed Andrew as he did the same thing. Soon they both clapped, first at the same time and then one after another. The teacher, more firmly, reminded them to settle down.

And so the fun began. All the grade seven students got their equipment. Some went skiing while the others went snowboarding. Elijah chose the snowboard, like most of the students. For the rest of the morning, they went sliding downhill. The sun was shining but the cold air maintained, but that didn't stop them from having fun. Elijah snowboarded up and down the hill repeatedly. Each ride not only had excitement but also a moment of peacefulness. As Elijah slid smoothly downhill, the activity cleared his mind, for that it was just him and the mountain. He didn't pay attention to any of his fellow students around him. There was no pressure or obligations, just freedom. And he enjoyed every minute of it.

It was also Sabrina's first time snowboarding. It was a winter sport that she never gave much thought of but she was open minded. And as it turned out, she was a natural. She and her girlfriends started off small because they were beginners as well. Sabrina taught Carly how to snowboard until she got the hang of it. From there, they went further uphill with their peers and slid down, which grew more fun. Sabrina, at one point, enjoyed the feel of the wind flowing passed her and then she raised her arms up, pretended that she was flying.

Elijah saw Sabrina and her friends at the bottom of the hill. So he turned his board slightly to the right. He began to slow down as Elijah slid closer to the girls.

"Having fun?" Elijah asked, as he slid passed Sabrina and her friends.

"Yes!" she replied, with excitement.

Elijah finally came to a complete stop. "I see you got a snowboard too" he pointed out.

"Yeah, before I thought about trying it at one point" Sabrina admitted, "I've went sliding with a crazy carpet and a sled, but never with a snowboard"

"I think everyone wanted to snowboard" Carly added, "Because everyone else chose that"

"Better than skiing" Elijah added, "I tried that years ago and I hated it"

"Honestly, I didn't mind skiing" Melanie told him.

"I kept falling down and my feet were hurting"

"It is tricky, I know" Melanie agreed, gently, "But I think all it takes is some practice"

Elijah just nodded. After brief silence, he looked at Sabrina. "Hey, wanna race down the hill?" he challenged.

"Sure" she agreed.

"Unless you're scared" Elijah said, as a joke, "Scared of losing" he added, to avoid the wrong impression.

Sabrina just looked at him, ready to smile, "Do I look scared?" she replied, playfully.

"You look…" Elijah tried to think of something clever to say, "Ready"

"Of course" Sabrina finally smiled. So then they both went up the hill, while the other girls were still at the bottom of the hill. "So…are we going with them or what?" Carly said to Melanie.

Elijah and Sabrina were making their way up the hill, with their snowboards in hand. The thought of him being alone with a girl was a perfect opportunity to ask her out. So he spent half his time trying to think of what to say and how to say it. Elijah tried to look back on where he saw this similar situation. In the movies, the boy would simply say the words; would you go out with me? That was an option but then Elijah thought in real life would be a little different. For some reason, he imagined that question might make him look and sound bad and he didn't even want to think of what Sabrina's response might be. Suddenly the idea scared him and just decided to think of another way to ask her.

"-sure is nice out" Sabrina was making conversation!

Elijah had to clear his mind before answering, "Yeah it is nice"

"I mean, I know it's cloudy but it's not snowing or anything. It's a good time for us to be outside and have fun".

Elijah nodded, "I think so, too".

Right then, he briefly thought about taking Sabrina's words and use it to ask her out on a date. But it was only that thought alone. No ideas were coming to mind. Soon that courage was gone. Elijah just decided to start over.

"Hey, you ever seen Jackie Chan's First Strike?" he asked, casually.

"No, I don't think I heard of" Sabrina said, "I know who he is but not the movie"

"Ah, well anyways, after seeing that movie I been wanting to try snowboarding"

"Oh nice"

Elijah hesitated, for that his next words were close to what he really wanted to say, "We'll have to watch it sometime",

That was it. He used to term we, hoping that Sabrina would get the idea. The short pause even built a little excitement. Elijah looked at her for an answer.

"Yeah, someday" she replied.

But that didn't sound very promising. It mostly sounded like Sabrina was just making conversation. Sadly, it didn't seem like she got the hint. Elijah silently took a deep breath and let out his disappointment. Even so, a little excitement went off when she said someday. That was something.

Next time, next time! He promised, with an ounce of hope.

So after walking for a short period of time, they figured they were high enough for their little race. Elijah and Sabrina attached their feet back on their snowboards and got into formation.

"Okay, ready?" he asked, looking down the hill.

Instead of answering, Sabrina posed a challenge, "I dare you to keep up".

Just like that she started snowboarding down the hill. The surprise prevented Elijah from starting at first. Then he tilted his board off the edge and started making his way down fairly fast. Sabrina was ahead of him, sliding smoothly. Elijah bend down a little, thinking that would make him go faster. Somehow, he was getting closer to her. Shortly, they were right beside each other. At first, they were competitors but then they spoke as friends.

"Hey!" Elijah called out, in a friendly way.

Sabrina looked over to acknowledge him, "Hey, you made it!"

Elijah just smiled as the excitement tickled him inside. Normally, he would continue the conversation but in that predicament there was no time. Nonetheless, it was fun. They just enjoyed the ride. Elijah decided to make the best of it and steered his snowboard into zigzags. First, he drifted away from Sabrina and then back to her. He attempted to do it again but this time he was losing balance. To his surprise, he was staggering too quickly. Sabrina noticed and grew worried.

"Elijah!" he could hear her voice clearly and then he heard, "Here, take my hand!"

He looked over and saw Sabrina's hand extended towards him. Elijah quickly grabbed it and held on. Now he wasn't staggering anymore, for that Sabrina gently pulled him back into balance. Elijah looked over at her and smiled in relief. She returned the smile. Even when he was okay, he didn't want to let go of Sabrina's hand. But as the race was getting close to finish, they had to let go of each other. As they were getting to the bottom of the hill, they started slowing down. Sabrina was ahead. She was the winner. But Elijah didn't care about the race, as long as he had fun with the girl of his dreams. Elijah tried to pull his board to a stop but it was a little tricky as he was still sliding along. Then he tried too hard and ended up falling in the snow. Sabrina looked over only to realize that Elijah wasn't there. She turned around and saw him lying in the snow. Sabrina was mostly amused than concerned, since they were far from danger.

"Watch out!" a voice called out.

242

PHILIP PATRICK

Sabrina faced forward and realized she was about to hit one of her fellow student, who quickly backed away. But from out of panic, Sabrina decided to fall into the snow, voluntarily, thinking it was the only way to stop herself completely. Luckily, nobody was hurt. Elijah saw the whole thing. He was concerned at first but after Sabrina allowed herself to fall to avoid an accident; they couldn't help but look at each other and laugh.

Elijah didn't get the date that he wanted or maybe this was already a date.

After the main event was over, it was time to go home. But first, they stopped at the local Dairy Queen to get something to eat. Elijah sat by himself, since Andrew and Paula's class were elsewhere. But that was okay. Since he got to spend some fun time with Sabrina that morning, Elijah didn't mind the alone time. He just relaxed and enjoyed his meal.

The classes began their road trip back to Burns Lake. After sitting in silence, Elijah decided that he wanted to make best of the time he had. He couldn't socialize with Sabrina because she was sitting a few seats down, next to Carly. All the other seats around them were taking. Then he remembered that he still had his camera in his backpack. Perhaps a picture-a memento of this trip, it would be something special. He pulled it out and waited for the right moment. Just as they were leaving the town of Smithers, Sabrina sat up, rested her arms on top of the seats between her, taking in each scenery they were passing. It was perfect because she was looking in Elijah's direction. He saw the right pose and pulled out his camera, aimed it at Sabrina without her knowing. Just when she sipped from her drink from the fast food restaurant, Elijah took the picture. Sabrina wasn't aware because the chatter of her fellow students filled the air. The photo from the Polaroid camera slowly developed. Once the picture became clear, Elijah sat there and admired it. Sabrina looked just as cute as she was beautiful. He was actually about to show her but he ended up keeping it to himself, at least for now.

Later that evening, Elijah went to the kitchen to look for something to eat. He browsed the cupboards and the fridge, but didn't find anything. So he then scanned the counter and saw a bowl of fruit in the corner. One fruit caught his attention, a red apple. Suddenly it became so profound, that it had Elijah hypnotized, as he went up and grabbed that particular fruit. That brought him back to his one moment with Sabrina Clarin. He could hear her voice as he gazed at the apple.

You're a good apple.

Out of nowhere, that just brought a smile to Elijah's face.

"Sabrina" he muttered.

"What?"

A different voice caught Elijah off guard. He turned around and realized his dad was standing there. Acting as normal as he could, Elijah cleared his throat and even hid the apple behind him.

"Nothing" he told his dad. He then tried to think of an excuse but nothing came to mind. So Elijah just ended up walking out of the kitchen, silently.

That memory with Sabrina and her apple remark put a smile on Elijah's face for the rest of the evening as he thought about her on and off. Then he started to think about what could be, particularly his desire for her love. After trying to ask her in a subtle way, Elijah wondered if he was getting closer to that goal. After all, she replied with the words: yeah, someday. It was easier said than done. Even so, perhaps that was merely another step towards a relationship. Elijah kept telling himself that, as another opportunity would come.

After the weekend, Monday morning had started. It was different like no other. The weather was one thing, for that it was nearly minus forty, the coldest it's been for the season. And Sabrina Clarin was late. It was a little unusual because she was always on time. Elijah thought he would've seen her once he arrived but she was nowhere in sight. Even Carly and Melanie were surprised that Sabrina wasn't there yet. Elijah couldn't help but feel a little empty inside, knowing that his friend might not be at school today. But just when the grade seven classes were entering the school, Sabrina finally showed up. Elijah could recognize her hair from a distance. She stepped out of the car and made her way up the steps.

"Sabrina, you made it!" Elijah greeted, triumphantly.

As she got closer, Elijah realized that something was wrong. Sabrina looked sad. In fact, it looked like she just finished crying.

"Hey, Elijah" she replied, rather weakly.

She walked passed him just as their classmates were going inside. Elijah's heart just dropped. That was the first time that he saw Sabrina Clarin cry. She was the last person that Elijah expected to be so emotional. Whatever it was that was bothering her, Elijah was sad for her. And there was no time for them to talk about it because the school day had started. So Elijah had no choice but to continue on and hope that Sabrina was going to be okay.

It was a busy morning; a little too busy that Elijah didn't get a chance to talk to Sabrina alone. Mrs. Parker was already there in class, so there wasn't any time to waste. Waiting patiently was the only thing Elijah could do. Throughout the morning, he would peer over at Sabrina, just to make sure she was hanging in there. She looked normal, on the outside at least.

After waiting patiently all morning, the students finally got to have a break; since it was too cold to go outside, the school principal decided that everyone should stay indoors for the day. So then the students hung around in class and talked during their free time. Now was Elijah's chance to talk to his friend. He got up from his desk and approached her slowly. She sat there, flipping through her schoolwork blankly.

"Sabrina" Elijah said, gently.

Their eyes met. There was no tear in Sabrina's eyes.

"Hey" he greeted.

"Hey" she sounded okay.

"Are you all right?" Elijah asked, in a low voice just so it wouldn't catch anyone else's attention.

Sabrina nodded slightly. "I am now"

"Yeah, I guess things weren't okay this morning?"

Sabrina broke eye contact as her mind wandered back to what happened. Voluntarily, Elijah knelt down at her desk like a teacher helping a student. "What happened?" he said gently.

"Well..." Sabrina was about to speak but then she realized the students in her group were having a conversation of their own and didn't want to intrude with something that ought to be private. So then Sabrina gestured Elijah to follow her. They got up and went to the other side of the classroom where the lockers were. But then Elijah noticed that the door was opened. And there were students from next door were wondering around the hall, for that some of them were playing on the computers.

"We can talk out here?" he suggested.

"Yeah?" Sabrina replied, reluctantly. Something seemed a little wrong about it, but she didn't feel like questioning, "Yeah...sure" she finally agreed.

Elijah and Sabrina exited their classroom. They found themselves wondering towards the boot room. As they entered, the sound of the rest of the world was going silent, and they could feel cold air coming from the outside where it was covered in snow.

"You're not trying to get me sick, are you?" she asked, as she wrapped her arms around herself, "Its cold in here"

Feeling a little guilty, Elijah reconsidered his suggestion and maybe head back to where they came from. "Oh, we can always talk somewhere else, over there maybe. There are some kids there but we can talk quietly..."

"Elijah" Sabrina interrupted, "I was joking. The cold air is not so bad"

"Oh" Elijah muttered. It was silent for a moment. Since Sabrina was feeling a little humorous, he decided to add something. "That's too bad. I was gonna warm you up with my hand" Elijah then gently put his warm hand on Sabrina's forearm. She just chuckled. It was definitely a moment between the two of them. Elijah thought about putting his hand on Sabrina's cheek, but he didn't. It was tempting. It would've been something special though. But Elijah had to remind himself why they were there. Once they had the silence, they began talking.

"So...what happened?" he repeated, gently.

"Me and my family got into a little fight" Sabrina admitted.

Elijah didn't know what to say.

"Yesterday, my mom was heading to town. She was driving down hill and she couldn't stop because the road was icy. And just as she reached the bottom, the car ended up going farther than it should've and then another car accidently rammed into her-my mom wasn't hurt thank goodness-but the back door was dented. My mom was confident that it will get fixed but then she found out my dad spent most of our savings from pre-ordering a new TV. Mom wasn't very happy and they started arguing. And then this morning she got mad at my brother Jonathan because he was complaining about breakfast. Then I got mad at him for making mom so angry and then we ended up in a fight. And that was just before I got dropped off this morning. So…that's why"

"Oh. I'm sorry" Elijah said, with sympathy.

Then for a moment, they both pondered around the boot room and gazed out to the outside world.

"Yeah, well, I'm sorry you had to see me like that" she added, "It's just I love my family and I don't wanna see them sad. And I felt bad that I put everyone in that position this morning. I must be a horrible person"

"No, no, don't be sorry. You picked a fight with your brother but you didn't mean it. All families get into a fight, but they're your family" For a second, Elijah wasn't sure what he said was good enough, so he tried to think of something else to say to comfort her, "They will always love you and the fight won't last forever".

Sabrina nodded, "Thanks, Elijah".

"And you're not a horrible person" he added, "You're a great friend, you're nice, and…I don't see anything wrong about you. I'm sure your family thinks that too"

Sabrina slowly formed a smile on her face. "Thank you. That actually makes me feel better".

That feeling inside Elijah sparked. He wondered if Sabrina was feeling the same thing. It grew brighter as they exchanged looks. It was something that Elijah felt no control over. He actually wanted to give Sabrina a hug, just to make her feel better. Nothing happened. The feeling faded away, until next time. Sabrina looked away for a moment.

"I guess that means I'm not getting a visit from Santa this year" Sabrina said.

Elijah was a little puzzled, "Was that another joke?" he asked.

"Yeah" then Sabrina couldn't help but laugh, "I was just thinking, you know when they say Santa only comes if you been good?"

"Oh yeah, I remember that"

"You ever tried so hard to be good just so you can get Christmas presents?"

"I did, actually" Elijah admitted.

"Me and Jonathan were sensitive about it" Sabrina explained, "I just remembered something that we did a few years ago. That's what made me laugh. But I guess…not everyone can be good"

"Or perfect" Elijah told her, "Like you told me that one day, we have flaws but that doesn't mean you're a bad person"

Sabrina nodded, "That's right"

"Yeah, we're not perfect but we're not bad either. We're…something else, in a good way"

Elijah was trying to say something nice and insightful but didn't know how. Sabrina peered over her shoulders just to make sure their classroom door was still open. "Well, I guess we better get back to class before indoor recess is over"

"Yeah, right" Elijah agreed.

"But thanks for listening though. You made me feel better"

"Glad I can help" Elijah said, with a little smile.

Throughout life we would think that friends and family, the ones close to us, would be emotionally strong and nothing would hurt them. But one day, you'll realize that everyone has feelings. They would be fighting a battle that no one knows about. Sabrina Clarin was one of them. From day one, Elijah thought that she was a happy person. But then he learned that Sabrina had bad days as well. He was worried at first, but in the end, the confidence in her voice convinced him that she was okay.

Later on, the school continued to have an inside day because the cold weather wasn't planning on going away soon. So for lunch break, the students were allowed to use the computer room at the library. Luckily, Elijah was able to hang out with Sabrina. He wanted to show her to computer games that they had. They sat next to each other as they were surrounded by their peers also playing on the computers.

"We got a lot of cool games here" Elijah explained. He went on and on, for that he really wanted to show Sabrina his world. "We got Cross Country Canada and Sim City. Oh and Oregan Trails. Too bad the computer in our class was taking because not all of them have that"

"Oh, well this one is just as fun" Sabrina said.

They were playing the game Gizmos and Gadgets. They each took turns. Once Sabrina had a chance, Elijah explained the controls eagerly like she was going to mess up.

"I'm a first learner" she told him, "Don't worry"

"Oh, I'm not worried" Elijah said that to be a little clever.

Sabrina glanced at him, "Good" she said with humor.

For the next few minutes, Elijah watched her master the controls and passed one level after another, almost perfectly. "Nice playing".

"Thanks. When me and Jonathan were little, we played one of the hockey games on Super Nintendo. Just the first time I beat him, he was already getting mad"

"Really?"

"Yeah, I had to lose on purpose a few times just to make him feel better"

"Almost sounds like Andrew" Elijah added, "He doesn't usually get mad but when he plays video games, he gets a little serious"

"I wouldn't doubt it"

Then Elijah said as a joke, "Maybe Andrew and your brother should get together"

Sabrina chuckled, "Yeah, I'm sure that would be interesting"

They spent the next moment playing the game together. It was silent. Only existing sound was from the computer game. It made Elijah contemplate his opportunity to ask Sabrina a certain question. He kept glancing over at her, hoping to say something. But the more he thought about it, the more discomfort he felt.

I really wish me and Sabrina could read each other's minds right now.

"So, uh, what did you do for the weekend?" he asked, casually. Then he remembered what he told her earlier and felt bad, "I-I mean other than…what happened". He could only hope that his voice was normal enough to convince Sabrina that it was just a friendly conversation. Fortunately, she didn't seem startled at all.

"Not much just hung around at home. We helped our dad shovel snow like old times. How about you?"

"Hmm, same thing, stay at home, wasn't as fun as the field trip"

"Yeah, that was pretty fun" Sabrina agreed, showing a little excitement in her voice. Hearing that lifted Elijah's spirits, knowing that she was comfortable with him. Now he lost himself in his emotions.

"You know what would be nice?" the words just blurted out. It was like leaping without looking.

"What's that?" Sabrina replied.

That was it! Elijah was getting close now that he had her full attention. He turned his head slightly to the left and almost caught her gaze but then he found himself focusing on their computer game.

"Ahh…" Elijah said, only to break the silence. Finally, he sat back in his seat and slowly turned to his girl, "To have someone to hang out with" he added, reluctantly. Sabrina just stared at him, like a regular student would in a classroom. So really she was only listening instead of trying to uncover the layers of Elijah's suggestion.

"I guess Andrew was too busy over the weekend?" she asked.

It was one moment that could've gone one way or the other. He wanted to tell her what he truly meant. It was either that or play along with Sabrina's question and pretended that he never even asked that question. Fate was in Elijah's hands but there will always be fear and doubt.

"Yeah" he replied, using his own disappointment to pretend that he was upset with Andrew, "You know him, he likes to sit back, eat cereal while controlling the game with his toes".

CHAPTER SIXTEEN

Mystery Valentine

One month had passed. Elijah had treated each day like it was normal. Like a normal kid, he got up every morning and went to school, and did his schoolwork like a normal student, and hung out with his friends and talked about normal things, nothing too exciting. Sabrina Clarin still said hi to him, so that was always a good sign. Sometimes they walked around the school or even just talked. Any day with Sabrina was a good day.

Valentine's Day was getting close. It was a day of love. And it got Elijah thinking long and hard. It could be his chance to tell Sabrina how he really felt about her. It would be liberating and a big step up in their relationship. It was possible and it had Elijah dreaming every day. He'd imagine having a private conversation with Sabrina Clarin.

Sabrina, would you wanna go out with me?

The words that he wanted to say so badly repeated in his mind along with every possible scenery; it didn't have to be a private conversation, if Elijah wanted to he'd let the whole world know that he was in love with Sabrina Clarin by approaching her in front of her girlfriends.

Sabrina, I like you, like a lot and I wanna be with you.

As the days passed, Elijah treated his imagination like a blank canvas and painted more pictures. He then imagined trying to get Sabrina's attention in a creative way by drawing different pictures of her and put them around the school and have it say If found please return her to Elijah Khoda. Regardless of how silly his approach would be, all Elijah could think about was seeing Sabrina's eyes and look into her soul and connect.

Hey Sabrina, there's a movie that I wanna see and wondered if you wanna see it too. Do you wanna go together?

A night at the movies with Sabrina Clarin would be extraordinary, with the two of them sitting next to each other in the theatre, sharing popcorn and enjoying the cinema experience. Every now and then, they would glance at each other and smile.

Do you wanna go for a walk sometime? Not just around the school, but all over town?

Elijah would be more than willing to show Sabrina around Burns Lake since it was the place he grew up in. He would show her his old primary school, the reserve, and almost every location in town. Each time these ideas crossed his mind, he became more excited. He hoped that at least one of them would happen someday.

Picturing the possible outcomes became a regular thing. Even when Elijah was interacting with his friends in daily life, his thoughts became deeper and so did his words. One day in particular, it sent his feelings higher than it ever did. Elijah was walking around the school with Paula and Andrew. As they were busy talking amongst themselves, Elijah's mind was far from reality for that his thoughts became deeper and so did his words.

Sabrina, I never met anyone like you. You're the first girl I ever liked.

Before I met you, I was a kid looking for trouble but I don't want that anymore. I want you.

I want us to be more than friends.

I…want…you, Sabrina.

In the end, there was one picture he painted that explained all his thoughts and his words. Elijah imagined one thing that he never imagined before. He imagined himself kissing Sabrina Clarin on the lips, just like in a romantic film. That thought turned off his consciousness as that image stayed still in his head, Elijah Khoda holding Sabrina Clarin close like never before, like he actually tried to imagine how holding her body would feel. He might've had a clue, recalling the time when they hugged each other. He remembered wrapping his arms around her. It was a firm and yet delicate feeling. Even just thinking that was starting to feel real in the mind's eye. Next thing Elijah imagined was kissing her. He fantasized it for a brief moment from that one night. But this time, he wanted to see how real it would be. As Elijah kept on walking, he was mentally miles away as he saw himself standing in front of Sabrina. There he saw her face, eyes open and looking straight at his, and there were her lips. That was all the image that he needed. Then Elijah imagined himself leaning closer. The more real he wanted it to be, the illusion was starting to become real. At last, they kissed.

The daydream ended and Elijah was back in reality, still walking behind Andrew and Paula.

It was that moment; Elijah realized how much he loved Sabrina. That kiss he imagined sparked his emotions more rapidly than before. Elijah completely stopped, like the feeling became an uncontrollable force that he couldn't break away from. Andrew and Paula were walking further away, unaware about Elijah's predicament. He was actually about to tell them that he needed some alone time. But he wasn't sure and then it was too late as his friends were out of reach. So Elijah just turned around and ran in the opposite direction.

He ran all the way back to the front of the school and there was Sabrina, with her girlfriends as usual. Still feeling motivated, Elijah started moving towards her. It could finally be happening. He and Sabrina could be boyfriend and girlfriend any moment. Elijah was getting closer. Sabrina did not know that he was nearby. But before he went any farther, he thought of something else.

What if Sabrina didn't like Elijah the same way he liked her?

So the daydreaming became a nightmare once reality interfered.

Elijah stopped where he was, frozen stiff and suddenly unable to move. Everything in his mind changed once he thought of Sabrina rejecting him. That thought scared him more than anything. Just thinking about it made his heart drop a little and prevented him from focusing on the present. If Sabrina Clarin didn't feel the same way, it would just be the end of their friendship. The thought was more than Elijah could handle, so he turned around and went out of sight.

That night, Elijah gazed at the photo he took of Sabrina back in January on their field trip. It was the only moment with her that he could go back and enjoy. He still hadn't shown anyone that he took a picture of her. Only he knew.

Later that week, it was time for counseling. Elijah was actually glad to see Ken because he needed someone to talk to about what happened. For the time being, Ken was the only person that could give some perspective. They sat in the same room as last time. Elijah got straight to the point once they sat down.

"I was...kind of sad the other day" he explained, "I mean things are good. I didn't get into any fights and I stayed with my real friends. But...sometimes I get sad"

"Do you know what it is that's making you feel that way?" Ken asked, gently.

"I don't know"

Elijah hadn't spent much time on his problems and had to process them during the moment of silence. Then he shared what happened with Sabrina and her family, and how much it made him sad. After that Elijah recapped the day when he almost asked Sabrina out. He told Ken about it, but didn't bother sharing that one image he had in his head before the whole thing happened.

"I almost did it, Ken" Elijah said, "I actually almost asked Sabrina out...I-I thought about a few minutes before and suddenly I just ran, like I had to-it was like something told me that I had to-so I started moving. I ran to the front of the school to look for her and there she was. I was about to go up to her but then...I stopped. I stopped because... what if Sabrina said no?"

Ken didn't say anything.

"If she said no, then I would just feel more sad" Elijah added, "I started thinking what if she doesn't like me the same way I like her? I got so scared, I just couldn't move anymore. So I turned around and left before she saw me"

That was probably why he just couldn't say the exact words from the times he was alone with her. Before Elijah knew it, there was a little tear in his eye. He wiped it before the emotion could go any deeper.

"Are you okay?" Ken said.

It took a moment for things to settle down.

"Take a deep breath" Ken encouraged, "Remember deep breaths help"

Elijah did as Ken said and inhaled through his nose and breathed out through his mouth.

"How are you feeling?"

"A little better" Elijah admitted.

Ken nodded. "So basically, you're feeling pretty emotional because you're afraid that Sabrina might reject you?"

Elijah took his time and finally nodded. Then he stared blankly as he was going through his thoughts. "I didn't know I loved Sabrina this much" he added. That was the first time that Elijah said in his own words that he loved Sabrina Clarin. "If she said no, I don't think I can handle it"

"I can see you really care about her that much" Ken told him.

"Yeah, I do. And maybe it's not just her saying no; I'm also scared that she might not want to be friends anymore"

Ken nodded, "You can never tell what's going to happen"

"So I don't know what to do" Elijah admitted, "I want to tell her how I feel, it's just…I'm not sure if I should. I do care about her much more than a friend-a normal friend usually does. But I'm scared because I might scare her away. And I don't want her to go away; I want her to be part of my life. It's just…I just wish there was a way for Sabrina to know how I feel about her…"

After expressing himself, Elijah went into silence. He sat back and took another deep breath. Ken took his time before giving some perspective to his student.

"Well, Elijah, maybe something is telling you that it's not the best time. That might be why you couldn't tell Sabrina how you feel. Maybe you're not ready or maybe she's not ready. I'm not saying that you shouldn't tell Sabrina at all, I'm saying that everything happens for a reason. I don't know if that helps but sometimes that's how life is, you feel like you should do something but you just can't. You're not really sure why, you just feel it"

Ken wasn't wrong, but Elijah wasn't sure if it explained everything.

"Other than that" Ken added, "Maybe there is a way for Sabrina to know how you feel without telling her"

Intrigued, Elijah looked at Ken and listened.

"Keep being yourself, be there for her, and show how much you care through your kindness. That way, the relationship builds and the longer that goes on, the more you two connect".

There were no other alternatives. So Elijah took Ken's advice.

After that emotional phase, Elijah decided to express himself on Valentine's Day, in a friendly way. Giving store bought Valentine cards to friends seemed to be getting cliché. Having someone special like Sabrina Clarin in Elijah's life was different in a profound way. So he decided to make his own Valentine cards! He only had a few days to think of something to write. It had to be original and it had to describe his friendship with Sabrina. As soon as Elijah found some paper, he pulled out his pencil crayons and markers, and spent hours working on them at home. With all the paper, supplies, free time, and all the heart, Elijah then decided to make Valentine Cards for everyone, Sabrina, Paula, Andrew, and even Melanie, and Carly.

February 14.

The anticipation for giving friends Valentine cards never felt so exciting. A girl like Sabrina Clarin sure made it extra special like she did with Christmas and even just a regular school day. Making your own Valentine cards seemed only right. Elijah had all the cards in his backpack and acted normal throughout the morning. Normally, students would exchange Valentine cards just before their lunch break. But for Elijah it seemed a little too far away. So he decided that he would give his to Sabrina and Carly before anyone else gave out theirs.

It was time for Mrs. Parker's class to start their art subject. She encouraged everyone to grab their supplies and make their way to the art room. Elijah deliberately took his time just until the last of his classmates left the room. He didn't really want to be seen sneaking some cards into a girl's locker. Once he had the moment, Elijah immediately pulled out the cards from his backpack and taped them to Sabrina's locker and Carly's locker. Mrs. Parker was waiting patiently.

"One second" Elijah promised.

After he got the second card on the locker, Elijah quickly went and grabbed his art supplies, and finally made his way out of the classroom. As Elijah was walking out, he felt his teacher's eyes gawking at him, almost like she was waiting for an explanation.

"Please don't tell anyone" he said, politely, as he met Mrs. Parker's eyes, rather awkwardly.

After art class was over, it was almost time for recess. The students returned to class. Elijah decided to wait at his desk, as he watched both Sabrina and Carly. They spotted the cards taped to their lockers. Elijah began to feel a little edgy, nervous, yet excited at the same time. Things got more interesting when the girls gazed at the cards. Both were puzzled and intrigued. Being too shy to face the result, Elijah turned away and acted normal.

"Hey, I found this on my..." Carly tried to explain as she went up to Sabrina, only to realize that she had the same envelope, "Oh, you have one, too?"

"Yeah, somebody was decorating our lockers" Sabrina said, "How thoughtful"

"I wonder who it was from" Carly wondered.

"Only the card will tell us"

Carly started opening it, but then stopped herself. "Oh, should we wait until later? You know when we hand out our cards?" She was speaking in a low voice.

"Why are you whispering?" Sabrina asked,

Carly gave a little sigh and spoke at her normal tone, "We're the only ones who got cards stuck to our lockers and then everybody's gonna ask about it"

"Yeah, we become famous just for having mysterious envelopes taped to our lockers" Sabrina added, sarcastically.

Ignoring her friend's remark, Carly just decided to open the envelope, as well as Sabrina. Before they got a chance to look at it, more of their classmates were constantly passing through. It was becoming more crowded. "Let's go over here before we get crushed" Sabrina insisted. Both girls went towards the back of the room, leaning on the counter. Once they had their space, they finally realized that it was merely folded paper.

"I guess they're not cards" Carly said.

"I guess not" Sabrina agreed.

They both gazed at the paper, realizing that it had a drawing and a saying: Having a friend on Valentine's Day is just as special as petals on a flower. And then there were illustrations of red hearts on the outline of the paper. And at the bottom of the paper, it had Elijah's name. Sabrina quickly looked up, expecting to see Elijah at his desk, but he was gone.

Next door to Mrs. Parker's class, Andrew and Melanie received envelopes from one of their classmates, claiming that she was instructed to give it to them. And just across the hall, as one of the students was leaving to go outside, he noticed an envelope on the door that had Paula Hennig's name on it. Everybody made it outside for recess. Sabrina was with her friends and they were talking about the surprise Valentine papers they received. Paula and Andrew met by the entrance and they were wondering the same thing. They looked around but Elijah was nowhere to be seen.

"He gives us Valentine cards and now he's playing hide and seek" Andrew said, as they were looking around.

"I was just thinking a minute ago that maybe I was getting too old for Valentine's Day and now I feel bad" Paula added.

"Hey guys" Elijah called, from behind. Both of his friends turned around and there he was, standing next to the pillar, "Happy Valentine's Day".

Paula smiled and went up to give Elijah a hug. "Happy Valentine's to you too. I owe you a card now"

"Oh that's fine. Your friendship is all I need" Elijah told her, kindly.

Then Andrew went up to Elijah and gave each other the thumbs up-fist bump, and wished each other a Happy Valentine's Day. "Thanks bud, and the chocolate was nice too"

"Chocolate, how come I didn't get any?" Paula asked,

"Because I know Andrew would eat melted chocolate" Elijah explained, "But don't worry, I got yours right here". Then he pulled out a small package and gave it to Paula.

"Huh, and you only gave me a few" Andrew said, and then he looked at Elijah, "What did I do?"

"Being a good friend"

"Then where's my bag?"

Then Elijah pulled another bag and gave it to Andrew.

"Now that's more like it!" Andrew added with excitement.

After the celebration with Andrew and Paula, Elijah went to meet with Sabrina and her friends. They weren't that far. Once Sabrina noticed him, she began to approach, with the other girls watching. "Elijah?" she called.

Elijah stopped and met her eyes. "Yeah?" he replied, casually.

It was silent at first, but then the moment become comforting when a smile slowly formed on Sabrina's face and then she showed him the card. "That was very nice of you".

Then Elijah began to smile, for that he succeeded his Valentine's Day plans.

"You like it?" he asked.

"Yeah, it's great! And very thoughtful"

"Glad you like it"

Sabrina then gave Elijah a hug. He wrapped his arms around her in return. Once they let go of each other, Melanie came from behind, "Aww, thanks for the card, Elijah. That was very sweet!"

Before Elijah could reply, Melanie walked up with open arms and gave him a hug as well. He wasn't expecting that.

"Yeah, you're welcome. I'm glad you like it" Elijah said to her.

"More like love it!" she added.

Carly however was a little too shy to give a hug. So she merely gave a little wave, acknowledging Elijah, followed by a friendly smile. "Thank you. This was very nice"

Elijah smiled and nodded. "Yeah, sure. But hey, it's not over yet. I got some candy just for you guys!"

The girls couldn't help but get excited as they were offered the candy. Again, the girls thanked him, proudly. Then Sabrina went up and gave Elijah another hug. That was a bonus. He was more than willing to return the hug. So Valentine's Day was pretty much already over for him. His friends were happy, as well as Sabrina and her friends. And it turned out better than he expected. It made Elijah feel good. As he slowly walked away, he couldn't help but think, why stop there?

Buying treats for the girls became a habit after February 14th. Not only it made Elijah feel good but it also motived him to show Sabrina that he cared about her and her friends, through kindness. So after that day at school, Elijah went down to the gas bar and bought some more candy, just enough for all of them. From there, he planned his next day at school. It gave him something to look forward to and he could barely wait.

All three girls were at school, which was good. It meant a lot more when Carly and Melanie were by Sabrina's side. For the morning, Elijah remained casual as he secretly had the candy in his backpack. He decided that recess would be the best time. Once the time came, he grabbed the treats and stuck them in his coat pockets and then went outside to meet with the girls.

"Hey, Sabrina, Carly, Mel" Elijah greeted, as he approached, "How's it going?"

The three of them answered, almost at the same time. First, Sabrina said, "Good", and then Mel added, "Tired", and finally Carly, "Cold, but good".

"That's good. Hey, I got something for you"

The girls were a little surprised once Elijah pulled out a bag of candy for them,

"You brought us more candy? Again?" Melanie replied. Even though she was a little tired, she still managed to sound a little excited.

"Yes" Elijah replied, smiling politely.

"Well, this should wake me up a little" Melanie took the candy, "Thanks, Elijah!"

"Aww" Sabrina said, as she got hers, "You're sweet"

"Almost sweet as the candy" Mel joked.

Flattered, Elijah smiled. That day was just as good as Valentine's from the day before. The plan lived up to its expectations. He was feeling just as proud.

"Thank you" Carly said, gently.

The girls took their time to enjoy their treats. Melanie just devoured hers.

"Mmm" Sabrina muttered, as she swallowed the last bit of her candy. "Elijah, I been meaning to ask, those sayings on those Valentine's cards, did you come up with that yourself?"

Elijah nodded, "Yeah".

"Really? How creative"

"Thank you".

That put Elijah in the mood as he started bragging about being an artist most of his life. The girls kindly listened to every word. Since he was talking about art, Elijah was starting to wish that he brought his notebook where he kept his drawings. But even so, talking to the girls about was just as satisfying. Then the topic influenced Melanie to share her experiences with art. After her, Sabrina and Carly added a few stories. Each detail led to another. During a pause, Elijah looked over and saw Paula and Andrew hanging around alone.

"Well, I guess I better get going" Elijah said, wrapping up the conversation, "Glad you girls enjoyed the candy"

Just as he started walking away, he heard Sabrina calling out his name. At first, he was expecting her to say one last thank you or simply express her gratitude. But it was neither.

"Or you could hang out with us a little longer" she suggested.

Elijah certainly didn't expect that, being asked to hang out with Sabrina and her friends. His moment of surprise prevented him from saying anything.

"If you want" Sabrina added.

Elijah looked back at Paula and Andrew, as if he was asking for permission to hang out with the girls. He could feel Paula meeting his eyes and then suddenly felt obligated to go back to them. But then he thought that the offer could be a rare opportunity to get close to Sabrina.

"Of course" Elijah finally answered, sounding a little excited but then he toned it down to mild, "Yeah", he added, as he went back to the girls.

CHAPTER SEVENTEEN

Angels

Elijah and the girls decided to walk around the school, as a way to cope with the cold weather. Along the way, they continued their conversation about their art experiences. Carly admitted that was not all good at the activity, while the others had a natural talent. It was nice for Elijah to know that he had one thing in common with Sabrina's friends.

"-those boys got me pretty good" Melanie explained, "For a little while I actually believed that pumpkins were going to grow inside of me".

"That would be kind of scary" Carly added, "I don't even wanna think that".

"That sounds like something Andrew would joke about" Elijah said.

"I can see that, too" Sabrina agreed.

They were in the back of the school. They noticed one of the supervisors renting out crazy carpets to some of the students. Just seeing that got the group reminiscing about their field trip to Smithers from the previous month. They recapped certain moments. In fact, Elijah remembered the picture he took of Sabrina that day. He thought about showing it to her but decided to wait a little longer.

They walked in silence shortly after that. Elijah then suggested to Sabrina to show her friends the little game they made back in November. She agreed and so they began explaining what it was. The girls went

262

along with the idea, as he and Sabrina showed the other girls their little game when one walks forward while the other walked backwards. They did a demonstration before Carly and Mel did the same. The four of them altogether tried it. Elijah had Sabrina walking backwards in front of him, while Carly had Mel doing the same. As they were going along, some of their peers were coming toward them. Just like what Elijah and Sabrina did last time, they told each other which way to turn. Halfway through, they switched positions. They kept going until the end. After they were finished, there was laughter and excitement.

"That was kinda fun" Melanie said, "Thanks Elijah"

"Yeah" Elijah nodded, "That was pretty much Sabrina's invention. We should thank her"

"Well, thank you, Sabrina"

Sabrina chuckled, "You're welcome. I'm glad you guys enjoyed it as much as we did"

"Yeah, like Mel said, it was fun" Carly agreed.

"You're missing the word 'kinda' but whatever"

As they walked casually, they were slowing down, for that parts of the ground was covered in ice. Suddenly, Carly slipped. She lost her balance and was about to fall, but luckily Elijah was behind her and quickly grabbed her before hitting the ground. It happened so fast that the other girls weren't aware of it until they heard the commotion.

"Whoa" Elijah said.

Carly was panting in fear. Sabrina and Mel stopped.

"Are you all right?" Elijah asked, kindly.

He gently lifted her until she was on her feet again.

"That would've ended badly if she did fell" Sabrina said.

"I'm okay" Carly claimed, "Oh boy that was a close one. Thank you"

"Anytime" Elijah replied.

"I really don't like winter" Carly said.

"Yeah, not everybody does" Elijah told her, "But don't worry too much. Next month will be spring and we'll have the sun"

Carly smiled, a little more than she intended, "Yeah" she muttered, just to break the silence.

"But you're okay though?" Elijah asked.

"I'm okay" she told him.

That was when Carly Dawson was beginning to warm up to Elijah Khoda. Before they were just kids in the same classroom but now she found him friendly and considerate. Since then, she said hi to him on daily basis.

Elijah spent the rest of the recess with the girls. It turned out more enjoyable than he expected. He got to know Carly and Melanie a little better. Melanie was upbeat and Carly was kind hearted. The reason why Elijah decided to give them Valentine cards was because he wanted to show Sabrina that he was supportive to her and the ones in her life. By giving them the cards, it took Elijah somewhere he didn't expect, being in the company of girls.

As they were walking, Elijah decided to tease Mel after the humorous affection she showed him. Without her knowing, he snuck up behind and shoved her slightly. "Whoops, I slipped" he said, jokingly. Melanie stopped and shot a scowl at him, but in a playful way. Sabrina and Carly stopped to see what would happen next.

"Like to play rough, eh? Well, I can play rougher" Mel said. She returned the favor and pushed Elijah in the same manner, "Whoops! I must warn you, I'm pretty clumsy"

"What, do you knock things down, bump into people?"

"All the time" Melanie replied, in a sly tone.

"Try me" Elijah challenged, in a smooth voice.

Melanie's eyes widened, "Well, if...you...insist!" then she abruptly ran like an athlete and bumped into Elijah, a little hard than he expected, for that he nearly lost balance. Even Sabrina and Carly were a little surprised.

Elijah just chuckled, "Nice one, Clumsy"

"I dare you to do something better, Pushy"

"Pushy, eh?" he replied, gently.

Elijah was tempted to shove her again, but that seemed too repetitive. So one idea came to mind and without giving a second thought, Elijah quickly dashed around Melanie and lifted her up by wrapping his arms around her, and sprung her around.

"Whoa!" Mel cried, "Not bad"

The excitement was building up, that Elijah just had to bring Sabrina and Carly into it.

"Who's next?" he challenged.

Sabrina and Carly exchanged looks. Carly thought maybe the whole thing was a plain joke, but there was mischief on Sabrina's face as she smiled. Then Sabrina went up to Elijah and shoved him back a few inches. And so the play fight began. Melanie fought back and did the same thing. Elijah then began running from them in circles. It took a little time for Carly to gain the courage to join. With a little hesitation, Carly went up to Elijah and threw a punch, which caught everyone by surprise as they all looked at her.

"Um, that was the best I can come up with" Carly claimed.

After brief silence, Melanie formed a smile, "The best one yet!" she agreed. Then Melanie started throwing punches at Elijah, "Whoops, whoops, whoops!" she taunted.

"Oh come on, you fight like a girl" Elijah teased.

"I know you are, but what am I?" Mel said, as she kept punching Elijah.

Sabrina laughed and joined the fight, but shortly Elijah was able to escape for a moment. While he had the chance, he grabbed some snow off the ground and threw chunks of it at the girls.

"Snowball fight!" Sabrina declared.

All three girls created a distance between them and Elijah, as they went and gathered snow off the ground. They shaped them into small rounds and began throwing at each other. It was Elijah against Sabrina, Melanie, and Carly. Once he was able to hit three of them, he began running off, laughing as he went, and the girls began chasing him.

That wasn't the last time Elijah spent time with the girls. Since then, he would naturally meet them every day, in the morning and during recess. They would greet each other in a nice and sometimes playful way, and they would hang out until the end of their free time. And each time, Elijah had little bags of candy to offer them, just like what he did on Valentine's Day. They grew quite fond of each other. Both Melanie and Carly treated Elijah like he was part of their inner circle. Even Carly didn't feel as awkward around him anymore as she got to know him a little better. After a little while, spending time with the girls became more than just privilege. Elijah was doing it out of love for Sabrina. He treated her friends the same way he treated her, with kindness and warmth. It was always a good time whenever they were together. There were some days where Elijah was a plain friend and there were days where he would go out of his own way just to make one of the girls feel better, even if it meant standing up for one of them.

"What's wrong?" Sabrina asked, as she noticed Melanie had a sour face.

"Oh, nothing, it's just..." Melanie trailed off, "Now I can't really finish that sentence"

Melanie always had a smile on her face. Something was a little off that day.

"Come on, talk to us" Sabrina insisted.

Both Elijah and Carly became concerned.

"Oh, just now in the boot room, that one girl said to me 'hurry up!'. It was pretty unkind. But it's no big deal"

Mel claimed that it wasn't big of a problem, but Elijah could sense the hurt in her voice.

"Just ignore her" Carly advised, "I'm sure she has problems of her..."

"Which girl?" Elijah asked, promptly.

They all turned to Elijah, who looked like he was ready to do something.

"Uh, that Marissa Hartway"

"Melissa" Elijah corrected.

"Yeah, that was her. I didn't even do anything. And what bothers me more is that we both have the same initial".

There was a paused moment.

"I know Melissa. She was unkind to me too" Elijah admitted. Then without thinking about it, he added, "Allow me".

Just like that, Elijah took off. The girls exchanged looks with each other. "What's he gonna do?" Carly asked, trying not to sound too worried.

"I don't know" Sabrina replied, "But only one way to find out"

Sabrina went after Elijah. Shortly, Carly and Melanie followed. Sabrina caught up with Elijah.

"Elijah?" she called. But there was no reply, "What are you gonna do?"

"Nobody messes with friends of my friends" Elijah finally responded, as he kept walking with his eyes forward.

"Yeah, but what are you gonna do?" Sabrina repeated.

Elijah then glanced over at Sabrina, "Talk" he told her.

He knew that Melissa Hartway wasn't all nice when there were no grownups around. He hadn't forgotten the times that she judged and belittled him from the previous school years. Therefore, Elijah couldn't help but feel a little offended that she briefly antagonized Melanie. At first, he saw that as an insult to Sabrina Clarin. There was no way that could be overlooked. Melissa and her friends were hanging around the pathway when Elijah found them. He stopped for a moment to breathe in some confidence and then looked back at the girls who stood there supporting him.

"Time for bravery" he said. Then Elijah approached Melissa, who noticed him right away. Her face just dropped with disappointment, "Excuse me" he called.

Hiding her surprise, Melissa scoffed, "What do you know, he has manners now" she muttered to her friends.

"Melissa Hartway" Elijah called, rather gently. Before whenever he interacted with Melissa, he'd always be aggressive due to his dislike towards her.

"Never thought I'd hear you say my name, Elijah Khoda" she replied, strongly. She would say his full name, just like she did before. And from the way her voice sounded, she probably hadn't forgotten about their last interaction.

"Yeah, right" he muttered, "Is it true that you were being mean to that nice girl over there?"

Elijah gestured towards Melanie, who gave an awkward wave as she was being singled out. Melissa just ignored her and turned her attention back to Elijah.

"She was in my way, so what?"

"That wasn't very polite, you know" Elijah told her.

"Funny you say that because you weren't always polite to me, Elijah Khoda" she told him, "May I remind you that you and your friend Andrew pushed us off the ledge back in grade four". Melissa wasn't wrong. The firm tone in her voice threw Elijah off guard as he recalled the times he'd antagonize her and vice versa. Suddenly, his love for Sabrina interfered and softened him up. Now he lost his power and control of the situation as he realized the wrong he had done. The silence grew longer. So Sabrina approached Elijah from behind.

"So I guess that means you won't be apologizing" Elijah assumed, maintaining just a little authority in his voice.

"I wouldn't count on it" Melissa promised, shaking her head.

Sabrina tapped Elijah on his shoulder, "Hey, you don't need to do this" she told him gently, "We'll just walk it off"

Elijah almost turned around to walk away with Sabrina. But he could already see the embarrassment coming from a mile away. So he stopped to think for a moment. Standing up for Melanie Peyton was the original intention, but it ended up with Elijah having to pay for his mistakes. So the best thing to do was to admit it and call a truce with Melissa Hartway.

"It looks like you're about to say something else" Melissa said, "If so, just get it over with. I don't have all day"

Elijah exchanged glances with Sabrina and then to Melanie, standing in the distance. "Yes I do" he admitted. Then he turned around and walked up to Melissa, who was on the other side of the railing. It was rather discomforting silence, as they were expecting Elijah to do something reckless.

"You're right" Elijah admitted. Melissa flinched and her eyes widened for a brief moment. "Me and Andrew shouldn't have pushed you and your friends off the ledge. And I shouldn't have been rude to you all those times. So…instead of an apologizing to Melanie, you can draw on my face"

That caught everyone by surprise, even Melissa's friends froze.

"Yeah, you can draw something on my face and write something, which ever one you like", he actually hadn't thought that far ahead. The only thought he had going through his mind was that he might've deserved the punishment. So the next words just rolled of his tongue, "And I'll leave it like that until the end of the day"

Melissa took a moment to consider. "Do any of you have a pen?" she asked, as she glanced to each of her friends.

Whose funny looking now? That was written all over Elijah's forehead, along with drawings of a mustache and dark circles around the eyes. Elijah was sitting on the bench between Sabrina, Carly, and Melanie. He spent most of his time eyeing the ground, taking in the humiliation. Elijah couldn't help but think that Sabrina and her friends looked at him as strong right up until that point because he appeared weak and defeated.

"Hey" Sabrina said, gently, as she leaned in closer, "You okay?"

Elijah glanced at Sabrina and then to Carly and Mel, who were gazing in pity. "It's true, you know" he admitted, "I was a little rude to Melissa ever since grade four". He didn't bother telling them about the times Melissa was unkind to him because it was pointless. "So this is what I get" Elijah added, pointing to his face. Only Sabrina knew about Elijah's bad side. So he figured he owed Carly and Melanie and explanation. "Uh, actually, there were times when I did things that weren't really good" Elijah told them, "But I don't wanna be like that anymore"

The girls nodded and they understood.

"Well…" Sabrina spoke, "She may not have apologized to Melanie, but that was sweet that you stood up for her"

"Yeah, thank you, Elijah" Melanie said, with kindness, "At least now you made me feel a little better"

"Glad I can help" he replied, "Nobody messes with my friends, or I mean, my friend's friends"

"No, don't be silly" Carly encouraged, "We're glad to call you our friend"

"Really?"

270   PHILIP PATRICK

"Yes" Melanie agreed, "You gave us Valentine cards and some candy. You made us laugh and you made our recess a little more fun"

Elijah just smiled with flattery.

"Yeah, we're kinda like...Charlie's Angels" Sabrina said, "Because there are three girls by your side"

Elijah's smile grew even bigger. "I guess we kinda are"

"Elijah's Angels" Melanie declared.

"That's kinda cool" he agreed, gently.

Once recess was over, Elijah lined back up with his class. Paula and Andrew were passing through when they noticed the drawings on Elijah's face.

"What happened to you?" Paula asked,

"Melissa did this" he explained.

"Melissa?!" then her skeptical reaction dimmed, "I guess that's not really a surprise. But even so, this is new"

"Why did she go all Jigglypuff on you?" Andrew said.

"I told her to" Elijah admitted, with weak confidence in his voice. He felt proud that he won more affection from Sabrina and her girlfriends but at the same time he was also a little embarrassed by Melissa, even if it was his own doing.

And then back in class, Mrs. Parker was handing out their next assignments. Even she noticed the little graffiti on Elijah's face and became puzzled. He could feel his teacher's eyes gazing at him. So he shot a quick glance, "Payback" he told her. Elijah was about to add something else, but couldn't keep his mind and words together, "Let's just learn", he insisted.

In the end, Elijah lived up to his debt to society and washed off the ink from his face. He didn't feel as embarrassed as he did before. After all, there were upsides to that conflict. For one thing, it showed that Elijah Khoda really cared about the ones around him and that he didn't face the conflict to fulfill his own personal needs. And the other thing was, he disciplined himself for the wrong that he had done, attacking Melissa Hartway emotionally for no reason. That was a positive way to

ELIJAH AND SABRINA

271

look at it. So afterwards the hard feelings had passed and new day was on the horizon. The next morning, they were waiting for the bell to ring. Elijah went to greet the girls and then he noticed something that was a little off, which was alright because it was a chance to interact with Sabrina.

"Hey Sabrina" Elijah called,

"Yes?" she replied, kindly.

"Is it me or do you look a little taller?" Elijah wondered.

Uncertain, Sabrina gazed at herself and back to Elijah, "I don't know. Am I?"

"Maybe; I don't know, it's just I thought I was a little taller before or we both could be the same height"

"Well, let's find out" Sabrina suggested.

So Elijah stood tall and straight, and so did Sabrina. They both peered to the tip of each other's heads just to see if it matched the height.

"It might be because of my boots" Sabrina offered.

"Maybe"

After that, Elijah decided to stand on his toes, as a joke. Sabrina laughed, "That doesn't count", she told him.

"Of course, it does" Elijah insisted, "I wanna be tall. Let me have it"

"Now that easily, mister"

Sabrina too started standing on her toes as she was competing with Elijah. They stood as tall as they could. Shortly, Sabrina lost balance and nearly fell forward. Elijah feared the worse and actually grabbed her.

"Whoa" Elijah said, "Are you all right?"

"I'm fine. I guess I was trying a little too hard to be taller than you" Sabrina said, followed by a chuckle. Elijah smiled and then he found himself looking into Sabrina Clarin's eyes. That would be the first time Elijah experienced intimacy.

"I think you can let me go now" Sabrina said, gently.

Before he realized, Elijah still had his hands on Sabrina's waist.

"Oh, sorry" he replied, as he let go.

Then Melanie and Carly joined their little conversation, "I saw what you guys were doing" Melanie said, but yet she was uncertain, "What were you doing?"

Promptly, Elijah explained.

"Oh, sounds fun. Can we join?"

Again, Elijah and Sabrina stood on their toes, as well as Carly and Melanie. Shortly the silliness had them laughing. School started once the bell rang. Elijah went in with his classmates, but he never forgotten about that moment when he was practically holding Sabrina in his arms. Later that day, Elijah went to town with his parents to do some grocery shopping. The first thing he grabbed was four bags of candy.

"Whoa, that's a lot of candy" Madeline told Elijah as he put inside the shopping cart.

"It's only four" Elijah replied gently.

"Needo must really like his candy" she added.

"Oh, it's not just for Andrew. It's for the girls too"

Madeline was more uncertain than intrigued, "Girls?" she repeated.

"Just friends of mine" Elijah explained.

Spending time with Sabrina and her friends was a blast. Since Valentine's Day, Elijah made the best of it and each time he wanted to make it special and memorable, from having friendly conversations to having fun. Once every few days, Elijah spent time with Paula and Andrew as well. Then the next day at school, it was the best of both worlds, for that Elijah wanted his friends to hang out with the girls' altogether. He purposely waited until their lunch recess, so they would have more time to play. Elijah exited the school and met with his friends outside.

"Hey, Paulie and Andy" Elijah greeted, with a smile on his face.

"Hey, you're in a good mood" Paula said, gently.

"Yeah, normally you don't start giggling until I put the 'fun' in funny" Andrew added.

"Well, what can I say; it's been good these past couple weeks. I got you guys and I got them" Elijah then pulled the bags of candy from his coat pockets, "For you".

Andrew and Paula accepted their little treats.

"Sweet!" Andrew cheered, "You're almost like the tooth fairy, except you want us to have bad teeth"

Andrew ripped open the candy bag and started to devour it.

"Elijah" Paula called, "You know, I don't think I've ever seen you be this nice before"

"Well, maybe I didn't really care about it that much. All I cared about was having fun. But now I care about both, just as much as I care about you guys"

Paula smiled and gave a friendly nod, and it was all genuine. "We care about you, too" Paula told him.

"You and the treats you give us" Andrew said, with a little candy in his mouth, in which he shortly swallowed, "If I'd to choose between my best friend and the food, I'd chose you, as long as you bring the food"

Elijah chuckled with joy. "You can count on me for that. Come on, we're gonna do something a little different today"

"We're gonna put Paulie in a garbage can and roll her down the hill?" Andrew asked.

Paula only rolled her eyes because then she had candy in her mouth. "I'm eating" she told them.

"Maybe next time" Elijah said, as a joke, "Today, we're gonna hang out with the girls"

Elijah, Andrew, and Paula, were standing across from Sabrina, Carly, and Melanie. Elijah introduced the whole gang to each other. First he brought in Paula by gently placing his hand on her shoulder. "Some of you might know her, this is one of my best friends, Paula Hennig" Elijah told them, "We have been friends since primary school".

Over the years, Paula didn't seem to fit with the rest of the crowd. She was mature for her age, compared to most girls. So Paula stood just waved gently as she stood in awkward silence. "Hi…so how's girl's night going for you?"

Nobody answered at first. Then Sabrina stepped in, "Never better", she answered with a smile.

Then Elijah offered another little fact about his best friend, "Paula likes to read. One time she read an entire dictionary. Ask her about any word and she'll answer. Ask".

"Okay…" Mel replied, "What does the word abstract mean?"

Then Paula answered, promptly, "An existing in thought or an idea but not in a physical or concrete existence"

"Not bad. How about…" Mel paused to think, "Doppelganger?"

"A double that looks alike"

"That's great! Even my dad didn't know what that word meant. Carly didn't either"

Carly looked at Mel skeptically. Then Mel exchanged an apologetic expression. "Just slipped out" she added, shrugging her shoulders and smiling nervously.

Andrew walked up to them to mingle. "Hello, the name's Andrew Little, what's up?"

"Um, we know because Elijah just introduced you" Carly said, gently.

"But you didn't hear it from me" Andrew told her, "I'm Elijah's best friend, since grade four. I'm the funny and the weird one… I bring the laughs, the imagination, and the little pain you feel when you laugh too much"

"Well, it's funny you say that" Melanie spoke, "Because Elijah appointed me as the angel of humor"

"Does that mean you're the funny one of the…girl band-this girl band?" Andrew replied.

"Mhm"

"Oh yeah, well let's see who makes them laugh the most"

Melanie gave a grim smile, "You're on".

Andrew closed his right eye and pointed at Mel with two fingers. Melanie did the same gesture; except she showed her teeth and her eyebrows were narrowed down, like she was ready for any competition.

"Oh, I forgot to see hello" Andrew added, "Hello". He spoke politely to Melanie.

"Hello" she replied, in the same manner.

"You're Melanie"

"And you must be Andrew"

"Not just Andrew, I'm the Andrew"

There was a paused moment as they met each other's eye.

"Hello" Andrew repeated.

Melanie played along, "Hello" she said, casually, "Hey, are you the one who put a straw in a pizza pop and tried to suck out the ingredients not too long ago?"

"Yes" Andrew admitted, undauntedly. Melanie and the other girls looked at him, waiting for an explanation or even a joke, "It was an idea that came to me. Just had to try"

Melanie just nodded. It was silent again, as Andrew just looked at Mel. Every now and then he liked to repeat words or jokes. So he greeted her once more. "Hello", Andrew repeated, smoothly. And he was glad to hear that Mel kept playing along.

"Hello" she replied, slyly.

Their eyes met. Flattery and playfulness were written all over them. It looked like Andrew and Melanie were going to get along just fine.

"Alright" Elijah called, "Now that we met each other, whose ready to have some fun?"

"And annoy each other?" Andrew offered, "Paulie?"

"I miss my book already" she replied, sarcastically.

Then Elijah just played along, "Maybe cause mischief" he added.

"Play in the snow!" Melanie called out.

"Freeze our butts off" Sabrina joked.

"Wait for spring?" Carly suggested.

"Gang up on Andrew" Paula told them.

After all the ideas and suggestions were spoken, Elijah spoke cheerfully like he was hosting a sporting event, "Alright, so we got lots to do. So if you're ready, raise your hand". Just as everyone was about to do so, Elijah prevented it once he thought of another way to get everyone on board. "Wait, wait" he protested. He remembered one particular moment from the snowboarding trip, "If you're ready...clap your hands together".

Elijah was the first to do the gesture. Andrew and the girls did the same.

"How about twice?"

Then they all clapped twice. That was supposed to be the end of it, until Andrew joined in on the fun. "Now everyone stomp your feet!" he insisted but only as a joke. Surprisingly, the girls went along with it and stomped their foot on the ground once. Andrew decided to take advantage of it. No one seemed to have a problem. It was their way of starting off their time together.

"Stomp your feet twice" Andrew told them.

They did as he instructed, even Elijah did, and then he added, "Now clap again".

The whole gang clapped twice. Once it was Andrew's turn, he decided to change it up.

"Jump up and down!"

Smiles formed on all the girls' faces as they jumped off the ground, repeatedly. The boys could see the excitement taking formation. Elijah and Andrew stood there, laughing excitedly. They figured that was enough but then-

"Now let's race to the field" Elijah offered.

It was silent at first. The girls looked at each other briefly, until Melanie turned around and started running. Shortly, Sabrina and Carly ran after her. Then the boys did the same without hesitation. Paula went to catch up, thinking that they weren't really going to do it. But in the end, it was a great turnout. Carly was the first that made it to the field, since she was the athlete. Everyone else caught up, one by one.

"That was fun" Sabrina said, catching her breath, "You guys should teach gym class".

"That would be awesome!" Melanie agreed, "I would attend that".

Then Andrew replied with genuine excitement, as if the idea was doable, "Hey, I like!" He opened his mouth to add more to the idea, "Aww, I was going to come up with a name for it but I got nothing. E.K, I think those candy you gave me is messing with my brain".

"Huh, you didn't blame me for once. Thank you" Paula said.

"Haha, glad I could help" Elijah replied.

"Alright, so what's next?" Sabrina asked.

Both Elijah and Andrew's minds suddenly went blank. They hadn't thought that far ahead. So it took a moment for them to brainstorm ideas. "Well, I guess we can't play Frisbee or anything because they don't give those out in the winter." Elijah told them. Feeling uncertain, he turned to Andrew, "Or do they?"

"I forget."

Then Elijah leaned in closer to Andrew, "What else can we do?" he asked, in a low voice.

"You're asking me? You're the leader"

"Yeah but sometimes leaders need help, you know" Elijah's voice was getting lower.

"I'm the funny guy, I do my own thing" Andrew replied, in the same tone of voice.

"Can't the funny guy help?"

"Why are you guys whispering?" Carly wondered.

"I'm only whispering because he is" Andrew claimed.

"Oh, the heck with it" Elijah said, as he bent down to gather some snow and then he stood back up and threw it towards the girls, "Snowball fight!" But then his snowball went passed Sabrina and only hit the ground. There was a pause, a little awkward at first. But then the tension built up as everyone in the group exchanged glances at each other. It became clear they were all thinking the same thing. Finally, both boys and the girls quickly grabbed some snow and began their snowball fight. It started off as Elijah against Sabrina with their friends by their sides.

After that playful activity, the group decided to walk around without destination until they found something else to do. All six of them were walking side by side, in a line that spread across. But soon they divided themselves into pairs as they approached the wooden stairs. So Elijah led the way, with Sabrina right behind him, while Andrew and Melanie were in the middle, and Paula ended up beside Carly in the back of the crowd.

"Hi" Paula said, politely, as she found herself making eye contact with Sabrina's friend.

"Hi" Carly repeated.

They were looking eye to eye longer than they anticipated. It was already becoming awkward. Paula Hennig wasn't keen on making new friends. She always relied on Elijah and Andrew to do the socializing.

"So...you're Carly" Paula said, mildly.

"Yeah, Carly Dawson" Carly nodded, forcing a little smile.

Paula finally broke eye contact, but she still felt obligated to make small talk. Her mouth was open and ended up having to improvise.

"Well, I would say Elijah has told me about you, but he actually didn't say much"

"Oh" Carly added,

"Would you do the honors?" Paula suggested. That would be her way of interacting whenever she spoke to someone that wasn't Elijah or Andrew.

"Like about myself?"

Paula almost said that she didn't have to but Paula was thoughtful enough not to be rude.

"Yeah" she agreed.

"Well...I like sports and I like cats"

"Well that's good. You're a...sporty girl and a cat person. How many cats do you own?"

"Just one, her name is Peyton"

Paula nodded, "Cute"

"Yeah, I'm not really good at...naming things, so when I first got her I just named her after Melanie"

"That's me!" Mel said, as she looked back at them.

As they were walking, Andrew turned around to add something to their conversation. "For a second, I thought you were gonna say 'catty'" then he chuckled, "Because you said sport with a Y at the end"

"You sound like one of my teachers" Paula told him, "You would be a good teacher's pet"

Carly giggled at Paula's comeback. Paula couldn't help but feel proud of herself that she made a good first impression.

The gang ended up at the tire swings once they realized once one of them was available. Andrew was the first to try it, by lifting himself up and stood on two feet, and then he swung around. Not everybody had the courage to do such a trick. So Andrew offered to teach them. The first person he asked was Melanie. So she went up and did as Andrew instructed. Together the both of them started swinging as they were standing on their feet while they were holding the chains.

"Anybody wanna go for a little spin?" Andrew offered, "Let's fill the tire up with three of you"

Elijah, Sabrina, and Carly volunteered.

"Wanna go next Paulie?" Andrew asked.

"Nah, I don't trust you" Paula admitted, "You'll probably make me throw up"

"But it would be worth it"

Paula looked at Andrew a little weird, like she always did. "Pretty much everything amuses you"

"Almost everything"

Once Elijah, Sabrina, and Carly were ready, Andrew did as he promised and started spinning them around as fast as he could. Elijah and Sabrina cheered, while Carly was smiling nervously.

"Woo! That was fun" Elijah called.

"I'm feeling a little dizzy but it was worth it" Sabrina agreed.

"Now that is the consequence of fun" Andrew added, "Worth it".

After they exited the tire swing, Elijah noticed Paula was merely standing there watching them. So he decided to include her into their activity. "Wanna do some swinging, Paula?" he asked, gently.

"Definitely" Paula agreed, "Because I trust you"

"Paulie, I'm right here" Andrew said, jokingly.

"I know"

Together, Elijah and Paula stood on the tire swings and held onto the top of the chains as they were gently swinging. While the others were waiting, Andrew was having friendly conversations with Sabrina and her friends.

"This is cool" Andrew said, "We're kinda like our own bands, you know"

Intrigued, Sabrina looked at him and listened.

"Like you and your friends are a girl band" Andrew added, "And me, Elijah, and Paulie are...both"

"Oh, you mean like pop artists coming in one?" Sabrina said, "I like that"

"We would be the Spice Girls!" Melanie insisted.

"Oh, so you're 'Wannabes'. Get it?"

"Oh we get it" Mel told him.

Elijah and Paula were slowing down on the tire swing as they overheard the conversation. "I guess that makes us S Club 7?" he asked.

"Might as well" Paula replied, "Since our group is a mix of guys and a girl"

"S Club 3?"

"Sounds more accurate"

They both got off the tire swing as the topic of the conversation caught everyone's attention.

"Hey Sabrina, which do you think is better, Backstreet Boys or N'sync?" Elijah asked.

Sabrina paused to think.

"Say N'sync, say N'sync" Melanie told her.

"Backstreet Boys" Sabrina answered.

Melanie gave a disappointing groan.

"I only listened to a few N'sync songs. So…"

"So you're saying you have one of their CD's but only like a few songs?" Mel asked.

"Well, not really. I just saw a few of their music videos. That was about it"

"Well, I know what I'm getting you for your next birthday"

As the girls were talking, Elijah reached to the ground and grabbed a chunk of snow and then threw it at Sabrina. The snowball hit Sabrina on the chest. All three girls looked at him.

"It was him" Elijah said, pointing to Andrew.

"No, it was you" Carly pointed out.

"Are you asking for trouble, Elijah?" Sabrina asked, playfully.

Elijah shrugged his shoulders not sure what to say at first, "Trouble is a friend of mine"

Sabrina quickly grabbed some snow off the ground, and then threw it at Elijah. "Well, tell Trouble that was for him"

Suddenly, another snowball came firing at the girls but it was a near miss. "Now it was me"

Before Andrew knew it, a chunk of snow came splashing on the side of his face.

"Gotcha!" Paula called.

"Get her" Andrew insisted.

"Get them" Elijah told him.

"Get everybody" Melanie added. Then she threw a snowball at Carly, who then returned the favor. So began another snowball fight. There were really no teams, just boys and girls attacking each other for fun.

At the end of the day, Elijah was at home still thinking of the fun day he had with both his friends, and Sabrina and her friends. Together they seemed to get off on the right foot and Elijah couldn't be more proud.

He went upstairs to get himself a snack from the kitchen. Madeline Khoda came walking in to return the glass that she was using.

"Eli" she called.

Elijah stopped once he heard his name.

"Are you still hanging out with those girls?" she asked, gently.

Even though she spoke gently, the power of her words made Elijah froze. There was no running on this part.

"Yeah?" he admitted.

"I wanted to talk to you about that"

A bad feeling was creeping all over Elijah. But in actuality, he didn't do anything wrong. Maybe there was a possible chance to convince her. Madeline stood face to face with her son as she got straight to the point.

"I think it's best that you stop hanging out with them"

Elijah nearly stuttered, for that he wasn't expecting such a demand. He thought for sure that his mom was merely checking up on him. How wrong he was.

"Why?" Elijah replied, trying to act normal as possible while being a little concerned.

"Because you're too young to be hanging out with girls" she told him.

Too young; that was exactly what Elijah was afraid of, not getting a chance to have a friend like Sabrina in his life because he was simply too young.

"B-but...nothing's going on" Elijah assured, "We're-we're just friends"

"Sometimes you never know" Madeline added, "Elijah; you're getting to that age where you become a little curious about girls. Sooner or later, there's going to be hurt feelings, whether it's you or them, or even both. I don't want you going through that"

Just when his friends began bonding with Sabrina's friends, suddenly it was over, just like that.

"That's just one thing" his mom said, "I remember you telling me what you and Andrew did to those girls a few years ago"

That day in grade four when Elijah and Andrew pushed Melissa Hartway and her friends off the ledge, Elijah came home bragging about it like it was okay to pick on kids in his class. But he learned from it once his mom was displeased with what he did. And as it turned out, she never forgot about it.

"I think you need to learn how to respect a girl before becoming friends with one. Okay?"

Madeline was done talking and turned around-

"But mom, I..." Elijah called.

His mom stopped and looked again.

"I...It's..." he muttered. Elijah couldn't find the right words. He was devastated at first, but then he realized that his mom was asking him to stop hanging out with the girls, as in Sabrina and her friends' altogether. Maybe he could still be friends with Sabrina.

"Never mind" Elijah said, calmly, "You're right. I'll stop hanging out with them"

Again Madeline was surprised that her son was more than willing to do what she said. Elijah couldn't hang out with girls anymore but he wasn't told that he couldn't hang out with Sabrina. So that was the one he chose to spend time with, like he did in the beginning.

CHAPTER EIGHTEEN

Rhythm of Souls

March.

The days of being in the company of girls were long gone. Elijah was sad at first but the feeling later passed. On daily basis, he spent his time with Andrew and Paula. Every now and then, he'd still visit with Sabrina; even if it was just brief moment to say hi. The fact that she was still part of his life was enough for him to look forward to.

Music was one thing that floated around in Elijah's mind, ever since he and Sabrina talked about it in November. That memory was a favorite because it was the one day that they both truly connected on an emotional level. For a while, Elijah had thought that music was another opportunity to get close to his dream girl. After all, it was one of their interests. When Elijah showed up at school, he waited until his class lined up since it's one of the times that he could talk to her alone.

"Hey" Elijah greeted.

Sabrina turned and smiled gently, "Hi".

"Hey, uh, I wanna show you something".

She didn't say anything but she looked at him, intrigued.

"Not now but maybe at recess?"

"Sure"

When the time came, Sabrina met with Elijah outside. She came to him instead of the other way around. She remembered. That was admirable. "So what do you wanna show me?" she asked.

"You like music, right?" Elijah replied.

"Of course"

With his backpack in hand, he guided her to the nearby bench. After sitting down, Elijah opened up his pack and pulled out his discman and showed it to her.

"Wow, a discman" Sabrina said, jokingly.

Forming a smile, Elijah gave a little chuckle. "It's cool, isn't?" Then he gave the electronic device for her to hold. Sabrina examined it. "Right? Wonder what they're gonna make next", she added. Then her tone went from playful sarcasm to sincerity, "But this is cool"

The bottom of the backpack had a few CD's. Elijah pulled out one of them.

"I wanted to show you the music I like"

Those exact words were one thing he had wanted to say for a while. And just as he imagined, it came out nicely and Sabrina being by his side and interested was just perfect. Thoughtfully, she returned the discman for him to put the CD in. Elijah opened it and placed the disc in and then he plugged in the earphones. He gave one side of the earphones to Sabrina, in which she accepted and placed it in her ear. Elijah took the other side of the earphone. And then he pushed the play button. The CD started to turn and the music played.

"This is from the Small Soldiers movie" he explained.

"Okay" Sabrina acknowledged.

"You ever seen it?"

"I remember seeing previews for it but never seen it"

"It's so good! I used to love it when it first came out, especially for boys who were obsessed with toys. And the music is pretty good, too"

Sabrina nodded, "I look forward to hearing it".

The song itself, War remix, was bitter-sweet and catchy. Elijah and Sabrina met each other's eyes as they were getting into the rhythm. They began nodding their heads back and forth. The music continued from there. Elijah showed Sabrina more of his CD's and played at least one song from each of them. The rest of the world around them was on mute as the music took over their minds and hearts.

"That was pretty good, Elijah" Sabrina said, "You have quite a taste in music"

"Mhm, I sure do" Elijah agreed.

"Yeah, I love music. Sometimes I like to close my door and just dance away"

"Sometimes I like to listen to music to take my mind off things"

"Music is good for that too"

Music was good for more than that. It was a way to look at life and bond with the ones around us, a profound way to communicate. "When did you start getting into music?" Elijah asked.

"When I was little" Sabrina explained.

"Me too"

"Nice. Yeah, it all started off with kid's shows and Disney films and I would sing along to it, although I couldn't pronounce some of the words correctly".

Elijah gave a smile as he imagined a young Sabrina Clarin in his mind, singing. It would be both adorable and beautiful. Briefly, he then thought about her singing right now but she probably wouldn't go for it. "I'm sure you did good" he told her.

Sabrina smiled, with a little shyness. "How about you?" she asked.

"Well, pretty much the same as you, except I didn't sing"

Elijah was about to mention that he would probably be a bad singer. But instead, he played the next song and they both listened together. After the song was over, they took a little break to talk more about music in general.

"You ever watch Hit List? You know the show on YTV?"

"Yeah! I remember watching that. That's when I first got into Aqua"

"Same here!"

Then Sabrina playfully sang the song Barbie Girl. She was bobbing her head, which made Elijah smile, genuinely. "My brother hated that song" she added, "I often sang it just to annoy him, same with Britney Spears. He doesn't like girly music, but you know, boys".

"Yeah, but me I don't mind some of them. There's actually one, or two I should say, called M2M. They were on the Pokemon soundtrack. I kinda like them".

Sabrina paused to try and remember those particular artists. "Sounds familiar but I can't put my finger on it. I've seen the movie too but it's been a while"

It was one of those moments where Elijah realized that they had more in common than he thought, such as music and an old favorite TV show. Even just two offered so many subjects to choose from to start another conversation. Sitting on the bench, talking to his crush was another scenario Elijah imagined. He became lost in that thought while Sabrina sat in silence. "Anyways, I kinda like that one song that they sang".

Next thing they did was looking at the other CD's that Elijah brought. Although they didn't listen to them, for that they started talking more about the same topic. First they talked about having to save some money to buy a single CD and how some of them only have one song that appealed to them. And Sabrina admitted that she never really heard any rap music. Shortly, having the discman out seemed less important. But the conversation itself was just as good. Elijah didn't mind it at all.

"I like to dance, sometimes" he admitted, in a low voice as if he didn't want any of his peers to know.

"You dance?" Sabrina replied, conversationally.

"Sometimes" It was silent, a pause really, like Elijah was about to say more. Sabrina gazed at him, patiently. Dancing was one thing he kept to himself for years. Not even Paula or Andrew knew about it. Some people would usually that dancing was for girls but that didn't appear to be true, at least from what Elijah had seen on TV. Aside from drawing, dancing was a way to express himself, creatively. "Yeah…I guess that I like music so much, sometimes it makes me dance".

"There's nothing wrong with that" Sabrina said, "If you love music that much, sometimes you just have to show it. Even I do".

Elijah couldn't help but think about the dance scenario he fantasized about months ago. It almost made him smile but he didn't allow himself to get lost in that daydream but even just sitting next to her in reality felt close to that fantasy. Elijah decided then that he would have to ask Sabrina for a dance, when the time was right.

"Well…" Elijah started, feeling more comfortable about the topic, "I do dance, like what we did in gym class when he danced to Cadillac Ranch"

"There you go"

"Although, some kids don't really like it"

Sabrina shrugged her shoulders, "Can't blame them. It's not for everybody".

They both sat in comfortable silence. They've had to be sitting there for almost ten minutes. Elijah naturally assumed that Sabrina would end the conversation any minute so she could catch up with her friends. But she didn't. Even Paula or Andrew didn't come along to join in on their conversation. It was one of those days where Elijah had Sabrina all to himself without any interruptions; perfection.

"Which band is your favorite?" Elijah asked.

"I like Savage Garden, All Saints, Hansons, Backstreet Boys, Spice Girls. There's quite a few of them; how about you?"

Elijah paused to think.

"Uhh, I don't think I have a favorite band. I know I like a lot of singers"

"Well, singers are just as great as bands" Sabrina told him.

"Yeah, you're right. Well, I like Will Smith, after listening to Men in Black. John Fogerty. And Eminem"

Sabrina nodded, "They're cool. I like Britney Spears, Bryan Adams, Cher, Christina Aguilera…"

She paused to think of more.

"Aaron Carter" Elijah added.

"Yes, him too! I almost forgot about him. Thanks"

That brought a smile to their faces, probably because that particular artist reminded them of their conversation they had last fall. It felt like that day all over again, just the two of them talking but more singular and connected than ever before.

"And which one's your favorite, doing the Macarena or Cadillac Ranch?"

"Mmmm" Sabrina replied, "I always enjoyed the Macarena. So I'd probably go with that"

Elijah nodded, "I think I'd go with Cadillac Ranch"

Elijah and Sabrina continued talking about music. They started with naming different singers from the 90's and the new ones that were just starting and then they mentioned movie soundtracks, which led them to brief conversation about the movies themselves. "Music is life" Sabrina said, in the end.

Then recess was over. Elijah couldn't be more proud that he spent it with the girl he really cared about. As they got up to lineup with their class, a last minute idea just came to Elijah's mind. So he caught her while there was still time. He pulled one of his CD's out of the bag.

"Oh, Sabrina…" he called, as he was offering her the CD, Much Dance 2001, "You said you don't listen to rap music. So here's your chance. It's got some rap on it"

"You sure?" she replied, feeling uncertain.

Elijah met her eyes, "Yeah" he nodded, "I trust you".

"Okay" Sabrina agreed, as she gracefully accepted the CD.

The music echoed for the rest of the day, the rest of the week, and most likely the rest of Elijah's life. Since then, the music continued to play in the mind and heart. During his most private moments, he played the songs he liked and began dancing. It lightened the mood and gave a positive vibe as Elijah stepped back and looked at life in a profound and imaginative way, which filled in the gaps of emptiness.

When Sabrina got home after that day, she went to her room and put the CD into her stereo and allowed the songs to run its tracks as a way to get acquainted with it. Afterwards, she replayed it to hear what the music was really saying. Soon it grabbed her attention and before she knew it, the music was moving her. Her mind went blank and she was in her own world. Sabrina moved, slowly and gracefully around her bedroom.

Meanwhile, Elijah allowed himself to be carried away to the songs he listened to and the music videos he watched on TV. There he started mimicking the dance moves, which became an interest almost immediately. He was learning more moves that were much more exciting and exaggerated. Elijah found himself doing it constantly that was becoming a habit. Even at school, when no one was looking, he would dance a little as he walked passed his peers.

A few days had passed. Elijah and Sabrina were able to have a follow up conversation about their latest experience with music. She went up to him during the lineup in the morning.

"Hey" Sabrina greeted, "I listened to the CD you gave me"

Excitedly, Elijah replied, "What did you…"

"I liked it" Sabrina said, promptly. The smile on her face made it extra special. So he couldn't help but return the smile.

"That's cool"

"It is cool. That one rap song sure had a nice beat to it. Quite catchy"

"Which one?"

"The, uh, Eminem one"

"Oh, the Real Slim Shady"

"Yeah, it's a good one"

"Yeah, honestly I didn't think much of Eminem when I first heard of him. But sounds like he's got great music"

Elijah nodded. He then cleared his throat, for that it was his turn to speak, "I been dancing a lot. I learned a few new things"

"Yeah? Would you like to show me?" Sabrina suggested.

That put Elijah in a rather tough position; dancing in front of his peers where there was no music. "Yeah?" he answered to kill the silence, "I mean, not here, uh, maybe later."

She looked at him and decided to tease, "You're not scared, are you?"

Then he spoke with sudden confidence in his voice, "I'm not the one who's scared" he said.

Sabrina just raised an eyebrow, "You calling me scared?"

Again, there was hesitation, "Maybe"

"Only one way to find out, if you're up for it"

"Of course I am" Elijah assured, "Not scared"

"Well, whenever you're ready" Sabrina said with sincerity, and then she turned around to wait for their teacher to open the door.

That was a different kind of conversation. It was not friendly or heart to heart, where they would understand each other. They were rather taunting and calling out their egos. It was another challenge. The whole class was still waiting in line. Elijah began contemplating that this might be an opportunity to take advantage of, while Sabrina was right in front of him.

"Hey Sabrina?" he called, without giving any further thought.

She turned around and gave her attention. Then Elijah started moving his legs with rhythm. He only showed off for a few seconds and then ended with a twirl, carefully because there was another student behind him.

Sabrina was greatly entertained. Instead of saying anything, she merely smiled and clapped her hands silently.

Then Elijah returned the smile, "Not scared" he repeated, with confidence.

Later on, at the end of gym class, everyone was changing back into their casual clothes. Elijah had the CD with him. He was able to hide it. Luckily, the stereo was out, for that it was used from the other class. Elijah stepped out of the change room and there he saw Sabrina, loitering with Carly. Many of his classmates were still in the change rooms, so they had little time to spare.

"Hey, Sabrina" Elijah greeted.

"Hey, Elijah, what's up?"

Instead of giving a verbal answer, he decided to be clever and show her the CD that she just returned to him, "This" he told her.

"And?"

"More of this?" Elijah then gave another twirl like he did that morning.

"And what is 'this' exactly?" Carly asked.

"Dancing" he replied, honestly.

"Oh, right" Carly muttered.

Elijah faced Sabrina again, "I see the stereo is out. Good thing too, because now is your chance to see a little more of my moves"

She gave a friendly smile, "I look forward to it"

"Let's go"

"Be right back" Sabrina said to Carly before taking off with Elijah.

The couple went straight to the stereo that was on the bench. There was already a CD in it, along with its case beside it. "Looks like someone forgot to put it away" Sabrina said.

"Yeah, looks like it" Elijah agreed.

He took that CD out and put in his Much Dance CD. As he turned it on, he turned the volume down low just to be safe. The music started to play silently. After that, Elijah didn't think any further. He only saw the opportunity and went for it. First, he searched for the right track, Ooh It's Kinda Crazy by SoulDecision. Then he started to turn the volume high. Once it was fairly loud, Elijah turned around to Sabrina and started dancing. This time, he showed off more moves than before. Sabrina was getting into the rhythm as she watched her friend moving to the music. She even started bobbing her head to the song. At first, Elijah's mind was blank as he focused on his dance moves. Then at the corner of his eye, he noticed more of his classmates were exiting the change rooms. So Elijah thought that he would have to wrap it up. So after displaying just a few more moves, it was over as he gave a final pose. Sabrina just smiled as she met his eyes.

"Well, I guess it's time to go back…" then Elijah stopped once Sabrina started dancing as well. It was rather short but she did it beautifully. He was amazed by it. Once Sabrina stopped, Elijah just gazed at her.

"Come on, you two, gym is over" Mrs. Parker called over the music.

As they went back into reality, Elijah quickly turned around to turn off the music and took his CD out. "Wow, Sabrina, that was pretty good, or should I…" he clapped his hands sincerely. Then Sabrina just curtsied, "Thank you" she said.

Once they realized their class was leaving, Elijah put the CD back in its case and started walking with Sabrina.

"You know what, I forgot about those guys" she admitted, "SoulDecision"

"Yeah, I think their music is good"

"It's catchy"

"I'd like to see more dancing from you, Sabrina"

She looked at him "You dare me?"

Elijah paused to meet her eyes, "Yeah, I dare you".

So they kept their challenge in mind as time went on. Even during class, whenever Elijah met Sabrina's eye, they looked like they were up to something. Yet there was no discomfort. It was actually quite exciting, for that they had something to look forward to. But deep down, they both knew they were just playing together. The next day, as lunch recess started, they both agreed to isolate themselves. So they went up to the other side of the field. And there was less snow on the ground at that point in the season.

"So are you ready?" Sabrina asked, casually.

"Oh, I'm ready" Elijah told her, "But first…" he pulled out his discman, "This is why I wanted to do this today, so I could bring this. Just so we could actually have music to dance to and since we can't carry a stereo around."

"Good thinking. Okay, you go first"

Elijah was just a little surprised. He was about to protest but soon he decided to face the challenge. "Okay" he agreed, "I know this might be a little silly, dancing while one of us just hears the music"

Sabrina shrugged her shoulders, "I don't hate it".

So Elijah then put the earphones on and pressed the play button. With the music consuming his hearing, Elijah began with moving his feet into the rhythm. Once the music gained more momentum, he then shifted his upper body around with little movement with his arms. Elijah danced almost flawlessly. For a short moment, he happened to glance at Sabrina, who was amused. He remained focused and danced for as long as he needed to but there was a limit. It had a beginning and middle but an end was still in progress. Even so, he danced much more than the previous day.

Elijah stopped and turned off his discman.

"That's all I got for now" he said, showing disappointment.

"Well, either way, I thought you danced pretty good" Sabrina told him, with an assuring smile. Elijah only smirked and then he handed her the discman.

"Now your turn"

After putting on the earphones, Sabrina turned on the device and searched for a song that best suited her. After she found one, she took a deep breath and then she stepped forward with her head down and her hair covering her face. The music started, Sabrina moved her right hand, an inch at a time, like she was a robot. Her hand was closer to her forehead and finally pushed her hair back and looked up but with her eyes closed as her body shook rhythmically. Sabrina opened her eyes and began twirling around like a ballerina, almost excitedly but gentle. After that, she started walking by putting one foot in front of the other and moved her shoulders. At that time, she whipped her hair back and gazed at Elijah, who stood there in awe. After walking a few feet, Sabrina stopped to move her hips around while she lowered her head and sprung it in a circle. From there, all kinds of dance moves went off, like from a pop star's music video. Sabrina was a natural dancer. Hers was lengthier than what Elijah had displayed. For the next minute, she was stuck in her own world until she had nothing else further to offer.

"Ta-da" Sabrina said, mildly as she took the earphones off.

"Wow" Elijah said, in astonishment, "That was really..." He tried to think of a best way to describe it, "Perfect"

"Why, thank you"

She gave him back the discman and they started walking back towards the school. None of them said anything. Elijah found himself revisiting Sabrina's dancing ritual, mentally.

"I think you're a great dancer, Sabrina" he told her.

"You're not so bad yourself. When I was little, my mom started calling me Sabrina Ballerina because I danced a lot"

"Nice nickname. It rhymes"

"Haha, right? She still calls me that, sometimes"

Then Elijah tried to think of how to keep the conversation going.

"If only I had more dance moves" he added. Those were the only words that came to mind and slipped out.

"Oh, I'm sure you will and it will probably be just as good" Sabrina promised, "And one day, we won't have to worry about bringing a stereo, a stereo will be brought to us at the right time"

Elijah only nodded. He liked that idea.

Since then, Elijah practiced whenever he had a chance behind closed doors. During one day, Elijah was with Paula and Andrew. They were by the playground, loitering after spending most of their energy playing around. Andrew and Paula were tired out, but Elijah still had enough energy. So he briefly did a little dance move. Paula was able to catch a glimpse of it.

"Were you just dancing, Eli?" she asked, as she gazed at him.

"Yes" he admitted.

"Dancing?" Andrew repeated, "But there's no music"

"I know" Elijah told him.

Paula and Andrew said nothing, for that they felt they were looking at someone else, since they had never seen their best friend do such a thing. So Elijah slowly started walking backwards and he did it with style. He was showing off by moonwalking.

As time went on, the snow was melting away. The color of green spread everywhere, from the grass to the leaves on the trees. Just like nature, life had sparked inside Elijah. He never felt so good about himself, knowing that he had friends that loved and respected him, and there was so much gratitude Elijah had to return by spending time with his friends. And there were so many days to do anything and everything. Every now and then, Elijah would share with Sabrina their favorite snack. He went up to her during lunch time.

"Still like Dunk-a-Roos, Sabrina?" he asked.

"I still do!"

Together, they ate the cookies and dipped them in the chocolate.

"So you see any good movies lately?" Sabrina asked.

Elijah shook his head. "Just the ones I have at home. Have you been to our theater yet?"

"Not yet; just waiting for a good one to come out. Until then, it's just the movies I have at home and whatever we watch in class"

"Now that's a movie. We just need popcorn"

"Yes! Despite how educational the movie is"

"It's too bad that we're only allowed to watch movies that are rated-G"

"The joys of being a kid"

They looked down and realized there was only one cookie left.

"Oh, you can have it" Sabrina insisted.

"No, it's yours" Elijah told her.

"You sure?"

"Yeah"

Sabrina took the last piece, "Thanks, Elijah".

A few days later, Elijah and Sabrina were pondering around the field. The weather was a mix of sun and clouds. There were puddles covering up different parts of the field.

"Sabrina Ballerina, I got a new nickname for you" Elijah told her, as they were walking along.

"Uh oh" she replied, "Is it something embarrassing?"

"No, not really"

"Okay, let's hear it"

"From this day forward, you shall be known as: Sa-Boo"

Before she could reply, Sabrina took a moment to let in sink in. Then she slowly formed a smile and then broke into mild laughter.

"I guess that's not so bad. Kinda cute though"

"Ha-ha, yes!" Elijah replied, with joy.

"How did you come up with that?" Sabrina asked.

"I just kept thinking of your name and I changed it to that just for fun"

"How thoughtful"

They walked in silence for a moment. Elijah was just about to make conversation about the weather when suddenly he felt a little splash as he took one step. Looking down, he realized that he stepped in a puddle. The bottom of his pant leg was wet.

"Damn" Elijah muttered.

"Hey, no swearing!" Sabrina joked.

"Very funny, Sa-Boo"

Sabrina began walking around the puddle, gently and gracefully. Shortly, she was on the other side, across from Elijah. "You gotta walk around" she told him.

"Alright" Elijah replied, rather grimly. Instead of walking around, Elijah jumped across the puddle and landed right beside Sabrina.

"How's that for walking around?" he said, smoothly.

"Very clever; what were you gonna say?"

"I was gonna say something about the..."

Then Sabrina jumped across the puddle. "Sorry, I didn't hear you" she teased.

Elijah went along and then leaped over the water to catch up with Sabrina who then hopped away. Soon, they were chasing each other through the field, laughing, and taunting each other. Once the excitement calmed down, they both went back to pondering around. Elijah then didn't feel the need to make conversation because they were bonding in silence.

"Now I gotta come up with a nickname for you" Sabrina said. Then there was a pause, "E-I-Jah"

Elijah looked at her instantly, "E-eye-Jah?"

"I just thought of it" she admitted.

"I don't think anybody thought of that"

"So I'm the first; yay."

After they made it across the field, they arrived at the edge where the tetherball pole stood. Elijah and Sabrina took a moment to admire the view. "It looks nice" Elijah said.

"What does?" Sabrina wondered.

"All this" Elijah gestured towards the school, the parking lot, and the residential area on the other side.

"Yeah, it's beautiful" Sabrina agreed.

ELIJAH AND SABRINA

A beautiful view from a hill top reminded Elijah of his old primary days. He thought about it and then he had an idea. "How long until recess is over?" he asked.

Sabrina did the math in her head, "It's been like half an hour. So maybe like ten minutes or less, why?"

"I just thought of something" Elijah told her.

Sabrina waited to hear the answer.

"Wanna sneak off school grounds?" he asked.

Sabrina hesitated, "What do you mean?"

"It won't be far" Elijah promised, "I just remembered that..." A moment alone with Sabrina Clarin, he thought. Elijah couldn't take no for an answer, "You know, we don't have much time. Let's go!"

Elijah began running to the bottom of the hill, "Come on" he called.

Sabrina followed.

Just like Elijah said, they were off school grounds. They were in the small forest that filled the gap between both schools. Elijah and Sabrina approached closer and shortly, they were able to see the hill. There were dozens of children running around and playing.

"This is my old school" Elijah explained, "Muriel Mould Primary School"

"It's nice, looks friendly" Sabrina said.

"Me and Paula used to come way up here just to sit" he added, "Not up here in the bushes but just passed that playground over there"

Sabrina acknowledged by nodding.

"Yeah, when I was little, I was pretty shy. I couldn't even call my teacher by name. But that was until I met Paula. She helped me and we got through school together"

"Yeah, I kinda picked up on that when we first met" Sabrina told him, "But it's always nice to have friends that help. And you're much different now. I can tell."

Elijah only smiled, softly.

"Were you like that?"

"Maybe a little; I honestly didn't think much of it. When I was five, I used to think that everyone was friendly as much as my family was, so that made it okay for me to socialize with other people, although it took a little practice. I didn't know what to say at first"

"Ah" Elijah muttered.

"But when I first started school I was actually scared to death. You probably knew how it was; being stuck with a bunch of people you haven't met before"

"Oh yeah, I know that"

"I remember this one time; I actually told my teacher that I wanted to be in the same class as Jonathan so I wouldn't be alone. That's how scared I was. But because he's a year older than me, I couldn't. I cried like it was the end of the world. It was embarrassing"

Elijah paused to think of something to say, "But I'm sure it was cute"

"Haha" Sabrina chuckled, bashfully, "That's a way to put it. But I got the hang of it after a little while"

"Looks like we both did"

At the last minute, Elijah decided to put up his hand for a high five. Sabrina noticed and clapped her hand with his.

They both continued to gaze at the school kids playing around.

"There are a lot of memories here" Elijah added, "Like our school trip to the swimming pool in Smithers. Well, not here but I remember meeting Paula here and waited for the rest of the class before going on the trip."

"I've been there" Sabrina shared, "I loved that place"

"It's great, isn't it? Yeah, that was a fun day. So many good memories… It just makes life…good, that you have something to smile at"

Elijah only glanced over his shoulder and ended up catching Sabrina's gaze. She just smiled at him.

"Like this?" she asked.

It was a rather warm and joyful moment. It had Elijah laughing a little but he stopped himself before he went hysterical. "Yeah, just like that" he agreed.

Sabrina broke eye contact and continued to look away blankly. Elijah went back to gazing at his friend and just had the urge to say something nice and meaningful.

"You have..." he spoke slowly.

Sabrina turned her head towards him again once he spoke.

"...a beautiful smile"

That was the first time Elijah complimented one of Sabrina's features and she was quite flattered as she smiled again.

"Thank you" Sabrina replied.

Elijah just made her day. So he began to smile as well, from ear to ear.

"You have a pretty bright smile yourself, Elijah Soda"

The mood got more exciting as Sabrina showed her kindness and humor. Elijah could only imagine how silly his face looked and hoped that he wasn't blushing. But he was laughing, so much that he couldn't focus on the next topic, either Sabrina's compliment or the nickname she gave him.

"Did you just call me Soda for my last name?"

"Yes!" Sabrina laughed.

"I kinda like that one"

Is this how love works? Elijah wondered. He had so many funny and heartfelt moments with Sabrina Clarin, and just now he wondered if it was any step closer to developing a romantic relationship.

"Well, I think we should probably get back before the bell rings" Sabrina suggested.

"Might as well" Elijah agreed.

So they started walking back to school grounds. None of them spoke. As Elijah walked behind Sabrina, he was looking directly at her left hand and just thought about holding it, his hand in hers; would Sabrina mind that? It was a perfect time to make something out of that moment. After all, Elijah was alone in the woods with a girl that he truly liked. It was almost like a scene out of a movie, where the boy and the girl would have a heart to heart talk and would end with a kiss. However, reenacting that particular scene in real life was rather intimidating unless the girl was willing to play along. But Sabrina was unaware of Elijah's feelings. So maybe he couldn't hold her hand, but while they still had a few minutes to themselves, Elijah wanted to make something memorable before it was over.

"Hey Sabrina?" he said, gently.

"Yeah?"

"Sabrina Clarinet"

Sabrina turned around as she was still walking. She met Elijah's eyes. They acknowledged the nickname by slowly breaking into laughter. "That one was pretty awesome" Sabrina told him.

Then she started walking backwards, slowly, while Elijah walked forward, just like they did that one day during winter.

"Uhh…" Sabrina muttered, "Elijah…Koala Bear"

Smiling, Elijah continued playing, "Sabrina…Staring. You stare like a bear!"

"I guess we're both bears" Sabrina said, and then for fun she impersonated a roar, "Raawerrr!" in a deep gargle voice.

"Oh yeah?" Elijah replied. Then he gave his own impersonated roar, "Ah-er-er" he said, in a high voice, "That's what Koalas sound like, right?"

"Something like that"

After they continued their walking, Elijah again was gazing at Sabrina's hand. That time, he pretended that he was going to grab it gently and held it. He reached his hand out while Sabrina wasn't looking. He was only inches away from her hand.

Should I or should I not?

But Elijah waited too long. They were already close to school grounds. Then he began to feel nervous. So then he immediately pulled his hand away.

"Hey Sabrina?"

"Yeah?"

"What's one song you don't like but everyone does?"

"A song I DON'T like?" Sabrina replied, as she turned halfway.

"Yes"

Sabrina thought for a moment, "Ummm…I'd say Mambo No. 5"

Elijah's reaction was skeptical, "Really? I think it's a good song!"

"I thought so too when I first heard it" Sabrina admitted, "But after a while, they were playing that song a little too much and I was starting to get tired of it"

"Yeah, I guess it got tiring for some people"

"What about you, Sly-Jah?"

"Haha that's very clever of you" Elijah said, with a short chuckle and then stayed on track with the topic, "The one song called Short Skirt and Long Jacket"

"Really?" Sabrina said, surprised, "I kinda like that one"

"So does everybody else but not me" Elijah told her.

"Well, we all have different tastes in music"

There was a short pause.

"So I guess we don't?"

It sounded like Elijah was judging. So Sabrina stopped and turned towards him, "I thought we did"

"Yeah, or maybe we still do" Elijah explained, "It's just I like one song that you don't like and you like the song that I don't like"

Sabrina chuckled, "Elijah that doesn't mean that we can't be friends. We pretty much like the same music and that's what matters"

While Elijah had Sabrina's attention, it was chance for him to strengthen his connection with her somehow. It may not be a simple gesture as holding hands, but maybe it could be something about music that marks their friendship.

"Yeah? I guess we'll still be friends when the songs change? That we'd still be dancing or listening together?"

Uncertain, Sabrina just gawked at him, briefly, "Not sure what that means, but yeah"

Elijah was about to explain what his little speech might've meant or could've meant, but it was really something he made up-he really wanted to connect with Sabrina on a different level. But Elijah was young. He didn't know how to put feelings into words. Maybe someday he would.

The moment was over once the school bell rang. Elijah and Sabrina realized they still outside the school perimeter. So they started running back towards the school building.

CHAPTER NINETEEN

Absolute Dream

It was spring break. Sabrina was on her way to have a sleepover at Carly's. She arrived and got welcomed by the Dawson family. Soon after Melanie showed up and instantly began bonding in the evening. It was Sabrina's first time sleeping over at a friend's. So it was exciting for her, being in good company outside of school.

Halfway through the evening, the girls were sitting on the floor in Carly's room. Melanie had a teen magazine in her hand and they were all answering multiple choice questions. "Your best friend forgets her wallet at home" Mel said, as she was reading out of the magazine, "Do you…A: Run home and get it, B: Give her all your money, or C: tell her 'too bad'?"

All three of them laughed, for that they were amused by the little things such as questionnaires. "Too bad?" Sabrina answered.

Carly scoffed, "You're mean!"

"Just having a little fun" Sabrina explained.

"I'd probably run home and get it because I'd feel bad if I have to ask for money from a friend" Carly told them.

"True" Mel agreed, "Although me personally, I'd go with Sabrina's choice, just to see how you'd react"

Sabrina giggled, trying not to laugh too hard. Carly just gawked at Melanie, not having the energy to laugh, so she just forced a smile.

"We're both mean", Mel said.

302

"Next one!" Sabrina insisted, getting more excited by the minute.

Melanie turned her attention back to the magazine.

"Oooo" Melanie muttered, rather amused. Then she glanced at her friends with a little smile. It was getting interesting.

"You accidently bump into a cute guy" she told them, "Do you…A: start a conversation, B: say nothing but stare at him in wonder, or C: kiss him?"

Both Sabrina and Carly were speechless.

"I'll just stare at him in wonder" Carly said, after a moment of silence, "I'll probably be too shy to talk"

"Fair enough" Mel replied, and then she turned her attention to Sabrina, waiting for her answer. That particular question had Sabrina thinking for a long moment.

"Maybe A" she admitted.

"Nobody wants to kiss?!" Melanie said, in disbelief.

"Who wants to kiss a stranger?" Sabrina suggested.

"That's a good point" Carly agreed.

"Or maybe it doesn't mean it that way" Melanie added, "Maybe it means to get to know him first and then kiss him"

"Hmmm, maybe" Sabrina replied, as if she was reconsidering.

"Well, that's what I think at least" Mel assured.

Then Melanie put the magazine down and then she gently lied on the floor to stretch her arms and legs, groaning while she did it. "I'm not sure about you guys, but I'm feeling a little snacky"

"I'm still feeling energized from these sweets we had earlier" Sabrina said, "So I am for one"

"Maybe a little for me" Carly told them.

"That's all I need to hear" As she was still lying on the floor, Melanie decided to press her feet against her friends, playfully. "Whoops, whoops, whoops". She did it repeatedly until Sabrina and Carly started to giggle. They both grabbed her feet and then Mel pulled away and got up, "I shall return. You know, Carly, it's not too late to put up a blanket fort"

"I'd rather sleep on the lawn" Carly replied, sarcastically. Melanie just laughed and then excused herself from Carly's bedroom, and closed the door only halfway.

Carly got up to her feet as well. "Oh" she groaned, "I need to sit on the bed. My bum is starting to hurt"

Then Sabrina couldn't help but chuckle.

"What?" her friend replied.

"Nothing, it's just you never said the word 'bum' before"

Carly responded with only a mild laugh, "Well, I wasn't sure if I wanted to say butt. So…yeah"

"Mhm; better than the worse, even so, it was quite cute"

Carly went and lied on her bed to relax. Sabrina soon joined her.

They went back into silence as Sabrina's mind wandered off. She thought about that last question from the magazine, particularly the one about kissing, for that love was something that had been floating in Sabrina's mind.

"Hey Carly?"

"What?"

"Can I ask you something?"

"Sure"

Sabrina hesitated. She couldn't believe she was about to ask her friend, "Have you ever…kissed a boy?"

Carly didn't answer, not right away. First she looked up at Sabrina, who waited patiently. "Sorry, can you say that again?"

"Have you ever kissed a boy?" Sabrina repeated, slowly and undauntedly.

They were staring at each other. Carly had never been asked that kind of question before.

"No?" she finally answered. She didn't know what to say next, "Have you?"

Sabrina shook her head.

"Uh, why are you asking me this?" Carly said, gently as if she didn't want to offend her. Then she sat up on the bed. Now Sabrina was feeling a little guilty for asking, but she tried not to show it.

"It's just something that's been on my mind for a while" Sabrina explained, casually.

"Is there someone you like?"

"No, not yet"

"Are you even old enough to date?" Carly asked.

She seemed more concerned than intrigued. It wasn't the reaction Sabrina was expecting. At first she thought maybe Carly was wondering the same thing for her own benefit, since they were at that age.

"Maybe not, but..." Sabrina trailed off. She spoke like she knew what she was going to say but realized her words weren't really leading to anywhere. "You know what, never mind" she added with a crooked smile just to show that she was still in a normal state.

"Okay" Carly agreed.

Then Melanie rather kicked the door open, but gently. "Whoops, whoops, whoops! My foot slipped" she joked. Then she walked back into the room with a small plate of baked treats in her hand.

"You dad was kind enough to show me where the plates were" Melanie said to Carly, "So now I brought back enough for the three of us to get even MORE hyper! Dinner is sweetly served"

Gently, Melanie put the plate on the bed between Sabrina and Carly. She took a bite out of the treat, while the girls helped themselves.

"So good" she added, with the food in her mouth. Mel was on her way to close the bedroom door. First she turned around to Sabrina, who was just taking a bite of her food.

"Oh, by the way, Sabrina, I heard everything!"

Then Melanie finally closed the door. Sabrina Clarin froze as she became the center of attention in the room. She just chewed her food, regretting that she even said anything. Melanie went to sit on the floor like a child eager to hear a bedtime story. She looked directly at Sabrina..

"So....who does Sabrina like?" she asked.

"Tuxedo Mask" Sabrina joked, hoping it would be the end of that topic.

Melanie just burst into laughter. "That's a good one" then her tone of voice changed to a gentle but almost serious tone, "No really, I'm curious".

"It's nothing" Sabrina explained, right away, "I was just telling-or asking Carly something; well, you probably heard because you said you heard everything"

"It involved a boy" Melanie told her.

"Not any boy" Sabrina added, promptly, "I mean that I haven't met anyone that's cute"

Melanie then approached Sabrina, "Move over, so I can sit" she joined her friends on Carly's bed and was just dying to know Sabrina's hidden agenda. "Doesn't mean you shouldn't start looking" she told her, continuing the conversation.

"Well, maybe Sabrina doesn't want to and we shouldn't put her on the spot" Carly said, politely.

"Car, she's probably gonna find someone anyway. And she will because I just happened to know that someone!"

Now Sabrina couldn't help but feel intrigued, "Yeah?" she tried to remain nonchalant.

"Yeah! He's actually in my class. His name…is…Logan Austin"

"Logan Austin?" Sabrina repeated.

"He's cute and funny, and sensitive. If you want, I can introduce you to him?"

Sabrina didn't expect Mel to do such a thoughtful gesture. It was happening a little too fast.

"I don't know, or…" Sabrina glanced at Mel and Carly, "I guess I'll think about it"

April.

So during the rest of spring break, Sabrina thought about Melanie's offer, to meet a boy from her class and possibly start a relationship. It had been daunting Sabrina since the sleepover. During the wait, Melanie decided to point the boy she was referring to. It was just before school started. The girls were outside.

"Well, Sabrina have you decided yet?" Mel asked.

"Not yet"

"Wanna see what he looks like before meeting him? Would that make you feel a little better?"

Sabrina started considering her friend's suggestion. Since Melanie was being quite generous, she didn't really want to be rude.

"You don't have to say anything, just-"

"Sure" Sabrina finally agreed.

"Oh…okay"

Melanie looked over her shoulder; just to be sure Logan was still there beside the entrance. He was. "Good, he's still over there" Mel said, "He's the one in the yellow sweater"

"Kay" Sabrina said, "I don't have to say hi or anything, right?"

"Nah, just look at him for a second and then turn away before it gets creepy"

So then Sabrina, Melanie, and Carly acted normal as they walked passed the entrance where there was a group of boys, hanging around. Sabrina could see the one in the yellow sweater. They approached closer, Sabrina kept her eyes on the ground and then she looked up slowly. There was the yellow sweater. She lifted her head up higher and there she saw a rather handsome face, dark curly hair that caught her attention, longer than she anticipated. She finally turned away. The girls were around the corner. As soon as they got a little privacy, Melanie met Sabrina face to face, waiting for a feedback.

"The one in the yellow sweater, right?" Sabrina asked,

"Yesss" Mel replied.

Sabrina took her time, that didn't feel creepy at all, she was about to say. "He is cute" she admitted.

"See? What I tell you?!" Melanie cheered.

Now there was a feeling inside Sabrina that made her fall into silence. It was a feeling of excitement and also nervousness.

"So now what?" Carly asked, in a low voice.

Melanie noticed the curious look on Sabrina's face as she briefly peered back to the corner, "Would you like to meet him now?" she offered.

"Sure" Sabrina agreed, "I think so"

Then Melanie gave a big smile as she was fired with excitement. Then she grabbed her friend by the arm and gently guided her.

"Hey boys!" Melanie greeted, as they approached them. Just like that, she had their attention. Mel didn't waste any time. She got right to the point, "Hey Logan?" she called.

Sabrina didn't make any eye contact with him or any of his friends.

"This is my friend, Sabrina"

Their eyes finally met. The next thing Sabrina noticed was a pair of blue eyes staring back at her and that pushed her mind out of reality for a moment. He was perfect, she thought.

"Hi" Logan finally spoke. His voice was light and friendly. The next thing Sabrina saw was his boyish good looks now that she was up close.

Sabrina cleared her throat, even though she didn't really need to, "Hello" she replied, kindly.

The eye contact continued. It went for a little too long. So Melanie stepped in and raised Sabrina's right arm out for a handshake. Being polite that he was, Logan reached out and put his hand in Sabrina's and shook hands.

"I'm Logan Austin" he said.

"I'm Clary-Clarin" Sabrina cleared her throat again, "Sabrina Clarin"

"That's a pretty name" Logan said.

Sabrina smiled with genuine flattery, "Thank you".

A few hours later, when the students were dismissed for recess, Elijah was outside, waiting for his friends, Andrew and Paula shortly made it out. But there was no sign of Sabrina. After a few minutes, Elijah figured every student was out of the school. So they were back in front of the entrance, where Elijah looked and finally saw Sabrina, but something was different. She was talking to another boy! It immediately caught his attention. There they were, sitting next to each other, along with Carly and Melanie. The longer he looked; Elijah noticed the genuine smile on Sabrina's face. And the boy had the same expression.

"Who's that guy?" Elijah asked, casually.

Both Andrew and Paula looked to where Elijah was pointing.

"Logan" Andrew told him, "Austin, I think. He's in my class. Can't say I've talked to him much. Either he's quiet or I got food in my mouth"

Elijah looked back at Sabrina and her new friend. Suddenly some cruel words went through his mind; I like to shove food down Logan's mouth.

It was different to see Sabrina mingling with another boy. Elijah wasn't sure how to feel about it, after spending so much time with her.

Before his mind went any further, Elijah reminded himself what happed with Jeff Tomley back in the fall. He promised that he wouldn't go that far again, especially if Sabrina was involved.

But later on, Elijah wanted to be certain that he and Sabrina still maintained a connection. So for the next recess, he decided to make a little conversation. As soon as Sabrina walked out, Elijah went up to her, promptly.

"Hey Sabrina" he greeted, casually.

"Hi Elijah" she replied.

"How's it going?"

"It's going good"

She didn't ask him the same question.

"So, see anything new on TV lately?" Elijah asked.

Sabrina's mind wasn't exactly in the present, "Uh, no not really"

"Well, I did. It's an anime show about these giant robots"

But then Carly and Melanie came out and met with Sabrina. Did she even hear me? So their mutual interests weren't working. Elijah went to last resort.

"Hey Sabrina" he called, while he pulled out a tray of Dunka-a-Roos. This time she heard him but something wasn't right, "Uh, sorry, Elijah. I gotta go. See you later"

She walked away with her girlfriends by her side, probably going to see a certain boy.

"I thought maybe you wanted to have some Dunk-a-Roos with me" Elijah said, hoping that Sabrina would've heard, but she was further away. Soon, Andrew and Paula came out.

"Hey, Dunk-a-Roos" Andrew said, "I'm gonna steal a piece while you're not looking"

Elijah looked at Andrew, "You know what, you can have it" he insisted. Then he gave Andrew the small container.

"Really?

"Yeah, I'm still feeling kinda full from my lunch"

"Sweet!"

Elijah tried to act normal and maybe bonding with his friends would take his mind off things. So for the time being, Elijah decided to give Sabrina her space. During that time, her friendship with Logan was developing, instantly. Every time Elijah saw them, it would add more weight to his shoulders and soon grew heavy. Even if she would say hi to him, it would be enough to convince Elijah that they were still at least friends. One day, he waited for Sabrina. For once, she wasn't hanging out with Logan. She and her girlfriends were coming around the corner, where Elijah was waiting.

"Hello!" he said, smoothly.

No response. The girls didn't look at him. Maybe he didn't speak loud enough.

The next day, Sabrina was with Logan. They were walking slowly outside the school's main entrance. Melanie deliberately gave them some alone time.

"So Mel says you're into hockey" Sabrina stated.

"Oh yeah, I totally am" Logan admitted, proudly, "Best sport ever"

Without their knowledge, Elijah was right behind them, listening to every possible word to see if he could outshine Logan in any way.

"You ever play hockey?" Logan asked.

"Only when I had to in gym class" Sabrina said, "And I watched it with my dad. He's into it"

"Well, I'm sure he'll like me" Logan joked.

He spoke like was going to go over to Sabrina's house one day. They both laughed. Elijah remembered the times he put a smile on Sabrina's face.

"Good enough for me" he added.

Intrigued, Sabrina stepped in closer to listen.

"What is?" she asked.

"I'm into hockey and you're sort of into it. Maybe I can show you how to play someday"

Logan was talking to her in a way that Elijah didn't. He was flirting with her but not in a playful way. Somehow it felt a little more real, and she could see it. For a minute, it made Elijah question his friendship with Sabrina. Was it all real?

"Well, as long as you get to teach me" Sabrina said. Did I really just say that? She thought.

The conversation was going a little too far and the feeling started to sink lower. So Elijah went in close and tried to interfere. He stood behind Logan, who was standing across from Sabrina. Elijah tried to get her to notice.

"For sure" Logan told her, "I'd be happy to teach you. In fact, I can show you a lot of things"

So the first move Elijah did, was giving the peace sign behind Logan's head, making it look like he had bunny ears. But it was hard to tell if Sabrina saw it or not.

"Like what?" she said, like Elijah wasn't even there.

"Oh, I don't know, hockey…"

Then Elijah began making different faces behind Logan, who was still unaware.

"…the car my dad is helping me build"

Wow, a young boy who's talented and practically had his own vehicle. Sabrina didn't show but she was quite impressed. And then Elijah started dancing randomly, but still didn't get any acknowledgment.

"I sure like to see all those things" Sabrina said, "Well, it's just two things, but you know…"

"Two is good" Logan added, "I think"

Finally, Elijah gave up and just left the scene to avoid the embarrassment. But he stayed near just in case. Logan and Sabrina smiled at each other.

"Logan!" one of his friends called. A group of boys came from behind. One of them was holding a football.

"Are we still playing?" he asked, "We're not playing without you"

"Of course!" Logan said, "I been waiting long enough for the grass, you know"

"Then let's do it"

Logan turned his attention to Sabrina, "See you later", he said, smoothly.

Sabrina just chuckled and smiled from ear to ear, "I'll be around".

Finally, Logan was gone. Elijah stepped in once he had a chance, "I used to be into hockey"

"Yeah?" Sabrina said, only glancing at him.

"But that was because I watched the movie Mighty Ducks. You ever seen it?"

Taking her time, Sabrina shook her head. Something was wrong. The connection wasn't really there like it should've. Then Elijah started dancing again. He moved around Sabrina to try to get her attention. She smile but it wasn't as natural as before.

"I learned new moves" he told her.

"That's great" Sabrina said.

He felt the need to express his feelings somehow, to try and feel that connection again.

"Would you dance with me, Sabrina, one day?" he asked, in a low voice.

Elijah remembered seeing couples dancing together in music videos. He definitely wanted a moment like that with Sabrina. But she didn't answer his question. Was she even paying attention? The courage was fading away. Elijah just stopped dancing and acted casual. He tried walking side by side with Sabrina, hoping to start a conversation about anything.

"So...done anything inappropriate, lately?" he asked, jokingly "Get it?"

He paused to wait for a reply. The answer he got was not satisfying at all.

"I'm gonna go catch up with my friends" Sabrina told him. She practically ran from Elijah, who completely froze. He couldn't help but feel ignored. Last time that wasn't Sabrina's intention. This time it almost looked like she meant it.

"Well, that was inappropriate" Elijah muttered in sadness.

Sabrina wasn't actually meeting up with her girlfriends. She went up to the field to see Logan play with his friends. She stood in the distance and watched in awe.

"Dreamy" she said.

CHAPTER TWENTY

The Professor and The Comedian

Days and days had come and gone by, and Elijah barely spoke to Sabrina. It was just like what happened back in October, only it felt like Sabrina really was forgetting about Elijah, or maybe she wasn't. He tried to give himself positive vibe and not allow the negative energy get to him. But the silence went on, longer than he anticipated.

After just a few days, Elijah figured he'd waited long enough. The one morning, the class was lining up. Elijah waited until Sabrina joined their classmates. He went up to her.

"Hi, Sabrina" Elijah said, sincerely.

For the first in a few days, Sabrina actually looked at him. "Hi, Elijah" she replied, in the same manner. Then almost right away, she broke eye contact. Elijah opened his mouth but didn't know what to say. Then he thought it would be unwise if he tried to make her feel bad for neglecting him. After that, Elijah just went to the back of the line. So he got a sincere response out of Sabrina. But was it enough? Perhaps it was a start. Surely, it wouldn't be the last time he would interact with her, but for how long?

The next day, Elijah thought about it and decided that he wanted Sabrina to hang out with him, Andrew, and Paula, and hopefully play some tetherball together. So he was on his way to meet with her and noticed right away that Sabrina was already with Logan. Taking a deep

313

breath, Elijah decided to be polite. Melanie and Carly were there with them.

Sabrina and Logan stood face to face.

Elijah started to approach. Without realizing, Melanie snuck up behind Sabrina and gently shoved her towards Logan. Elijah stopped. There was just enough force for Sabrina to fall into Logan's arms. They looked at each other for a moment and there was that genuine smile on Sabrina's face.

Elijah suddenly felt the urge of rage, as the jealously took over, thinking that it could've been him holding Sabrina. Would Melanie ever do that for me, to push Sabrina into my arms? Apparently, you'd have to be good looking!

There was just a moment of happiness between Sabrina and Logan that Elijah just couldn't bear to watch. So he left. Sabrina didn't know Elijah was even there.

Life had become silent again. Elijah lied there in his bed. He couldn't even think about Sabrina because then Logan would also appear in his mind. So he just stared blankly and dealt with the emptiness he was feeling. It was a good time to talk to someone, but Ken was the only person Elijah could talk to, but he had to be at school in order to see him. If Elijah couldn't talk, maybe he could do something. It was the only solution he thought of from that evening to the next day at school.

The day wasn't feeling normal like it used to be. Just thinking about Sabrina and her new friend put Elijah in a sour mood. He didn't realize how much it affected him. He was moody and every little thing was irritating him. Truthfully, he was waiting to see if he and Sabrina were still friends. He waited for an acknowledgment, something that's not just saying hello to fill the silence. Elijah kept telling himself to be patient and that she would come along, but when? It felt like it was going to be a long wait. What if a month went by and this time Sabrina wouldn't say hi to him? Probably because she and Logan might be holding hands!

Mentally, that thought broke Elijah in half. The feeling of rage erupted and flowed through his sadness and was about to come out in tears. With little luck, he was able to keep it bottled up but he knew it couldn't hold forever.

Breathe, he then encouraged himself.

Perhaps Elijah was overthinking and maybe he needed to spend time with Andrew. Paula was sick that day. So it was only the two boys. Elijah and Andrew were on the field, playing tetherball by themselves. They both talked about the usual, their favorite shows, games, and upcoming movies. But it wasn't enough to cure the rage that Elijah was hiding. Not to mention he was still peering back and forth to the lower ground, to make sure a certain someone was down there. Elijah felt that he was out of options. So there was only one idea come to mind, making Logan look bad in front of everyone. Would that be too far? Elijah wondered. There wasn't much time to think, for that the tetherball came flying towards him. Elijah immediately ducked.

"Ha!" Andrew taunted, "I win again, sucker!"

After their little game was over, Elijah and Andrew walked back to the supervisor to return the tetherball. It was quiet. It was a good time to ask Andrew for a little help that could be an addition to Elijah's plan.

"Hey Al, can I ask you something?"

"Okay, but my mind might wonder off any minute" Andrew told him.

"Uh, about Logan, do you know anything about him?"

Andrew paused, "Like what, his favorite movie, fast food restaurant, or if he ever did something stupid like put a whoopee-cushion on the teacher's chair?" He looked at Elijah, "Don't tell me you like him!" he joked.

"No, of course not" Elijah was slightly irritated, "I mean-I don't know, like something he doesn't like or any embarrassing moments he had?"

"There might be at least one" Andrew stood there to think, "Let me try to remember. Oh, just so you know that whole whoopee-cushion thing was made up"

"I know" Elijah told him.

While they were waiting, the boys went to return the tetherball to the supervisor. "You know what, I need food!" Andrew said, "Food helps me remember"

Elijah had no comment.

"Luckily, I usually keep one chocolate bar in my pocket, for an after snack"

Andrew checked his pockets. Elijah waited patiently.

"Ohhh no" he muttered, "It's not here!"

Elijah gave a little sigh. "Should we go look for it?" he offered, reluctantly.

"It's the only way I can help you, E.K."

From there, Elijah and Andrew re-traced their footsteps. As they went along, they kept looking to the ground, hoping the chocolate bar would appear in sight.

"Do you remember where you had it last?" Elijah asked,

"I didn't have to touch my pockets until a minute ago. Who knows, it might still be on the field or the boot room"

Elijah was getting impatient. "If it's in the boot room, I'll just shove food down my throat" he muttered.

They passed the monkey bars and then around the corner.

"Better make this quick before the bell rings" Elijah insisted.

"Just keep your eyes to the ground" Andrew added. Then he gave a chuckle, "We look like idiots walking like this"

Finally, they found it.

"Ah-ha! There it is" Andrew started running towards his chocolate bar, "Oh, now I remember something" He stopped and explained to Elijah.

"Back in grade five, Logan couldn't pronounce Mississippi. So we called him 'Mrs. Hippy'" Andrew started laughing. It also made Elijah chuckle a little.

Elijah nodded, "Anything else?"

Andrew paused to think, "None"

Then Elijah began to ponder in thought, if that little info could be enough.

"I better grab my chocolate before someone else does" Andrew said. It became quiet for a moment as Elijah was in deep thought, while Andrew was eating away.

"Oh wait, there is another thing" Andrew claimed.

Elijah listened closely.

"His name isn't really Logan"

"What? Really?" Elijah was surprised as he was confused.

"No-no; well it is, just not his first name"

"So Logan is actually his middle name? What's his first name?"

"Robert. Yes, I remember one day I was handing in my work and saw his name on the attendance sheet. It said, 'Austin, Robert Logan.' But everyone calls him Logan, even the yearbook"

For a moment, Elijah was both puzzled and intrigued. "Huh, how did the school keep that a secret?"

"I don't know" Andrew took a moment to enjoy his chocolate bar, "Maybe he bribed the teacher. 'Hey, Mr-Mrs. Whatever, I don't feel like being called Robert. I'll give you a quarter and a piece of gum I just found under my seat if you call me Logan'."

That joke made Elijah laugh a little.

"So what did Logan do, anyway?" he asked, after swallowing a small portion of chocolate.

The jokes were over.

Don't mention Sabrina. Elijah paused to try and think of an excuse that was simple, "Uhh, he's been annoying me" he told him.

"Really? I didn't know you guys were friends, well not friends, but you guys knowing each other"

"We're not. I…got to know him a little through Sabrina"

That was the best explanation Elijah could come up with and not revealing his true feelings about the girl of his dreams.

"Are we gonna bash one of our fellow students like old times?" Andrew asked.

Elijah took his time, "Maybe".

"Maybe I can help?"

"I appreciate the offer, but I don't want you…getting in trouble"

"Depends how bad we're gonna be"

318   PHILIP PATRICK

"Hold on, give me a minute" Elijah needed time to think. Did he really want to humiliate Logan in front of Sabrina? There was a chance he could lose her or what if he already did, since they barely spoke for almost a week. It was still a mystery if Elijah and Sabrina were still friends. A simple hello wasn't enough. Then Elijah remembered the one day Sabrina ignored him and ran off. That wasn't a very nice feeling. It only took one thought to change the mood and that gave Elijah the motive.

"Still wanna help, Andrew?" Elijah asked,

"Hey, if my best friend needs help, I'm there to give the gift of helping!" Andrew promised.

"Cool, you sure?"

"Let's just say this: I'm no religious freak, but if one of god's creatures becomes annoying, he creates us to stop them!"

Later that day, Sabrina was with Logan, Carly, and Melanie. They were all sitting together on the field, which was a place Elijah hung out with Sabrina once. They were talking amongst themselves. Elijah stood on the lower ground, looking up at them and then Andrew joined him, shoulder to shoulder. "Is that your boy?" he asked,

"He's not my boy" Elijah told him, trying to sound calm, "But yeah, that's him"

"Damn rights" Andrew replied, strongly, "I'm your boy".

Elijah didn't reply because he was focusing on their mission. *But that's MY Sabrina!* Right then, he turned off his mind and got into character.

"Logan Austin" Elijah called, loud and clear. Everyone in the circle looked at Elijah, who stood in front of them. He did now know what to expect because he didn't have the decency to think ahead. Perhaps that decency was taking from him. "I've heard a story about you, something that's worth telling, I think". Then he sat across from the group. Nobody spoke. "But before I do, Mr. Little would like to give a little presentation". Then Elijah gestured towards Andrew, who stood next to them. Sabrina and the rest of the gang turned their attention on Andrew. He was standing straight and tall, and had a pencil in his mouth, pretending it was a smoking pipe.

"All the way from England" Andrew replied, in a weak British accent, "Now, there's something unique about that word, 'pree-sen-tation'. I think it's a word that encourages you to show off. So allow me"

Andrew had a sketch book in his hand. He opened it and showed a drawing of a robotic being. "This is an android or some of you might call it, a robot. He's a rather troubled fellow but he can change shapes and has many tools programmed inside of him"

Andrew turned the page. The next drawing was a humanoid lizard, wearing a cape, a crown, and armed with a sword. "This one is a Lizard King! A creature who rules the caverns of Rac-Ta, and Rac-Ta's a place. And don't ask me what or where. We're still trying to look for an idiot-I mean a brave young man to discover for us"

Turning to the last page, it was a drawing of a sea creature. It was a massive eel-like predator. "A rare photo of the legendary sea monster; I don't know much about it, only that it feeds off curly-haired boys. If you look closely, the little weasel is trying to fight this monster with a hockey stick". Still in character, Andrew scoffed in disbelief, "Like the monster is going to grow a soft spot for that little fellow. I mean, it's got sharp teeth for a reason!"

There was a little pause, as Logan felt singled out. He had a feeling that it didn't sound like a compliment.

"Oops" Andrew said, in his British accent, "Did I say curly-haired boys?" He started laughing directly at Logan, "I meant curly-haired boys who dared to spit in the face of this creature"

Then Andrew went up to Logan and patted him on his head, "There, there, Pork Chop, you're all right. Thank you for your attention. Now back to Mr. Khoda"

Andrew dashed away. Sabrina didn't look too pleased. But at that point, nobody else mattered, not to Elijah.

"Thank you, Mr. Little" Elijah said, "That was a good presen-ta-tion. Now Logan, I once heard you had a little accident back in grade five? Yes, you accidently said Mississippi wrong. Then kids started calling you Mrs. Hippy?"

Logan frowned and broke eye contact. Then Andrew, who sat right beside him, started laughing rather hysterically. "Isn't this guy hilarious?" Andrew said, putting his hands on Logan's shoulders, "You should see his other act. It involves mice"

Elijah was running low on ideas. He had no choice but to improvise. In that moment, he spoke like he had the power, a power that carried him away. "So is your name, Logan Hippy?" There was no response, "Or is it Robert?"

Logan couldn't move like he was paralyzed.

"Yes, Robert Austin is your real name" Elijah added, "But I think Logan Hippy sounds more fun. Hey, it almost sounds like you can use it for a food product, Logan Hippy Beans"

Melanie nearly burst out laughing but she stopped herself.

"Logan Hippy Beans" Elijah repeated, "It's kinda fun to say. I can see it on the shelf right now. A little kid comes along, 'mommy, mommy, can we get some Logan Hippy Beans?'"

Andrew continued to laugh and even slapped Logan on the shoulder. Nobody said anything. Sabrina actually started feeling embarrassed. She glanced over at Logan, who put his head down in shame.

"Well, that's all I have for tonight but before I go" Elijah added, as he got up to his feet, "I just like to say, I think hockey sucks... Pork-Chop!"

Andrew continued laughing like he was in a comedy club, "What do you know, he acknowledged you!" he said to Logan, "Don't worry, it's a cool thing. The fat chicks will be all over you". Once again, Andrew slapped Logan's shoulder and held it tightly.

Feeling discomforted, Logan got up to his feet "Excuse me" he said, gently. Then he walked away. Sabrina scowled at Andrew briefly, but she was mostly upset at Elijah.

"Elijah, can I see you for a minute?" she asked. She got up to her feet and left with Elijah. But Andrew was still with the other girls.

"Good show, right?" he said, casually, trying to make conversation.

"Your accent wasn't bad" Melanie told him.

Elijah and Sabrina were further away from the others. She stopped and glared at him, "What was all that about?"

There was no proper explanation, "Just playing around?" Elijah offered.

"Playing around? How about hurting Logan's feelings?!" Sabrina snarled.

What about my feelings? Elijah almost said, "You mean Robert"

"You think this is funny? Besides, that's not the point. Elijah...I gotta say, I'm pretty shocked right now. Out of all the people in this school, I didn't think you would do such a hurtful thing".

There was no more sweet talk. Everything from there was all bitter. And the words finally came out of Elijah's mouth. "Well, what about the other day when you ignored me? I tried making conversation and it didn't look like you were paying attention". This time, he let the anger go off in his voice.

"Elijah, I gave you a lot of my attention for a long time. Why can't I do something different?"

"I just wanna know if you and I are still friends. That's all" Elijah said, sincerely.

Sabrina scoffed, "Not when you're acting childish"

Something was wrong. This wasn't the same Sabrina Clarin that he met back in September, the one he fell in love with and the same person that made a difference in his life and gave him something to look forward to each day. Sabrina was mad. Not only she was mad, she changed somehow. No, it was all wrong. Elijah didn't like it.

"Hey, back in November you said that we can hang out once in a while"

There was barely any time for Sabrina to process everything that was going on, for that she was too furious, "Well, maybe things are a little different now" she explained, rather bitterly.

Elijah froze.

He didn't like the way that sounded. Was their friendship officially over? "What does that mean?" He almost wished he didn't ask that, but he couldn't help himself to get answers after all the silence.

322 PHILIP PATRICK

Sabrina continued scowling at him, "It means that I have something good going on, something I've been wanting for a while. And Elijah…" she went up to his face and yelled, "…you're ruining everything!"

Then Sabrina turned her back and stormed away. And Elijah's heart dropped more than it ever did. Andrew walked passed Sabrina, but neither of them said a word. Sabrina only glared at him, briefly. Elijah didn't move a muscle as he watched his special friend walk away. Andrew regrouped with his best friend.

"Well, that went well" he said, mildly.

"Maybe a little too well" Elijah replied, without any emotion.

"You okay, bud?"

Elijah paused and slowly started walking away, "Just need to be alone for a bit"

"Hey, if it makes you feel any better, Sabrina also gave me the evil eyes"

Well, I'm glad we're still friends, Sabrina.
We'll always be friends.

CHAPTER TWENTY-ONE

Far From Finished

Back in the fall, it was all a misunderstanding when Elijah thought Sabrina was being forgetful but now it was real. That was the first time she got mad at Elijah after what he did to Logan. And Elijah had nothing but guilt and loneliness. That was just one thing; the distance between them grew longer. And the other thing that probably hurt the most, Sabrina Clarin wouldn't even look at him.

Two days after the incident, Paula was back at school, feeling much better. And Elijah needed someone to talk to, badly. So the first thing was to meet with Paula. Both she and Elijah were on the curb near the parking lot, for a little privacy.

"Paula, am I bad person, like really?" Elijah asked. Paula heard the distress and became concerned.

"No, of course not!" she told him.

"I thought I was doing good. I really tried but some days I just couldn't handle it"

"Doesn't mean you should stop; Elijah, you're a good person, much more than you think. What's bothering you?"

"I...did something bad" Elijah actually almost cried when he admitted it. He told Paula about what he and Andrew did, and the fact that Sabrina was unhappy with him in the end. Paula didn't say anything, not at first.

"Elijah, I'm sorry" she said, sincerely.

"I just wanted to know she was still my friend" Elijah added.

"Well, to be honest with you, that was an immature approach"

"Yeah but Sabrina ignored me that one day. So I...humiliated Logan"

Paula didn't know what to say. "Well, I can't really speak for Sabrina. But one time, my dad told me that the person who gets mad usually talks than thinks."

That was a fair point and gave Elijah something to think about. He looked away to the parking lot, blankly, for a moment.

"Elijah" Paula called, "Look at me"

So he did.

"Believe me, you are a good person. It's not too late to show it. You did something wrong and all you can do right now is say you're sorry. And maybe you and Sabrina will still be friends after this whole thing".

So one weary thought was dealt with, but the weary spirit still needed to heal. For the time being, Elijah just took in the silence and behaved like a regular student. This time, he didn't look over at Sabrina like he usually did. Luckily, the next day, Ken actually came to check on Elijah. They went to their usual room, where Elijah told Ken what happened.

"I don't know if she'll ever talk to me again" Elijah added, sadly.

"What makes you think that?" Ken asked,

"Because of what I've done, even after I told her that I didn't wanna be like this anymore. And I didn't mean to hurt her feelings. I just wanted..." Elijah couldn't find the right words because he couldn't fully process what happened. "I don't know. Things just happened and I feel bad"

"Well, Elijah, it sounds to me that you didn't really mean to hurt anyone. Sometimes we humans get a little shaken up by something or someone and it gives us that negative energy. Most of the time we don't know what to do with it, so we look for a place to put it".

Now that was a metaphorical explanation.

"I think you were feeling threatened by Logan" Ken continued, "So you used him to take your anger out on him. And maybe it's also because you didn't want to take it out on Sabrina"

"I guess it was a good thing it didn't happen that way"

Both Elijah and Ken sat in silence.

"Hey, Ken, does this how love works?"

Ken took a moment to figure out what to say because no student had ever asked him that kind of question before. "Sometimes" he admitted, "Sometimes love makes us do crazy things. We'd do anything to get that one person's attention"

"Even you?" Elijah wasn't sure why he asked that. It was probably just a natural way to keep the conversation going. And Elijah didn't expect such a response from Ken, who chuckled at the question.

"Yeah, even me" he answered, honestly. For the next moment all the problems were turned off as Elijah couldn't help but wonder.

"Now I'm a little curious" he said.

"Well..." Ken sat back in his chair, "I first met my wife in high school. Back then, my main priority was to get her attention. This one night, all of us were partying at someone's house. I decided I wanted to pull a stunt. So I brought my dirt-bike and a ramp that I had. By the time I got the courage to ride, none of my friends were around. I was gonna get them to introduce me because I didn't have all the courage just yet. I was quite shy back then. So I had to introduce myself and came up with my own nickname at the last minute because I wanted to surprise them-they thought I was being clever-anyways, I said to them...'introducing...Crazy Dog!'"

Both Elijah and Ken couldn't help but laugh. The image of a teenage Ken with a dirt-bike just planted in their minds.

"Immediately, I went and started the dirt-bike and there I went up the ramp, and over the fence, and landed successfully! But unfortunately, I rammed into the table and spilled the drinks"

They laughed again.

"Well, at least nobody got hurt" Elijah said.

"Yes! That was a good thing"

They enjoyed what was left of the excitement. But that was a good conversation. Just mentioning the word love had Elijah thinking about Sabrina, along with the memories they made together. He missed her.

"I guess I just have to talk to her and tell that I'm sorry. That's what Paula was telling me"

"That's probably your only option"

What if Sabrina doesn't wanna be friends anymore? Elijah was tempted to ask, but then he wasn't sure if he really wanted to know.

"And...maybe this whole thing is not as bad as you think" Ken added, "Maybe there's something in Sabrina's life that's troubling her. But that's just a thought"

It was hard to imagine a girl like Sabrina Clarin having problems that could possibly destroy her wellbeing. She seemed so happy most of the time, but then again, no one couldn't tell. The meeting with Ken was over. Elijah thought about what he had to do, he simply had to right his wrong, and hopefully re-connect with his special friend.

School was over. Elijah was eager to see Sabrina, as he waited outside. Paula and Andrew were there. He told them what he was about to do. After a moment, Sabrina was out of the school building, talking with her friends. Without wasting any time, Elijah raced towards her.

"Sabrina" he called.

He had her attention, but Sabrina gave him a sour look.

"Can I...see you for a moment, please?" Elijah asked, politely.

She hesitated.

"I just wanna talk to you and tell I'm sorry" Elijah added. The discussion barely started and it already sounded like he was reaching the end. It had to be because he was afraid that his dream girl might walk away on him.

"Sure" Sabrina reluctantly agreed.

That was a mild relief. It did help Elijah to focus but yet he was still getting anxious by the minute. As he was guiding Sabrina to a more private location, he took a deep breath and told himself of his dad's saying: men were born to be brave. Once they were finally alone, they looked eye to eye. She still didn't look very pleased. It was the same expression she had that day when Elijah humiliated Logan.

"Sabrina, I…"

Just when he was about to patch things up, someone from the past lurked behind him.

"Hello bro" a voiced called out.

That wasn't just any voice. Elijah turned around and it was actually the last face he expected to see.

"Miss me?" Quinton Malcolm said, grimly.

Elijah frowned. Sabrina felt neglected.

"What do you want?" Elijah said, bitterly. Suddenly, he overlooked his personal issues as he felt that he was transported back to the days when he hung out with Quinton Malcolm.

"To catch up with my bro, what else?"

The anger Elijah was feeling diminished once he remembered that Sabrina was still in front of him, waiting. The pressure was already getting to him. Quinton noticed the worry on his former friend's face and that revealed his soft spot.

"I'm not your brother, Quinton" Elijah was able to say, firmly, "I'm pretty busy right now. I'll always be busy"

He then quickly gestured Sabrina to walk away with him.

"You must be her"

Oh great, Quinton talked to Sabrina, who looked at him in awkward silence, as she sensed some hostility in his voice.

"Quinton!" Elijah snapped.

"The girl, the one he likes" Quinton pointed to Elijah, "The one HE likes"

Sabrina said nothing. Elijah closed his eyes, hoping that Quinton would just disappear.

"Sabrina" Elijah sighed, "This is the reason I got suspended a few months ago-this pipsqueak loser!"

"I-I'm sorry, I gotta go" Sabrina shrieked, trying not to look at either of the boys. She then turned around and walked away.

328 PHILIP PATRICK

"Sabrina!" Elijah called, desperately. Then he cocked his head towards Quinton, "Get out of here! Now!" Then Elijah went to chase after Sabrina.

"Sabrina?" Quinton said.

She then stopped once she heard her name. *Just walk away, girl.* But for some reason Sabrina froze. It was Zachery Epstad all over again. Elijah froze when he realized that Quinton Malcolm was trying to communicate with his special friend.

No! Not Sabrina! Enough was enough. Elijah turned around and stormed after Quinton before-

"You like her, don't you?" Quinton said, as he looked directly at Elijah, who then couldn't move any longer for that he felt trapped, mentally.

Paula was only several feet away when she realized what was going on. She recognized the distress in Elijah's face.

"You do" Quinton said.

Sabrina was about to turn around and continue walking.

"You hear that, Sabrina, he likes you!"

Elijah looked at her and felt a heavy guilt coming down on him. I'm sorry, he desperately wanted to say.

"No, really, he likes you" Quinton added, "In fact, he was looking at a magazine with naked woman"

With great fear, Elijah's eyes widened. He turned back to Quinton, who was holding his hands out in front of his chest, pretending he was holding breasts. Sabrina felt mocked and humiliated. Furiously, Elijah dashed towards his former friend, grabbed him firmly by the shoulders.

"Stop it!!" Elijah growled, "Stop it right now!!"

Paula and Andrew were about to interfere but they just couldn't move.

"Go on, hit me, like you did before" Quinton challenged.

"No!" Elijah refused, "Not this time"

Elijah glanced back at Sabrina, who was still worried. He knew he had to do something, without resorting to violence.

"I wanna talk to you right now!" Elijah strongly urged. He pushed Quinton away from the crowd until they were around the corner. Paula and Andrew followed.

ELIJAH AND SABRINA   329

"Quinton, I want nothing to do with you and I don't wanna talk to you" Elijah snarled, "So get of here!"

"You can't get rid of me that easily" Quinton claimed, "I'm stronger than you think"

"I don't care!"

"Oh, you will"

"What does that mean?"

"Because you and I, we're not finished yet" Quinton promised, "I just wanted you to know that" The tone in his voice turned bitter. It became clear that Quinton was still mad at Elijah.

"Quinton, if you got a problem, you talk to me, but leave Sabrina out of it!"

"No promises"

Elijah froze, regretting the fact that he even revealed Sabrina's name, thinking that he was going to do something to her. Now Quinton Malcolm got to Elijah's head, making him lose control and concentration of the situation. The only possible solution was throwing a punch but Elijah couldn't do that. He already caused enough trouble when he humiliated Logan Austin, which was another thing that was holding him down.

"Just get outta here!" Elijah repeated.

Quinton pointed at him "For now" he warned.

Then he turned and finally left. Once it was safe, Andrew and Paula met with Elijah, who was clutching his fists hard and gave a heavy disappointing groan.

"Elijah, are you okay?" Paula asked, with deep concern.

"No! I'm not okay! That damn Quinton!"

"I didn't see that coming" Andrew said, "Wow".

Paula patted Elijah on his shoulder and encouraged him to take a deep breath.

"Sabrina" Elijah said, once he remembered. Then he quickly turned around ran back to the front of the school. There were still several students around. Elijah looked and even went in further but there was no sign of Sabrina. She was gone. Elijah was speechless. He just gave a sigh and put his head down in shame.

Just when Elijah was about to patch things up, Quinton Malcolm just had to make things worse; now Sabrina Clarin was humiliated and probably wanted nothing to do with Elijah anymore. The weight on Elijah's shoulders grew heavier, for that he blamed himself. He kept looking around, hoping to see Sabrina. Denial was running its course. She probably fled the school once she saw one of her parents. But Elijah had so much passion that he refused to believe it. His mind was still racing from what just happened, for that he was barely paying any attention when Andrew spoke to him.

"Sorry, bud, I don't wanna miss my bus..."

"It's okay, Andrew" Paula said, gently, "Just go"

"See you guys tomorrow"

So Andrew left. Elijah turned around and went to sit at the bench, trying to take it easy.

"Geez, that Quinton!" Elijah kept saying to himself.

"Elijah, deep breaths, remember?" Paula reminded.

So that was what he did. Paula sat next to him on the bench, with her hand on his shoulder. As the whole dramatic effect was fully processed, Elijah put his head down, almost wanting to cry. There was hurt just as much as anger. He couldn't believe that he just brought his problems to Sabrina. Paula stayed with him until she had to go. She reminded her best friend that she was only a phone call away. Elijah deliberately took his time just so Quinton would be long gone and the walk home would be safe.

That evening, Elijah tried to act normal as possible. He was eating dinner with his parents. His mom recognized the silence.

"What's wrong, Eli?" she asked.

Elijah looked at her, briefly. "N-nothing, I'm fine".

"You haven't said a word since you came home"

"I'm okay. It's just...school"

His mom paused, "Okay"

Elijah took a few bites of his meal. After a minute or two, he found himself only stirring his food as he couldn't stop thinking about Quinton and the damage he done. Geez, that Quinton!

"You know what" Elijah said, as he looked at his mom, "I'm not feeling hungry".

Then he got up from the table and left the kitchen. Elijah closed the door to his room and started pacing around, as more rage began to build up. He grabbed his pillow and squeezed it rather hard. It was tempting to yell but he couldn't. For the next hour, Elijah just lied on his bed and buried his face in the sheets.

After getting some alone time, Elijah called Paula. He went to grab the cordless phone and went to his room. He sat on the bed, dialed the number, and the line started ringing. After three rings, Mrs. Hennig answered and Elijah politely asked for Paula.

"Hello?" Paula greeted,

"Paula" Elijah replied, softly.

"Eli, how are things?"

"Okay, I guess" Elijah lied flat on his bed, as he had the phone to his ear, "It's been pretty...quiet"

"Sometimes quiet is all we need" Paula told him.

There was a short pause. Then Paula heard Elijah give a little sigh.

"Just when things couldn't get worse, it gets worse!" he said.

"I'm sorry, Eli. I know it sucks but sometimes life is full of surprises even when you don't want it"

"Yeah, and I don't want to start a fight like last time. I know it's something you don't like"

It was kind of nice to hear Elijah admitting that fighting was wrong when before it was a habit for him. "No, I don't" Paula agreed, "You know you can still stand up for yourself without having to throw a punch, right?"

So fight by using words. That wasn't Elijah's first choice when it comes to facing a bully. He would rather run and be left alone; otherwise he would have to take a beating.

"I guess that's the only thing I can do" Elijah said.

"Fighting is what the bullies want. It's just as becoming a prey to a predator"

No one could predict how a situation could get worse. Even once Elijah imagined how the outcome would be, but it never went as planned. "Yeah, yeah" he muttered.

There was one long silence on the phone.

"Elijah" Paula said.

"Still here"

"I want to help" she offered, "Is there anything I can do?"

He paused to think. There were barely any options at that point. "Be by my side? Be ready for something, hopefully nothing bad. But I'll make sure that doesn't happen"

"Hey, we'll try together" Paula promised, "We're a team".

Elijah nodded, "A team".

"Always"

There was another paused moment. Paula could hear him breathing as she waited patiently.

"Is there anything you wanna talk about, Eli?"

"Maybe...I...just can't think of anything right now"

"That's okay. Even if you just wanna sit in silence, then I'll sit with you. That's what I'm here for"

Anything and everything was going through his mind; both all the good and the bad. Yet, Elijah chose to stare blankly at the ceiling for a long moment. The only thing he wondered was if he and Sabrina would still be friends after all the trouble. But he figured that was something he had to find out for himself instead of asking a friend for an answer. Elijah knew Paula would help him in every way she could. He wanted to ask, but he hesitated because he also knew that Paula couldn't solve everything. And then he thought maybe Sabrina's friendship was something that he didn't earn after his bad behavior.

"Paula?"

"Yeah?" she replied.

"Uh...after all the bad things I done, did you ever...not want to be friends with me anymore?"

"Of course not, Eli; you haven't done anything to me that made me angry. You've always been kind to me. I know you been through bad times but I still see you coming to school. I mean, look at us; we made it to grade seven together, all the way from kindergarten. And you enjoy all the little things like laughing at Andrew's jokes or just having fun. You know what I mean?"

"Yeah"

"That means that there's still some good in this life and you made the best of it"

"I did, didn't I?"

"You sure did, Eli. And if you hadn't admitted your mistakes, I probably would doubt our friendship by now. So you done good things and because of that, you still have my friendship"

"Thanks, Paula" For a moment there, Paula's words made Elijah forget about his problems and it relaxed him. "It means a lot" he added.

Elijah breathed in and breathed out, feeling more liberated. He then started reflecting on the good he accomplished the past year, putting smiles on his friend's faces, meeting Carly and Melanie, and most of all, Sabrina Clarin.

"Eli?" Paula called.

"I'm still here. I...I do wanna talk, it's just I...I can't think of how to say it right now"

"That's okay. It takes time. And it's probably because you're still shaken up about what happened. Just let that sink in and when the time is right you'll know what to say"

Again, Elijah looked passed his problem with Quinton and talked about something else after gathering some thoughts.

"Yeah, I probably wanted to say a lot of things when I was little...I was so shy...Didn't always know what to say" There was another pause, "But now I think I do, it's just...bad timing I guess"

"And your time will come"

They sat in silence again for a short period of time. He thought about talking to Paula about the truth, about how he felt towards Sabrina and how her relationship with Logan took a toll on him. But he still wasn't sure if he was ready to share that just yet.

"I was actually just thinking about all the good things that happened this year" he said.

"Yeah?"

"Yeah, since you said that there was some good in this life. I've seen it...and...it was something great, maybe better than I expected. I...can't really describe it but I think it made me a better person"

That was probably as close as Elijah was going to get to telling about his feelings for Sabrina.

"Well, that's good. I'm glad to hear that, Eli. I could probably tell because I don't think I ever seen you being that social. You know, you just put yourself out there, make the best of it and you leave a good impression. I'm proud of you"

"Thank You"

"You're welcome"

They sat in silence again.

"Well, I'm sure my sister will need the phone any minute. Was there anything else you want to talk about?"

There was nothing else, not at that point. The only thing left to think about was his problem with Quinton. Now that burden was less heavy, Elijah could think more clearly and needed the time alone. "No, I don't think so"

"Okay, try to get some sleep now"

"Okay and thank you for sitting in silence with me"

"You're welcome. We'll talk again tomorrow. Good night, Elijah"

"Good night, Paula"

The phone call ended. Later that evening, Elijah was in bed and eventually fell asleep.

At the beginning of the school year, Elijah used to be excited to get up for school, just to see Sabrina. But now he didn't want to go to school, just like back in grade five to avoid Brian Kidman, only this time it's Quinton Malcolm. So it took a little while for Elijah to get ready for school. Once arriving on the field, there was Paula and Andrew waiting for him by the wooden steps. It was nice to have support from friends who were willing to face against bullies.

"Hey Eli" Paula greeted, "We thought we'd wait for you"

Elijah nodded, "Appreciate it".

Andrew approached Elijah and stood by his side, "When a friend is in need, we put the S at the end of friend, because we're here for you".

"Thanks, it means a lot".

"You're all right?" Paula asked,

"I'm a little nervous" Elijah admitted, "I don't really know what's gonna happen"

"Hey!" Andrew spoke promptly, "When you're nervous, we're all nervous. We're in this together. When you fight, we all fight and hope together that THEY go down..."

"I don't think your speech is going anywhere, Andrew" Paula interrupted.

"Well, at least I have a speech"

"Well, I don't need a spee-"Paula shook her head, "This isn't about us"

"This isn't about us?!", Andrew replied, in disbelief, "I thought we were in this together"

Paula sighed, "This isn't the time for jokes, Andrew!"

Elijah chuckled, nearly bursting out laughing but he stopped himself in order to take situation more seriously, although deep down, he'd rather not.

"See?" Andrew said to Paula, "It was worth it"

Paula didn't bother arguing, since Andrew's humor at least brought a smile to Elijah's face.

Elijah cleared his throat, "I wish I can laugh longer. I really do, but with that damn Quinton out there, I can't. I can't really do anything".

"Well if anything, let Quentin come to you" Paula insisted, "There's no reason for you to start a fight. Quinton's the bad guy here, not you"

"Okay" Elijah agreed, "So what do we do now?"

"Be ourselves, enjoy it while we can?" Paula said.

So keep living like nothing was wrong? Elijah wasn't exactly keen on the idea, "But I'm gonna have to face him, eventually" he added.

"And we'll be there by your side" Paula promised him.

Then all three of them walked down from the field, trying to act as normal as possible.

"'Spee'" Andrew said, amusingly, "That was pretty funny, Paula"

Paula let out a little sigh, "I was gonna say speech"

"I know"

For the morning, the team stayed in front of the school and they hadn't seen Quinton, not yet at least. After that, they enjoyed the silence in class while doing school schoolwork. Elijah however couldn't really relax, knowing that Quinton was going to come up to him sooner or later and force him to fight. Not to mention Sabrina was a few feet away from him, which made him emotionally vulnerable. Like he always did, Elijah peered over his shoulder to glance at Sabrina, wishing he was able to talk to her, but with Quinton Malcolm out there, it didn't feel safe.

During the first recess, Elijah still didn't have much courage to face his bully and with all their peers around, it might be unwise to make a move. So Elijah, Paula, and Andrew were at the pathway, where it was close to a supervisor that was patrolling one of the areas up front. And just as Elijah predicted, Quinton and his friends came around the corner.

"They're coming" Elijah said, unhappily, "I knew it"

"Relax" Andrew encouraged, "The supervisor is still close"

Then Andrew turned around and noticed the supervisor was a little further. "Sort of", he added. Elijah couldn't help but be disappointed, as he gave a sigh.

"Elijah, you don't need to face them today, if you're not ready" Paula told him.

Remaining silent, Elijah didn't have any words to describe his predicament. He only wished that his problems would go away.

"Well, well" Quinton called, as they walked by Elijah and his friends, "If it isn't the group of…" He paused to search a word, "Babies!"

The gang stopped, as the unexpected standoff took place. Elijah said nothing, for that he didn't want anything to do with Quinton Malcolm, especially after he taunted Sabrina. Roscoe, June, and Devon all stood by Quinton's side. The boys didn't look too happy. Most likely their leader fed them lies about Elijah.

"What, tough guy is not so tough today?" Quinton challenged, "Has he gone deaf?"

Elijah kept his eyes forward, hoping that he wouldn't have to fight.

"Why don't you keep walking?" Paula insisted, calmly.

Quinton laughed, "Isn't that cute, a girl standing up for another girl"

Paula just scowled at the bully. Quinton noticed the supervisor up ahead, "This isn't over" he warned. Finally, they left.

"How about I just don't wanna fight?" Elijah said, in a low voice.

"He's probably just saying that to sound tough" Paula told him.

Elijah already heard that before. What else was new? After school, Elijah quickly ran home before Quinton even left the school grounds. As he was running passed houses on Sus Avenue, Elijah kept looking in every direction of his surroundings, to make sure Quinton wasn't around. Luckily, it was a safe trip home.

For the next few hours, Elijah turned his mind off and just enjoyed the peace and quiet. But at the end of the day, his problems would cloud his mind again. He was missing Sabrina and wished that Quinton would simply smarten up.

Elijah reminded himself that he had to face him sooner or later. So then he brainstormed different alternatives to fighting. First, he thought of talking to June Disher and see if she could possible talk Quinton out of his bullying behavior. But there was too much doubt there.

The second idea Elijah had was to settle the conflict in a NON-violent way. It was hard to think that the bully would go for it. Most likely, he'd prefer the violence. It seemed like Quinton Malcolm only wanted to beat up Elijah Khoda. Maybe if they faced each other a year or two ago, Elijah would've had the confidence to fight. Even then, there were times Elijah would feel too overconfident that he wasn't prepared for the worse and ended up facing the consequences. But those days were over.

The third idea Elijah thought of was explaining to his mom what had been really going on and maybe she would do something about it. But what good would that do? Even if Quinton was stopped before doing anything, he probably wouldn't listen and still go after Elijah anyway. And most likely Madeline Khoda would punish her son for keeping secrets from her. She would find out about Sabrina and forbid him from seeing her ever again. The same thing goes for the teacher or the principal. There was no way Elijah could rely on the grownups to help him, not like the old primary days where the students were merely children and misguided by their thoughts and feelings. Whenever there was a conflict, it was settled by a simple talk, followed by an apology. The thought was too much to bear; it was starting to give Elijah a headache as it mingled with his emotions.

Deep breathes, he thought.

Elijah took a deep breath and exhaled, and repeat. His mind was calm. Why did life have to become so difficult? A life filled with enough violence to wipe a smile away. Elijah Khoda never wanted this; he was just as simple as any other kid that wanted nothing but to play and have fun. Things were simpler then, but somewhere along the way, life changed. Ever since grade five, Elijah dealt with only pressure from his peers, his teachers, and his mom. It seemed to become a regular thing and just made Elijah a fighter that took his problems out on everyone, especially when he felt he was being treated unfairly. Elijah had never been so serious when he said that he did not want to be like that anymore. But it seemed like his problems would never go away. Elijah lied on his bed, for that it was the only safe place in his life right now.

"This isn't me" he told himself, I don't think this was supposed to happen. What did I do? Is there anything I can do to fix it? He gave out a little sigh, closed his eyes as he emptied his mind. "Sabrina" Elijah whispered. If only she could hear him. "Sabrina, I miss you".

Sabrina, Sabrina Clarin. The name echoed in his head, just like it did after the day he met her. Right then, she was the only person he was thinking about, excluding all of his problems. Elijah never met a girl that he liked so much. In fact, he never really liked any girl before he met her. Elijah opened his eyes and kept muttering Sabrina's name, and then the memories came back to him, from the day he met her to the last heartfelt conversation they had. Sabrina Clarin was the one that gave Elijah's life a purpose…She gave him a heart, which was something he didn't really have before.

Then everything fell into silence, as Elijah realized something.

Sabrina Clarin came into his life and changed him as a person; to the person he was once before, young and loving life. The only difference was that he was better, better than his old angry self. That was it! Sabrina showed Elijah that there was still good in this life and it was worth fighting for! That was probably one of the reasons why he fell in love with her.

So Elijah was convinced there was another way. So he got up from his bed and went down to the basement to search for possible ideas. There he found his old basketball. He picked it up and it was still firm enough to play. Elijah remembered playing basketball back in the fall with Quinton and his friends. So settling the conflict in a sporting event, it was an option.

"A basketball game?" Paula said, after Elijah explained his idea.

"Yeah" Elijah admitted, "I thought about it last night and I think it's a way to beat him without actually fighting him"

Paula considered the option.

"It would be us versus them" Elijah added.

"It might work" Paula replied, doubtfully.

"I'm all for it" Andrew volunteered, with his hand up, "Anything to help my best friend, E.K."

Andrew stood by Elijah, who then waited for Paula's contribution.

"You know what…" she spoke, "I second that. This is probably the only way"

"Okay" Elijah agreed, with surprising confidence in his voice, "So it's decided, we face Quinton and his friends in a basketball game!"

"Sounds good" Andrew said, "Well, maybe not all good. So later on at lunch recess, maybe?"

"I guess we could" Elijah was uncertain at first. Then he shook his head to get his mind in the right frame, "You know what, the sooner the better. Lunch recess it is"

"Or wait" Paula suggested, "Sorry, I just had a thought. What if we did it AFTER school, like in the evening?"

Elijah and Andrew glanced at each other.

"I think it might be better because we'll have the schoolyard to ourselves and lots of time to settle this once and for all"

Elijah considered it and agreed that the evening was better to face the bully; so then all three of them went to search for Quinton to challenge him in person. They were at the back of the school building. Both groups ran into each other. Elijah and his friends were standing across from Quinton's gang.

"You come to fight, finally?" Quinton said.

It was silent for a moment.

"Are you still deaf, tough guy?"

"No" Elijah finally spoke, "And no, I didn't come to fight." He approached the bully, "I've come here to challenge you…to a basketball game"

Quinton scoffed. His reaction was no surprise, "Seriously?"

Elijah paused, dramatically, "Yes!" he told him, strongly, "It's us versus you guys"

"How about I just beat you up right here, right now?"

"No, Quinton!" Elijah yelled, "I. Am. Not. Fighting you! Not like that. I'll only fight you by beating you at basketball"

"Or maybe you're just chicken to face me"

"I'm not fighting you because I'm not like you, Quinton!"

"No, I'm better than you" Quinton told him, right up to Elijah's face. Elijah was rather too tense to keep his mind straight, and that he couldn't convince him.

"Or if you like…" Andrew spoke, "We can always play pin the tail on the donkey"

Quinton chuckled, "What are you, five?"

"Only the donkey will be you" Andrew added.

Quinton frowned.

"Oh, I'm sorry. I didn't mean you, I meant you, you, and you" Andrew gestured to the boys in the gang. Then he saw June Disher, "Except you, I wouldn't be mean to a girl. The name's Andrew by the way".

For a brief moment, June was actually tempted to smile, for that she was flattered by his charm. Whatever trick Andrew had up his sleeve it was throwing the bullies off guard. Both Elijah and Paula could only hope that he wouldn't take things too far.

"But with this one, I'll make an exception" Andrew said, pointing at Quinton.

"I think he just called you a girl, Quinton" Elijah told him.

Now more confidence was being restored, as they were facing Quinton together. "Yeah, didn't you say that you pose for a magazine or a shopping catalogue?" Andrew taunted.

Quinton's face turned into a scowl. Devon however giggled at Andrew's remark.

"See, that guy gets it" Andrew pointed out.

The bully cocked his head back to Devon, who then fell silent. Elijah had a certain temptation, one he just couldn't resist.

"Who's the girl now, Quinton?" Elijah said.

Slowly, the bully looked back at him.

"Shut up" Quinton snarled.

"You're saying it wrong" Andrew stated. Then he impersonated a high pitched girlie voice, "Shut up!"

"Shut up" Quinton yelled.

"Shut up!" Andrew repeated, in his girlie voice.

"I swear to god..." Quinton tried to pose a threat, but couldn't keep up with Andrew's wit.

"Duck season!" he said.

Quinton was getting extremely annoyed, "Seriously, you better..."

"Duck season!" Andrew repeated.

The bully had no reply, for that he was being filled with rage.

"You're supposed to say rabbit season"

"That's right" Elijah agreed, standing his ground, "It's Quinton season and I wanna find him and smarten him up!"

Now Quinton had to face the fact that he lost control, as he stood there facing Elijah, with a cold expression.

"Excuse me" Paula stepped in and stood beside Elijah, as she was about to talk to Quinton, "You said you were better than Elijah, better than him at what exactly?" There was no answer from Quinton, which was amusing "How about a basketball game?"

Again there was no response from the bully.

"So I suggest that you take Elijah's offer and keep walking" Paula insisted.

"Fine!" Quinton finally agreed, "We'll play your stupid basketball game"

"I thought you liked basketball" Elijah said, as he was a little surprised.

"Just shut up and tell me when" Quinton insisted.

The date was something they hadn't chose yet. So Elijah had to think for a moment.

"Friday evening, here at the back of the school"

"Okay!" Quinton yelled, "But I'm gonna beat all of you" He turned and told his followers to walk with him. As they were leaving, Quinton looked at Andrew, "You better watch your mouth, white boy"

"Watch my mouth?" Andrew said, jokingly, "How can I watch my mouth? I can only see the tip of my nose but not my mouth. It's just impossible. Hey, I'll pay one of you to be my mouth watcher. Would that make you feel better? And by pay I mean shredded cheese. So don't get excited about the paying part"

Annoyed, Quinton just waved him off and left. Elijah was surprisingly relieved and he didn't even make fists with his hand. But they weren't out of the woods yet. "Whoa. I can't believe we just did that"

"Like I said before..." Andrew replied, "We're not just friends, we're a team"

Paula went up to Elijah and patted him on the shoulder. She gave a proud smirk. "This just might work" Elijah said. Then he paused as he thought of something. "But I think we're gonna need some help".

CHAPTER TWENTY-TWO

A Clarin's First Challenge

"No, really, he likes you" Quinton added, "In fact, he was looking at a magazine with naked woman"

Elijah went and grabbed Quinton firmly by the shoulders. "Stop it!" he growled, "Stop it right now!!"

Even when he was laying down the law, Sabrina still felt frightened. Just after Elijah and the bully went around the corner, that was it. There was already too much pressure for Sabrina to handle. So she turned around and left, to get farther away from the crowd of students. She didn't exactly feel proud of it, but she didn't give it much thought. So she just waited for her mom to pick her up. As soon as they went home, Sabrina pretended that little conflict didn't happen.

She didn't really want to talk about bullying because she feared that she would have to face one sooner or later. It was best to stay out of trouble, she thought. The next day, Sabrina met with Logan during recess. He came out of the school building with his friends.

"Hey" Sabrina greeted, sincerely.

"Hey there" Logan replied. His friends left him alone with Sabrina, "So what's up?"

"Coming to see you" she told him with anticipation.

"Well, great! I'm here"

343

"Cool" Sabrina giggled, "Do you…wanna hang out for a bit?"

"I'd love to"

Sabrina and Logan walked further away from the entrance, rather slowly, for that Sabrina didn't really have a destination in mind. But she didn't care.

"So…uh, how's life?" she asked.

"Oh, life's great. It's actually getting excited by the minute" Logan looked at her once he said that. It just made Sabrina's anticipation more exciting.

"How's yours?" he asked.

"Oh, it's going fine, except yesterday" Sabrina said and then purposely trailed off.

"What happened?"

Sabrina was trying to hint Logan that she wanted a little comfort after the hostility she experienced from the day before. Sabrina was surprised that Logan didn't hear about it. *Is he even there?*

"Nothing too crazy" she replied.

"Oh…okay"

Logan still didn't get the hint. Sabrina was hoping for him to be at least a little concerned and maybe charm it out of her.

"Anyways" he continued, "I actually been wanting to ask you something.

"Yeah?" Sabrina acted natural. Logan took his time.

"Do you…wanna do something sometime?"

Sabrina became intrigued, "Like what?"

"I dunno, anything?"

They made eye contact. Sabrina's next words merely slipped out.

"I would do anything with you"

"Well, that's great. I'll give you my number later" Logan promised.

Sabrina was still surprised. She knew where the conversation was going. But her mind was only in one place. "Really?" she was genuinely surprised, but in a good way.

Logan nodded, "Really".

"Alright, I look forward to it!" this time she wasn't afraid to show her excitement.

"You got it, Princess" Logan replied, with a smile.

Then Sabrina's smile slowly faded, "Princess?" she repeated.

"Yeah"

Sabrina was just about to let it slip from her mind but her hesitation made it awkward, "Can you please not call me that?"

"What? Princess?"

"Yeah" she replied, right away, "Don't call me that"

Logan looked at her, funny.

"Why?"

"Just don't"

He then looked at her, apologetically, "Okay, sorry".

Afterwards, Sabrina pretended that didn't happen.

And just as he promised, Logan wrote down his phone number and gave it to Sabrina later on, during the second recess. She couldn't believe it. It was really happening! Sabrina only acted natural when she got his phone number. She was speechless. And she just couldn't hide her excitement when she showed the number to her girlfriends.

Melanie gasped in excitement, "That's awesome, Sabrina!"

"I know!"

"Amazing" Carly added.

"I have a feeling about you two" Melanie told her.

Sabrina gazed at the piece of paper with Logan's number on it, with a proud smile. "I think I do, too" she admitted.

The moment was all Sabrina could think about. And it was only the beginning at the path to a perfect life, new home, new friends, and a handsome young man by her side. Sabrina couldn't ask for more.

After school, she just had the urge to celebrate. But Sabrina wasn't sure if she wanted to tell her parents just yet. She probably would have to, soon. After dinner, Sabrina spent her time in her room, daydreaming of all the possibilities of her and Logan. They would be just like the couples she saw on movies and TV shows, young, good looking, going on adventures together. The dream was becoming a reality. Sabrina was so happy and proud that just had to put on music and dance her life away.

The song she listened to was about love. It was deep but yet upbeat. And Sabrina allowed herself to get lost into the rhythm and the story of the song, as she imagined just her and Logan as the center of the universe. As the song was reaching its climax, Sabrina began eyeing the poster above her bed. The poster was the one that Melanie gave her back in the fall. There she walked, slowly and gracefully. She stepped onto her bed, approaching the young man on her poster, pretending that he was real. Sabrina pinned herself against the poster, closed her eyes and kissed the picture of the young man.

There was knock on her door but Sabrina didn't hear.

"Sabrina?" Leah called, as she let herself in the room, with some neatly folded shirts.

The sound of her mother's voice caught Sabrina by surprise. Leah noticed right away what her daughter was doing and just couldn't move. Sabrina met her mom's eyes in awkward silence. The music was still playing. So Sabrina quickly went to turn it off.

"Hey" Sabrina greeted, gently. Her mom continued gawking at her. Sabrina then grabbed the small pile of shirts from her mom's hands and then went to put it away in her dresser.

"What were you doing?" Leah demanded.

Slowly, Sabrina turned around and noticed those eyes still watching her, "Nothing" she claimed, "I was just dancing".

Leah continued giving that firm look. Sabrina couldn't even breathe. "Sabrina, I saw what you were doing. I just wanted to hear you say it. Sit down". Finally, Sabrina gave in and did as her mom said and sat down on her bed. Leah went up and stood in front of her daughter. "Now why were you doing that?" she asked. Leah couldn't even say the word, for that it was the last thing she expected her twelve year old-daughter to do.

Sabrina hesitated, "I was just dancing and it got me in the mood" She was tiptoeing around the truth but didn't feel comfortable talking about it.

"Why?" her mom demanded,

"I…" Sabrina muttered. She didn't expect to be telling her mom about Logan that soon and she could tell that her mom already didn't approve. She could already feel the disappointment creeping around the corner.

"You know what, Sabrina...Look at me"

Slowly, Sabrina looked up to her mom, directly into her cold eyes.

"You don't need to tell me" Leah warned, "Because I think I already know. You just tell me if I'm wrong". Sabrina felt like a convict in a courtroom, while her mom was the prosecutor, and a life sentence was in order.

"You met someone" her mom stated. Sabrina didn't say anything. She just sat still. "A boy" her mom added. It was almost like Leah could see right through her daughter's head.

"And you're developing a relationship. You know which kind I'm talking about. Go ahead, tell me I'm wrong"

So it was the truth. Leah could see it in Sabrina's eyes, a truth that she would have to face someday, that her daughter wanted a boyfriend. It was too soon. It took one long moment for Leah to accept it. She almost wished it was something else. Finally, she broke eye contact with her daughter and sighed.

"Wow...wow"

Leah then sat next to Sabrina on her bed.

"Frankly, I don't know what to say. Yet there's so many things I want to say" She then looked directly into her daughter's eyes, "Sabrina you're too young for this sort of thing. I'll admit, love is a beautiful thing, but to you it's just a fairy tale. You don't know what's underneath that surface. You can't just dive right in. There are so many things about this life you still haven't learned yet. I can go on for hours about it, but right now I guess it's come to this. And honestly, I thought you were smarter than this!"

"Mom" Sabrina finally replied, "Nothing happened"

"Not yet" Leah added, firmly, "Sabrina, love isn't something you feel on your lips, it's what you feel inside you. I know it's a nice feeling but it can also be dangerous. Sometimes it makes you do things, even if you don't mean to. And the exact same thing goes for that boy. One day, things will go too far and in the end, you AND him end up being hurt. Those kinds of wounds are not easy to heal, Sabrina. And I don't want you going through that, not at this age. So whatever you got going on, it may be best to put a stop to it, while you're ahead. Do you understand?"

"But mom, before you said that someone will see me for the good person I am..."

"I was talking about a friend, not a boyfriend!"

There it was, that word slipped out of Leah's mouth.

"I didn't say boyfriend" Sabrina argued.

So now her daughter admitted it. It was so heartbreaking and it made Leah's blood boil at the same time.

"No, of course not but you're thinking it"

"I...I'm not" Sabrina tried to explain.

Leah put her hand up, which threw Sabrina in silence.

"Did you hear everything I said before you said the words 'But mom'?"

Sabrina didn't say anything. She was trapped and thought she could fight her way out by convincing her mom somehow. So then Sabrina got up from her bed to give herself breathing space and collect some thoughts.

"Mom" Sabrina spoke, gently, as she locked eyes with her mother, who was still sitting on the bed. Even though she was a little nervous, Sabrina was able to remain calm, "He's a nice person. I think dad might like him. He's into hockey like he is"

"I don't think your dad would feel the same way" Leah said, promptly.

That answer crushed Sabrina, for that it wasn't what she wanted to hear. And the confidence in her mother's voice was so strong, it just might be true.

"Well..." Sabrina hesitated, as she was about to admit it, "I like him"

There was a long pause, as her mom just stared at her. It wasn't the first time it happened. Each time it happened before, it usually didn't end well. Yet Sabrina remained patient and confident because the passion she had for Logan strengthened her heart. Before Leah spoke, she crossed her arms.

Think about Logan.

"Why?" Leah demanded, "Why do you like him?"

It was a test. No matter what Sabrina would say, it would just end up being the wrong answer. She almost didn't want to reply.

Logan.

"Well, he's cute"

"And?"

"He has…nice hair?"

Leah didn't even blink.

"And?"

"We get along very well" Sabrina added, promptly.

Leah didn't say anything else. But Sabrina could tell that her mom was waiting for another explanation.

"Well, Sabrina, I think you're just looking for reasons to find love"

Sabrina was puzzled but she didn't like the way that sounded. It started to make her angry. It actually made her raise her voice a little.

"So you're saying I can't…"

"That's exactly what I'm saying" Leah declared.

Out of all the people in her life, Sabrina thought for sure that her mom would be the one who would understand. She was so wrong. Sabrina stood there, defenseless. She began blinking as she was getting emotional.

"Sabrina" her mom called, "Sit down"

Reluctantly, Sabrina did as her mother said and sat beside her on the bed, with her eyes forward.

"As your mother, I am rather angry but I'm also very conscious right now. So don't think that I'm gonna realize that I done something wrong and let you have your way. Don't count on it, Sabrina. What I just said a couple of minutes ago, I meant it. So I'm going to ask you again: Do you understand?"

Sabrina looked away, blankly, facing the fact that she had to give up her relationship with Logan. What would happen after that? Nothing! Now Sabrina could see that her life was over and there was nothing that could make her happy. On the outside, Sabrina was quiet and weak, while on the inside there was disappointment, along with passion that may never get the treatment it deserved. Sabrina wasn't particularly thrilled about it. In fact, she was getting angry at her own mother, feeling that she couldn't do what she wanted. It was tempting to refuse but her mom's persuasive power was too strong. It made Sabrina feel imprisoned.

"Sabrina?" her mom called, calmly, "I know you heard me. Now answer me"

Nothing but silence.

"Sabrina" her mom was getting impatient.

Her daughter was still sulking.

"Sabrina!"

Finally, her daughter responded by yelling in her face.

"Yes!" she shouted, "I understand!!"

Leah could sense the attitude. So then grabbed her daughter firmly by the chin and made her look into her eyes. Fear alerted Sabrina's mind and shut off every thought as she was facing reality up close and personal. She thought her mom was going to slap her or yell into her face. Either way, it was crushing Sabrina's spirit.

"You talk to me like that again, I'm gonna do something that I'm gonna regret!" her mom snarled, "So don't test me!"

That gave the emotional breakthrough, for that Sabrina's innocence got the best of her and made her emotions fragile. Sabrina tried not to breakdown as she looked into her mom's eyes. A part of her wanted to apologize for making her mad but Sabrina couldn't speak.

There was more, much more that Leah wanted to say in case her daughter wasn't paying full attention. Any mother would do such a thing if her young daughter fancied for a romantic relationship. To Leah Clarin's eyes, she would always see Sabrina slowly turn back into the infant she once held in her arms. There was a part of Leah that did not want Sabrina to grow up at all, but there was nothing she could do about it. She loved her children more than anything and that complicated her emotions when looking after them. So it was tempting for Leah to teach Sabrina a lesson, but the fear in her daughter's eyes had softened her. Therefore, Leah just couldn't do it.

She let go of Sabrina's chin.

Then Leah took a moment to ease the tension she was feeling. She glanced at her daughter who was holding her chin, innocently. And when Leah heard Sabrina breathing in through her nose; she was about to cry. It made her feel guilty because she could tell that Sabrina was trying not to breakdown. At that point, there was no heart to heart conversation that could re-connect them. So then Leah just got up and slowly made her way to the door.

"Sabrina" her mom said. The authority in her voice went away, "I know you're growing up…Just don't grow up too fast"

Leah left the room. Tears were flowing down Sabrina's face. It took her a moment to let it all sink in, her mom's words, the dream of a perfect life being shattered, and the feeling of disappointment. Sabrina turned her head back to the poster above her bed and just couldn't look at it the same way. There was nothing but burden and humiliation displayed. So Sabrina then kneeled on her bed to try and take the poster off gently with just one hand. It was taped to the wall. So it ought to simply peel off. . There wasn't enough force, so then she tried pulling it off firmly and ended ripping half of it. With frustration, Sabrina just ripped the whole poster off the wall of shame.

The next day was total silence. Sabrina woke up, trying to treat life like a new day but couldn't stop thinking about her conversation with her mother. Yes, she was still dealing with the disappointment and hid in the shadow. Most of the morning Sabrina felt obligated to act normal, even that put a little pressure on her once she was in the presence of her mother, who barely said anything. Maybe she too was trying to forget that whole incident. Sabrina though didn't have the intention to find out, fearing that she might start another argument. Therefore, she remained deep in her thoughts.

Afterwards, Sabrina arrived at the school where she had to face a difficult task, to end her relationship with Logan. As soon as she saw him, she asked to see him alone. "Hey Logan" she said, carefully hiding her sadness, "I'm sorry, but I can't…do this anymore"

He looked at her, uncertain, "What are you talking about?"

Sabrina's mind still wasn't in the right frame. There was only little time to put her feelings into words. "I mean, I can't do anything with you, like what we talked about yesterday?"

Logan finally got Sabrina's message and couldn't help but feel a little sad, "Why?"

Sabrina was already getting tired of explaining. To her, it would've felt a little embarrassing if Logan knew that she was practically being controlled by her mom. "It's…just too soon", she muttered.

"What?"

"Too soon" Sabrina repeated, a little louder.

Silence came between them.

"Okay" Logan agreed, reluctantly, "Can we still be friends, at least?"

That's what I was trying to ask before my mom tried to break my jaw!

Would Sabrina's mom approve that part? There was some doubt there, but Sabrina's kindness convinced otherwise, but at that point her kindness was as weak as her emotions.

"Sure" Sabrina said, hopelessly.

"You don't sound sure"

Sabrina just shrugged her shoulders, "I don't know". Now the agitation was emerging in her voice. Then her eyes, filled with sorrow, met Logan's worried look, while he felt a heavy discomfort that weakened his heart.

"Was it something I did?" he asked, cautiously.

Then Sabrina practically yelled, "No!"

The frustration was getting to her. So she just turned her back and walked away, without looking back. Logan stood there, alone, watching her leave. After that, they never spoke to each other again.

It took Sabrina a little while to keep up with everyone else in class. All of her thoughts were scattered and it was hard for her to concentrate. The only thing that Sabrina was able to focus on was the one question on her worksheet she had been staring at for more than five minutes. The words of her mother automatically replayed in her mind. It wasn't long until words became the images it originated from, being in her bedroom with her mom, giving the lecture. Sabrina saw her eyes and her words became louder. It felt so real; it began to feel tense and interfered with the present. Even for a brief moment, Sabrina tried to pull herself together. Realizing that there was little time, she finally started writing again-

Mom, nothing happened.

I was talking about a friend, not a boyfriend!

I didn't say boyfriend.

Whatever you got going on, it may be best to put a stop to it, while you're ahead. Do you understand?

The answer to her worksheet was coming to her but her mind kept going back and forth.

You talk to me like that again; I'm going to do something I'm going to regret!

Without realizing it, the frustration was putting pressure on Sabrina's pencil, as it shortly broke the led. As her thoughts flushed away, Sabrina let out a little gasp. Then she scanned her surroundings, making sure nobody heard. While facing down, she rubbed her eyes making sure there weren't any tears and took a deep breath.

Surviving the morning was just the start. For half the day, Sabrina pretended like her problems didn't exist. She was able to engage in conversations with her girlfriends. She made it passed the first recess without thinking about Logan or her mom. But once lunch recess began, it was a little different.

"Hey, Sabrina" Melanie said, as they were heedlessly walking on the side of the school, "Logan said you guys aren't really friends anymore. What happened?!"

Logan told Melanie?

Sabrina wasn't expecting that. She thought that she and Logan built enough trust in their relationship to keep personal matters between them. Now she felt exposed to the world like her mug shot appeared on every news channel and the first instinct was to run, just run away from everything and hope that nobody would find her.

"Nothing" Sabrina replied, trying to sound natural, "It's just…I can't"

"You can't?" Mel repeated, expecting a little more.

Explaining heavy burdens felt like explaining it to a toddler after the first time. It was the last thing Sabrina wanted. She would rather put it to rest and move on with her life, even though there was nothing to move on to, for that the other half of Sabrina wanted things to go back the way they were. If only it was that easy.

"Well, it was nice getting to know him and all, but maybe it's not the time" she added.

"And?"

That word reminded Sabrina of her mom.

Of course, it meant a lot to Melanie because she was the one that set Sabrina up with Logan. It was like her pet project that she expected to construct itself. And Sabrina wasn't ready for Mel's reaction. What if she didn't want to give up that easily and insisted on giving another shot? What if both of her friends laughed at her for following mom's orders? The pressure was already there.

"I just can't" Sabrina explained.

"Come on, Sabrina" Carly said, "Talk to us"

At that moment, Sabrina felt like she was in a jungle where dozens of eyes were scowling at her from the bushes. And no matter which direction she would turn to run, there was no way out. So Sabrina Clarin just gave in.

"Because my mom won't let me!" she yelled, startling her friends. The outburst took a toll on Sabrina. So she stormed away before causing any more damage. Melanie and Carly exchanged worried looks. Sabrina stopped after walking a few feet, realizing what she had done and all she felt was guilt. She turned around and locked onto her friends' eyes. Tears were trying to emerge but Sabrina held it for as long as she could, but not for long. She ran back, where Carly wrapped her arms tight around her.

"I'm sorry!" Sabrina cried.

"No, Sabrina, it's okay" Carly replied, slowly.

"Yeah, you don't need to apologize, Sabrina" Mel said, sincerely, "You're upset and I shouldn't have pressured you. So…I'm sorry"

Melanie then opened her arms and Sabrina went in and accepted Mel's hug. Sabrina felt liberated. Now that the tension eased, she was able to put her mind back into focus for the afternoon. She maybe feeling better, emotionally, but now it felt like her life was uneventful and had nothing to look forward to, nothing but her education. Having only that and two friends didn't exactly comfort Sabrina. Being with Logan gave her something to look forward to but now she couldn't even look at him, without the fear of her mom watching.

After school, Sabrina was by herself once her friends went home. Since there was literally nothing to do, she took a seat at the bench and gazed at the nature in front of her, the trees and the sun, and admired the whole scenery. She still couldn't accept the fact that she couldn't see Logan anymore. Since that conversation, Sabrina was secretly hoping that her mom would have a change of heart and let her be friends with Logan at least. But that didn't seem promising, nothing did. Life at that point just seemed blank. The only thing that Sabrina Clarin could do was just gaze upon nature and hope. She knew that somewhere out there, there was greatness waiting for her.

"Sabrina" a voice said.

She turned around. It was Elijah Khoda. It was a little surprising only because she nearly forgotten about him. But she hadn't forgotten about what he did to Logan that one day. Yet there was no way that she could ignore him or walk away, since that whole incident was hardly important now that Logan was out of her life.

"Can I talk you, please?" Elijah asked, politely.

She paused, "Sure".

"Look, I know you're probably not happy with me for what I done" he told her, sincerely, "And I'm sorry. Sabrina" He paused, briefly, "There are so many things I wanna say but just don't know how…"

Many things, like not just an apology but everything, how he felt about her and the times they spent together. If Elijah could, he'd rather sit on that bench next to Sabrina and talk it over, sit in silence, reminisce and truly connect. So basically pick up where they left off last time, before antagonizing Logan and getting confronted by Quinton. Only such thing exists in a perfect world and one thing they learned, that the world they were living in was far from perfection.

Sabrina just stared at him in silence. *Say something! Elijah was your friend after all.*

Elijah noticed the pain in her eyes. Something really was bothering her, just like what Ken said. It was probably because of what he did to Logan and maybe Sabrina still wasn't happy about it. As hard as it was to accept, Elijah could not deny what he did, for that he had bigger problems to worry about.

"All I know that you saw the bad side of me" Elijah continued explaining, "And I hope that we can still be friends"

Sabrina didn't say anything, not right away. Elijah wasn't all fond of the words that he just expressed to her. It sounded like the usual excuses that was heard or said before, like a coward who tried to prove himself a friend but did not know the value of life or friendship, nothing but his own self. Nonetheless, Elijah really did mean what he said and only hoped that Sabrina saw him as that value.

"Of course we can" she finally answered, but her voice was emotionless as if she only said it because she felt obligated to.

That probably wasn't enough…, she thought.

"Yeah?" Elijah replied. Then he waited to see if there was more she had to say, for that it wasn't convincing enough. In secret, Elijah was hoping that Sabrina would offer a thoughtful gesture, like inviting him in her company, sitting next to her on the bench or hang out like old times, whether it was just the two of them, or the whole team. But sadly, that didn't happen. And he'd rather not put any pressure on Sabrina.

Of course we can, her words echoed. It was a start.

"Sabrina" Elijah said, calmly. Now it was time for the second reason why he came to see her, "There's something else. You remember…that bully who was picking on you-on us the other day? Me and my friends are going up against them this Friday, in the evening, probably around seven, in a basketball game. And we can use your help. It would be us against them"

He paused to hear a reply. But Sabrina remained silent.

You mean you want me to help you fight him? Fear struck her and froze her for a long moment. It was something that she would have to think about long and hard but Elijah seemed a little desperate. Sabrina felt obligated to give him an answer. As soon as he asked for her help, the first thought that came to her mind was that she would have to fight physically. It was dealing with bullies after all.

A car honk went off in the parking lot, multiple times. It was Mrs. Clarin, signaling her daughter that she was there. "I gotta go" Sabrina said. She tempted to give an honest answer but hesitated, "I'll think about it". She grabbed her backpack and started to leave.

"Sabrina" Elijah called.

She was thoughtful enough to turn around and meet his eye. At first there were too many words to choose from:

I know you're probably still mad at me but...
I'm sorry about everything.
This is all my fault.
If we're still friends, I...

"It would mean a lot if you came" he ended up saying, sincerely.

That was it. Elijah had nothing further to say. He hoped that Sabrina would say something, but he still got nothing, only silence. So he then walked away before any more disappointments that would sink his heart lower. Sabrina watched Elijah leave and couldn't help but feel a hint of sadness that struck her, perhaps it was pity. She didn't mean to be rude but her inner feelings were too complex that it put her mind elsewhere and just couldn't interact with Elijah properly, not at that time. Not to mention the fear that took a hold of her, thinking that she had to help Elijah face a bully. Sabrina hadn't forgotten about the day she had to deal with Zach Epstad back in Granisle, a day that she would prefer not to re-live.

The thought floated around in Sabrina's mind as the week was passing. She felt obligated to help a friend. It was a natural response whenever friends asked for help, as much as being told an apology and respond with the words *it's okay or apology accepted*. But now life was becoming more complicated.

Growing up, Sabrina Clarin was always told to be kind to others and she always had been. It was much simpler when being a child, before realizing that life had bullies that would not stop until they wanted to stop, which felt like it would be a never ending trip.

So how could Sabrina show kindness to ones that didn't have any? Just stand by and watch her friend get beaten half to death? Certainly there had to be another way and it sounded like Elijah had a plan. Even so, it was mostly daunting for Sabrina and it made her neglect her friend in need and as the hours passed, she was feeling bad, for herself and for Elijah.

The day came when it was time to face their fears. Elijah wasn't really looking forward to it but it had to be done. It was just like the early days of Brian Kidman picking on Elijah, not wanting to go to school and trying to find the best possible excuse or just run from everything. Over the years, Elijah learned that running away wouldn't solve anything because eventually all of life's problems would catch up to him. It seemed like no matter what he'd choose, he would have to stand and face it, whether he wanted to or not.

The time was getting closer. It was nice and sunny out, but there was a dark cloud covering Elijah's heart and it was about to get darker when approaching the school. At least Paula and Andrew would be by his side, so that created some confidence. Elijah needed to remain focused as he took his time, sitting on the bed. Men were born to be brave, he kept saying.

Bravery was the one thing anyone had to provide for one's self. While being a kid, you'd think that you had to wait for a man in a cape to fly in and save your life, and then inspire the world to be brave. You'd feel like you could do the same in your reality, being strong and confident, and helping others. Then you grow up and realize that reality was a gloomy place to live because there was always someone that would grab your life and crumble it like it was just a piece of paper. That was another thing that Elijah Khoda learned, that not everybody would be there to help, parents, teachers, or peers. The only person that could help you is yourself! Help yourself by giving confidence to your heart, help yourself by asking your friends, and help yourself to stand back up after getting knocked down. At this point, there seemed to be no other way. Now…it was time.

Waiting outside the school building, Elijah sat on the bench. There was no peers playing around, no supervisors watching over. It was just him, and soon his friends and his enemies. It was the calm before the storm. Elijah let it all sink in as he contemplated everything from the start. This whole thing happened when he took his best friends for granted and chose to hang out with a gang of hoodlums. It was his own doing. Many times Elijah wished he hadn't befriended Quinton Malcolm; otherwise Sabrina would still be part of his life. Everything would've been different if he hadn't fallen into that anger when he first dealt with that pressure back in the fifth grade. It was a version of himself that he hated and wished he could change it. That kind of wishful thinking was never possible, not in real life. Elijah had to accept reality and what he had to do, even though it wasn't an easy way out.

Paula showed up. She was dropped off by one of her parents. After bidding farewell, she went up to meet with Elijah.

"Hey" she greeted.

"Paula" Elijah replied.

She sat down next to him on the bench.

"How are you holding up?" Paula asked,

"Okay, I guess. I just want this to be over"

"I don't blame you. Sooner or later someone has to do something. I guess that's part of growing up, when you realize that someone is you"

That was true, too.

"You know what; I was actually just thinking that before I came here" Elijah told her, "Like before, when I was little…I used to think: what if I could do what superheroes could do, and face bad guys in real life? But once it actually happened, I was just too scared. Even back in MMPS, I was even afraid of kids who were the same height as me. Then I realized I wasn't like the heroes in the movies, I wasn't going to have my own cape or mask and be brave. Although, I…I thought I could but I wasn't. Now I realize that I have to help myself"

Paula merely looked at her best friend, pitifully. "Well, reality is not like the movies we see. I'm sorry to say, Elijah, but if it's real life, there's real fear, and we can't hide from it forever"

He just looked away, hiding his disappointment and Paula could see it.

"Hey" she called, gently.

She had Elijah's attention. "You know what I been thinking about lately?"

He didn't answer, but Paula wasn't expecting him to.

"The day we met" she added, "You remember that day, right?"

Elijah remembered the day they first got acquainted. It was their first year at Muriel Mould Primary School. Paula was constantly being picked on by older boys. She was only a kindergarten student. One day, she was just reading and the boys came along and took her book away. They wouldn't give it back. Elijah Khoda was near and saw the whole thing. A young Paula panicked and demanded her book back, or she would tell the supervisor on them. But the boys continued to laugh and taunt her. Elijah tried to ignore the situation. And when they ran, Paula couldn't find any grownups in sight, so she decided to run after them in case they would do something harsh like tear her book apart. Elijah saw them running further, towards the woods. He knew what it was like to be picked on and that was when he decided to help.

Paula ran after them into the forest area, where they were practically isolated from the school. Elijah remembered hearing Paula raising her voice when he was halfway to there and fear almost made him turn back. He thought about just finding a supervisor and reporting the whole incident. Then he turned around and saw one of the boys gripping Paula's wrist and yanking her around like a poor dog on a leash. That image was still fresh in Elijah's mind, like it was yesterday. That was when the anger flared up inside him and decided to handle the situation himself.

He ran to the bully who was about to rip apart Paula's book and aggressively shoved the boy to the ground and then attacked the boy who was holding Paula hostage by tackling him. There were three of them. Elijah made sure that he wasn't about to get beaten up, so he fought off those boys without getting too violent. By showing his temper, Elijah scared the bullies away and they never bothered Paula after that. Without thinking about it, he grabbed the book and returned it to Paula, and there she spoke to Elijah Khoda for the first time.

That was very brave of you, she said to him.

"You see Elijah, I still think you're that brave little boy who helped me that day" Paula said, "I think that maybe you are the hero that you need! Because if you faced those boys back then, you can face Quinton and his gang"

Elijah hadn't forgotten about that day when he first met Paula, but never saw it from her standpoint. It was rather insightful and heartfelt. Knowing that Paula believed in him, maybe he was stronger than he thought and that gave more strength and confidence. It also brought some comfort and that maybe he could face the whole situation with Quinton. The impossible began to feel possible.

"I know things seem bad..." Paula continued, "But maybe all this is happening for a reason. Who knows, it could be because it's helping you to became stronger"

She then gently placed her hand on Elijah's shoulder.

"Just know that you don't have to face it alone"

"Thanks, Paula"

After a moment of waiting, Andrew showed up. He came dressed in a black t-shirt and camouflage pants, and he was carrying a duffle bag.

"Ready for battle!" Andrew declared. Then he gave a salute and dropped the bag in front of him.

"Good, I think we all are" Elijah replied.

"What's in the bag?" Paula asked.

"Dirty laundry" Andrew joked. He was hoping to get a chuckle, but there was only silence, "I thought maybe that we could scare them away with my smelly socks" he added.

There was still no laughter.

"Tools we might need" Andrew finally answered, "For Operation: Quinton Sucks. And by tools I mean sporting goods"

"More sporting goods?" Elijah repeated.

"Yeah, you know, in case they don't play fair and we go on and on"

No one wanted to think about the conflict going longer than expected. He'd only hope that Quinton would accept defeat and move on.

"We should probably wait in the back of the school" Paula suggested, "Just so we'd be ready when those hoodlums come"

"Might as well" Andrew agreed.

Everyone else was ready but the team was incomplete. It was tempting for Elijah to wait for Sabrina. He was counting on her to show up. Sadly, there was no sign of her, which began to put doubt on their friendship. It was rather heartbreaking because Elijah trusted her with his life. Now more guilt was caving in when he couldn't help but think about humiliating Logan. That was probably why she wasn't coming.

"Alright, let's go" Elijah finally agreed.

At the Clarin residence, Sabrina was lying on her bed. She knew Elijah was asking for help but there was too much pressure and unresolved issues that was preventing her from facing the present. She kept thinking about her intense conversation with her mom. The burden wasn't as heavy as it was before, but she just couldn't face the results of disappointment. Sabrina always thought that things would go her way because she'd always been kind to people and her mother trusted her for it. But she didn't realize how wrong she was after that day when her mom caught her fantasizing about a boy. Since then, Sabrina's kindness was wearing thin and didn't know who to show allegiance to.

She ought to help her friend in need or if she wanted to she could disobey her mom and go back to Logan. At the same time, whenever Sabrina thought about her mom, she felt the need to punish herself, considering that she didn't end up being grounded. Maybe the disappointment was her only punishment. Her thoughts continued piling up and falling all over the place. Hence she just did not know where to place her heart. It was a battle between her conscious and the threats in her mind. And her mind had the advantage.

Without being able to think straight, Sabrina decided to do something to take her mind off things. It probably wasn't the best choice, as it was an alternative to being selfish, since she wasn't really considering Elijah or anyone else or it was simply because she was getting tired of carrying the burden and wanted to put it somewhere. There was nothing to do in her room. So she went to see her brother

"Jonathan?" she called, as she gently knocked on the door. She let herself in, "Hey, wanna play some..."

Sabrina stopped once she saw that Jonathan was actually napping. He was lying on his stomach, just sleeping away. Slightly disappointed, Sabrina scanned her brother's bedroom, blankly and noticed his TV was still on and his video game controller was lying across the floor looked like he was playing not too long ago. She turned towards her brother, who was still breathing and lying motionless. Maybe he's faking it, she thought. Sabrina needed some attention, and Jonathan was the one person she could count by spending time with him and share little secrets. So Sabrina went up closer and clapped her hands together right above her brother's head. No response. Giving it one more try, clap!

Nope, Jonathan really was sleeping. Sabrina sighed, loud enough, hoping it would slowly wake him up, still nothing. She looked around her brother's room again until she laid her eyes on the night stand next to Jonathan's bed. There she saw his hacky-sack. Sabrina grabbed it and rubbed her fingers through it. She turned to Jonathan and just pretended that he was awake.

"Jonathan, can I borrow your hacky-sack?" Sabrina asked.

Her sleeping brother let out a snore.

"Thank you"

Leah Clarin watched her daughter playing with the hacky-sack in the backyard from the kitchen window. After doing the dishes and putting everything away, Mrs. Clarin couldn't help but stare, absently. For the past week, she and Sabrina barely spoke, only when they needed to but it wasn't enough to bring them close again. Leah kept thinking about their strong conversation they had from the other day, wondering if what she said was enough or too much. She never liked the fact that she had to be mean to her kids, but just like any other mother would do, she had to speak loud and clear in order for them to learn. At the end of the day, Leah only hoped that her daughter would even look at her again. After a silent moment, Michael Clarin walked into the kitchen, with a tool box in hand.

"Well, you wouldn't have to worry about the closet anymore" he told her, "The downside is one of our kids will probably spy on us" Then he looked up and saw what his wife was doing, still watching their daughter outside, "Or vice versa"

Leah said nothing.

"What's on your mind, Lee?" Michael asked,

"Our kids, like always" she finally spoke, "She's been a little quiet all week"

"That would make sense. She's probably still embarrassed when you caught her the other day"

Leah reluctantly turned away from the window and briefly glanced at her husband. Then she stepped forward so her own daughter wouldn't catch her stare. Michael started to become concerned.

"Babe?" he called.

She leaned against the counter and met Michael's eyes.

"I knew this day was going to come. I just didn't think it was going to come sooner, our daughter thinking about boys-a boy. This feeling is heavier than I thought"

Michael nodded, "So it's too soon. I get where you're coming from and I don't blame you for being worried. What else?"

"She tried to hide it" Leah added, "I'm scared that she's hiding more"

"What else do you think she's hiding?"

"Love letters, a secret hideout at school or somewhere? But I know for sure that she's hiding from me, like everything about her, her interests, her dislikes, her thoughts and her feelings. Sabrina's become her own diary, which I can't read, even by looking at her"

So Leah was worried that she and Sabrina were drifting apart. And it was hard to tell if it was because that she couldn't see Logan anymore or that she might be still seeing him, in secret. Leah palmed herself on her forehead for creating such a thought. Her daughter being hurt put her in a dilemma: give Sabrina her space or give the boy a chance, for that Leah was starting to feel bad. Michael saw and felt his wife's emotional state. He went up to her and gently grabbed both of her hands and held it.

"Leah, first of all, you're not a bad mother. Second, you and I both know that this is just a phase Sabrina's going through" Michael paused for a moment to glance outside to see if Sabrina was still there, "Maybe she needs a little dad-talk"

Sabrina was still playing hacky-sack outside in the backyard. Suddenly, she kicked a little too far and it hit the ground, just a few feet away from her. Slowly, she went and reclaimed it. The little fun that she had was able to take her mind off her problems for at least a few minutes. But during the silence, her thoughts came back to her like owls after the sunset. Absently, she continued playing by letting the hacky-sack roll down her leg, hoping to make it launch from her foot by then it easily slid off before it even touched her shoe. Sabrina unwillingly bent over to grab it. Instead of continuing, she looked around the yard, mentally elsewhere, and just thinking about life. She could've sworn that she was meant for than disappointments and sulking.

"Show's over already?" her dad's voice caught her off guard. Sabrina turned around and immediately caught his warm eyes. It took her a moment to jump back into the present, for that she didn't know what he was talking about but it shortly hit her. He was referring to her playing around with the hacky-sack.

"Intermission" Sabrina said, forcing a smile. Her dad smiled as well, only it was natural. It was genuinely nice to see that his daughter hadn't gone away. Michael's presence brought comfort to Sabrina. She always felt safe around him, like nothing could ever happen to her. It also brought that warm feeling, something she hadn't felt in a while. In silence, Michael slowly approached her. It was tempting for Sabrina to start just a friendly conversation, as a way to take her mind off things. But she couldn't help but notice the way he glanced at her, almost like he was on a mission, which changed the mood a little.

"You're here to talk to me?" Sabrina asked.

"What makes you think that?" her dad responded naturally and politely. That made it safe for Sabrina to say almost anything. It wasn't the first time it happened. When Sabrina was a little kid, making simple mistakes like spilling juice on a rug or forgetting to clean up her toys, her mom would get irritated when that routine became repetitive and probably yell at her and Jonathan, her dad would be someone she'd go to for comfort. It became an instinct after all those years, for that Sabrina started to tell whenever her mom was mad just by the lack of communication. Like when she was cleaning the house or running errands, she would give a disappointing sigh or a groan. It was a sign that her mom needed some space. So she left her alone. With her dad, Sabrina knew that he had his bad days but most of the time he was kind, warm, and strong. Even when he was tired out, Michael Clarin always made an effort to give his kids the love and the attention they deserved.

"Because you're quiet" Sabrina answered.

Her dad just gave a little chuckle.

"Yeah, I picked that up when I was six" she added.

"Smart" her dad said.

They both gazed at each other for a moment. Even in silence, Sabrina could feel the comfort of her dad's presence. Now she felt safe and not so alone.

"Want some ice cream?"

Sabrina gave a surprised look, for that she wasn't expecting a treat to begin with.

"Ice cream?" she repeated.

"Yeah, it's a way to relax and take our minds off things" Michael told her, "You have heard of ice cream, right?"

Slightly annoyed, Sabrina answered promptly, "Of course"

"Good" her dad teased, "Just you and me, going for a little drive, and eat ice cream. Ready, spaghetti?"

Sabrina quickly met her dad's eyes, for that the last part rang a bell. "I haven't heard you say that in a long time"

Her dad just shrugged his shoulders. "Last time I said it, you didn't think it was that funny anymore"

Ready spaghetti, was a funny saying that Michael came up with years ago, when Sabrina and Jonathan were little kids. It was a humorous way to ask if they were ready. They would just laugh about it for a little while. He even got them saying it, especially when Sabrina and her brother would tease each other and sometimes they would say it to their mom. But just after a few months, it got tiring, and both the Clarin siblings weren't tickled by it anymore. Those memories came back in her mind like turning a TV on. Sabrina couldn't help but feel bad as she was thinking how it made her dad felt, probably a little sad.

"Oh…" that was all she could say.

"It's all right" her dad said, "Come on"

Michael and Sabrina walked out of the gas station, with ice cream in their hands, just like they planned. They took their time, enjoying their little treat and the beautiful sunny weather.

"Mmm" her dad moaned, "Good ice cream, nice weather"

"Mhm" Sabrina replied, with ice cream in her mouth, "And brain freeze"

Her dad laughed, "Can't forget that. Wonder what's next?" he looked at her daughter, "How about a trip to the beach?"

Sabrina automatically remembered that they were supposed to check out the beach at the beginning of the year but Jonathan wasn't really interested.

"Okay" she answered, almost right away.

Next they were in the car, on their way. Sabrina was sitting in the passenger seat, while her dad was driving. Michael had one hand on the steering wheel while he held the ice cream on the other hand. Shortly he needed to make a turn, so he had to turn right with on hand. It took a little longer and he nearly hit the curb.

"You sure you don't want me to hold your ice cream, dad?" Sabrina offered.

"Nothing I can't handle" her dad replied, with confidence. That wasn't the first time that he said those words. Michael Clarin was always willing to go the extra mile for the ones he loved. "Besides, we're almost there. I think".

They arrived at the beach. Michael parked the car. Then both he and his daughter got out and explored the beach. The lake was there with some white docks lined up from the shore, as well as a playground which was occupied by little kids that were playing around, next to it was a gazebo, a large ball field in the distance, and plenty of trees in the area.

"Radley Beach" Michael said, "Doesn't look like much but it looks nice"

"Yeah" Sabrina agreed. She continued eating her ice cream as she peered across the lake and noticed there was a residential area, "Huh, there are some people living on the other side"

"You're right. Wouldn't that be nice, living across from a beach? Let's take a closer look"

Sabrina and her dad went closer to the lake. They walked on the sand and could hear the lake splashing on the shore as the tide was coming and going, repeatedly. Since there was no one on the docks, they decided to walk onto it and see the lake up close. Sabrina and her dad stood there, taking it all in. The houses across the lake were right in front of them, acres of forests were all around, and the bridge was to their right. No words were spoken, as they enjoyed the scenery. After gazing at the lake, Sabrina and her dad went further away and came across some picnic tables that weren't far from the playground. They sat down and enjoyed the view of the beach.

"Well, we're here, just you and me with a little peace and quiet" her dad said, "Think now is a good time to talk"

Sabrina glanced at him to acknowledge. The tension in her eyes disappeared and the weight on her shoulders were balanced. It was more of a safe environment, no doors opening all of a sudden, no walls of shame, just nature surrounding them. It was their own little world, a home away from home. Maybe a little getaway was something Sabrina needed, even something as simple as going to town with her dad and enjoying some ice cream together. Sabrina now felt free from all the pressure and felt like she could tell her dad anything.

"Start anywhere" he encouraged. It was almost like he was feeling what his daughter was feeling, which was comforting for her.

"I can't describe how I feel right now" Sabrina admitted, after a moment of silence, "Not with one word. There's just so many of them"

By *them*, she meant the problems she been facing recently or the words to describe her predicament, guilt, fear, anger, and loneliness.

"I always thought mom trusted me" she added, calmly and sincerely, "I remember her telling me: do what makes you happy. But now it seems like she doesn't want me to be happy"

Sabrina knew where the story was leading to, which meant that she had to tell her dad about Logan, although he probably already knew. Before when she fantasized about love, she imagined that her dad would be nice enough to care about her happiness. But sitting next to him in reality had her worried about how he might react because she was simply his daughter. And of course after being caught by her mom for what Sabrina was doing, his feelings might be a little different, just like what mom said.

"I met someone, dad" she told him, in discomfort. For maturity, Sabrina slowly turned her head and met her dad's eyes, which appeared gentle but could never tell what he might be feeling underneath, "By someone, I mean…a boy. But I can't even be friends with him"

"Mom said you couldn't?" Michael asked,

"Pretty much" The disappointment was still in Sabrina's voice, almost as if she wanted to make her mom the bad guy, "I just…don't know. I thought we were all meant to be happy, like I love you guys, you, mom, Jonathan, and our new home. Before I wasn't sure how to feel about the move but then I made some friends that I like. Then I thought maybe this whole thing about coming to Burns Lake was leading to something great and I just got excited. But I guess that's a bad thing"

For a moment, the sound of the kids playing at the playground substituted the silence, along with the lake splashing water onto the shore.

"So all this happened because you were caught making out with a boy on a poster" her dad stated. It wasn't a question. Almost right away, Sabrina scowled at him as if her dad said it intentionally in front of her friends. Anger was written all over her face but Michael also saw the hurt in her eyes, like she could start breaking down any moment, and then perhaps a *I don't wanna talk about it remark*. Undauntedly, Michael faced his daughter's scowled look.

"Hey, I'll always be your friend but I'm still your dad" he added.

There was no point in arguing with that. So then Sabrina merely turned away, putting her attention back on the lake in front of them, with the hope of not being criticized in front of the world.

"Sabrina, one thing doesn't define everything. We're all meant to be happy, especially you" Michael then put his hand on her shoulders, "Hey" he called.

He had his daughter's attention.

"There's nothing more I want in this world than to see a smile on you and your brother's face. Believe me; your mom feels the same way. Just because she won't let you do this or that, doesn't mean you're not allowed to be happy. It's our jobs as parents to know who you are and help you become the person you're meant to be, and growing up, sometimes means losing a sight of ourselves just to live someone else's life. It's like wearing clothes that don't fit"

"Someone's life? What do you mean?"

"I mean, like the person that you think you are, if that makes any sense"

After uncovering the layer of her dad's words, there was a hint of sadness in Sabrina's eyes, as she was about to accept the truth that not everything would go the way she wanted.

"I guess" she replied, softly, "What if it was something I really wanted?"

That question made her sound petty. But she was dying for some answers.

Her dad took a moment to think of what to say.

"If it's something you really wanted, and if something or someone stops you from getting it, then it's not the time"

Sabrina sighed, quietly. "I guess that makes sense".

She couldn't help but let her sadness cave into her voice. Her emotions were getting to her. Sabrina turned away slowly once she felt tears leaking out of her eye. So then she gently wiped it away.

"Sabrina" her dad said, gently, "Just like everyone else, you're destined for greatness. You are growing up but you're still pretty young. Not everything comes all in one place. Life is a journey. Your happy ending is still far away. Right now, you're at that age when you see greatness in everything. But looks can fool you. You have to learn to tell them apart, just like the things you want are different from what you need"

"But how will I know?"

"Trust your instinct. If it feels right, go for it. If it feels wrong, stay put"

Sabrina didn't say anything but she hung onto her father's words.

"Another thing is…" Michael added, "Sometimes we don't know what we really want. In those times you're actually just looking to escape, like say you get into another fight with your mother and then you just decide that you want to eat supper in your room. And then you decide that you eat in your room for the rest of your life. But really, you're just doing that out of anger. Deep down, you'll always want to eat at the table"

Right away, Sabrina's mind scattered into a few places at once. First, she came to a full realization that she had been treating everyone around her, poorly, particularly her mother, Elijah, Melanie, and Carly. She yelled in all of their faces, rather disrespectfully. Now Sabrina began to think of how her friends and family felt altogether. I must've made them feel so bad, she thought. They and most likely every figure from the past thought that Sabrina Clarin was a great girl and spoke highly of her. She thought about that for a moment and imagined that they probably threw all those positive vibes away from when Sabrina lost her temper. She was never like that before. Now all was left with Sabrina was guilt.

"Sabrina?" her dad was calling her. It sounded like it wasn't the first time. Sabrina tried to pull herself together right away just for her dad.

She barely had any time to hide her emotions, but like water in a glass, they dropped in her mind and spilled all over.

"Are you okay?" her dad asked, patiently.

Sabrina finally met her dad's eyes and before she knew it she was ready to cry.

"What's wrong?" Michael was getting worried.

The thought of her being a bad person kept hitting her repeatedly. Then tears began dripping from her eyes. Michael put his arm around her and pulled her closer. Sabrina hid her face in her dad's chest as she started to sob.

"I've..." Sabrina managed to say but she couldn't keep it together, "I...I've been..."

Michael Clarin felt her daughter's pain. It was so real it almost made him tear up. He then had both arms around her and held her tight.

"Just let it all out, Sabrina" he told her.

Sabrina Clarin cried her eyes out. And most of all, it was the burden washing away.

After her good cry, Sabrina took a moment and relaxed in her dad's arms. She took deep breathes and exhaled. Once she finally pulled herself together, she looked up to her dad and admitted: "I'm a bad person".

Startled, her dad stared at her for a moment.

"No" Michael shook his head, "No, Sabrina, you're not"

"But I am, I...yelled at mom and I did the same thing to my friends..."

"Sabrina" her dad replied, almost right away, "Look at me, you wanna know how many people think you're a bad person? No one! Not me, not your mom, and not Jonathan. You have a home, surrounded by people that love you and care about you. We wouldn't trade you for anything, even if you yell at us. We all have bad days. You're a smart and beautiful soul, Sabrina. And I'm very blessed to father you"

Michael held her daughter's head gently and kissed her forehead.

Sabrina fell back into her dad's arms and took in the great comfort.

"Anything else you want to talk about?" Michael asked.

"Yeah" Sabrina admitted, after a pause, "Dad, do you think all this happened because of Zach Epstad? Because you said that sometimes we do things just to escape..."

Her dad thought for a moment.

"Maybe; are you still troubled by that incident?"

Sabrina and Jonathan were able to keep that secretive until the one day their mom noticed Sabrina's silence and eventually talked it out of her.

"Maybe" she admitted.

By that, she meant yes because Michael saw it in her eyes.

"Well, sometimes when you run from your problems, they chase after you and they won't stop until they destroy you. At one point, you have to face it"

"And...what if I do face it and things get rough?"

"Well, you can never tell when things could get worse. If something bad happens, all you could do is try to talk some sense into that person. When you think about it, bullies are just kids who are lost. Some of them are so troubled, they can't even think, they just do things. Whatever they got going on in their lives, they take it out on everyone around them"

There had to be more than that, Sabrina thought. "What if things do get worse?" she asked, in a calm and confident voice, just so her dad wouldn't think that she was up to something.

"Defend yourself, if you have to" Michael told her.

Once they locked eyes, Sabrina could tell that her dad was showing a little concern but he was also serious, and there was probably more he wanted to say.

"Only if you have to" he rephrased.

There was still that confidence and fatherly tone in his voice, as he hadn't taken his eyes off Sabrina. That meant he trusted her. It was best not to break that trust. So in silence, Sabrina imprinted her dad's advice in her mind and gathered some fresh confidence. But then shortly, one thought struck her as Sabrina started to think that she might get into a fist fight sooner or later. Michael saw the mood change, for that he recognized her silence.

"You're okay, kiddo?" he asked.

"I'm fine" Sabrina nodded. She managed to keep her voice steady, "I'm actually feeling a little better just from talking to you. It's just... maybe I'm a little nervous"

Michael suspected that she was nervous in regarding her concern about bullying. So he went with that instinct instead of questioning her.

"Being nervous is part of trying to conquer your fear. Facing your problems isn't always easy but it's the only way to make you stronger"

"What if I can't do it? Like just can't?"

"Hey..." her dad called.

They met each other's eyes.

"We're Clarins. Challenge should be afraid of us"

When Michael gave that advice, he said it with strength, like not only through his advice but he was passing that strength onto Sabrina. Their connection grew stronger as father and daughter. It was comforting and quite liberating.

"And when the time comes to stand up to someone, you give them the Clarin stare" her dad added.

The Clarin stare, the words echoed. Sabrina repeated it and then suddenly she froze but her mind went blank.

"Sabrina?"

She faced her dad again.

"You sure you're okay?"

"Yeah" she replied, honestly, "I didn't know what happened there"

"Ah, well, anyways, the Clarin stare" he repeated, "I just came up with that recently. To be honest, your mom has been giving me that look. It's when your eyes are in focus and your eyebrows slant lower and lower by the minute, like you're ready for a fight. And I swear you're exactly the younger version of her"

Sabrina Clarin really did look a lot like her mom. They both had the long dark brown hair, clear white skin, dark eyebrows and eyelashes that made them standout.

"And just like her, you're strong and caring, beautiful in every way"

Flattered, Sabrina smiled. And it never felt more genuine. Now with the weight lifted off her shoulders, she felt like she could do anything. She felt so loved and supported that she just had to throw herself into her dad's arms. They hugged each other tight and held on for a long silent moment.

"I love you, Sabrina"

"I love you, dad"

And they both said it with love and sincerity. Once they let go of each other, Michael saw the love he planted just by looking at Sabrina, with the smile that had love written all over it and the affection that she showed really acknowledged his pride that brought a smile to his face as well. He really was blessed.

"Well, ready to go home?" Michael asked.

"Sure" she agreed.

They both got up from the bench and started making their way back to the car.

"Oh, felt like we been sitting on there forever" Sabrina groaned, "Feeling pretty sore"

"Well, that's cute. Wait till you reach my age" her dad joked.

Sabrina wanted to laugh but couldn't.

"Hey dad, do you think we can drive around for a bit just to listen to the radio?" Sabrina asked, just as they were exiting Radley Beach.

"Sure, only if you put up with my singing voice" Michael said, jokingly.

"Haha, it's fine with me as long as you don't change the station all of a sudden"

Her dad chuckled, "Again, I was only checking the score on the hockey game"

Sabrina giggled quietly-

I guess we'll still be friends when the songs change? That we'd still be dancing or listening together?

Just like that, Sabrina stopped.

Because they were talking about music just now, Elijah Khoda's words called out to her. It was that day when they were outside the school grounds and talking about their taste in music. At first she didn't know what he meant by those words. But looking back at it now, she realized that Elijah was trying to tell her something, something that he couldn't really put into words so he used music to express himself.

Still friends when the songs change.

Sabrina deciphered it in her mind. It could mean that Elijah wanted to be friends even through bad times like recently with their sudden fight and the conflict with Quinton Malcolm.

Next thing that came to mind was the day in November when they first talked about music and that connected them on a new level. Sabrina started to feel emotional but yet strong. She realized the wrong she did, yet it also made her think of the good days and just how precious they were. That was Sabrina's life. She had to maintain it.

"Actually, dad..." she called.

As her dad approached the car, he turned around to meet his daughter's eye, only to realize that she wasn't by his side. She was far behind him.

"I just remembered something..." Sabrina admitted.

CHAPTER TWENTY-THREE

E-4 versus The Serious Bunch

William Konkin Elementary school drifted in one long silence. It was the absence of the sound of students chattering and playing. There were no grownups whatsoever in sight. Sometimes there would be kids just coming to play on the playground but not for that Friday evening, only Elijah, Andrew, and Paula. They were pondering around, waiting for their competition to arrive.

Elijah's mind was blank, even though many thoughts were turning on and off, such as the conflict with Quinton and most of all, Sabrina Clarin. He was still hoping that she would come, but he came close to giving up, yet he didn't want to. Other than that, he was training his mind for the upcoming situation, channeling his anger into focus and preparing himself for the worse.

During the wait, Elijah was sitting at the log that surrounded the tire swings, which were near the basketball poles. Paula sat beside him in silence. After a moment, Andrew joined them after stretching his legs.

"So what are the names of this punk's friends? And what did they do to you?" Andrew asked. It sounded like he was going to start a fight. That seemed like a noble gesture. Elijah didn't hate it.

"Devon Welks" Elijah explained, "He's the short one. He made me stay out in the cold just to look for a moose that was gone before we even got there"

Paula gave a small chuckle, "If he wants to see a moose, there are plenty of National Geographic books in the school library"

"Devon the Short, loves moose tracks" Andrew confirmed, "Who's next?"

"June Disher. Actually she didn't do anything to make me mad, unlike the other ones. The last one is Roscoe Lewis, the tall one. I think he and June are dating"

"You mean like boyfriend and girlfriend?"

"That's what dating usually means, so yes" Paula said, calmly.

"Roscoe wouldn't even let me talk to June because he was scared that I was gonna steal her away" Elijah added.

"He must've had a lot of stuff stolen from him" Andrew joked, "His bike, his favorite pants, and the last slice of pizza he was saving". He paused. "I could go for pizza right about now".

"Can we please stay focused?" Paula told him.

"Well, I don't say you lightening the mood" Andrew replied. He looked over at Paula, who stared at him and suddenly lost his authority, "I mean not that you...destroy the mood...uh...What are we talking about his for? Stay focused, Paulie!"

Then he reached over and nudged her on the shoulder.

Paula sighed, not having any intention starting any petty arguments with Andrew, "Well, as long as we're focused".

"So how are ya holding up?" Andrew asked.

"I'm holding, I guess" Elijah replied, feeling doubt and uncertain.

"Well, that's a start"

There was optimism and confidence in Andrew's voice. Elijah wished he was that strong but going through that much trouble, it just made him assume the worse in everything.

"Well, whatever happens, keep holding on" Andrew encouraged, "If you let go, we'll catch you"

Elijah just nodded and said nothing. It was silent for a short moment.

"Well…" Elijah spoke, casually, "We been waiting for a little too long. I'm gonna go check and see if they're here". He got up from the log and went towards the basketball area to peek around the corner. There was nobody in sight, just the school itself sitting in silence.

They didn't wait too long after that.

The Serious Bunch had arrived, Quintin Malcolm, June Disher, Roscoe Louis, Devon Welks, came around the corner. They could be seen in the distance, walking passed the monkey bars. Elijah warned his friends that they were coming, in an emotionless voice. The gang saw their competition ahead and none of them took their eyes off them. And there wasn't a single smile. They really were a serious bunch.

Elijah almost went out of sight, only to have a moment to catch his breath and gather confidence but what if Quinton would tease him about it, calling him a chicken and tease every little thing about Elijah, just to spite him? He'd rather not give Quinton the satisfaction.

"This is it" Elijah said, in a low voice.

"Hey" Paula called.

They looked at each other. "We can do this" she told him.

"Team" Elijah replied.

Paula said the same thing.

"Team" Andrew repeated.

Elijah glanced at Andrew and nodded. Quinton and his gang were closer and they arrived. Both groups stood across from each other. No one spoke, no one even breathed. And Elijah locked eyes with Quinton, who didn't look too thrilled, probably because he couldn't handle the conflict his own way. Most likely his way would end with blood. With the way his behavior had been going, Elijah wouldn't be surprised if that was all Quinton had craved; Before Quinton wanted to play basketball with Elijah when they were friends. So he ought to be at least a little genuine about it but he probably just wanted to beat people up.

"Ready?" Elijah asked, casually.

"I'm always ready" Quinton claimed.

"Alright, but before we start, I want you to know that if we win, you never bother me again"

"And what if I win?"

380 PHILIP PATRICK

Elijah didn't think that through, even handling a conflict with a bully had its responsibilities.

"I don't know"

"How about I own you?" Quinton suggested.

Elijah knew what he was trying to say but didn't want to believe it. So he played dumb.

"Own me?"

"You know, you do whatever I say. You left me to get beat up, so you have to pay for it"

That thought froze the world for a moment. Elijah saw the power in Quinton's eyes and feared for his life for a moment, like Quinton was for sure going to win. But realistically, Paula and Andrew probably won't let that happen. If it got worse, Elijah would just have to be ready.

"Alright, fine" Elijah reluctantly replied, only because he didn't want to start any debate that could lead to an argument. There was already so much on his mind.

Everyone positioned themselves in front of the basketball pole. Elijah gave himself some space in order to get his mind set.

"Hey" Paula approached Elijah, "If we lose, we're not giving him anything. Not even you"

Elijah just nodded. It was easier said than done.

"I'm surprised you guys didn't dress up for this main event" Andrew said to the gang. Quinton and the others looked at him. Most of them didn't seem happy to even hear Andrew's voice.

"We don't need to dress up. This isn't Halloween, white boy!" Roscoe snarled.

"No, I mean DRESS up" The gang just gave a confused and funny look. June however was intrigued of where Andrew was going. "You know, like jerseys-basketball jerseys, you know?"

"We don't have any-"Quinton was about to yell.

"Neither do I. So I dressed up as an army guy. Stand down, boy. That's an order!"

Andrew spoke loud enough; it startled the Serious Bunch just a little.

"MY point is…" he continued, "You wear certain clothes for a purpose. Army men wear camouflage, doctors wear white coats, maids wear dresses; the muffin man has the apron. You could've worn one of those to this little game"

Furious, Quinton walked up to Andrew and planned to destroy every property that belonged to Elijah Khoda. "You listen to me, white boy" he demanded, "I'm getting sick and tired of your jokes. Nobody asked you to be funny…"

"Exactly" Elijah interrupted, gaining more confidence, "No one asked him to be funny. Andrew is funny"

"Let him speak!" Andrew insisted, pointing at his best friend.

"You can't control everything, Quinton!" Elijah said to his face, "And you'll never control me. These are my friends. This is me, I'm not like you but I'm probably angrier than you. So watch it!"

The bully said nothing. He just scowled at Elijah, disappointed that he got interrupted.

"You think you're so tough" Quinton said, calmly, "But we'll see"

Then out of nowhere, Andrew burst out laughing. It was hard to tell if it was genuine or without humor. "Sorry" he said, after chuckling, "After I mentioned maids wearing dresses, I just imagined Quiny wearing one and walking around like…" he started imitating a certain walk by taking little steps and waving his hand in the air, almost like he was dancing.

"'Quiny?'" Quinton replied, offended.

"What? Aw, don't tell me nobody gave you a nickname" Andrew spoke, like he was having a friendly conversation, "Your friends never bothered? Then I guess they aren't really your friends"

Quinton went up to Andrew, pointing a finger directly at him. "I'm serious, if you mess with me again, then your nickname is going to be Mouth-Shut!"

Andrew just looked at him. He didn't seem startled at all. "Is that the best you got? If you suck at one thing, it's making jokes"

"It wasn't a joke, it's a threat!" Quinton claimed.

"That was a threat?" Andrew acted like he was puzzled.

"Come on, let's get this over with" Elijah insisted.

There was no point in arguing. After all, the whole point of playing basketball was to avoid a fight, at least that was the plan, for that the conflict wasn't over yet. Anything could happen. Both groups spread across the area. It was decided that they would go for ten points. Whichever team scores a ten, wins; simple as that. Elijah glanced over his shoulder, imagining Sabrina Clarin coming around the corner. But no, they were on their own. It was three against four.

Everyone got into positions like how they did in basketball games. Elijah and Quinton were in center, face to face.

"We need someone to serve" Elijah suggested. Since no one answered, he just picked the first person that came to his mind, "June?"

Almost everyone turned their attention on June, who was willing to serve. She began walking towards them-

"I'll do it" Roscoe insisted, strongly.

So instead he approached Elijah and Quinton. While he was walking, he looked at June as if he was telling her to stay where she was. He probably just didn't want her getting close to Elijah, who he glared at briefly. Quinton Malcolm probably wasn't the only one who was interested in beating up Elijah Khoda. Once he was between the two leaders, Roscoe grabbed the ball, with force like someone was trying to take it.

It was silent all around.

Andrew and Paula were sided near Elijah, ready to play, as they locked eyes with June and Devon, who stood behind Quinton. There was no motivational speakers, no speeches, no one explaining the rules. They just went right into it.

Roscoe finally threw the basketball in the air.

Elijah and Quinton leaped into the air and the game had begun.

It started off casual, like it did in an ordinary gym class, students simply just playing for fun, but in this case, there were hard feelings. Some would use the activity to psychically antagonize their opponents.

And no one would notice until someone got seriously hurt. With no grownups around, Elijah and his friends had to survive on their own.

The basketball itself constantly changed hands as the game commenced. One of the members of the Serious Bunch would have it until someone from E-3 would steal it, and vice versa. Quinton and his friends were already getting competitive, while it took time for Elijah's team to get into the game, naturally thinking that it was a friendly competition.

Once Elijah had the ball, he quickly ran with it like his life depended on it. Andrew and Paula jumped in the clearing, waiting for their leader to pass the ball to one of them. But Elijah was rather focused on beating Quinton, he ran straight to the pole, threw the basketball up, hit the rim, and missed.

Now the ball was in the bullies' hands.

Roscoe claimed it. As much as he wanted to try to score, he ran to avoid Andrew or Paula, who were pursuing him. He bounced the ball on the ground as he dashed through the area. Roscoe was quite fast. It wouldn't be surprising that he might've played other sports as well. Finally, he passed the ball to Quinton, who then quickly threw it to Devon, like he already knew he was there. Devon had the ball, went straight for the hoop. It happened so fast, Elijah didn't believe how lucky there were as they scored their first point.

One-nothing, for the Serious Bunch; they had a brief moment of celebration.

This is only the beginning. We still have a chance, Paula said to Elijah. So they kept going. Quinton didn't plan on losing, for that he quickly reclaimed the ball and wanted to score again, but Elijah prevented by trying to take the ball, which was shortly passed to June. She ran with it for a moment and causally bounced it towards Devon.

But luckily...

....Andrew jumped in and caught the basketball. *Too slow, pipsqueak,* Andrew taunted as he remained focused. He didn't have the ball for long, as he was surrounded by his competitors. So Andrew threw the ball up in the air. Coming towards the other side, Paula went after it as the ball was rolling away. But she grabbed it. The Serious team was already coming after her.

"Bring it on" Paula challenged, in a low voice.

Running with confidence, Paula ran with the basketball in hand. She dodged each of their opponents. But she knew the longer she held the ball, the more vulnerable her team would be. So she managed to throw it to Elijah, who again went straight to the hoop. Roscoe immediately went ahead to block Elijah's path.

"E.K!" Andrew called, almost desperately. It was almost as if he could sense another defeat coming near. If Elijah had known, he would've passed the ball to him because Roscoe easily took it away, just when they happened to be near the pole, and just like that, the Serious Bunch scored their second point. They cheered again, only this time it was a little louder. That's how it started. Soon they would start taunting them and shouting insults.

"Damn it!" Elijah blurted out, in frustration.

"It's sad, I know" Andrew explained, quickly, as the game was about to continue in a second, "But think about it: they still got eight more to go. We might get lucky"

That's if luck was on their side. Elijah could only hope. Instead of saying anything, he just nodded. And they went for another attempt. After a short moment, things weren't looking good for Elijah and his friends. He tried his best to focus but all he thought about was how much he hated Quinton for everything he done, using him, teasing him, hurting him, and scaring Sabrina away. And there were also his friends, Devon and Roscoe, who were on his nerves for too long. His thoughts mixed with his emotions and that caused a great distraction that was beginning to slow Elijah down, physically and mentally.

Easily, Elijah lost the ball before he could even pass it to his teammates. As Quinton was getting away with it, Elijah was losing hope. He practically gave up. At the end of the round, his bully scored the third point.

"Yes!" Roscoe cheered.

"Wooo!" Devon added.

Quinton just laughed with pleasure as he felt confident that they were winning. The boys celebrated, but only June was the modest one. Unlike them, June would rather not antagonize Elijah in any way.

"I guess you and your friends are not so tough after all" Quinton taunted, just as Elijah predicted, "Because you guys are sucking each minute we play!"

Elijah said nothing. He just stood catching his breath but was lacking confidence. Paula noticed his emotional state. She'd rather not give up that easily.

"Timeout" she insisted.

"Timeout!" Andrew shouted.

Quinton didn't really care much about the timeout. He stood there with his friends, with the basketball in hand-Elijah's basketball. It looked like he owned, just like he was about to own him. Paula suggested that they forget about them for a second, for that she needed a word with her best friend. Andrew went to his duffle bag to grab a drink of water while Paula led Elijah away from the crowd.

"Be honest with me" Paula told him, gently, "Are you all right?"

Slowly panting, Elijah answered, "I guess not"

"Yeah, I'm guessing the same thing. I know it seems like we're already losing, but this is just the start. Game's not over yet"

"But they're getting lucky" Elijah added, with disappointment. He spoke like he was ready to give up any minute. There was a paused moment, for that Paula was trying to figure how to work around her best friend's emotional state.

"Yes, that's exactly what it is: luck" she replied, "Luck doesn't last forever"

She waited to hear a positive feedback but Elijah kept glancing back to Quinton and his company. It appeared that her advice didn't really help. From the glare in his eyes, Paula could tell he was caving in on his emotions. Andrew shortly joined them in silence, with a water bottle in hand.

"Elijah, look at me" Paula urged. And so he did. "Forget about them. You're letting them get to your head. It's what they want. So don't just focus on trying to score, focus on passing the ball to me and

Andrew. They can't stop us all at once. And when the time is right, one of us aims for the hoops"

So basically outsmart them was what she meant. Elijah didn't know how but he knew he had to try. So he decided to trust Paula. Luck doesn't last and focus from a different angle. Elijah took a deep breath and repeated Paula's words as he channeled his mind into focus.

"Okay" he agreed, in a calm but heavy voice.

"Here, bud" Andrew offered his bottled water, "Secret Stuff"

Elijah accepted the water and took a sip. "Thanks" he said.

"Pour some water on yourself. Feel refreshed" It was almost like Andrew became a personal trainer for Elijah, who did as he was told. He gave the bottle back. Then Andrew lifted the bottle of water over Paula's head and gently poured a little on her. Slightly irritated, she merely scowled at him, but not as deadly as she usually did, for that she was too focused on their situation.

"Trust me, you're gonna need it" Andrew added, gently. Then he poured some water on himself. Once the bottle was empty, he threw it away.

Now that Elijah was focused, the game continued.

With a little more confidence, Elijah put many efforts into the play as he focused on one thing at a time. First was trying to reclaim the basketball. Eventually, he did once he stole it from Devon. Elijah kept his mind blank as he ran with the ball. The opponents were between him and the pole. So he had to go around.

Paula was open.

So Elijah went with his instinct and passed the ball to her. Luckily she grabbed it without fail and she was near the pole! Go Paula, throw it in! Elijah was thinking. So she did, but the ball unfortunately bounced off the board and back to the ground-

Andrew got the ball but Quinton was already beside him, trying to steal it. He could see Quinton's hands trying to reach for it. So Andrew quickly dashed away. He could sense his competitors coming up behind him. There wasn't any time to waste. Andrew Little took the risk and threw the ball up...and it went through the hoop!

E-3 got their first score!

"Yes!" Elijah cheered, in a low voice. He thought it was best not to get too excited.

"First, baby!" Andrew shouted.

The boys were happy but Paula said nothing, feeling that it was too soon to celebrate. The Serious Bunch didn't give any comments, probably because they were two points ahead and thinking that they're going to win. The game went on. Elijah and his friends put their minds back to focus.

And with all the efforts that were put in, E-3 got their second score as Elijah took the shot and the ball bounced off the rim and into the hoop. They were catching on. The score was now 3 to 2, with the Serious Bunch in the lead but Elijah and his team were feeling more optimistic, especially Andrew who started chanting during the play.

"E-3...come on let's do this...and be-be-be the great...and let them see!" he shouted, as he was pursuing the basketball. He noticed some of their competitors looking at him funny but Andrew didn't care. Then soon he became the player and the commentator, like the ones you'd hear at a live sporting event.

"The goes the ball being manipulated by a bunch of buzz-killers" Andrew spoke out loud, while they were still focusing on the play, "Now it's in the hands by a guy name Ross"

And by Ross, he was referring to Roscoe Lewis, who currently had the basketball.

"Hey, Andy, what does 'Ross' stand for?" Andrew said, impersonating a different voice and then went back to his natural speaking voice, "I think it's Ross-cal? I think he's from Egypt or Spain, some place like that?"

The longer Andrew was goofing off, the more irritated their competitors were getting, especially Roscoe.

"Hahaha, it almost sounds like 'Rascal'" he added, "There goes that little rascal!"

Suddenly Roscoe stopped playing and turned to Andrew, furiously.

"God, will you shut the hell-"

Before he knew it, some water was being squirted into his face. Andrew had a small water gun in hand. The whole game stopped once they saw Andrew pulling a silly stunt. He stopped and noticed all the eyes staring at him. Andrew shrugged his shoulders, "I wasn't gonna bring this for nothing".

The thought was there. Elijah went with his instinct and stole the ball from Roscoe. Without giving a second thought, Elijah ran to the pole-not realizing that Quinton was calling for him-and took another shot which should've gotten them a third point.

"Whoa, whoa, whoa!" Quinton called, firmly, "That doesn't count"

Elijah stopped. The basketball was rolling away as a serious discussion took place.

"Your needo friend distracted Roscoe. You don't get a third point"

Disappointed and irritated, Elijah glanced at Paula, who rolled her eyes. Now Elijah had to think of something firm to say but he wasn't expecting to and had no desire to argue with Quinton.

"So?" he replied. It wasn't going to stop the bully from getting flustered.

"It doesn't count!" Quinton repeated, getting more irritated.

"You're not making the rules here" Elijah added, casually. He ought to sound stronger than Quinton's but his mind was still spinning from all that play.

"Then I guess I'll just have to beat up you and your friends, right here right now!" Quinton yelled. From the way his voice sounded, troubled and hurt, he wasn't talking like an ordinary tough kid. There was a sense of danger as if a predator was lurking in the bushes. Paula could tell that Quinton Malcolm had a hidden agenda that he really wanted to beat up Elijah.

"No!" Elijah yelled back, pointing his finger at Quinton, "You leave them alone. Fine, we don't get a third point. Let's just continue playing"

Paula strongly disagreed but didn't say anything, even though it was tempting to rattle Quinton's cage. Andrew thought briefly that it was his fault but since Elijah didn't point it out, he let it slip his mind. The game went on like nothing happened. Now Elijah had to try to forget about that little argument that was sabotaging his focus.

Sadly, Quinton and his friends scored a fourth point.

Elijah was strongly disappointed and irritated that Quinton would just not play fair for once. He thought that the world revolved around him, that he just had to control everything! Quinton Malcolm probably got his way all the time and never once gotten a reality check. Elijah most likely had to be the one to teach him a lesson. He took a deep breath and continued playing.

From there, the Serious Bunch was getting rougher. Every time, Elijah and his friends had the ball, either Quinton or one of his friends would knock the ball out of their hands violently. They took every advantage to antagonize E-3 by pushing them and shoving them. The threat grew larger. Elijah tried to remain confident but things were not looking good for him and his team.

And of course the Serious Bunch got their fifth point.

They were all celebrating as if they already won. Elijah, Paula, and Andrew were keeping their distance like they were a pack of wolves ready to bite any minute. None of them said a word, for that they felt vulnerable. The three of them glanced at each other doubtfully. Elijah was starting to get concerned that his best friends might suffer for his actions. With all the strength that he still had, Elijah wasn't going to let that happen.

Quinton locked eyes with Elijah, with a sinister smile. He had the basketball in his hands-Elijah's basketball.

"Not feeling so tough now?" he taunted.

Elijah only continued to glare at Quinton.

"Aw, what's wrong? Do you want your ball back?"

Quinton held out the basketball to Elijah, who then slowly approached him.

"I'll let you shoot for free" he added.

Roscoe and Devon were standing behind their leader, with mocking smiles on their faces. But June was the only one that had sympathy for Elijah and his friends. Feeling that he was out of options, Elijah just went up and took Quinton on his offer. Just as Elijah's hands almost touched the basketball, Quinton threw the ball away, away from the area. Quinton burst out laughing, laughing without humor. Elijah didn't take his eyes off his bully. He was ready to fight. Andrew and Paula sensed that something was about to happen.

"Hey!" a voice called. It was a girl's voice.

The laugher stopped. Everyone, including Quinton and his friends turned their attention to the unexpected visitor. All of Elijah's negative energy disappeared once he realized who the girl was…it was Sabrina Clarin!

She stood there with the basketball in hand. Nobody said a word. But Elijah was greatly surprised. *She came! She really did!* He couldn't believe it. A rush of excitement waved through his body and formed a smile on his face. But Elijah put his hand over his mouth, hiding his excitement. But he was so happy to see Sabrina. She gave a strong firm look, showing that she wasn't just there to support her friends but also that she was ready for anything!

Sabrina approached Elijah, who was still speechless. "I decided to help" she said, casually.

"No!" Quinton strongly disagreed, "No! It's too late for that"

Rolling his eyes, Elijah cocked his head toward Quinton.

"Shut up Quinton!" he yelled, "You're not making the rules here"

"Alright, then I guess I'll have to…"

"NO!" Elijah replied, strongly, "You listen to me, Quinton. We let you get away with one point. So we're putting Sabrina on our team!"

There was no reply from Quinton.

"Just shut up, deal with it, and the play the damn game!" Elijah added.

Andrew and Paula came and sided with Elijah.

"Sabrina is on our team" he repeated, "And we are NOT starting over!"

"Welcome to the team, Sabrina!" Andrew said loud and clear, just to spite their competitors.

Quinton shook his head with disgust, "This is such garbage!" he muttered.

They heard what he said but they didn't care. So E-3 had become E-4 again. First thing they did was having a huddle. As the others turned away, Sabrina happened to lock eyes with Quinton Malcolm. She hadn't forgotten the day when he was calling her out just to get to Elijah. Sabrina stared at him with cold eyes with her eyebrows slightly lowered. It was tempting to say something, a sarcastic remark or something intimidating to throw Quinton off guard, but she just stuck her tongue out at him before turning away. Sabrina joined her teammates in the huddle and they brought her up to speed. She was now aware of the score and Quinton's behavior.

"Now that there are four of us, I think that evens things out" Paula said, proudly.

"When all else fails, Sabrina shows up!" Andrew cheered. He looked at her and gave a nudge on her arm, "And I mean right on time"

Elijah proudly nodded, "Let's teach Quinton a lesson" he said, with a slight bitterness in his voice.

"It's 5 to 2" Paula reminded, "We still have a chance"

"Let's take that chance" Elijah insisted. Then he put his hand in the center of the huddle, "Together" Then Andrew placed his hand firmly on top of Elijah's, showing his commitment, and then Paula's and finally Sabrina's.

"It's time for teamwork" she added.

It was just like what sport teams do before a game. And that's what they were a team. And as for a final gesture, Elijah placed his other hand on top of Sabrina's hand and just couldn't help but hold it firmly as he locked eyes with her, especially after all that he had been through, her companionship meant much more than it ever did. Sabrina could've turned her back on Elijah, forgotten about him, after all the flaws she witnessed...But she didn't. Sabrina really was that friend, caring and supportive, maybe a little more than that, more than what Elijah saw in her.

"Let's teach" Sabrina said, strongly.

The game continued. This time Sabrina was on Elijah's team. It felt great to have another friend on his side. Both groups got into positions like they did in the beginning. And this time, Andrew served the ball.

He stood between Elijah and Quinton, and threw the ball in the air. They began with luck as Elijah felt the basketball fall into his grasp while in the air and tossed it behind him, where Sabrina stood. She went after the ball and shortly caught it.

Her instincts kicked in as Sabrina felt the bully and his friends coming after her. In the brief time that she had, she turned her head and saw them getting closer and quickly ran and dodged the faces of danger with the basketball in hand. Sabrina moved surprisingly fast. It was just like that day when she and Elijah were racing on the monkey bars.

Devon was catching up to Sabrina. She glanced over her shoulder and saw him at the corner of her eye. So then she immediately stopped and quickly twirled to her right before Devon could get closer. Once the chance came, Sabrina passed the ball to Paula, who was on the other side of the crowd. Paula deliberately ran in circles, to tire out Quinton's team. Then the ball changed hands as it was passed to Andrew, but didn't hold it very long because he promptly threw it to Elijah. And his bully just happened to be a little further away from the pole. So Elijah went and threw the ball and finally got their third point!

During the next round, Quinton's team nearly got another point but E-4 prevented them from doing so. After that attempt, both teams took a brief moment to control their breathing. Almost everyone was starting to get sweaty but they remained ambitious. Paula went to Sabrina and whispered in her ear: "Try to run in zigzags. That should tired them out" she told him.

Sabrina nodded. Now it was time for the next round.

The ball constantly changed hands. Both teams came close to putting the ball throw the hoop but nobody succeeded just yet. Only Sabrina and Paula knew about their game plan. That way they wouldn't stress about it, trying to accomplish it. Once Sabrina finally received the basketball, she did as Paula suggested and boldly ran into the crowd of both teams. She moved quickly passed her opponents without delay, even when one of Quinton's friends tried to steal the ball. After outrunning them, June went after Sabrina, who then leaped into the air and passed the basketball to Andrew, in whom she spotted at the last minute.

ELIJAH AND SABRINA   393

But Andrew couldn't catch the ball, for that it was barely going into his direction. It rolled away as soon as it hit the pavement. Quinton went and pursued it, as well as Andrew. Before they knew it, they were both running aside from each other. One quick glance into one's eye, it became a challenge, a race. Both boys were running equally fast as they put all their energy into it. Andrew and Quinton were close, but the bully put all the effort into running like his life depended on it. Andrew was falling behind. So he made a last minute decision and just dived towards the ball and successfully grabbed it, even though he landed firmly on the ground. Quinton unwittingly ran passed it. Andrew had the ball and then immediately threw it back towards the others.

Elijah reached for it but then Roscoe grabbed it first.

Suddenly Paula approached and stole the ball. The pole was right ahead. Quinton went after her, promptly, while Paula just took that chance and ran towards the hoop. Once she was far enough, Quinton was getting closer, but she launched the ball, which then hit the board and bounced off. Sabrina came around and grabbed the basketball and threw it up carefully.

Elijah's team got their fourth point.

They were catching up and Quinton was already getting agitated as if they were losing.

"Great shot, Sabrina!" Elijah said.

"Thanks" she replied, modestly.

Both teams had no intention of stopping or losing. So they kept going.

Andrew was able to get the fifth score. Elijah and his friends couldn't help but celebrate just a little, knowing that they made a good team and that they just might win.

It became a time game, five to five. Now it was all downhill from there.

Neither Quinton nor the other boys didn't like the fact that they were scoring. Once they stood together for another attempt, they fought back, aggressively. He encouraged Roscoe and Devon to crush them. Little that Elijah's team knew, time was about to sabotage them. Roscoe shoved Andrew to the ground and claimed the ball. Pain inflicted on

Andrew's arm. It took him a moment for him to get back up. Devon blocked Elijah. So he couldn't do anything to retrieve the ball. Paula pursued Quinton, who was outrunning them. Then he passed the ball to June, who then gave it to Roscoe and then got their sixth score.

There was no time to pick a fight. So Elijah and his team walked it off and tried again. If there was such a thing as luck, it wasn't with them at all. The bullies were getting even more aggressive. Next thing they did was huddling together and just ran through Elijah and his friends. Both he and Paula were knocked down. Sabrina and Andrew nearly lost their balance. They were getting weaker by the minute. But they weren't giving up.

Elijah gathered the strength he had, eventually reclaim the ball. And there he was able to tie the game once he put the ball through the hoop.

For the next few rounds, E-4 put up with the Serious Bunch's aggressiveness and both teams got their scores.

First it was a tie game, six to six.

Devon scored a seventh for his team.

But then Elijah and his team got the next two scores.

It was now eight to seven. Quinton wasn't happy.

"Alright! Everyone stop!" He yelled.

"I think you're supposed to say 'time out', bro" Devon told him.

Quinton sighed, "Whatever!"

Everybody on both teams stopped where they were.

"This isn't fair" he complained.

"What isn't?" Elijah replied, "I think everyone here is playing fairly"

"No! You guys keep scoring"

"So?"

"I think one of you is cheating!"

Elijah then exchanged glances with his friends. They seemed just as confused. Quinton automatically met Andrew's eye, who looked rather mischievous, like he was about to do or say something.

"Don't you say a word, white boy!" Quinton yelled.

"I was just gonna say there's a bug on you" Andrew explained, and then he just gazed at a random spot on the bully's upper body. It took Quinton a moment, for that his mind was racing. But he looked all over his shirt and then his arms. Andrew laughed, "Made you look", he said, proudly.

"Quinton, what is your problem?" Elijah said, getting irritated.

"You guys got lucky from the last two shots" then Quinton had to think of the right words to criticize, "You're-you're…fast…You're…helping each other…You're…"

Elijah just had to shake his head in disgust. Paula chuckled, without any humor. She said to him: "It's called being a team. Didn't you learn anything from gym class or anything at all?"

"Are you calling me dumb?" Quinton replied, offended.

"I think you're calling yourself dumb" Paula responded, strongly, "Because it sounds like you don't pay any attention at all"

"Hey…" Quinton pointed at Paula-

"I second that, Paula" Sabrina spoke abruptly and firmly. The bully stopped and looked at her as she approached and stood in front of everyone, "I think Quinton here only pays attention to whatever he wants to, like winning, being in charge, bossing people around, making sure things go his way" Sabrina was talking like she was a teacher telling her class something important, "At least that's what he THINKS. So he stops everything just to complain, even it's true or not" Then she looked directly at Quinton, "Am I wrong?"

Quinton said nothing, like a child who lost his credibility after hearing the authority through the voice of a grown up. Thing became silent. Everyone waited. Then June stepped up to speak her mind.

"Quinton, I don't think they were doing anything. They were just playing like the rest of us" June told him.

Quinton cocked his head towards her, "Well, why don't you go join them if you like them so much?!"

"I didn't say I like them" June said, firmly.

While they were distracted, Elijah threw the basketball to the pole. Once it hit the board, Quinton's mind suddenly went back on the game, "Hey!" he shouted. He took a few steps to go after it but then he stopped once he realized that nobody was moving. Again, Elijah shook his head, irritated.

"You know what I think is funny, is that Quinton is complaining when the game is not even over yet!"

The bully was speechless, now feeling like a fool.

"Go ahead" Elijah insisted, gesturing towards the basketball, which had rolled away, almost off the perimeter, "We'll give you a head start"

His decision didn't startle any of his teammates. So they were up for the challenge. First, Quinton hesitated, thinking that they were playing some sort of trick. But then his mind began racing again. Go, go, go! He told himself. So he ran after the ball, with his teammates behind him.

"Okay, go!" Elijah called. Then he, Sabrina, Paula, and Andrew ran back into the game. Both teams played like the timeout didn't happen, for that they remained focus to pursue victory. This time, Quinton himself wasn't as aggressive as he was before because of all that negativity he used. Roscoe became that athlete of their team once he claimed the ball and eventually tied the game, eight to eight.

The end was drawing near.

Both teams were playing much harder than they were before, maybe harder than they ever did in gym class, except there were no marks, no teacher, and most likely no safety. It was a creative way to settle a conflict between two troubled boys. If it was just normal kids playing, they'd play for as long they needed to. Then sooner or later, one would lose interest, thinking that they weren't talented enough to win a rather friendly competition, all because there was always one person who would get competitive. Sometimes they wouldn't play all the way to the end and no one would ever know who would've won.

No, it wasn't like that. It was more of a battle really, a battle that started when Elijah walked away from Quinton that night on the reserve. He thought for sure it was over then, but it was far from it. Now Sabrina Clarin, his special friend, suffered for his mistake. There was no walking away this time. Elijah had to face it and fight. And with all the distress and humiliation they been through, Elijah Khoda still kept his head up, for that it was near the end of the tunnel.

Now E-4 scored their ninth goal!

They were getting close. Quinton knew he had to give it all he got and he wasn't giving up that easily, even with all the sweat running down from his head. For the next round, he focused more on teamwork, only to get what he wanted. And there, Quinton's team tied the game, nine to nine.

Right away, after Roscoe scored the goal, both teams stopped for a moment, not only to catch their breath but to wrap their heads around the fact that they were both close to victory. Only the sound of breathing went off during the dead silence. Elijah and his friends stared at their opponents. No one spoke for that moment. Not even Andrew bothered to give any taunting remarks. When Elijah looked directly at Quinton, he could tell they were thinking the same thing, *This is it. It's either me or you.*

Elijah himself was rather too focused to give any words of encouragement to his friends. Instead he just gave a quick glance at each of them, Andrew, Paula, and Sabrina. He was grateful to have all three of them by his side and he would never take that for granted ever again. So then they all stepped forward, for their last round.

"Well, are you ready?" Quinton called out.

"We've been ready since before you guys came here" Elijah told him, "Are you?"

Quinton didn't answer. Everyone was ready. Elijah possessed the basketball, which he then served it into the air. He and his team ran for it, as well as Quinton's. The ball bounced off the pavement once before it feel into the hands of Devon, who ran with it while being pursued by Elijah's team, but Quinton made sure they weren't going anywhere near him. But soon he lost the ball when Sabrina came around and claimed it. She ran further away purposely to lead them away from the pole.

Quinton knew what they were doing, so he ran back towards the hoops. Sabrina realized right away but had to give up the ball in order to help her friends. So then she threw it towards Paula and Andrew. Quinton watched closely to where the ball was about to land. Andrew caught it but didn't have it for long, for that the bully came and took it away. And there, he ran towards the pole, being chased by his competitors. The ball went up but it missed. Then everyone ran for it as it hit the ground. And that was when the game became a little more physical than it should've been. Roscoe had the ball but Elijah stepped in right away and pulled it out of his grasps. He was surrounded by both his friends and his enemies, shoving and blocking each other. He had little time to think, so he just threw the ball away in a random direction. Paula ran as fast as she could and grabbed the ball. First thing she did was leading the bullies away. She quickly scanned her surroundings. Quinton's team was upfront, while Elijah and the others were scattered around, waiting for the opportunity to come along. So Paula came up with a solution, as she raised the ball above her head.

"Andrew!" she called. Paula passed the ball to Sabrina instead, while Quinton's team was partially focused on Andrew, thinking he really was about to receive the ball. But just as Paula planned out, Sabrina got the basketball and she ran with Elijah by her side. Of course, Quinton's team was right behind them. So Sabrina developed a plan of her own. She ran to her right and once she was further away, she quickly turned around-

"Elijah!" Sabrina called, as she passed the ball towards him.

Just like that, Elijah had the ball and was close to the hoop. He ran towards it.

"You go, E.K!" Andrew shouted.

Elijah was close, but just when he was about to shoot the ball, he felt himself being pushed to the ground with strong force. Quinton tackled him. So sadly, Elijah lost his chance and the ball rolled away. But then Andrew chased after it and was able to grab it. Everyone was at the pole now. Andrew made an attempt to score, he missed. The ball went back to the crowd, constantly changing hands. Elijah and Quinton quickly got up to help their teams, as both sides shot the ball quite a few times but each of it was a near miss. There was no score yet.

Paula was able to claim the ball. Since Elijah was the one that was further out, she passed it to him. Elijah ran in the opposite direction, but he couldn't go far because he was being chased. So then he threw the ball and hoped for the best. It was quite a gap between him and the hoop. As the ball was going airborne, Quinton was able to throw it off course slightly as his fingers touched it. The ball was falling back to the ground. Sabrina caught it and made her way towards the pole. Her opponents were catching up to her. Sabrina was getting close.

"Do it! Do it! Do it!" Andrew said.

Once she was close enough, Sabrina jumped and tossed the ball upwards.

"No!" Quinton cried.

But it was another near miss, for that the ball bounced off the board, passing above the hoop. In that moment, Elijah ran for his life and time slowed for him as the ball passed the rim. He ran passed Quinton and his friends. The ball was on its way to the ground. And then…Elijah leaped into the air, with both hands above his head. He got the ball! While he had it, Quinton was about to steal it. But then Elijah pushed the ball back to where it came from and he did it carefully.

The basketball bounced off the board again.

Everyone stopped.

The ball went into the hoop!

Elijah's team had won! They did it!

"Yeeaahhh!!" Andrew shouted, "Ahhhh!"

Elijah and Sabrina stopped. They quickly looked at each other, as the ball hit the ground and no one bothered to claim it. Slowly, smiles formed on their faces. A tired Quinton froze, for that his heart dropped and his mouth lowered into a frown. Roscoe and Devon were just as disappointed. But June just stood there and watched Elijah cheer with his friends.

Elijah, Paula, Sabrina, and Paula, regrouped, patting each other's backs, and hugging each other. They did it, they beaten bullies in a basketball game and they did it fairly! Quinton gave his friends a firm look and threw his hands in the air in disappointment. None of them said anything.

CHAPTER TWENTY-FOUR

The Final Round

"This is garbage!" Quinton yelled, as he eyed all of his friends, "Why couldn't you guys do any better?!"

"Hey, we tried" Devon replied, softly.

But no words were not comforting Quinton at that point. They never did. He stood there, feeling angry and defeated. Then he started pulling on his hair as he gave a heavy groan. June couldn't help but feel disgusted.

"Jeez, it's just a game, Quinton!" she told him, firmly.

He could hear the attitude in her voice and looked at her weird. "Just a game? It wasn't just a game, June. It was my chance to win"

"Win what?"

"Everything!"

"What do you mean by that?"

"I-I don't know! I just wanna be taking seriously for once!"

Quinton didn't realize how loud he was talking until he turned around and saw Elijah and his friends, looking directly at him. Quinton was speechless as he was disappointed.

"Well, Quinton, game's over" Elijah said, "We won. Now you get to leave me alone"

It was silent.

"Okay?" he said, almost strongly.

400

"No" Quinton replied, coldly, "No, I'm not giving up that easily!"

Then he began approaching Elijah, menacingly. How predictable. Elijah knew that was going to happen and he wasn't a bit surprised. He stood and let out a big sigh.

"We had a deal, pipsqueak" Elijah spoke firmly, "What more do you want?"

"I want YOU and your friends to lose, humiliated, beaten, and weak!"

It was almost pointless to argue but with someone like Quinton Malcolm, there was really no other choice.

"What do you want, Quinton? Do you wanna fight me?" Elijah asked,

"Yeah, I wanna go!"

"I thought we settled this last year in November. I guess that wasn't enough for you"

There was no response.

"Or I guess nothing is ever enough for you" he rephrased.

Quinton still said nothing but he waited for Elijah to make a move first. It was like he needed an excuse to fight. Elijah seriously did not want to start a fist fight and there was no other lesson he could put into words. He then exchanged glances at his friends, who were just as concerned, but he'd rather not have his friends fight his battles for him.

It was silent.

Quinton stood in the center, waiting for his opponent to approach. So Elijah really had no other choice. Before making any move, he peered over at Paula, with an apologetic look. He knew that she hated violence. But Elijah had no intention of throwing a punch. Instead, he was secretly thinking of an alternative. There was nothing yet but Elijah had to think of something soon. After a moment of silence, Elijah finally stepped forward and met Quinton in the center. He took a deep breath while Quinton braced himself as he put his hands up in fists. They locked onto each other's eyes.

"Well, you wanted to fight" Elijah said, with strange confidence, "What are you waiting for?"

So first Quinton took a dramatic pause and then he raised his fist, for what Elijah saw clearly from a mile away. It was almost like time slowed down for him. Then Quinton took a step forward and threw the punch, but then Elijah dodged it. But the bully wasn't stopping there, for that he began throwing more punches. And again, Elijah avoided it. They moved around in circles. After a few attempts, Elijah began leaping and twirling around, almost like he was dancing. Now the fear was fading away, for that Paula and the others were staring in wonder. Elijah continued avoiding the punches by leaping away. After a moment, he even started laughing, not in a mocking way, but out of joy. He was having fun.

"Are you tired yet, Quinton?" Elijah taunted.

First the fear was gone and now the anger was slowly fading. Elijah felt like he was in control of the situation.

"What are you…?!" Quinton wanted to yell more than anything, but just couldn't find the right words, "Why aren't you fighting? Are you too chicken or something?"

Sabrina nearly laughed because of the way Quinton said the last part, almost like a little kid because the anger in his voice was rather mild.

"If you wanna call it that" Elijah said and then he did his moonwalk, and then twirled as he leaped into the air, "Or I just don't wanna fight you. I'm not like you, Quinton"

It was such a relief that Elijah was handling the situation as himself and not as a fighter who craved for trouble. Quinton was irritated and still much anger. It was tempting for him to yell or fight but just couldn't. He wasn't in control as he hoped he would. So his mind needed time to process that, hence his lost for words.

"I'm not finished with you yet!" Quinton snarled.

"Well, when are you finished?" Elijah replied, with a little irritation.

"When you're beaten up" Quinton added, as angrily as he could.

"Yeah, yeah, you mentioned that before. I wish I can yawn because you're making me sleepy"

It was silent, for a fairly short moment. Quinton never took his eyes off Elijah.

"Well, are we gonna fight or what?" he asked, impatiently.

Elijah's first instinct was ultimately refuse and maybe that would be rid of Quinton's ambition. But then he remembered that they were going to teach him a lesson and he might've found a way to his problems: fun! So Elijah then went over the facts: Quinton Malcolm wanted to do his own thing and be in charge like an adult. But he overlooked the truth that he was still a kid, a kid who wanted to grow up. And what would a normal kid do? Play, like all the others. Quinton wasn't like them at all, for that he thought he was more mature and better than everyone else. But only he didn't know how wrong he was.

"You know what, Quinton?" Elijah said, as he stood up straight, "No"

The bully didn't say anything. He just continued scowling at Elijah.

"The answer is NO! We're not gonna fight"

Then Elijah quickly glanced over at Paula and then back to Quinton.

"We're gonna have some fun" Elijah promised, without a grimly tone. He spoke like he was about to show his peers a time of their lives.

Quinton looked at him, weird, "What is this?"

"It's a NON-violent fun filled activity" Elijah said, promptly, "There's going to be games and maybe a little dancing" Then he showed his dance moves in front of everyone. Then he stopped and stared directly at the bully, "How about a game of tag?"

Again, Elijah glanced over at his friends. They could tell he was onto something. So they trusted him.

"Tag!" Elijah called. Then he quickly ran up to Quinton and shoved him, hard enough for him to lose balance and fall. Elijah then started backing away.

"Catch us if you can?" Elijah challenged.

It was the same exact stunt that he pulled on Brian Kidman in his friends from the year before. Now Quinton was getting the same treatment. Filled with rage, Quinton got up and started running after them. Elijah turned around and ran towards his friends. Together, he, Paula, Andrew, and Sabrina were running from the bullies. Roscoe, June, and Devon went to catch up with them.

"To the tire swings!" Elijah told his friends and so that's where they bolted to. Once they made it there, they ran in zigzags as they passed the structure, making it a little more difficult for the bullies to catch them. At the last minute, Elijah decided to push the tire swings and hopefully it would slow down Quinton. After the tire swings, Quinton eventually caught up to Elijah and tackled him but they were able to keep balance. Elijah felt the bully's arms wrapped around firmly, in which turned into a wrestle. Sabrina, Andrew, and Paula, stopped to be sure the play wouldn't turn into roughhousing. Luckily, he was able to break free before Roscoe and the others showed up.

"I guess I'm it" Elijah called.

"Hey bud, tag me, tag me!" Andrew strongly insisted.

So Elijah did by patting Andrew's shoulder firmly. Then right away, Andrew dashed back towards the basketball poles. On his way there, he tagged Roscoe.

"You're it, Rascal!" Andrew said and then he stopped just to taunt him, "Oh by the way, you stink like sweat. You smell worse than my socks!"

Roscoe just scowled at him and then began to chase him.

"That's the sprit" Andrew said, as he started running.

As they were running, Quinton wasn't really paying attention to the game. He didn't care about it, only trying to get to Elijah, who then ran back to the basketball poles, with his friends following.

"Come on, slowpoke" Sabrina teased, as she ran ahead of Quinton, who growled while trying to catch them.

Andrew made it back to where his bag was, leaning against the pillar beside the entrance. With the little time he had, he opened the bag and pulled out a plastic bag full of water balloons, and then he continued running when Roscoe was getting closer. Andrew took the moment to untie the bag and pulled one out. The others caught up. Devon was right behind Roscoe, while Elijah was still by his friends while Quinton was running after them.

"You like water balloons, Rossy?" Andrew asked, as he was running around the perimeter. There was no answer, "Oh, I love water balloons, Andrew" he added, in a deep voice, although it didn't really sound like Roscoe's voice.

When the time was right, Andrew immediately stopped, faced Roscoe with the water balloon and threw it right at him. Suddenly water splashed all over Roscoe's upper body. Just like everyone else, Roscoe stopped and looked at his wet shirt in shock, and then glared at the culprit in front of him.

"It's almost summer time" Andrew said, shrugging his shoulders. And then he ran passed him and threw another water balloon, this time at Devon.

"Waa!" Andrew cried, just after splashing him.

There was only two water balloons left. Andrew pulled one out and gave it to Elijah, who then threw it at Quinton behind him. Next thing Quinton only saw blurs of water splashing into his eyes, which slowed him down for a moment until his eyesight returned. Then Andrew threw the last water balloon at Quinton's back. Everyone stopped. Roscoe and Devon were too irritated to go after Elijah or Andrew, for that they were all soaked in water, except June.

"What the hell is with you and your kids' games?!" Quinton yelled, as he was furiously rubbing the water out of his eyes.

"Uh, maybe it's because we are kids?" Paula suggested, "You ever think about that?"

"I don't think Quinton really thinks about anything" Elijah added, as he walked into the center of everyone, "He doesn't think about how others feel, even when they say something. And he doesn't have any imagination and he only laughs when he teases someone, non-stop! He's not a kid. He said so himself that he was more grown up than the rest of us, but really he's acting like a big baby"

"Shut up!!" Quinton shouted. Then he ran after Elijah, threw a punch, but only hit the air, for that Elijah moved out of the way. After that, Quinton peered over at his friends, who were suddenly just bystanders, "Why aren't you guys helping?!"

Roscoe and Devon stood in silence for a moment and then exchanged glances with each other. Each of them gave a deadpan expression. "What's the point?" Roscoe said, "They beat us in the game and they humiliated us. Do you really wanna keep going?"

Quinton said nothing. There was no way he could express his disappointment for the ones he always counted on. From within, there was only rage.

"Argh! The hell with you guys, you're useless, I'll do it myself!" Quinton once again charged at Elijah, who only laid his hands on the bully to push him away.

"Look…" Elijah spoke strongly, "We had beaten you in the basketball game. I thought us acting like little kids would make you lose interest. So Quinton, I have no other way to say that's enough! So stop it!"

But that didn't help, for that the bully tried another attempt to fight. As Quinton charged, Elijah quickly stepped aside, putting one leg out, making Quinton fall to the ground. He felt his gut and his chin land on the pavement. Without giving any thought to the inflicted pain, Quinton got back up and tried throwing more punches, but was unsuccessful.

"Come on, fight me, you wuss!" he challenged.

Again, Elijah just shoved Quinton away. There was enough force to push him back to the ground.

"I said that's enough, Quinton!" Elijah yelled.

"No!" Quinton snarled. That was when he pulled out a pocketknife. Nobody knew about it until Elijah saw it at the last minute, coming towards him.

"Holy…!" Elijah replied, loud enough and with enough aggravation to warn his friends.

Everyone stood in shock as Quinton was swinging the knife at Elijah. Even, Roscoe, Devon, and June, were frozen stiff. Elijah was tempted to run. Paula and Andrew slowly stepped forward, attempting to do something. Before they could take another step, Sabrina quickly ran in, without hesitation. She went up to Quinton and firmly grabbed his arm, in which he was holding the knife.

Surprised, Quinton peered over his shoulder and met Sabrina Clarin's eyes that were glaring back at him, "BACK OFF!" she said, strongly. In that moment, Sabrina couldn't help but feel proud that she seized the courage from within. At the same time, she imagined she said that to Zach Epstad's face.

Elijah stopped, for that it seemed like it was over. For a brief moment, Quinton really was intimidated by Sabrina. Then the fear went away, along with his conscious. He pushed Sabrina away with his other hand. Elijah noticed immediately and suddenly just felt rage take a hold of him. Bullying Sabrina with words was bad enough. But laying a hand on her was too far. That moment was too unbearable, even for the mind's eye. Sabrina must've felt scared. What if she got seriously hurt? Quinton Malcolm couldn't stop and won't stop. Somebody had to discipline him and Elijah Khoda was the only person there willing to.

Before Quinton even turned around, Elijah made fist with his hand.

And as soon as he met Quinton's eyes, Elijah fired his punch and struck Quinton right in the mouth!

Sabrina Clarin remembered back from November when she first found out that Elijah got into a fight. She was both surprised and worried. Violence was forbidden. Any normal kid would know that. It was just after Sabrina encountered Quinton, she learned that life couldn't maintain control over such actions. She learned that sometimes, one person had to take action to stop another. That person could be anybody, even a friend. So once Sabrina heard Elijah's fist making physical contact with Quinton's mouth, she didn't even blink.

The sound of the impact was loud enough to startle everyone. Even June, Roscoe, and Devon flinched. Quinton Malcolm fell to the ground. The knife was out of his grasp. Sabrina quickly grabbed the knife before the bully would even move. Quinton lied there, cupping his hands over his mouth. Paula and Andrew were a little relieved, but not enough to start breathing again. And that went both ways, for both two teams.

Elijah stood above Quinton, glaring down at him. The feeling of rage wasn't the first time that consumed him. It happened when Elijah faced Brian Kidman, when he wanted nothing but to hurt him. In fact, he wanted to hurt anyone that wronged him. As Elijah was looking down at Quinton, who was starting to cry, he realized that he could've become just like him, a bully. Right then, the tension was fading away and Elijah looked over at Paula, and just felt human again. And then he turned towards Sabrina, met her eyes. There was a look of relief and sincerity. That was when love met humanity within Elijah Khoda.

Sabrina herself was gazing at Quinton. She didn't think that she had the courage to stand up to a bully but she did. The first thing that came to mind was that day in Granisle when she was antagonized by Zachery Epstad. And she remembered her brother Jonathan's words, *I'll make you cry like a little baby!!* Sabrina felt a great relief because in a way, it almost felt like she went back to that day and faced her fear.

"Did you guys know about this?" Sabrina asked, after a moment of silence.

Roscoe shook his head; Devon hesitated, while June said nothing.

"No" Devon finally admitted.

"How can you guys hang out with this kid?" Paula demanded.

"We didn't know, okay?" Devon replied, almost yelling.

Sabrina broke eye contact and just shook her head in disgust. Finally, Elijah bent over to look directly at Quinton, who was still lying on the ground, defeated.

"Quinton" Elijah called, firmly, "Look at me. You look at me now"

Their eyes met. Quinton had tears floating down his face.

"You lost!" Elijah told him, "You wanted a fight, I just gave you one and you lost. If I was you, I'd just get up, walk home, and don't say anything. Now get up!"

Slowly, Quinton did as he said.

"Now let me remind you, we win the game and you don't bother us anymore. And by us, I mean me, Sabrina, Paula, and Andrew. That was the deal. You leave my friends alone, but if you don't, I'm coming after you. We're not friends and we're not brothers"

Quinton said nothing. He only nodded.

"Now before you go, I want you to apologize to Sabrina, for what you done"

Sabrina wasn't really surprised but she was relieved because Elijah was being so considerate. Deep down, she was grateful for his support. The bully looked at Sabrina, who stood behind him.

"I'm sorry" Quinton said, trying to hold it together,

"Sorry for what?" Sabrina replied, as she crossed her arms.

Quinton's emotions were getting fragile, "For...for shoving you" he said, poorly.

"And?"

"And for...t-teasing you...in front of the whole school"

Sabrina was about to make Quinton apologize for picking on her friend Elijah. But then she felt that he already paid for that when he got punched to the ground.

"Good" she said.

Finally, Quinton broke down, feeling weak and embarrassed. He began to sob.

"Can I have my knife back? It's-it's my... my dad's" Quinton managed to say.

Elijah couldn't help but shake his head. *Pathetic*, he thought. He probably wasn't the only one thinking it.

Sabrina slowly gave back the knife. Quinton grabbed but Sabrina was still holding onto it, tightly. They met each other's eyes. Sabrina leaned in, as she glared at him.

"I have a big brother" she warned, "Unless you want to meet him, don't EVER touch me again!"

Just like before, Quinton felt intimidated by her, only this time he couldn't do anything about it. He had the knife back. Suddenly, June approached and quickly took the knife away from Quinton. "I'll hang onto this until you get home" she told him. Her voice was a little firm but gentle. "I don't think I trust you with it". He didn't say anything. He was rather too emotionally weak and defeated. So June put the knife in her back pocket for safe keeping.

"Quinton" Elijah said, emotionlessly, "Get out of here"

So Quinton walked away, still crying. It was all quiet. Elijah had nothing else to say. As they were following their defeated and troubled leader, June and the others were speechless. They probably wouldn't look at Quinton the same way again, after that violent act he just committed. Not only that but neither Roscoe and Devon wouldn't even dare to look Elijah in the eye. In that moment, they were rather intimidated by Elijah Khoda, like he was the grownup that laid down the law on misbehaved children. After the Serious Bunch was gone, Elijah Khoda never dealt with Quinton Malcolm ever again.

E-4 was still drifting in silence. Elijah turned around and saw all of his friends looking back at him, Andrew, Paula, and Sabrina. Once their minds processed the events they just went through, from winning the basketball game to dealing with Quinton, they accepted the peace and quiet. As the three of them gazed at Elijah, they could tell that he was the same person but also different. Elijah himself felt different. First he was afraid of dealing with the conflict and ought to run away from it. Instead he stood in his place and fought it, all the negative energy that consumed him and the bully's rage, and won.

And for the first time since last June, the dark cloud in Sabrina's mind had cleared.

"Peanut butter pop tarts" Sabrina spoke, after a moment of silence. Everyone turned to her.

"It's something you say when you can't think of anything else" she added, casually.

Nobody said anything, not right away. Then Andrew chuckled under his breath. It was loud enough for them to hear and that brought joy upon them. Slowly, Elijah smiled and so did Sabrina. Finally, Andrew burst out in laughter. Paula exhaled and relaxed. The laughter was their cue to go back to being themselves, as kids. After going through that drama, they earned a joyful moment.

"Well, we did it" Elijah said.

"We did" Andrew agreed.

"Damn right, we did" Paula said, proudly.

"Haha!" Andrew cheered, as he clapped his hands together, "Wooo!"

Then Andrew went up to Elijah and did their thumbs up-fist bump. But it wasn't just that, there was also a high five, two of them, followed by a low five, and then a firm pat on the back. It was so exciting that Andrew couldn't help but hug his best friend. Elijah did the same and wrapped his arms around Andrew. Elijah let out a chuckle. Paula and Sabrina smiled, and then exchanged looks with each other.

"Boys" Paula said, "Sometimes they have their moments". She then went up to her best friend, "Hey"

"Hey Paula" Elijah replied, almost cheerfully but then he remembered something important that he had to explain, "Look, I uh, didn't want to punch him but..."

"I know. He went too far"

They met each other's eyes.

"But I'm proud of you" Paula told him, sincerely, "You did it. You faced your problems, even when you were nervous. You just as brave as the first day I met you"

Paula and Elijah hugged each other.

Elijah Khoda was so surprised that he couldn't believe it. Even after all that doubt and hard feelings, he was still able to overcome a major, emotional, challenge. He was lost for words but he was truly grateful. And he couldn't have done it without his friends. It was tempted to say something nice to each of them, especially Sabrina who he thought for sure wasn't coming but she did. But he couldn't think of what to say that could justify their friendship. But instead he just met each of their eyes as they smiled and he smiled back.

"So what do we do now?" Elijah asked, after the moment was over.

"Go home, I guess" Paula suggested.

"Oh yeah about that, E.K., I probably have to go to your place and call my parents to pick me up" Andrew said.

"Yeah, for sure"

"Maybe we don't have to go home" Sabrina said, "We can hang around for a bit, or play around, whichever. I'm only saying because my dad said he'll pick me up in about hour. I got like maybe thirty minutes left"

Elijah cocked his head at both Paula and Andrew. They seemed okay with staying at the school for a little while longer.

"I do have some other sporting goods in the bag" Andrew told them, "I got the frisbee"

"I don't mind staying a bit" Paula agreed.

"You know what, I kinda like the idea too" Elijah admitted, "So come on, let's go to the field"

"Yes!" Andrew said.

412   PHILIP PATRICK

Then he went to grab his bag, while Paula went to reclaim the basketball, which was sitting the gravel outside the school's perimeter. Elijah purposely waited until Sabrina joined them and started walking together. He walked beside her, while Andrew and Paula led the way.

"Got the whole school to ourselves" Andrew said, "So let's enjoy it"

"Yeah, I don't have to worry about making eye contact with other students" Paula added.

As they were walking, Elijah glanced over at Sabrina. "Thanks for coming, Sabrina"

She looked back at him, "No problem" she replied.

After breaking eye contact, Elijah peered forward, rather blankly. There was much more he wanted to say to his special friend. "You know, I was starting to think that you weren't coming" he admitted, in a low voice.

Sabrina started to slow down. Elijah noticed and stopped right away. Next thing she stopped. Andrew and Paula were still walking. She knew that her best friend needed a moment, so she insisted Andrew to keep going and without looking back.

"I almost didn't, actually" Sabrina told Elijah, who said nothing, "But then I thought about it and I started to feel bad. So here I am"

"Well, better late than never"

There was a pause after that.

"Sabrina, I...I didn't mean to hurt you, you know what I did to Logan..."

"No" she replied, promptly, "You don't need to..." she trailed off and then he met his eyes and turned away again, "Me and Logan aren't really friends anymore".

Elijah didn't say anything. He wanted to ask why but after what he did, it would just be too silly, doing some damage that he may or may have caused, and then wondering how it happened. But then he saw the hurt in Sabrina's eyes. She seemed troubled by it. Maybe it wasn't him. And it was hard to tell if it was good or bad that she wasn't associated with Logan Austin anymore.

"Elijah..." she called, gently. Then their eyes met, this time longer than before. "I've been a terrible friend..."

Her mouth was open, ready to speak, but yet Sabrina paused to debate on whether or not she wanted to tell Elijah about her conversations with her parents and how she learned that she was being self-centered and pushed her friends away. And the time that a boy named Zach Epstad troubled her at school that prevented her from helping Elijah in the first place. Sabrina wasn't sure if she should have a long discussion about those topics. Maybe it wasn't the right time.

"I'm sorry that I called you childish and for yelling in your face, and for ignoring you". Saying that out loud almost made Sabrina cry; she quickly looked away trying to hold her tears back. She wiped them away and then she added, "I know, I'm a bad apple". Her voice was weak like she was about to breakdown any second. Even so, Sabrina managed to keep it together but kept her head down in shame.

Just like normal people, Elijah wasn't about to say it's okay or apology accepted. For one thing, saying that it was okay that Sabrina pushed him away just didn't seem right, not realistically. He could tell that Sabrina felt bad but yet he couldn't stay mad at her. Sabrina's sincerity was enough. And Elijah ought to say apology accepted, but he heard so many people say it that it's become a little too formal. Elijah Khoda wanted to be more than that, as much as he wanted to be more than a friend to Sabrina Clarin. There had to be more to life than just a straight line, like what he just experienced. Surely he fought Quinton Malcolm and won, but that probably wasn't going to be the last bully he would encounter for years to come. If being normal was optional, there had to be something different, something greater that only a special someone can see that it sometimes it wouldn't need words to express one's self.

"I know" Elijah finally replied and then what he said next brought back a certain memory, "We all have flaws"

Sabrina gazed at him as she heard her words echo back to her. She remembered that conversation like it was yesterday. Thinking about it just brought her back to that moment and she remembered how much heart Elijah Khoda had shown, not just from that day, but from day one.

They broke eye contact. Elijah felt emotionally close to Sabrina that he just had the urge to give her a hug but he wasn't sure how she'd feel about it. Even so, he wanted to acknowledge her, physically. So Elijah reached over. He was about to pat her on the shoulder. Sabrina noticed from the corner of her eye but wasn't really paying attention, for that she just raised her hand. Next thing she knew, she was feeling Elijah's hand against hers. They looked at each other. There was sincerity all over their faces. It was so profound; it almost felt like Elijah was looking at Sabrina for the first time. The feeling made him wrap his hand over Sabrina's hand. Then she positioned her hand properly by interlocking her fingers through his and there they held it for a long moment.

There was something special about that gesture. There was a certain feeling that emerged from inside. It wasn't just comfort. It was also warmth and strength. Altogether those feelings were mingling like water soaking on a shore during a bright sunny day. It was nothing like they felt before. It was beautiful.

Slowly, Elijah smiled, softly, and Sabrina smiled back.

They went to catch up with Paula and Andrew. They were up by the field. Once they arrived, they noticed Andrew was trying to spin the basketball on Paula's head.

"Hold steady this time" Andrew told her.

"I been holding steady all along" Paula claimed.

Andrew then gave the ball another twirl but it nearly fell off.

Elijah laughed, "What are you guys doing?"

"Taking the ball out for a spin, on Paulie's head!" Andrew said.

Giving another attempt, Andrew twirled the ball again, this time it spun around a few times until Andrew made it spin a little faster and fell off Paula's head.

"Aww" Andrew cried.

Elijah and Sabrina just laughed.

"Alright, now that you guys are here, let's play some frisbeeee!" Andrew called.

"Wanna do the same thing as last time?" Elijah asked, "You throw the Frisbee and me and Sabrina go catch it"

"It sounds like a good start" Paula agreed.

Elijah and Sabrina went into the field to be ready. Andrew threw the Frisbee hard and it went flying across the field. And the couple went to chase after it. So the game had begun. The four of them played until it was time to go home.

PART THREE
Lost and Found

CHAPTER TWENTY-FIVE

Another Step Forward

After that evening, Elijah Khoda and Sabrina Clarin maintained their friendship. Each day was a new day. It started off with a simple hello. Sometimes they shared their favorite snack, Dunk-a-Roos, during lunchtime. Every now and then, they'd hang out, whether it was with Andrew and Paula, or just Elijah and Sabrina alone. It was pretty much the same, like nothing had happened but yet something did feel different, in a good way. They grew closer to each other than before, especially after their friendship experienced the worst and still never lost sight of their best. From there, whenever they made eye contact, there was a genuine comfort that expressed a smile on their faces, almost like they were thinking about each other and it turned out greater than they expected once they met at school every day. Elijah was so happy that he still had Sabrina part of his life, and she seemed just as grateful.

During that time, Sabrina Clarin didn't bother thinking about love or dating. She simply enjoyed the time she had with her friends and her family. Most of all, she reconnected with her mother. After dealing with the bully that evening, Sabrina went home and just gave her mom a hug and she returned the hug. Right then, their little argument became ancient history. Sabrina couldn't ask for any more, for that she felt she had everything she needed. She was blessed.

Before any of them realized, time was going by so fast. April had come and gone. For the month of May, it was quiet. Nothing but school days and each day they all worked as their days of being grade seven students was almost over. When June started, nobody just couldn't believe it, it was the last month of school.

As always, Elijah thought about Sabrina. He only thought of her as a friend, but when the school year was almost ending, he was starting to feel sad, not just the fact that he wasn't going to see her for two whole months but he was also sad that he never had her as a girlfriend, even after he determined to romanticize their relationship. He wanted to but he just wasn't sure how or if he should. That was just one thing. Another thought was planted in Elijah's mind: What if Sabrina moved? Throughout the school years, he saw students come and go. None of them he never gave much thought to, but with someone special like Sabrina, he'd be very sad if she did move away during the summer and wouldn't know for sure until the first day of school in September. He already imagined the scenario in his mind, being at the high school, with all the other freshmen, desperately looking for Sabrina but nowhere to be found. The scenery felt so real, Elijah could already feel the emptiness inside him growing bigger and just made him cry. Maybe Sabrina Clarin wasn't planning on moving. He was too scared to ask her because of the wrong impression that he might give her. Then again, why would Sabrina move after coming to Burns Lake at the beginning of the year? Elijah just left it at that and didn't think about it any further.

The month of June turned out to be eventful. The entire school had sports day where all the students and teachers divided into teams and played many sporting activities around the school. At the middle of the month, it was 7-up day, where all the grade seven students would spend the entire day touring the local high school LDSS (Lakes District Secondary School), which would their next stop in their educational journey. Once 7-up day was done, it was time to enjoy their last days of elementary school.

ELIJAH AND SABRINA

One day, Mrs. Parker and her class had a discussion on what to do for a year end celebration. The first thing someone suggested was a movie and students could bring their own snacks. A possible field trip was the next idea but that seemed unlikely considering there wasn't enough time to fundraise money for it. One student suggested a barbeque outdoors and everyone could play around at the field. And the last idea that was pitched was a school dance. Half the class was interested in the barbeque and the others were interested in the dance. It was a rather tough decision, so they had a vote. In the end, the dance won the vote.

Elijah actually had no problem with the school dance. The first thought that came to him was the opportunity to get close to Sabrina. It made sense because they both had the same interest for music. It could be a great evening of bonding. Elijah could see it already, both he and Sabrina dancing together. Each day he grew more excited about it. Therefore, Elijah was counting down the days.

"Hey Sabrina" Elijah greeted. He met with her once another day of school was over.

"Hey Elijah" she replied.

They stood outside the entrance where their peers were exiting.

"How was your day?" he asked.

"Day was good. I was tired at first but I made it through. How about you?"

"It was good. Nothing too exciting but I liked it, wouldn't have it any other way"

Sabrina nodded. Then Elijah made conversation by talking about the weather. It had been sunny for some time and only a few cloudy days, but neither of them didn't mind the rain. Even so, it was a beautiful time of the year where the sun was shining more than ever. Sabrina was excited for summer.

"Oh, I gotta go" Sabrina said, as she realized her mom was in the parking lot, "My ride is here, See you, Elijah"

"Sabrina" he called, promptly.

She stopped and looked at him.

"I just wanted to ask, are you going to the dance next week?"

There was a short pause.

"Of course" Sabrina told him, with a little smile.

"I am too" Elijah admitted.

"Awesome!"

"Alright, well I better let you go. I'll see you tomorrow"

"Same to you"

And she was gone but Elijah knew he would see her again. Once he found out that Sabrina was officially going to the school dance, he just couldn't wait. Later that evening, Elijah was at home, spent most of his time daydreaming or more like planning out every move for the school dance. He imagined that the first thing he'd do was mingle with his closest friends, just hang out for a bit and then start dancing. That was only the beginning. The one thing that would make the evening complete would be having a slow dance with Sabrina Clarin. Elijah saw himself putting his arms around her and moving slowly to the rhythm of the song. That put a smile on his face. That would be beautiful.

For the rest of the week, Mrs. Parker and her class were planning out the dance. She actually discussed it with the other grade seven teachers and they agree that their classes would be happy to join. Sabrina and her friends offered to provide the music. They would simply use a stereo and plug it into the speakers in the gymnasium. And one of the students suggested decorating the gym, perhaps with lights and/or balloons all around. So it was all decided when Mrs. Parker agreed to all of the ideas. Now everything was set.

Later that evening, Elijah was at home. He went to tell his mom about what his class had planned. And then something unexpected happened. There was another event going on that same day as the dance, a family dinner. The first thought was that it interfered with Elijah's plans. Initially, he didn't say anything because he still needed to wrap his head around it. If the dinner started a few hours later, it might work out.

"Hey mom, what time does the dinner start?" Elijah asked.

"Probably around six or it might start a little late" she answered.

A little late? Elijah thought. Now he started to fear the worse, that he might not be able to make it to the dance. But maybe it was still possible.

"Mom, would it be okay if I left the dinner a little early to go to the dance?" Elijah said, gently.

Madeline Khoda looked at him, long and hard. It was rather suspenseful.

"No" his mom replied.

Elijah didn't breathe. Things became tense once he realized that his mom was serious.

"No?" Elijah replied, helplessly, "Why?"

"Why?" his mom repeated, "Because I don't think you deserve to go"

It completely shocked Elijah as the truth was revealing itself. "Why can't I go?" he said, innocently.

"Because you haven't been really honest with me at all, Eli" Madeline was speaking firmly. She was clearly upset about something. For a second, Elijah thought she might've found out about Sabrina somehow and was totally unprepared to live up to a certain demand, but instead his mom said: "To tell you the truth, I'm not sure if I even know my own son because you keep hiding from me"

"Mom, I'm not hiding anything" Elijah said, carefully.

"Then how come you're so quiet all the time? Especially that one day when you left supper without finishing it because you were mad. What was all that about, anyway?"

That was when Elijah was furious about Quinton Malcolm antagonizing Sabrina just to get to him. He never thought he would have to re-visit that day again. Madeline Khoda was the one person who was strongly against Elijah causing trouble, especially when it involved violence.

"I was…having problems at school" he said to his mom, covering the truth with many layers.

"What kind of problems?" Madeline demanded, after a moment of waiting.

424 PHILIP PATRICK

"It-it doesn't matter now" Elijah claimed, "It's not bothering me anymore"

"Eli, it does matter. I can tell you were troubled that day and you ran off without saying a word. But that's just one thing, how about back during Christmas; something was bothering you at the store..."

"Mom-"Elijah interrupted. That was the night he bumped into Sabrina at the grocery store. He was only surprised because he literally thought Sabrina was mad at him for a problem that wasn't even there.

"Stop interrupting me!" his mom was nearly yelling. From there, Elijah just stopped talking. "And the one thing I was really worried about was when you got into a fight with that Quinton Malcolm. I don't know what it was about, because you don't tell me anything, but I knew that were you hanging out with him and his friends, and now you're back with Paula and Andrew? When did that change up? See, you won't tell me! I worry about you, Elijah. Ever since you first got suspended from school, I just naturally think that you're somewhere up to no good. I do wanna help you because I'm your mother, but you won't let me in on your life. So why should I let you go to a dance?"

There was nothing but silence. His mom's words hit Elijah so hard, that he started to shed a little tear from his eye. And Madeline was just as unhappy. The sad part was that it was just as far as they would go. Elijah felt speechless and his mom didn't bother pressuring him for the truth, thinking that it was pointless. That's what it was, an estranged relationship between mother and son.

"I just think you should spend a little more time with family" she told him, "I think you owe me that much"

Later that night, Elijah went to bed and cried himself to sleep.

The next day, Elijah's mind just went blank, basically on autopilot. He got up, had breakfast, got ready and arrived at the school. But during that time, Elijah just wasn't paying attention, for that he had no choice to deal with the consequences. Sadly, he didn't talk to Andrew, Paula, or Sabrina, most of the time. He acted normal until he got a moment with Paula during recess.

"I can't go to the dance" he admitted.

"You can't?" Paula said, in disbelief, "The other day you were getting excited, why not?"

"I'm not allowed to go" Elijah said, sadly.

"Aww, Eli" Paula said, with sympathy, as she noticed the sadness in his voice and in his eyes.

"Do you wanna talk?" she offered.

So then they took a walk around the school. Elijah had been holding it for so long that it was coming out in tears, but he did his best to keep it together. He told Paula about what his mom had said to him.

"Aww, I'm sorry" Paula said, sincerely, "To be honest, you can't really blame your mom. She just cares about you that much"

"I know. It's just I was looking forward to..."

Elijah was dying to go the dance just to be with Sabrina. It was a chance to spend time with her after school hours, where they didn't have to worry about schoolwork. Elijah saw that moment fading away and that struck him in the heart. He took a deep breath to prevent himself from breaking down.

"Looking forward to going, you know"

Paula nodded, "I know".

There was nothing else to add. Elijah just sighed and looked away, blankly.

"Well, Eli, the only thing I can tell you is that sometimes the best thing to do is just be honest" Paula told him.

It sounded simple, but there was always some doubt.

"Do you think my mom would let me go if I told her?" Elijah asked.

"I don't think either of us can tell. So there's only one way to find out"

Even if Elijah did tell his mom the truth about all the things that had happened all year, there's a chance that he would be punished for it. And Sabrina, what would his mom think about her? That was one thing that was stopping him; he still wanted Sabrina Clarin in his life. Since his talk with Paula, Elijah's been going from one option to the other, tell or don't tell. And he's been imagining what kind of outcomes for either decision. What if he didn't? Would his mom eventually forget about it and move on? But at the same time, Elijah really wanted to go to the dance but it seemed unlikely that he'd be let off the hook that easily. So for the time being, he thought it would just be pointless altogether and carried on with his day.

As the week was going by, Elijah thought he would forget about it or let the feeling pass. None of that happened. His thoughts were turning on and off. There was no denying or pretending. It was a rather huge deal because whenever he thought about Sabrina, his feelings would urge him to make a decision, and so the dilemma continues. Elijah didn't bother telling her about the fact that he couldn't go to their year-end celebration. He thought about it just for him to get some comfort but that wouldn't really help. Every time Elijah looked at Sabrina, he just wanted to be with her more and more. Maybe it was still a possibility that he might go to the dance.

Being at school was different than being at home. When you're at school, you'd feel that it's your own world, being surrounded by your peers, and ought to do what was best. But at home, there were orders to follow, doing what your parents would say. So when Elijah came home, he just lost all confidence when he fell into the silence that maintained between him and his mom. Sure, she spoke to him but only because it was expected. There were no serious discussions but Elijah still didn't feel any love and he was afraid to say anything.

The wait went on. It was getting tiring and caused a headache for Elijah as he sat in class. He took it one day at a time. Thursday evening, there was nothing but isolation and that brought one long silence. Elijah remained in his room, still sulking about that fact that he wasn't able to go to one social event. After sitting in silence with nothing to do, Elijah found a way to cope with the situation.

He grabbed one of his notebooks, turned all the way to the end to find a blank sheet of lined paper and tore it out. Elijah decided that he was going to write a letter to Sabrina. He wrote down his own words as if he was talking to her in person. It was one way to ease the tension he was feeling and since he probably won't get a chance to spend time with Sabrina like he wanted to, writing a letter was his top priority.

ELIJAH AND SABRINA

So Elijah sat on his bed and wrote the date: *June 21, 2001*, and below that, *Dear, Sabrina Clarin. How are you? Me I'm good. I'm just sitting here, thinking about you and…*

It was a little too silly, just writing how normal people would do it. Elijah didn't find it very satisfying. So he then erased it and started over.

Dear, Sabrina Clarin

There was a short delay, for that Elijah was trying to think of what to say. Maybe writing down what was bothering him might led somewhere.

I'm sorry to tell you this but I can't go to the dance. My mom won't let me, all because of me. I didn't think I was doing anything wrong but I guess I was. I'm sorry if this bothers you because I know I said I wasn't going to be…

That one was too repetitive and petty.

Dear, Sabrina Clarin,

I think you're a great person and very beautiful

Elijah sighed and started over. Next thing he tried was writing something nice.

I'm really glad that we're still friends after all the trouble we been through. I enjoy all the times we hung out. You, me, Andrew, and Paula. I think it would be cool if all of us hung out during summer. At least one day would be fine.

Running into another delay, Elijah began to question himself on whether or not he was really going to give Sabrina Clarin this letter. Was it really worth it? Elijah almost gave up as he went back into his own exile. He kept looking back at the paper he wrote on.

"Sabrina" he muttered.

Then almost right away, Elijah went back to writing a letter just because he wanted to say something so badly to the one girl he truly loved.

Dear, Sabrina Clarin,

I'm writing you this because I want to tell you something but I don't know how. Ever since I met you, a lot of things happened. I was actually mad at your friends because they took you away from me. And I didn't want to hang out with my friends anymore, so that's why I made friends with

Quinton Malcolm. But when I saw you at the store and you talked to me, I actually couldn't believe it. So I'm glad we were still friends after that.

All that excitement was making Elijah a little tired, mentally, because the words were speaking loud and clear in his mind. Once he took a deep breath, he looked over the letter and still didn't live up to his expectations. So he then gazed at the letter, waiting for some sort of magic to happen, like the words would just appear as he thought of it. Letting out a sigh, Elijah realized that it was pointless. There was so much pressure that he couldn't even focus on talking to the one girl he enjoyed talking to. So in the end, Elijah just fell back on his bed as he lost all motivation.

It was finally Friday, the day of the dance. Sabrina was still unaware that Elijah wasn't going to be there. At that point, he considered giving up because it was getting too much to handle. In fact, when school was over, Elijah met with Sabrina outside the entrance. He pretended to be happy but just seeing the beauty through Sabrina's eyes and smile made it genuine.

"Well, tonight's the night" he said.

"I know. Me and the girls are getting excited. Maybe a little nervous, but excited"

Elijah paused to try and find their next conversation.

"So you'll be in charge of the music? That's cool, especially if you-we like music" he told her.

"Yeah, I just hope the other students wouldn't mind it because not everyone likes pop"

"Ask them if they prefer country" Elijah joked.

They both laughed.

"Haha, that's funny" Sabrina replied.

"You know, I'm glad they chose you and your friends to play the music because...you guys like all the good songs"

Elijah was trying to live up to his plan and tell Sabrina that he couldn't go but instead her charm put him in another direction and now Elijah couldn't really keep a conversation going because his mind was just piled with his thoughts.

"Well, we're not the only ones" Sabrina claimed, "Because Mel said a few students from her class were also bringing some CD's. But thank you"

"Oh" Elijah replied.

Their eyes met and didn't say a word for a moment.

"Are you still going?" she asked.

Elijah paused, thinking that it was time to decide. For Sabrina, he would always be honest with her. But he hesitated. For a second, Elijah thought maybe she was counting on him to be there and could be upset if he wasn't. Suddenly he was thinking: do it for her.

"I'll be there" Elijah finally said.

Sabrina smiled, "Great"

"Yeah, cool" he replied.

"Very. Well, I should get going. I'll see you at the dance!"

Sabrina's excitement was so genuine that it awed Elijah. Once she was gone and he turned around, reality came back as he realized what he just did.

"Oh, I'm in deep trouble" Elijah whispered.

As he slowly walked home, Elijah tried to wrap his head around what he just did. He wasn't allowed to go to the dance but he just told Sabrina that he would be there. Of course Elijah cared about her a lot, so much that he'd do anything, even if he rebelled against his mom and go to the dance anyway?

What have I done?

Later that evening, the family dinner was about to commence. Elijah was at home, being forced to dress up. He reluctantly took his black suit and red dress shirt from the closet. After laying them out on the bed, Elijah stared at it, realizing that once he puts it on, he had no choice but to go to the dinner. He was about to break Sabrina's heart. Elijah just sighed with disappointment and began to sulk.

"Why does this have to happen?" he said in a low voice.

Then his mom's voice called from the other room: "Eli, are you ready?"

So it was decided. Elijah's heart sank as he grabbed the dress clothes and put it on.

"I'm sorry, Sabrina" he said, having the urge to cry.

The family dinner was taking place at the Margret Patrick Memorial Hall on the reserve. About a dozen vehicles were parked outside as many family members were arriving. Some of them brought home-cooked meals to the gathering. Elijah helped around for a little while and mingled with his relatives, aunts, uncles, and cousins alike. He shook hands and gave hugs to half the people there. Elijah forced a smile for every meet and greet. There were some friendly conversations he had with the family that helped him take his mind off things. Maybe the evening wouldn't be so bad. For a little while, Elijah was starting to forget about the dance and just acted casual for the dinner. Everyone started to eat after saying a prayer. Elijah had a few plates. The food was good for sure. It was all casual. And then there was one interesting conversation that put Elijah's mind elsewhere when he crossed paths with one of his cousins.

Elijah! Wow, you're getting big. Do you have a girlfriend yet? She teased.

It made him think about Sabrina right away. Elijah just responded with a laugh and gave an honest answer, no he told her.

After that, Elijah's mind left the dinner as Sabrina Clarin was back in his head, along with the dance, followed by his feelings. He looked at the time. The clock displayed quarter to seven. The dance was about to start and he was going to miss it. Then he took out the picture he took of her back in January. The picture was the only access to seeing her.

"Sabrina".

There was nothing he could do about it, even though he promised Sabrina that he was going to make it. Elijah fell deeper into thought. He began to wonder if he should just sneak away. But that would not end well. The more he thought about it, the more eager he was getting. Maybe it was too late. Elijah just sighed and sat back in his seat and slowly ate the scraps from his plate. His mind just went blank again. After a moment, he peered over at his mom, who was socializing with relatives. They were talking and sharing jokes. Just seeing the smile on his mom's face made him realize how much the dinner meant to her and probably meant a lot more having her son there. Now Elijah began to think that maybe he was wrong to neglect her and even started questioning himself, if he had done any good for that year or the years before. He remembered all the bad days when he acted out of anger, which led Elijah to think of how things were before all that. There was happiness, innocence, the simpler days of just being a kid and that was when Elijah found his younger self and the good he had done.

Sometimes the best thing to do is just be honest.

Paula's words replayed in his head. She always saw the possibilities because Elijah didn't always see the big picture for that he was often lost in his emotions. Right then, Elijah realized what he had to do. So he then got up from his seat and went up to his mom.

"Hey mom, can I talk to you?" he asked, gently.

Madeline was quite astonished but also a little nervous, thinking that he might possibly rant out. She led her son outside, where they had some privacy. They both stood on the wooden porch. They looked at each other. Elijah took a deep breath.

"Mom, you were right, about everything"

His mom just stared at him.

"You want me to tell you everything. Here it goes: I met someone"

Elijah remained focus as he locked eyes with his mom. He was finally about to tell her.

"A girl, on the first day of school; her name is Sabrina and she's great, and I like her…I like her more than that, actually. Mom, I fell in love with her"

Deep down, Madeline was aghast, for that she did not expect the truth to involve love.

"I didn't really know it at first, but…it's true. Since then, all I wanted was just a chance to get to know her and I did. We became good friends since September. She actually hung out with me, Paula, and Andrew. But then she made other friends and spent more time with them. I…I was so sad because I didn't get to see her as much as I used to. After a while, I thought maybe she forgot about me. And that was when I decided to hang out with Quinton because I was tired of things being the same. But then being friends with Quinton was a big mistake! I wanted things to go back the way they were but Quinton wouldn't leave me alone. He was the one that started the fight and I fought back because that's how angry I was"

Elijah paused just to work his way through the story. He glanced at his mom, who was giving a sympathetic look.

"That was why I got suspended" he continued, "I felt bad because for the first time I was worried of how the other students looked at me for who I was, especially her. That's when I decided that I didn't want to be like that anymore. And when we went to the store that night in November? I ran into her and she remembered me, like nothing changed! That was why I was so quiet because I was surprised but also grateful.

And the time I was hanging out those 'girls' that was them. I didn't mean to do anything bad. I just wanted to show her that I respected her friends and I guess I got a little carried away. And that day when I left supper because I was mad? It's because Quinton came back to pick on me and he actually picked on Sabrina and that's why I was so angry because of him.

And mom...a few days later, me, Paula, Andrew, and the girl I like, we all teamed up to play against Quinton and his friends, in a basketball game. We won but Quinton just wouldn't stop. So I..." Elijah stopped for a moment as he was about to tell his mom that he done something violent, "I punched him. I punched Quinton. I didn't want to fight, believe me, because I know you don't like it and I'm trying to change that. But Quinton went a little too far and someone had to stop him. After that, he never bothered me or my friends again"

Just telling the story made Elijah feel emotional, so he paused; he actually expected a skeptical reaction from his mom but she remained silent.

"Today she asked me if I was still going to the dance. I was about to say that I couldn't go but then I guess I lied and told her that I was gonna go. I don't know why, I-I just didn't wanna hurt her feelings. I really did want to go to the dance because I thought..." He was about to explain that he might have a chance to be with her, but he wasn't sure if that was promising. So he rephrased: "I just want to see her. This girl made things special. She made my life special. And no other girl has ever done that…So that's it. That's all of it"

No other words could express what Elijah was feeling. So he ended up giving his mom an apologetic look. Madeline was quite speechless and relieved but also sympathetic.

"Elijah…" she finally replied. Her voice was emotionless. For a second, it sounded like she was about to raise her voice or give a lecture, "That's…" she trailed off, for that she had a hard time finding the right words. After another silent moment, the emotional breakthrough happened. Madeline practically chuckled with joy and emerged a tear at the same time and Elijah's heart had lifted.

"Oh, Elijah!" she cried and went in to give her son a hug. Elijah Khoda now felt pretty liberated as he returned the hug. They held each other for a moment. He could hear his mom crying, crying out of joy. It even made him emotional.

"Elijah" Madeline said, as their hug ended, "This is all I ask from you, just to be more open! Thank you for telling me"

Tears burst from Elijah's eyes, but in a good way, "I love you, mom"

"I love you, too"

They never felt so close in their lives. Madeline and Elijah just had to hug each other again.

"So that's what it was all along, love?" she said, sincerely.

"Yeah" Elijah said. He wanted to say more. He wanted to tell her about Sabrina and just how amazing she was but he was just speechless at that point after telling his story.

Madeline chuckled, "Wow, you're growing up. I don't believe it, but it's also amazing, especially when you found someone that shows you love".

It was a great relief because all that time Madeline thought her son was filled with hatred. Now she knew that he discovered the beauty in life.

"Yeah" Elijah repeated, "Oh mom, I'm sorry, for all the bad things that happened, the fights and all the arguments. I'm sorry"

His mom just held his face for a moment. That was probably her way of accepting his apology.

"Well, I guess we better head back in" Elijah suggested.

He went up to open the door. Madeline however stood to think for a moment. Since her son finally made up for everything, maybe he earned something special.

"Eli" she called.

Elijah turned around and caught her eye.

"Do you still wanna go to the dance?"

Amazingly shocked, Elijah froze and his eyes just widened. "Really? Right now?" he said.

His mom just nodded, "It starts at seven, right?"

"Y-yeah, I think it's seven o'clock right now actually. So I can go?"

"I think you earned it" Madeline told him.

Elijah started to smile. It was so genuine; it made him excited, almost made him want to cheer. After everything was settled, the relationship between Elijah and his mom was no longer strained. It was another step in Elijah's growth. Now he didn't need to hide from his mom anymore. Since he was granted permission, Elijah just had to get to the dance. So he asked his dad to drop him off at the school.

CHAPTER TWENTY-SIX

Dancing the Night Away

"Thanks for the ride, dad" Elijah said, humbly.

"No problem. Are you gonna need a ride later or are you gonna walk?"

"I think I'll walk" Elijah opened the passenger door to step out, "See you later"

"See you. Have fun"

Elijah closed the door and pretty much ran towards the main entrance of the school. After coming up on the steps, he gazed through the glass windows and saw a couple of teachers loitering around and a few students just entering the gym. Once Elijah entered the building, he could already hear the music echoing.

"Hello" one of the teachers greeted, kindly.

"Hi" Elijah replied, in the same manner.

"Ready to have fun?" she asked.

"Oh yeah"

Then the other teacher added, "You look like you're ready".

She was referring to Elijah's suit. He almost forgot that he was wearing it. It wasn't exactly the attire he thought he'd wear to the event but it was hardly important at that point.

"Yeah, pretty much" he agreed.

It was time. Elijah went up to the gym doors; he quickly glanced through the windows and noticed only a few lights within the darkened gym, followed by a few silhouettes in the background. He opened the doors and stepped into the dance but what he saw wasn't what he really expected.

The music was playing fairly loud, maybe not as loud as he imagined. That was just one thing. Nobody was really dancing, except a few girls that were on the dance floor. Elijah cocked his head to the left and saw everybody else just standing around. It was hardly exciting.

"Huh" Elijah muttered.

He took it all in and then he went looking for his friends. First place Elijah went to was to where the other students were hanging out. It wasn't just his classmates but the other grade seven classes as well.

"E.K!" Andrew called, loud enough for Elijah to hear. It took him a moment to see Andrew because it was quite dark and he could be anywhere in the crowd. He scanned the whole area until he saw Andrew approaching him, followed by Paula.

"Eli!" she called, "You made it!"

"Yeah, I was allowed to come after all" Elijah told her, proudly, "After I talked to my mom, she said I could go"

Paula was just happy for him, "Well, that's great"

"Very great"

Andrew noticed Elijah's suit, "Look at you, James Bond".

That compliment made him feel more comfortable in the suit. "Why, thank you" Elijah replied, casually. Then he noticed that his friends were dressed more casually, along with half the students there. Elijah couldn't help but feel a little exposed.

"Am I the only one that dressed up?" he asked.

"Uhhh" Andrew peered around and saw a few students dressed semi-formally, "Nope, doesn't look like it"

"Phew"

Now that he had Paula and Andrew, the only one missing was Sabrina. Elijah looked around. Most of the gym was shaded, so it was hard to see the faces around.

"Well, this looks like fun" Elijah said, sarcastically. He was about to ask if his friends seen Sabrina anywhere but he didn't want to sound too desperate.

"Yeah, it's not really a dance" Paula added, "More like a hang-out event and the music is just to kill the awkward silence"

The music stopped for a moment, putting the gym in silence. Elijah looked and saw a few girls at the stereo that was hooked to the speakers above the gym. The stereo was on a table, along with a lamp next to it.

"Just trying to find another song!" one of the voices called out. That familiar voice caught Elijah's attention. It was Melanie. If she was there, Sabrina had to be there as well. Shortly, music started playing again. The girls immediately started dancing. As the song was getting excited, the girls turned around and with a little light, Elijah saw Sabrina. She was there!

"Sabrina!" Elijah called, as he approached her, with Paula and Andrew following.

"Elijah, hey!" Sabrina replied, loud enough over the music.

Melanie and Carly were still dancing as Sabrina was mingling.

"You're here" Elijah just couldn't hide his excitement.

"Of course; nice to see that you made it" Sabrina said, kindly.

"Why are you guys the only ones dancing?"

"I know, right? It seems like everyone doesn't want, even after they voted for the dance"

They quickly glanced over at the other students, who were still loitering on the other side of the gym. Then Melanie danced her way to the group.

"Elijah" she said, as she was still dancing, "Wanna help us get the dance going?"

"Me?"

"Yeah, if they see us dancing, our classmates just might want to do the same. Plus, Sabrina said that you were a good dancer"

Elijah automatically looked at Sabrina, who smiled and shrugged her shoulders modestly. That compliment got him considering the girls' idea.

"Alright" he agreed, then he looked over at Paula and Andrew, "You guys up for this?"

"I'm up for anything!" Andrew replied, almost excitedly.

"You guys can go ahead" Paula told them, "I'm gonna get something to drink"

Then Elijah nodded his head to acknowledge, "Okay".

And so the dance began. Elijah looked at Andrew next to him, who was already warming up. Then he glanced to Sabrina, who still had the smile on her face as she went to regroup with her girlfriends. None of them spoke. Only the lyrics were about to be the only voice in the gym. Now the sound of music had consumed the place. Elijah and Andrew both started to move slowly to the rhythm. As the song picked up, they danced a little more excitedly and then they joined the girls, who were having just as much fun.

After the song was over, they all stopped to rest for a brief moment. They allowed the CD to keep playing as they spoke. "Well, that didn't really work!" Melanie exclaimed, as she gazed at the other students that still loitered around.

"Yeah, might as well send them home and have the place to ourselves" Carly said, jokingly.

"That's fine with me"

"I'm sure they'll join us soon" Sabrina assured.

Then Andrew expressed his idea, "Let's just tell them that this will affect their grades or else they will have to become play toys for gorillas at the zoo"

Melanie began to giggle, while Carly just looked at him, oddly. "What?" she replied. And then Andrew just started laughing at his own joke.

The dance continued. A few other students from other classes finally joined the dance floor. It was picking up.

The next song that played was Happy Boys and Girls by Aqua. Elijah spent the next moment gaining confidence as he allowed the music to feed energy to him. It started off with him alone while the others were dancing. Elijah developed his own routine as he went from moving slowly to a fast pace. He made sure that his dancing matched the rhythm of the song. Elijah soon found himself dancing around the group, for that he was in his own world. It was upbeat and energetic. Once he felt that it was time, Elijah leaped into the air and onto the dance floor and used every move he learned from the past few months. Everyone around him was surprised just how natural Elijah was as he was stealing the show. Some of the girls even started cheering for him.

Once the other students heard the excitement, they became intrigued. Once more students joined the dance floor, everyone finally joined.

"Wooo!" Melanie cheered, after the song ended, "Now that's more like it!"

The next song started and the dance began. Now the event became more fun when everyone finally danced. They all crowded in the center of the gym floor. All three grade seven classes were pretty much dancing together. A few of them moved from one place to another.

As the CD continued playing, some of the students left the dance floor to take a break. There was a table against the wall that held plenty of baked treats, followed by some juice and water. That's where Paula was most of the time. Elijah grabbed himself juice and took a sip. Both he and Paula stood and watched everyone else having a good time.

Elijah leaned over to his best friend, "How come you're not dancing?" he asked, over the sound of music.

Paula leaned closer to talk into Elijah's ear, "I can't dance" she said, honestly. Elijah could've left it alone, but a thought occurred to him almost right away.

"Come with me" he encouraged.

Elijah and Paula stepped outside the dance and into the hall where it was quiet.

"So you can't dance" Elijah stated.

"You say that like you're onto something" Paula told him.

"I can teach you"

"N-no, it's okay" Paula explained it, gently. She wasn't ashamed to admit it. "Really, just as long as I'm here with you guys, I'll have just as much fun as everyone else"

Elijah paused to think, "What if we're all dancing, which we are, and...you're just standing there?"

"It wouldn't bother me" Paula promised.

The need wasn't as desperate as Elijah thought but he felt like he should leave Paula with something.

"Okay, but how about I teach something at least?"

In silence, Paula was considering the offer, "Sure. I don't see why not"

"Yeah, okay" Elijah said. He then cleared his throat as he was about to show a little lesson in dancing, "Well, uh, I never actually had to teach someone to dance. So..."

Paula waited patiently.

"Well, you don't have to be a great dancer. You can just start off slow. You know, let the music move you"

"Okay?" Paula replied, like it wasn't convincing enough.

"It can be something like this..."

Elijah had to think for a moment. Then he started turning with his waist, left and right, gracefully. And then he began nodded his head to the music, which didn't sound very distant. The rhythm had Elijah going, for that he added another move to his teaching. He started circling Paula by walking sideways, and then he twirled and started jumping up and down, twirled again, and finally ended it with a landing.

"Ta-da?" Elijah said, mildly.

"That was pretty good, Eli"

"Thanks. So yeah, you just pretty much do it, don't have to think about it, just go along. If you have to, just copy everyone else's dancing. That's what I did from watching music videos on TV"

"You gave me something to think about"

Elijah nodded, "Alright".

The dance went on. Elijah made it back to the crowd, where Andrew was. Both of them danced side by side, with everyone around them. Each of them were lost into the music, for that they were not in class, no lessons, no schoolwork, just fun. Shortly, Elijah made his way towards Sabrina, who was dancing away with her girlfriends. He acted casual until she saw him. So then Sabrina gestured Elijah to come join them.

Of course he did without hesitation. He danced with her, Melanie, and Carly. The gang was together again, like when they hung out a few months ago. Before the song was over, Andrew decided to jump in the center and show off. He was doing rather silly moves. Some of the girls laughed, but Melanie cheered him on. Elijah did the same by shouting, *Go, Andrew!* The song ended. The girls celebrated their fun by cheering and that sent a good vibe to many of their peers.

As soon as the next song started, Elijah made his way to Sabrina. She noticed him and they both started dancing together. It was just those two. Andrew was with Melanie and Carly in their circle. Elijah and Sabrina danced face to face. They were showing off each other's unique moves like they did a few months ago. This time, Elijah's dancing had a beginning, middle, and an end. Sabrina was impressed. It was a perfect moment, the kind that Elijah once imagined, both he and Sabrina in their own world. If only it would last forever.

After all the excitement the students built up, many of them were starting to tire out. So that was when the girls decided to start a slow song next. Not all the students were keen on slow dancing. Therefore, half the crowd stepped aside while the others paired up with a partner. This was one opportunity Elijah just couldn't let pass. He was about to run towards Sabrina to ask for a dance, until he glanced over at the side of the gym and saw Paula leaning against the wall. For some reason, he felt a little bad. Then he thought maybe she was waiting for him to teach any further dancing lessons. The slow song already commenced; it was Hope by Shaggy. So Elijah just decided to ask Paula and show her a good time. He went up to her, and without saying anything, he offered her his hand. Their eyes met for a moment. And out of kindness, Paula accepted. Instead of putting her hand in his, she gently reached for his wrist. Elijah escorted her to the dance floor and there they held each other and moved slowly to the music. It wasn't long until Elijah felt Paula's foot step on his. Gently, he backed away as they still had their arms around each other.

"Sorry" she said, casually, over the music, "Told you I couldn't dance"

"But you're a good learner" Elijah told her, "After all, you taught me how to read, I'll teach you how to dance"

Paula formed a proud smile on her face. Her best friend really was different, from the way he spoke; he seemed wiser than before, pointing out facts from a different standpoint, a point where he learned a lot after going through rough times. It definitely wasn't the same Elijah from last October. Sabrina Clarin must've changed him for the better, Paula thought. She couldn't remember the last time that Elijah showed heart, but she remembered the times when he pretended he was okay. Even then, Paula sensed the distress in his voice. But at that moment, during the dance, Elijah felt human and proud. As she continued holding him, Paula could feel his warmth, a genuine feeling.

"Great" Elijah said, clapping his hand once the slow song was over, "You did great"

Paula smiled, "All thanks to you"

"Glad I can help".

The CD changed to the next track, where the song had a different tone, fast paced and energetic. Elijah and Paula just stood there, taking it all in. Before he knew it, Paula slowly started moving to the rhythm, using the exact move that he showed her. Their eyes met and smiled once the excitement picked up. Soon, Andrew found them and joined in on the fun. The team that had been best friends for years came together and started dancing. It was hard for Elijah to think that he once wanted to end his friendship with Paula and Andrew. As he danced with them, Elijah realized how lucky he was to have them by his side. After all, they put up with his flaws over the years. So that meant they were Elijah's true friends.

After a little while, many of the students took a break. They went towards the snack table, grabbed a drink and a bite to eat, and relaxed. The music was still on to keep the vibe going. Elijah stayed with Paula and Andrew for the time being, until he saw Sabrina and her friends leaving the gym. He wanted at least one moment with Sabrina alone. So then Elijah excused himself and towards the gym doors. Through the window, he saw Sabrina talking with Melanie and Carly. He was literally about to come out to say hi to them but as the door was partly open, Elijah decided to wait at the last minute, thinking that was probably somewhat rude if he interrupted them.

So Elijah acted normal and stayed close to the doors. He glanced over every minute. Then one last look, he realized they weren't in sight. So Elijah went up to the door again, peered through the window and the back of Sabrina's head, but her friends were not there. Elijah pretended he was heading somewhere else as he walked through the doors. Her back was still turned, for that she was facing the main entrance. Elijah slowly walked passed her.

"Sabrina" he greeted, gently.

As she turned around, Elijah finally looked up and met her eyes.

"Hi, Elijah" she replied, with a smile.

"Hi"

"Are you having fun?" she asked.

"Lots of fun. You?"

"Maybe a little too much fun" she answered with a chuckle, "Just kidding"

Elijah stopped where he was once he had Sabrina's attention. He was about to make up a story on why he was passing through, for that he didn't want Sabrina to think that he was following her. Then he remembered what his dad told him, if you want to have a serious conversation with a girl, you have to mean what you say.

"I just wanted to say hi" he told her.

"Well, you're always welcomed to" Sabrina encouraged.

There was a little pause for that their little greeting reminded Elijah of their first interaction on the first day of school. After saying the word hi, he said to her, *I just wanted to say hi,* and she replied, *You just did.* Thinking about day one just brought a smile to his face. Sabrina noticed and just smiled back.

"Where are your friends?" he asked.

Without saying anything, Sabrina just pointed behind her, where the girls' restroom was.

"Oh" Elijah replied.

"Yeah" Sabrina went up to him and spoke in a low voice, "Carly doesn't like going to the washroom alone, at least not in a public place"

Elijah had no comment. Sabrina just froze once she realized what she did.

"I didn't know why I told you that" she admitted. Then she noticed that she was speaking fairly loud. So Sabrina quickly glanced over at her shoulder just to make sure her friends weren't standing there. "Hopefully they didn't hear me" she whispered.

"I don't think so" Elijah whispered back, with confidence, "Don't worry I won't say anything".

Sabrina mouthed the words, thank you.

From there, they acted normal and pretended like the conversation never took place. There was a lost and found box between the two restrooms. Sabrina leaned on it, while Elijah leaned against the wall across from her.

"Great music" Elijah said.

"Yeah" Sabrina agreed, "It's fun that we're in charge of the music. I just hope they like the songs that we play"

"Well at least I enjoy it. And I'm sure there are other kids who don't mind it"

"I guess that's all that matters, having fun"

Elijah nodded. It was silent for a moment. He had to think of what to talk about next. Then Sabrina was gazing at Elijah's suit.

"Nice suit" Sabrina told him.

"Oh" Elijah glanced down at his attire, "Thanks. I actually wanted to wear something else instead of this-these clothes. It's a little silly"

"Don't say that. Elijah, you look nice"

With that compliment coming from his special friend, it made Elijah felt more comfortable in his formal clothing. "Thanks" he replied.

Then he noticed the formal clothing Sabrina was wearing. She had a dark blue long sleeved blouse, with an image of a rose in the center. She also wore a skirt and nylons underneath. It was a different look that brought out the beauty of Sabrina Clarin.

"You look nice as well" Elijah told her.

"Thank you" Sabrina replied, with flattery.

"And the rose too, that's pretty cool"
"Yeah, I love it"

There were no words that could describe just how beautiful she looked. The smile on her face convinced Elijah that what he said was enough. He spent half his time admiring her. Out of boredom, Sabrina went from leaning on the lost and found box to sitting on the thin ledge. She even lifted her feet off the floor as she practiced balancing herself.

"Be careful not to fall in" Elijah told her.

"Yeah" Sabrina laughed, "I'll be joining all these sweaters and hats"

A bored thought came to Elijah and just went for it just because he wanted to be with Sabrina. He went up to the wooden box and sat beside her. Doing the same thing as her, Elijah sat on the thin ledge and balanced.

"We'll get lost together" Sabrina joked.

"Then we'll find each other" Elijah added.

They both laughed as they settled down and sat on the ledge gently. Elijah felt Sabrina's hand slightly touching his. He glanced at it and realized how close it was but he didn't give it any further thought and just enjoyed Sabrina's company.

"Or I found you" Elijah said.

Sabrina turned her head and met Elijah's eyes. "What?" she asked.

"I found you?" he repeated. It was a temptation to say something about their friendship and Elijah said the first thing that came to mind. "I mean the first day we met, I found myself a new friend, you"

Sabrina didn't say anything but she was starting to see what he meant.

"Well, it's not like you were lost or anything" he added.

Sabrina looked away as Elijah's words made her recap that time in her life when she moved away from home. She remembered all the doubt she had and the trouble that she experienced from before the move. Sabrina didn't realize how much she changed since then.

"Or maybe I was" Sabrina admitted.

"Yeah? You were lost?"

"Mhm" Sabrina looked at Elijah again, as she came close to telling him about what she had been through but just didn't know where to start. The opportunity was gone. Sabrina peered at the gym doors, thinking that somebody was about to come through any minute.

"I guess we better get off the lost and found box before a teacher comes and yells at us"

They did as she suggested. Next they heard Melanie's voice coming from the girls' washroom. "Sabrinaaaa?" Mel sang.

"Whaaat?" Sabrina replied in the same manner.

Then Melanie came around the corner and continued singing, "Carly wants your opinion on something!"

Sabrina turned to Elijah, "I'll catch up with you later" she promised.

"Okay, see ya" Elijah replied.

Sabrina went with Melanie into the girls' washroom and Elijah went back into the gym. He was glad that he had a moment with Sabrina Clarin…And it certainly wouldn't be the last.

Elijah made best with the time that he had and kept on dancing. At one point, his dance moves were quite unique that he stole the show. It was Andrew who started chanting his best friend's name and the girls chanted along.

Elijah! Elijah! Elijah! Elijah!

He certainly didn't expect that but he had fun.

Once everyone got into the spirit of the event, Melanie asked if they were interested in dancing to Cadillac Ranch. Not only half the class expressed interest but one of the teachers was also keen on the idea. So the song started and the students and their teacher began dancing just like what they learned in gym class.

In the end, all that fun was taking much energy out of the students. The girls figured it was time to slow things down again. Once Elijah heard this, he thought it was time to share a dance with the one girl that he cared about the most. The song was already starting. Some of the students were pairing up. Elijah quickly went to find his partner. Sabrina was near the stereo. He sprinted across the dance floor like it was an obstacle course. From the distance, Elijah could see that Sabrina was alone. It was definitely his time to have a special moment with her like he planned from the beginning. It felt like it took forever but Elijah finally arrived. He stopped in front of Sabrina, panting but he managed to keep it together. Once their eyes met, Elijah offered his hand. The song only started seconds ago, so it wasn't too late.

He was holding his breath until she took his hand, just like that! It felt like a scene from a movie, where the boy and girl had a special bond and they were about to express it in a beautiful and profound way.

As they were making their way to the dance floor, Elijah really couldn't believe that he was about to slow dance with Sabrina Clarin. It was felt like a dream that he was actually holding Sabrina's hand. And he couldn't believe the opportunity came that easily. That must mean that he was lucky to have built a friendship with a girl that he never thought he would meet and develop feelings for her. Maybe Elijah didn't really believe it at all…and it was all magical.

In the middle of the other dancing couples, Elijah and Sabrina faced each other, their eyes met and then he gently placed his left hand on Sabrina's hip, while she placed her right hand on his shoulder, and finally their other hands interlocked and held it. And so began this beautiful moment.

The lyrics of the song, Truly Madly Deeply by Savage Garden, called to them and moved them gracefully. To begin with, Elijah and Sabrina acknowledged each other by locking onto each other's eyes. There was just enough light to see the beautiful soul looking back at him, like it did from day one. Seeing was just one thing, but feeling truly expressed a lot of emotions. Just by holding Sabrina close, Elijah could feel the comfort, joy, and there was a certain level of love that they both felt, a love that they couldn't really express.

They were simply two kids, who hadn't experienced such a thing. And after all they had been through in that point in their lives, they earned that moment of happiness, for that they were about to take another step in a new part of their lives, their teenage years. It was nice to know that there was still some good in this life and it was something to hang onto as they were about to become something greater.

Sabrina knew that love would take the pain away. Before she realized she was thinking of intimacy but what she needed was love from a friend. And Elijah was that friend. Knowing him, she felt safe, stronger in a way, and appreciated for who she was, especially all the doubt she had for herself on the first day of school. She was grateful that he went up to her and said hi. So as they danced slowly, Sabrina went in closer and wrapped both her arms around Elijah and he did the same. Sabrina closed her eyes, as she rested her head on Elijah's shoulder, and took in all the comfort.

All the time in the world had slowed down, long enough for the couple to enjoy. Elijah felt the warmth of Sabrina's upper body as he held her close and her long dark brown hair blanketing against the side of his face. It was much greater than he imagined, holding someone that special close to him. And for a minute there, it actually felt like that moment was going to go on forever. In that moment, Elijah only saw himself and Sabrina as the only ones in the gym and no other soul in sight. It was the kind of life he wanted, just the two of them in their own perfect world.

After holding each other for a little while, Elijah broke apart and now he was holding Sabrina by her hands. He decided to make the best of it and twirled around and Sabrina did the same. Then he pulled her close and gently stepped back, repeatedly and rhythmically. They smiled at each other. After that, Elijah held Sabrina's hand above her head, while she started twirling around like a ballerina. It was just like what they saw in the movies where a man and a woman were ballroom dancing. Sabrina felt like a Disney princess and that brought a lot of pride to her. As the song was nearly over, Elijah and Sabrina went back to the simple slow dancing, putting their arms around each other and held each other for a long moment. If only time slowed down for Elijah to spend his youth with Sabrina, but sooner or later, it was time to go back into reality.

The slow song had ended and another song started. All the dancing couples around broke apart as they were about to dance to a different beat. Elijah and Sabrina stood there for a short period of time, looking at each other. They were both lost in thought after the wonderful dance they just had. Maybe they were still miles away from reality. Everyone else continued dancing around them, but for Elijah and Sabrina, it took them a moment to catch up with the others. Perhaps they didn't have to, not yet. While Elijah still had her close to him, he leaned to her ear, "Wanna hang outside?" he asked.

Sabrina didn't say anything. She just looked at him and nodded. Yes, it was going great. So Elijah left the gym with Sabrina by his side. They went through the doors, where the music faded once they were closed. Elijah relaxed, as he felt like he was breathing in fresh air after being in that gymnasium.

"Well, that was…" Sabrina was trying to think of a word.

"Beautiful" Elijah finished.

"I was gonna say great, but…yeah. It did feel beautiful. Thank you"

Elijah only smiled at her. Then he glanced towards the main entrance, realizing that nobody was around.

"Come on" he insisted, as he started walking.

Sabrina walked by his side. They walked in silence, in the empty school. Elijah was trying to think of something to say. Sabrina was gazing at the hallways at both sides. They were closed and locked off for the evening. Then she scanned the surroundings, where there was the main office and the library across from it, and between it was the entrance to the outside world. Sabrina looked at the hallways again and imagined the lives of their peers walking around in their daily life.

"Felt like I been going here for years" Sabrina said.

"Yeah?"

"Yeah, I know it seems a little crazy but it just kinda feels like I been spending a lifetime here"

"Well, there's nothing crazy about that" Elijah told her, "I guess that means Burns Lake is pretty much your new home"

Sabrina nodded, "Must be".

They went further down towards the hallway. Sabrina was examining the trophy displays. Then the couple stopped at the closed doors, facing the other side of the school where the lower grades resided.

"Can't believe it's been years ago since we were in grade four" Elijah said, "That's where it all started, down there to the right side is my old class room"

"I'm guessing that hall is the same as our side?"

"Yup, pretty much the same, all the tables and the computers"

"Neat"

After that, they continued walking. Just before the school library, there was a phone on the wall.

"You ever tried this?" Elijah asked.

"No, I haven't" Sabrina replied, "I noticed it on the first day of school but didn't think much of it. It's for anybody to use?"

"Yeah, one time Andrew used it to phone his parents after school"

Just for the fun of it, Elijah picked up the receiver, put up to his year and it still worked.

"Still works" he told her.

Then Sabrina joked, "Make a prank call"

Elijah chuckled, "Order some pizza".

They started laughing. Elijah hung up the phone, gently. After that, Elijah and Sabrina moved onto the school library. Together, they gazed at the interior where one side was filled with tables and chairs, while the other side had all the book shelves.

"The library here is nice" Sabrina said, "I like the windows and how we can see the outside world, just seems peaceful"

"Yeah, it's nice. You should see the one at Muriel Mould-well you probably won't because you don't have to go there-but the one there was nice also. It was right in the center of the building and it has four book shelves on the corner and in the middle of the floor there's a hole where we all sat"

"That does sound nice"

They both turned back to the library. "You know it's kinda weird" Elijah added, "When there's a book fair, I get excited about it, even though I don't really read. I always had a hard time reading and trying to finish it. But I always liked the book fairs for some reason"

"Nothing weird about that. I got a few books from a fair that I didn't finish reading"

"Oh, guess that's two of us" Elijah agreed, "I did get one of those I Spy books"

"There you go. Those are always fun"

"I think they were everyone's favorite book"

"I think so, too"

Once the conversation ended, Elijah led Sabrina towards the office and from there they stood and gazed outside the window. Going in for a closer look, they leaned against the beams. It was a beautiful evening. The sun was setting and there were only a few clouds in the sky. Sabrina relaxed and admired the view. Elijah couldn't ask for a better evening than having a girl next to him. He stood in silence and enjoyed the comfort.

During that moment, Sabrina started thinking about her past when her troubles could've put her on a different path. It was hard to imagine what kind of person Sabrina Clarin would be, had she fallen into that abyss of sadness. She felt like she took a leap of faith somewhere along the way and couldn't pinpoint where exactly. It took her a moment to think but ended up with nothing. It nearly frustrated her. In the end, she rested her head against the window. Elijah thought he heard a sigh, as if it was a call for attention.

"You're alright, Sabrina?" Elijah asked, gently.

"Oh, I'm fine, it's just..." Sabrina lifted her head up and reconnected with the nature in front of her and it put her mind back to focus, "Clarins are always up for a challenge" she said. Then she turned and faced Elijah, "It's our family motto. This whole time; I thought it meant something like just doing your schoolwork or doing chores at home when you think you can't do it. But last year, there was one challenge I didn't think I would have to face one day"

Before going any further, Sabrina turned away from the window and sat down on the bench. Elijah joined her and listened.

"There was a boy in my class. His name was Zach Epstad. He didn't like me that much. This one day, he got mad at me just for being smart in class. During recess I was just playing around and having fun. I wanted to climb the monkey bars. He and his friends were hanging out there and he wouldn't let me. He pretty much chased me away. I told my brother about it. He wanted to teach him a lesson, most likely by fighting. And I got so scared, I just told Jonathan to forget about it because I didn't want to see him get hurt.

We never had to deal with him again. We just left him alone and he left us alone. I thought it was over but then later on I realized it was still bothering me. So that day when Quinton was picking on me in front of you, that reminded me of Zach and that was why I ran off, but I felt bad after a while and I also felt scared, so scared that I was only worried about myself. A few days later, I had a talk with my dad and that made me feel better. He told me that if you run from your problems, they will chase after you.

You know, I used to think that my life was perfect. I have a nice home, nice family, and a sun in the sky. I'm always thankful when I go to bed at night and then I wake up the next day, I'm dealing with bullies all of a sudden. I didn't think I would have to face such a challenge. I guess all I needed was a little courage. So after talking with my dad, I came here. I'm sorry that I wasn't very helpful to begin with"

"No" Elijah replied, gently, "It's all right. I mean, after all, you came". Then he was about to explain how her absence affected him that day but that didn't matter. It was all in the past now. "And that's the part that counts" he added.

That gave the story a whole new meaning once Elijah saw it from Sabrina's perspective. That time, he literally thought that Sabrina ended their friendship but it was all because she had problems of her own that would've made her behave in unintentional ways. It was just what Ken said to Elijah during one of their sessions. It all made sense now.

"I'm sorry about Quinton, Sabrina" Elijah added, "It was actually my fault. We were friends last year but being friends with him was wrong. So I just left him. I guess I just left him at a bad time-it's a long story-but he was mad at me. He must've been that mad because he wanted to fight until he felt better. But he won't be bothering us anymore. Just so you know, Sabrina, I never told him anything about you. I...think it was Devon that might've...Like I said, it's a long story"

"Elijah, it's all right" she told him, "It doesn't matter now"

"I was running from my problems, too" he admitted, "I didn't wanna deal with them anymore. When I first started having problems, I was told just to walk away. So I guess that's what I was trying to do all this time but no matter how many times I did, they just wouldn't leave me alone"

Sabrina just looked at him with sympathy.

"Yeah, it wasn't fun and it also pretty confusing. I mean, how come I can't even walk away if my problems don't wanna stop bothering me, you know? All I want to do is just be me. I like who I am, I like the friends that I have and I like coming to school. I know there are bad days but sometimes you just gotta make the best of it. And that's what I'm going to do because I just wanna keep having fun, while I can"

Sabrina nodded, "Well, I think that makes two of us" she said, with a soft smile and Elijah did the same thing. Their deep conversation was over. They both sat there and let all their words sink in. Before they knew it, they were liberated from their sorrows, for that they had each other.

Elijah then glanced over at Sabrina, just to see how she was doing. She could feel his eyes looking to her. So she turned her head slightly and gazed at Elijah. Even though Elijah had made eye contact with Sabrina so many times, there was something about this one that felt different in a good way. Perhaps it was the sunlight that brought out the brightness in her eyes and/or she was looking in a genuine way. But this moment could be a lot more. Elijah opened his mouth, as he tempted to say the first words that came to his mind but he hesitated and ended up just keeping his eyes forward.

"What is it?" Sabrina asked.

"What is what?"

"Kinda looked like you were about to say something"

"I was but then I thought no it's kind of silly"

Sabrina was giving her full attention and then Elijah peered slightly to his left, only to see those beautiful eyes.

"I don't mind a little silly" she told him.

That brought Elijah's confidence back up. "I was gonna say...that... they say staring isn't nice, but it kinda is when you and I do it"

Mentioning themselves in particular just slipped out of Elijah's mouth; then the thought of Sabrina getting uncomfortable from him just for expressing himself and it would be a step closer to breaking out the truth that he was in love with her. But she in fact stared at him. Elijah caught her gaze but he was actually waiting patiently for her to say something until-

"I win" Sabrina spoke, nearly triumphantly, "You blinked"

Elijah relaxed with relief and also with joy, "Oh, haha, I guess I did"

"Yeah, staring can be nice, I suppose, depends on who it is"

"A friend?" Elijah suggested, "Or a good friend?"

Sabrina could tell that Elijah was having trouble finding the right word to describe it.

"How about a best friend?" she offered, sincerely.

Quite astonished, Elijah felt like he won that title. From day one, he always saw Sabrina as a new best friend and knowing that she looked at him in that way also meant a lot to him.

"I like that, actually" he replied.

Then they smiled at each other.

Probably the best thing about their relationship is that they been through hard times, although Elijah never thought that it would happen, but yet they still maintained their friendship and respect for each other. There was a great amount of joy within Elijah that he just had to let out somehow, whether it was giving Sabrina a hug, a pat on the back, or holding her hand. He even glanced at her hand for a brief moment, but the only response he could give was a warming smile. After that, Elijah glanced to his left and saw the empty office.

"Looks like we're in trouble" he joked, "You and me sitting here"

"We are bad, BAD kids" Sabrina added and then started giggling.

"Might as well suspend both of us"

"Yay! No school for us"

"Ha-ha, so long suckers!"

The sound of their laughter echoed throughout the hall. Soon after they settled down, Elijah started tapping his foot on the floor and he turned his head slightly towards Sabrina as he did. Sabrina responded by tapping her foot as well, but hers was faster. They both took turns tapping their feet and shortly at the same time, grinning from ear to ear and giggling under their breath. And as for a friendly competition, Elijah gently kicked Sabrina in her ankle and she returned the favor.

Now those moments were the best kinds, the ones that weren't planned. They just happen. And neither Elijah or Sabrina were thinking, only going wherever their hearts took them as they sat close to each other, as best friends.

"Now we're playing footsies" Sabrina said, casually, as she and Elijah had their eyes on the floor.

"Yeah" Elijah replied. He indirectly moved his foot against Sabrina's and she played along by tapping her foot against his ankle.

Shortly, the silence ended once the gym doors and the music in the background grew louder briefly until the door closed. It was Melanie and Carly.

"Sabrina?" Mel called, "There you are!"

The girls started approaching. Elijah and Sabrina got up from the bench.

"Did you miss me?" Sabrina asked.

"Of course" Carly admitted, "Dance is getting boring without you"

"So boring that I thought I had to make friends with the students I don't really talk to and they probably wouldn't be as Sabrina as you" Melanie told her.

Sabrina wanted to say something just as clever, "Can't think of anything cool to say" she said, "But yeah, me and Elijah were just hanging out"

"Just hanging out" Elijah agreed, "But we're pretty much done"

"Great" Melanie said, "Now I think we should do our little dance?"

"Yeah, sure" Sabrina replied, reluctantly, "I'll do it if you guys do"

"That's why we're here"

"I am a little nervous" Carly added.

"A dance?" Elijah asked.

"It's a dance show that we prepared for tonight" Sabrina explained, "We been practicing all week for it. We thought, why not?"

"We watched the movie Bring it On just to get a few ideas" Melanie told him.

"Sounds like fun" Elijah said, "And Carly, I think you'll do great"

"Thank you" she replied, kindly.

"Alright, ready spaghetti?" Sabrina asked.

Melanie just looked at her and started laughing.

"That's pretty clever" she told him.

"Yeah, it's something my dad usually says" Sabrina added. As her friends started walking back to the gym, she then gave Elijah a meaningful look, "Let's go have some fun"

They were all back in the gym, with their peers all around. Sabrina, Melanie, and Carly, were gathered together on the dance floor. Elijah even offered to provide their music while they were in positions. He pushed the play button on the stereo and the show had begun.

Sabrina quickly started dancing as if it was a reflex to the rhythm. She was showing off her own moves and then Carly cleared her mind and did her moves, even when she was nervous, she still performed like nobody was watching. Once her number was over, Carly froze just like what Sabrina did, and that gave Melanie her cue to dance. As the music picked up momentum, all three of them finally danced together. Some of their classmates began cheering for them as the girls danced gracefully. Sabrina was quite the natural, for that she moved to every beat of the song and she carried that rhythm until the song ended. Everyone in the gym applauded. Elijah was amazed by their musical number. He even went up to each of them and told them what a great job they done.

The girls took a break from all that dancing and mingled. Elijah decided to have a little fun, for that he discovered a particular CD over by the stereo. While no one was looking, he put the CD in and pushed play once he reached the song he wanted.

The gymnasium was quiet and then the next thing Sabrina heard was the song Mambo No. 5. Only one person came to mind when that song played. She turned around and saw Elijah with a mischievous grin on his face. As the song started to build up, he danced his way to her.

ELIJAH AND SABRINA 457

"That's right, you have to dance to this one!" he taunted.

Sabrina made a face at Elijah, as she started dancing, reluctantly. Then everyone else joined in on the fun. She went up closer to his ear, "Now you have to dance to Short Skirt Long Jacket"

Elijah just shrugged his shoulders and didn't say a word. In the end, he lived up to the agreement.

For the next song, all the students crowded the floor again. And this time, Elijah, Andrew, and Paula, got together and danced with Sabrina and her friends, and enjoyed every minute of it. It wasn't long until one of them remembered that day when they all hung out and did their own warm up routine. They did exactly that, with Elijah guiding them through different dance moves and they merely mimicked each of them.

Altogether, they clapped their hands, stomped their feet, jumped up and down, and many other little dance moves. As they went along, they danced with more excitement. Once their song was over, they all cheered and praised one another. Even Paula had a smile on her face, as she bonded with Sabrina and her friends.

As the dance continued, Andrew pulled out balloons from his pocket, blew some air into it, tied them up and started throwing them across the crowd, just for the fun of it. Some balloons were pushed back into the air by some of the students, passing it to each other like it was volleyball. Many of them seemed to enjoy it.

In the end, Mrs. Parker came along and politely asked to turn the music off for a moment. "Well, gang, I hate to ruin your fun, I really do, but it's passed 8:30 and I think we should wrap things up"

Many of the students gave disappointing groans and a few of them shouted out yes as a joke.

"Because by the time we finish cleaning up, it'll be nine o'clock. And don't forget we all agreed that would be the best time to end the dance"

"But can't we play at least one more song?" Melanie asked, kindly.

Her friends and along with some of their classmates sided with Mel. Mrs. Parker merely chuckled as she saw the joy and passion behind their eyes. She exchanged looks with the other teachers.

"Oh, what the heck, it's the end of the year. Might as well enjoy it"

Half of the students cheered. Sabrina and her friends went up to the stereo to find the right song.

"I think we should choose something that's more upbeat" Melanie suggested, "Something we can really dance to"

"I think so, too" Carly said.

"Funny, I was thinking the same thing" Sabrina admitted.

And then Melanie added, "I don't care if they don't like it"

"Gotcha" Sabrina confirmed, as she was searching through the CD's, "Something upbeat and slightly annoying"

They found the right song to end the night, Bring it all Back by S Club 7. Sabrina put the CD in and skipped a few tracks to get to the one they wanted.

"Alright, girls, let's make this count" Sabrina told them.

The final song started. There was no build up. The rhythm and the beat quickly got to the whole class and started moving them. Just like that, everyone got right into it. For the last dance, Elijah showed off his moves and had a dance off with every friend in sight, Andrew, Paula, Melanie, Carly, and Sabrina. The balloons that Andrew provided were still all over the place. Once he saw one near him, he leaped over, jumped on it and popped it. Then quite a few students did the same. Elijah grabbed one and passed to Sabrina, who sent it towards Carly and she passed it to Mel. Andrew gave more balloons by spreading them around. Elijah took advantage of the fun and popped one of the balloons by jumping on it and the girls did the same thing. They laughed and danced like everybody else.

They could sense the song was almost over. So then Sabrina quickly grabbed Carly by the hand and shortly recruited Melanie. The three of them held hands, formed a circle and started hopping up and down. Elijah saw them and it just made him smile, seeing how happy they were. Sabrina noticed him and quickly invited him to join their circle. Elijah felt a little silly just by hopping around in circles with the girls, but he didn't care. That was just the start. Soon Paula and Andrew joined the fun and held hands with the group. Altogether, they stopped and waved their bodies back and forth, pulled their circle closer and back out. The girls cheered, everyone cheered.

The circle had broken and each of them went back to dancing solo. And for the last minute of the song, Elijah danced right next to Sabrina. They gazed at each other briefly as they were showing off their moves. Just with a little bit of light, he could see the smile on her face. Their friends danced around them, while the couple in the center danced with each other. Soon there was physical contact when Elijah extended his hand to Sabrina, not knowing what to expect, for that all the energy motivated him to be intimate with her somehow. Sabrina took his hand and pulled herself closer. Neither of them were paying attention to the song, for that they just happened to hold each other, like they were about to slow dance like before.

But suddenly the song ended.

Elijah and Sabrina found themselves holding each other once they completely stopped.

The gym was silenced again and then all the students cheered.

The couple let go of each other. Both Elijah and Sabrina didn't feel any sense of discomfort by the intimacy. They just smiled.

CHAPTER TWENTY-SEVEN

An End and a Beginning

The dance was over. Many of the students had gone home. Only a few stayed behind to help the teachers to put everything away. Sabrina was one of them. Elijah volunteered to help. The decorations were taking down. All the garbage was collected. And both the teachers and the students took home the leftover treats. The stereo was unplugged and put away. The CD's were claimed by their owners. Once the gymnasium was spotless, it was time to go home.

Elijah offered to walk Sabrina out. Carly and Melanie were ahead of them, recapping their evening. The moment they stepped outside, their evening became silent, for that the music was long over. Elijah and Sabrina slowed down to take in the scenery in front of them. The sky was mostly dark, for that the sun was nearly gone and the cold air was floating all over.

"Well, that was fast" Sabrina said, "Felt like we were only in there for five minutes"

"Yeah, it's probably because we were having too much fun" Elijah added.

"Probably, or should I say PROPER-bly?"

They both laughed because she was quoting Paula from early that year.

"Hey Sabrina, are you coming?" Carly called.

"Yes, I'm coming" Sabrina replied and then went back to talking to Elijah, "We're having a sleepover, Melanie and Carly, at my place"

"That sounds like fun" Elijah was about to say a joke, asking if he could come. But he changed his mind at the last minute.

"Yeah, it should be; watch a movie and just...hang around"

They started making their way down the stairs. Sabrina saw her friends already getting into her mom's car. Elijah deliberately walked slowly as his way of saying that he didn't want the evening to end. Even though it was merely the weekend, Elijah felt emotional on the inside as his best friend was about to depart.

"Well..." Sabrina said, as she turned to see Elijah, but only to realize that he was standing behind her. He tried to think of something to say, other than good night or see you later, even if it was a short conversation. Elijah's eyes met Sabrina's eyes and just couldn't think of anything to say.

"Time for me to go home now" he said, sincerely.

"Yeah, you and me both"

Sabrina felt a little bit of sadness as well, probably because the evening was over and there was a part of her that was going to miss it, all the fun they had and the peers she spent it with, for that it was their own little world, their music and their school. Sabrina then went up to Elijah and gave him a hug.

"I had fun, Sabrina" Elijah said, as he had his arms around her.

"Me too, Elijah" she told him.

Their hug didn't last long. Sabrina slowly walked away, with her eyes still on Elijah.

"Have a good weekend" Elijah told her.

"Thanks, Elijah. See you on Monday!"

They waved at each other and then Sabrina finally left. Elijah turned around before it got more emotional. Keeping his head down, Elijah went back up the stairs. He turned around for one last look and saw the car just leaving the school grounds. Sabrina went home. And Elijah did too. He walked home just like he told his dad earlier. He entered the house. The sound of the TV in the living room was on. He gently took off his shoes and his jacket.

"Eli?" his mom called.

"Hey, mom"

"Hey, so how was it?"

Before answering, Elijah went up the stairs, entered the living room and saw his mom sitting on the couch.

"It was pretty fun" he told her.

"Good, I'm glad you had fun"

Elijah went and sat next to his mom on the couch. She turned the TV off and they sat in silence. Madeline put her arm around her son.

"She was there" Elijah told her. If he had the right words, he would add how great and memorable the evening was all because Sabrina was there. So he just sat there with his mind wandering. The smile on his face convinced Madeline how much the girl meant to her son. She was quite moved by it.

"So this girl, what's she like?" she asked.

That just made Elijah smile, for thinking about her. "She's great-I mean she's…she's so many things, a great friend, a smart student, funny and adventurous, and she's really beautiful. I…I care about her like a lot, much more than that, I love her

"There were…" he continued, "Some times where I got mad…in front of her. There were actually a couple of times I thought we weren't really friends anymore…But, it turns out we've been friends all along, even though she found out I had problems. It made me feel good, especially after I been bad, sometimes

"It's like…I feel like that I was being punished for all the bad things I done in the past because…I had nothing. I mean I had Paula and Andrew, it's just I wanted something else, something special and I think I found it when I met her

"And now I see that life is not just about dealing with bad days. There's something good and something beautiful out there. And I hope that one day, her and I will be holding hands"

"Does she know, about how you really feel?"

Elijah paused and then shook his head, "No, she doesn't. I want to tell her. That was actually my New Year's resolution, to make Sabrina my girlfriend but I was too scared, maybe it's because I'm scared that she won't like me the same way"

"If it scares you a little, maybe you shouldn't. Sometimes the truth hurts. Once you hear it or see it, you will never look at that person the same way. But you can never tell. And it might be because it's not the best time right now. So I'd say the best thing to do is keep treating her with respect. If anything, you can always express your love through little things, through gestures, mean what you say and just simply be there, and do it with heart. And if she feels the same way about you, she will show it. And one day, you two will connect and become more than friends"

"Yeah, maybe I will" Elijah agreed, not giving it a second thought.

"You said her name is Sabrina?"

"Yeah, Sabrina Clarin"

Madeline nodded, "That's a pretty name"

"It really is" Elijah paused, "She's...she's great", Then a smile formed on his face. It was a meaningful look. Then he remembered the picture he had of her. He pulled it out and showed it to his mom. "It's a picture I took of her" he explained as his mom examined the photo. "Back in January from our field trip; she doesn't know that I have it. I was actually about to show her but I didn't. I think it's because I wanna keep it for myself. You know, just to look at her when I'm not with her"

Madeline nodded. "She is pretty". Then she kindly returned her son's photo. "Your secret is safe with me" she added, with a warm smile. Elijah and his mom hugged each other and then called it a night.

He later went to bed, but stayed up thinking about his evening, along with Sabrina, and what the future might bring. He hoped that along the way he would have more heartfelt moments with her and that each moment would build a potential relationship. That gave Elijah Khoda a reason to live and love life again. Upon facing reality, anything could happen. But with the lessons learned and the new strength that was wielded, the idea of running away had been diminished. Elijah was ready for the next chapter in his life.

Meanwhile, at the Clarin residence, Sabrina lied awake in bed while her girlfriends were fast asleep. She thought about how wonderful the night was from the dance to the sleepover. But she couldn't help but feel that something was missing. Whatever that may be, left her in wonder as she looked upon the neighborhood from her window. Turing up towards the sky, there were layers of stars all around. Sabrina imagined that there had to be a beautiful world beyond from what she could see. At that point, that was her view on life that something or someone was waiting for her. That was one mystery she couldn't help but think about, of who could be the one that Sabrina would give her heart to. Right now, it was only a silhouette in her mind. Whoever that may be, she thought. The words kept repeating until they reminded her of something, the note, the note that she used to express herself last November! She quietly went towards her dresser to find the paper. After that night, she tucked it away. Sabrina nearly forgot about it. Now she was on her bed, with the flashlight on, with the note lying flat on a hardcover book so she could write on it. She added a new saying to it:

Here I am, waiting for you, whoever you are. Sabrina paused to read it over and over. Then shortly, more of her feelings expressed in words, *wherever you are, I'll find you.*

After that she put it down and lied in bed. She could hear her girlfriends' breathing as they were sleeping. Sabrina closed her eyes, although not feeling tired just yet. In fact, she began thinking about her little note and repeated the words. Then at one point, they scrambled into different places. Just like that, she thought of something different, something unique. So she got up, turned the flashlight on again and added more to her note, a note than soon became a poem

Here I am, whoever you are,
waiting for you, wherever you may be.
Once you find me and I find you,
let's make our own destiny.

The weekend was over. When Elijah arrived at school he saw Sabrina but didn't feel the need to talk with her. Just making eye contact with her and smiled as they were thinking about the dance. As school continued for its last days, Elijah interacted with Sabrina casually, during class and recess. Next thing they knew that the school year was coming to end. It was that time of year to clean out lockers. Many of the students were quite excited and there were some that were going to miss it.

The thought of school ending had Elijah thinking if he would see Sabrina again. Usually he'd never see any of his classmates during summer, except only Andrew and Paula. It was possible to ask Sabrina if she could hang out with them from time to time. But he was still worried that if he asked her for her number, he would give the wrong impression. And it's likely that Sabrina would probably be busy doing things with her family and her girlfriends. So now that idea didn't seem promising anymore.

Elijah knew he had to come to terms with the fact that school was almost over and wasn't going to see Sabrina for two months. If he was going to say goodbye, Elijah wanted it to be more than just words. The idea of giving something to Sabrina to remember him seemed pretty profound. Unfortunately, there wasn't any money to buy her a gift. At one point, Elijah thought about giving her one of his CD's but that didn't seem enough. Pondering in his room, Elijah looked around blankly, hoping an idea would come to him. As he was scanning across the floor, he saw a part of his notebook hiding under the bed. It was the same one Elijah used from the week before when he was writing a letter to Sabrina. Now that the pressure was gone and Elijah's mind was ready for focus, he decided to try the letter again, and this time he wrote down how he really felt about Sabrina Clarin.

The last day of school had come. Students and teachers couldn't believe it. It felt like the school year only lasted a few days. During the last day, Elijah just had the urge to do something with his friends. He could only think of the simple things, whether it was playing a sporting activity or just walking around the school. Once he consulted with Paula and Andrew about it, they agreed that they would play. Elijah asked Sabrina to join and thankfully she said yes. So the four of them chose to play tether ball just like they did at the beginning of the school year; this time it was boys against girls and this time Elijah didn't fail on purpose.

That whole time, Elijah had the letter safe in his back pocket. Every now and then, he took it out just to glance at it to make sure it was the right one and to be sure that it was still there. It was labeled: *For Sabrina Clarin.* After each time he looked at it, he would then peer over at Sabrina herself. The thought of giving her the letter was just as challenging as trying to tell her in person. Either way, it was hard to tell how Sabrina would react and that made Elijah nervous.

Nobody gave it a single thought, but once that last bell went off, Elijah realized he was about to walk out of William Konkin Elementary School and wasn't going to come back. For the next few minutes, the mind went blank to take it all in. The moment the bell rang and everyone got up, Elijah remained seated as he gazed at his desk and then scanned the classroom, accepting the fact he wasn't going to see it anymore. Then Elijah said goodbye to Mrs. Parker and thanked her for everything, and then he left the classroom.

Before going outside, Elijah stopped and turned his attention to the hall. It was the open space where he and other students spent half their time working on projects or using the computer. Then he went down further to see the hallway, where a lineup of students would walk to the gym, the library or the art room. They'll probably never walk in lineups again. After the hallway, Elijah finally left the school building. Outside, every student were giving each other hugs and bidding farewell.

"Well, this is it" Elijah said to Paula, after he caught up with her and Andrew.

"Yeah" Paula replied, sincerely, "It's crazy, feels like we were just at MMPS yesterday. Now we literally just finished elementary school"

"I'll say…" Andrew spoke, "Feels like yesterday we were just learning our ABC's and one-two-three's, and now we are learning to stand up and teach hoodlums a lesson"

That was definitely a way to put it.

"No comment required" Andrew told them, smoothly.

"Well…" Paula said, but she was quite speechless.

"Well" Elijah repeated, "I guess we don't need to say goodbye because we'll probably see each other during the summer"

"Yeah, I'm sure we will" Paula agreed.

"No goodbye required" Elijah told her.

"Hey, that's my line!" Andrew pretended to be offended.

"Haha, I'm borrowing it"

"That's impossible. How can you 'borrow' a line?"

"Take a piece of paper and draw a line on it. And boom, you got a line" Paula suggested.

Andrew laughed, "That's a good one, Paulie. Well, what do you say we look at Willy K. one last time?" Andrew insisted.

So the three of them turned around and gazed at WKE, which was now their former school. Elijah, Paula, and Andrew, had their arms around each other as they reflected on their memories.

"This is where we became friends, Andrew" Elijah said.

"And I couldn't ask for anyone better than you, E.K."

"Thanks Al, for all the good memories"

"And it certainly won't be the last" Andrew promised, "Especially bugging Paula"

Paula sighed, "I knew it" she replied, playfully.

They laughed and then they eyed the school building once again.

"And thank you Paula" Elijah told her, "For still being my friend, even after the times I wasn't acting like a friend"

Paula smiled, so proudly, it almost made her want to cry. "That's what best friends do"

Then Elijah, Paula, and Andrew, hugged each other. Together they been friends for three years and there was many more to come. Elijah promised he would never take them for granted again and enjoy what he had. After all, Paula and Andrew weren't just his friends; they were his brother and sister. Once the team departed, Elijah realized that Sabrina hadn't left yet. She was talking with both of her girlfriends.

"You know when I first moved here, I didn't think I was going to make friends at all" Sabrina admitted, "I actually thought that maybe nobody would care until I met Elijah and then you girls. So I don't know what else to say, but thank you"

"Aww" Melanie and Carly said simultaneously.

"We're glad that we made you feel welcome" Carly told her.

"And at home" Melanie added.

"Yeah, that's the other thing. It started to feel like home after becoming friends with you two. And now it kinda feels like I had been coming to this school for years. I'm sure gonna miss it"

"You know, I was just thinking the same thing" Carly admitted, "Even though I had rough days but there's also some nice memories here"

"Probably thanks to me" Melanie said, "Not to brag"

"Yeah, what Mel said and I'm glad that you're part of it, Sabrina"

Sabrina gave a heartwarming smile.

"And I'm just as glad as Car" Melanie told her.

The girls had a group hug and held each other for a moment. Shortly, Carly had to go.

"Well, I think my dad was waiting long enough" she told her friends, "Sabrina, you still have my phone number, right?"

"Of course"

"Awesome, I'll call you every now and then"

"Not unless I call you first" Sabrina replied.

"And I still have your number, Car, in case you were wondering" Melanie said, jokingly.

Carly chuckled, "I was just going to ask you the same thing. But yeah, I'll talk to you guys sometime. If we change our number, I'll let you know ahead of time...not that we're going to...I don't know why I said that"

The other girls laughed.

"Carly, I'm going to miss your blondeness" Melanie said, as she went up to give Carly a hug. Sabrina did the same. And almost right away, Carly Dawson went home. But they'll probably see her again soon.

"Well, it was nice meeting you, Sabrina" Mel said.

"Nice meeting you, too"

They hugged each other.

"See you in high school"

"I'll be there" Sabrina promised.

After her girlfriends went home, Sabrina absently turned around and saw Elijah standing nearby.

"Sabrina" he greeted.

"Hey" she replied, kindly, "Been standing there the whole time?"

"Just got here"

"Then what are you waiting for? I don't bite"

Elijah just laughed. As much as he wanted to say a comeback, he couldn't think of anything.

"Sabrina" he repeated, as she was approaching her, "So uh…This is…" Elijah was about to talk about the last day of school but he realized that would be a short conversation.

"How was your last day?" he asked.

"It was good. It started off as any other day, but now I see it wasn't so different. Last day, no school or homework for two months"

"Do you ever miss it, sometimes?"

"Hmm, not homework"

"Same here"

Elijah went and stood closer to Sabrina and gazed at the school together. Then the next thing that caught his attention was the top of the stairs. That was where Elijah and Sabrina first met, where it all started.

"Well, I guess this is it" Sabrina said.

Right away, Elijah cocked his head to her. His heartbeat nearly went fast, as he feared the moment was already almost over before it even began.

"It doesn't have to be" he said before she could say anything, "I mean, I…"

Sabrina still had some patience, even with her mom waiting in the parking lot. Since it was the last day of school, she figured she'd better make the best of it.

"I just wanted to see you before we take off for the summer"

"Well, I can probably spare another a minute or two" Sabrina assured.

They both looked at each other for a moment. Elijah was debating if he should make friendly conversation or something meaningful. Then he got lost in Sabrina's eyes and couldn't help but smile. She did the same thing. Elijah noticed her blink.

"Looks like I win this round. You blinked" he said.

"Oh" Sabrina giggled, "Well, congrats. Next time, I won't go easy on you"

"I'll be ready" Then they paused. Elijah almost didn't want to speak because he could feel the moment coming to an end, "Hey, wanna sign my yearbook?"

"I'd love to" Sabrina pulled out a pen as Elijah handed her the yearbook. "Wanna sign mine, too?"

"Yes" Elijah said.

She gave Elijah hers and they both started to write down sayings, followed by their signatures. "You should read what Andrew wrote" he told her.

Sabrina looked for Andrew's signing and found it, "Here's to another school year and the hopes of finding the golden...sink?"

Elijah laughed, "Yup, every now and then he says something random"

"I bet. It sounds like him alright"

They returned each other's yearbooks and went back into silence.

"Well..." Sabrina spoke.

"It's been a fun year" he told her.

"It sure was"

"Even though there were bad days" he added. "I'm glad we got through it because..."

Elijah had no idea that trying to make a heartfelt conversation from a friendly conversation was difficult. "I like you".

Sabrina stopped. Elijah came close to panic once he realized he was so close to telling Sabrina the truth. And having her eyes on him made it exhilarating. Saying the words like you was a step up, but Elijah wasn't sure if he wanted to go any farther. And it was too late to change the subject for that he was already in too deep.

"I like you" he repeated, "Because you like me, even after those bad days". He then paused just to meet Sabrina's eyes. She seemed intrigued and not feeling any discomfort. Now Elijah no longer felt nervous. "And that's what a friend is for, my friend"

It may have been too soon but Elijah was already reaching for his back pocket to pull out the letter.

"That's sweet" she told him and then she gave a smile.

In Sabrina's mind, she went back to the first day of school when she first met Elijah. From that day to the present, a lot had happened, much more than she realized. If only there was enough time to put it into words.

"Well, I don't think this is going to sound just as sweet as you put it, but I'm grateful to have a friend like you, Elijah. You said hi and welcomed me to Burns Lake. If it weren't for you, I probably wouldn't have had the courage to say hi to anyone and I wouldn't have become friends with Carly and Mel. And most of all, you helped face my problems. So thank you"

Everything happens for a reason. Elijah found it hard to believe that he was once against Sabrina befriending others. Now with new perspective, he realized that Sabrina becoming friends with other girls actually helped her. They both may not hang out as much as they used to, but as long as Sabrina still says hi like nothing changed, Elijah would be happy.

They had to say goodbye any minute now. He could tell her anything but he also wanted to say everything. Sadly, their time was running out. Truthfully, he didn't want her to go. If Elijah could, he'd keep her close forever.

"Sabrina…"

"Yeah?"

"I wish…I want to tell you a lot of things, you know just movies, music, hanging out, and…how much we don't like homework"

That was all Elijah could come up with, for a friendly conversation, while his mind was still on the letter.

"Aww, Elijah, we'll see each other again" Sabrina promised, "We can talk more when that time comes"

So Elijah was going to see her again; hearing it from her sounded promising. But he also couldn't help but think of the reality while time is moving. Even in two months, some things could change.

"Yeah?" he replied, gently, "So if we see each other again, you'll say hi?"

"As long as you say hi back"

Elijah nodded, "Always"

Time was almost up. It nearly startled Elijah that it made him break eye contact. Now he was getting more nervous as he was pulling the letter out of his back pocket.

"Sabrina" he muttered.

She listened closely. After a moment, Elijah was able to look her in the eyes again.

"Sabrina" he repeated. This time he spoke a little louder.

After a pause, Sabrina replied: "Elijah?"

She could tell that he wanted to say something but he hesitated.

Elijah was considering giving her the letter. He wanted to.

There was nothing else he wanted to say but how he really felt.

No small talk, no delay, no goodbyes, just the truth that he was deeply in love with her.

But then everything was ruined when Elijah asked himself the same question he did before: What if she said no? What if she freaks out and doesn't want to be my friend anymore? But Sabrina Clarin was a nice person. She might understand, even if she didn't feel the same way. But was friendship enough? Elijah wanted more than that. He wanted to hold Sabrina's hand, hold her in her arms, see her every day, share each other's lives, go on different adventures, simply tell her that he loved her and kissed her. It's what Elijah Khoda always dreamed of. And the way Sabrina made him feel, comfort, strong, and loved. She made Elijah see the beauty of life, a life he wanted to be a part of. Truthfully, Elijah wanted it sooner than later. But then he remembered his mother's words.

If it scares you a little, maybe you shouldn't. Sometimes the truth hurts. Once you hear it or see it, you will never look at that person the same way. But you can never tell.

So Elijah just gave in and left the letter in his back pocket.

"I'm going to miss you" he finally said, sincerely.

Sabrina smiled and went in to give him a hug. Elijah promptly wrapped his arms around her and held her, to enjoy the comfort of her presence before parting ways. Sabrina whispered into Elijah's ears...

"Thank you for being my friend" she told him.

Hearing her voice really moved Elijah. It almost made him want to cry for that he felt her love and could only hope that she felt his.

Their hug ended. They smiled at each other one last time.

Shortly, Sabrina took the last step and was off the curb.

Their moment was over, until next time.

"Bye, Sabrina" Elijah said, with a little wave.

"Bye, Elijah. Have a good summer"

"You too"

"Thank you"

Sabrina finally waved back and then she turned around and went to meet with her mom. She got into the car in the passenger side. Leah Clarin was in the driver's seat. She greeted her daughter and was joyful to see that she was quite happy. It didn't seem secretive and it felt genuine.

"Who was that?" Leah asked.

Sabrina glanced back at Elijah, who was still on the curb.

"That's Elijah, Elijah Khoda" she said, proudly, "He actually welcomed me to the school on the first day" Sabrina then turned to her mom, "He's my friend".

Leah smiled and gave a little nod. She started the car and slowly drove away. Elijah saw the car coming towards him. He caught Sabrina's eye looking back at him as she was departing. While they had little time, they waved at each other. Elijah stayed where he was until the car was out of sight.

"Sabrina" Elijah muttered.

Now the school year was officially over once Sabrina Clarin had gone home.

Elijah left the school grounds and started making his way home. While he was walking, he took his time, thinking about all that he had been through in grade seven, the good days and the bad days. Looking back at it now, Elijah didn't feel startled as he did during the rough times. It was amazing to think that he made it through, even when there was a lot of doubt. After all the fights and drama, Elijah Khoda still had his head up and took pride in the fact that there was good in this life.

As for the good days, there was something different about it, different in a good way, whereas before those days were just simple like any other, such as having a laugh with Paula and Andrew or passing a test with a good mark. But this past year was something special. It was beautiful, making a new friend, who decorated life itself with her humor, kindness, love, and beauty. Elijah saw life through Sabrina's eyes and it changed the way he looked at reality. Now he saw there was beauty in almost everything, a soul within a person that was just as extraordinary as a sun setting beyond the horizon. Even on his way home, Elijah slowed down just to admire the scenery around him, the grass, the trees, and the sky. There was beauty in all of them and it was shining through. At one point, Elijah stopped and saw a dandelion growing from the earth, like how Sabrina Clarin was born and grown into a beautiful girl.

What if Elijah didn't say hi to Sabrina at all on the first day? It was hard to imagine how things could've been like. Maybe it was meant to happen. Just when Elijah Khoda was losing interest in his own life, he met a girl like Sabrina. That couldn't be a coincidence. Perhaps Sabrina really was the one, for that fate had brought them together. Hopefully one day, they would be boyfriend and girlfriend.

Elijah was at home and it actually felt like a home for the first time in a while. He walked in and just felt the warmth and the comfort once his feet touched the floor. After getting settled in, Elijah went to see his parents, who were in the kitchen prepping for dinner.

"Mom, dad" he greeted.

Madeline gave a little smile as she approached him. She put her arm around him just to comfort him. "Well, you did it, Eli" she told him, "You finished grade seven. Congratulations!"

"Thanks, mom"

"Now in a couple of months, you'll be in high school" Sam added, "Are you nervous?"

Elijah slightly shook his head, "No, not really. You know what; I think I'm ready for anything"

Feeling all proud, Madeline Khoda gave her son a hug and gently kissed him on his head.

After dinner was over, Elijah had the whole evening to himself. He went outside to their backyard, with his discman in hand and brought a CD that had pop music on it. He sat in the lawn chair, put his headphones on, and played the disc. As the song commenced, Elijah relaxed and gazed at the forest in front of him. The fresh air was all around, mingling with the scent of the trees, and the clear sky floated above. He took it all in as the slow song was playing, a song about love.

Elijah thought about Sabrina. Her long brown dark hair, eyes so clear you can see the reflection of life all around. In his mind, he saw her face and her kind smile.

And that brought Elijah Khoda back…to the beginning…

"I'm going to miss you" he finally said, sincerely.

Sabrina smiled sincerely and went in to give him a hug. Elijah promptly wrapped his arms around her and held her, to enjoy the comfort of her presence before parting ways. Sabrina whispered into Elijah's ears…

"Thank you for being my friend" she told him.

In the middle of the other dancing couples, Elijah and Sabrina faced each other, their eyes met and then he gently placed his left hand on Sabrina's hip, while she placed her right hand on his shoulder, and finally their other hands interlocked and held it. And so began this beautiful moment.

Next thing she knew, she was feeling Elijah's hand against hers. They looked at each other. There was sincerity all over their faces. It was so profound; it almost felt like Elijah was looking at Sabrina for the first time. The feeling made him wrap his hand over Sabrina's hand. Then she positioned her hand properly by interlocking her fingers through his and there they held it for a long moment. Slowly, Elijah smiled and Sabrina smiled back.

"Yeah? I guess we'll still be friends when the songs change? That we'd still be dancing or listening together?"

Uncertain, Sabrina just gawked at him for a brief moment, "Not sure what that means, but yeah"

"Elijah?" she called.

Elijah stopped and met her eyes.. "Yeah?" he replied, casually.

It was silent at first, but then the moment become comforting when a smile slowly formed on Sabrina's face and then she showed him the card. "That was very nice of you".

Then Elijah began to smile, for that he succeeded his Valentine's Day plans.

"You like it?" he asked.

"Yeah, it's great! And very thoughtful"

"Glad you like it"

Sabrina then gave Elijah a hug. He wrapped his arms around her in return.

"Elijah!" he could hear her voice clearly and then he heard, "Here, take my hand!"

He looked over and saw Sabrina's hand extended towards him. Elijah quickly grabbed it and held on. Now he wasn't staggering anymore, for that Sabrina gently pulled him back into balance. Elijah looked over at her and smiled in relief. She returned the smile. Even when he was okay, he didn't want to let go of Sabrina's hand. But as the race was getting close to finish, they had to let go of each other. As they were getting to the bottom of the hill, they started slowing down. Sabrina was ahead. She was the winner.

"You know what; I know how to make this work". Then she gently pulled the candy cane until the plastic broke in half. Sabrina offered Elijah the other half of the candy cane.

"Merry Christmas" she said, with a beautiful smile.

Elijah certainly wasn't expecting that, a thoughtful gesture from Sabrina Clarin, especially when the moment almost went downhill. Elijah, more than willing, accepted the other half of the candy cane.

"Thanks!" he replied, "Now you're being thoughtful"

Sabrina smiled and broke eye contact for a brief moment. "Ho-ho-ho" she replied.

They both laughed.

"Merry Christmas, Elijah"

"Merry Christmas, Sabrina"

As they were gazing to the white sky, Elijah slowly looked back at Sabrina. Their eyes met. And then Sabrina stuck her tongue out just to catch some snowflakes. A little happiness lit up inside Elijah and came out in laughter. Then Sabrina laughed with him. Elijah did the same and started catching snowflakes with his tongue. But that was only the beginning, for that they both paced around to wherever the snow was falling, trying to catch more, almost like they were competing against each other, but in a playful way.

"Be careful or you'll slip" Elijah warned, ignoring her story.

Then they stopped. Sabrina glanced to the ground and back to Elijah. "I know. YOU be careful"

That sounded like a challenge. Elijah tried not to smile, as he wasn't sure if she was joking or not. He continued walking but Sabrina was still walking backwards, like she did it for sport. Then Elijah slowed down as he realized that his new friend was being playful. Sabrina walked in the same manner as he did, slow and then casual.

"What are you doing?" he asked. For a brief moment, Elijah thought maybe Sabrina was trying to prove a point.

"Having a little fun, what are you doing?" she replied, with a little proud smile.

"And I know that you're not a bad person" Sabrina added, "I know because I saw the good side of you. And you admit all your faults. Not a lot of people do that"

To her eyes, Elijah felt like he was one of a kind and that flattered him. "Well, thanks"

After a moment, he finally decided what he wanted and grabbed it, then he went to exit the aisle, but there was a few other customers crowding the area, so Elijah had to go in the opposite direction. Elijah was almost at the end and just as he turned the corner, he saw a face he did not expect to see...
"Hi, Elijah!" Sabrina Clarin said.

"I'm Elijah...Elijah Khoda" he told her, as he extended his hand.
The girl glanced at his hand and then extended hers. Things got more interesting once Elijah felt her hands mingling with his. It was soft and warm, that sent a certain vibe through his body. Something that was indescribable.
"Sabrina Clarin" she said.

After the memories floated in Elijah's mind, he finally said:
"I love you, Sabrina Clarin".

Printed in the USA
CPSIA information can be obtained
at www.ICGtesting.com
JSHW082334010823
45740JS00006B/22